ELECTRIC

STORM

A RAVEN INVESTIGATIONS NOVEL

STACEY BRUTGER

Copyright © 2012 © 2020 **Stacey Brutger**

Cover artist: Merry-Book-Round

Editor: Erin Wolfe
Proofreader: Jan A.

All rights reserved.

ISBN-10: 1475109075
ISBN-13: 978- 1475109078

To my husband, my biggest supporter, my best friend.
Thank you for helping me realize my dreams.

And to all those who have encouraged me to never give up.
This book is for you.

Chapter One

DAY ONE: AROUND MIDNIGHT

*T*alons.

The paranormal hot spot where the fanged, furry, and spell slingers went to blow off steam.

Raven tapped her leather-clad fingertips on the steering wheel, waiting for her friends to emerge from the club's steel door. They were thirty minutes late and counting.

The prospect of going inside, risk being in public around other paranormals, twisted a small thread of excitement through her—that was if she ignored the dip in her stomach that threatened to bring supper back up for a revisit. Doing the best to disregard her swinging emotions, she assessed the building.

The non-descript warehouse appeared innocent enough. There were no lines, no bouncers. Nothing overtly threatening that would explain the way her mind screamed that going after her friends to pry out their asses was a very bad idea.

Another minute ticked by, and she blew out a breath, unable to ignore the dangerous lure of curiosity.

She got out of the car and cautiously approached the club. The building was crouched in the shadows, as if would pounce and squish her like a bug the moment she dared to enter...as if it knew she didn't belong. She eased closer to the entrance and pried open the heavy metal doors with a little shove of electricity from her gift. The industrial sized magnets that sealed the door ensured only the right kind of people were admitted.

As precautions went, it wasn't bad. No humans, or what the shifter community called normals, were admitted without someone vouching for them. Prejudiced? Maybe. But it guaranteed that whatever happened inside would be handled by their own laws. The club was neutral territory for paranormals. No one dared pick a fight on the property. It could get you killed.

A long, shadowy hallway greeted her. The air rumbled with music, the pounding rhythm slapping her in the face. Heat blasted along her body, brushing the chill from her skin, but did nothing to warm the cold lump in her stomach. There was no décor in the confining space except for one prominent word clawed into the heavy wooden panels.

Talons.

Raven lifted her hand, noting how her fingers sank in the deep grooves. Whoever created it had to be huge. Another frisson of doubt curled about her, but she quickly shoved it away before it could take root. She could hold her own against these people.

But not without a cost, her mind whispered.

She ignored that, too.

Her next case was due to begin all too soon. Humans oversimplified the paranormal world, wedging all things supernatural into their too narrow viewpoint. Too bad it didn't work that way. That's why they hired her when they needed something done. She lived on the fringes of both cultures, and knew enough to get things done, but not enough to be a threat.

Despite the protest she gave her friends when they first invited her to the club, a little R&R sounded perfect. Too bad this place felt more like work and less like rest and relaxation.

Her friends had assured her that she'd find a suitable lover here if she dared to take a chance. Not an easy objective when her very touch could kill if she didn't keep on constant guard.

And who better to choose from than a pack of paranormals? They weren't immortal, but they could take a lot of abuse and survive. Although inflicting pain, even accidentally, didn't spawn any romantic interest for her, she couldn't turn tail for the seductive reason that all she had to do was choose someone inside to find the key to learn control over her own gift.

During sex, shifters were vulnerable, their beasts close to the surface. They had to exert tremendous control to keep from shifting.

If she could learn how they did it, she knew she could fix her own control issues. Unfortunately, that meant firsthand experience. Physical contact. Her heart thumped hard, imagining what it would be like to finally allow herself to touch someone without the fear that she'd kill them.

None of this would matter if her damn gift didn't morph every time she got close to mastering it. If she didn't get a handle on it soon, it wouldn't be much longer before her secret became exposed to the paranormal world, and she would be hunted in earnest. A conduit was too valuable, too dangerous to all sides to be left unclaimed.

If tonight's plan didn't work, the very short list of possible cures would grow even shorter. At least in this experiment, the byproduct wasn't a bad exchange. Rumors said shifters were intense and generous lovers.

She took a deep breath to calm the shimmering power that rose at her initial unease. The energy that hovered over her slowly settled and soaked back into her skin, wrapping her in a warm blanket as if to offer comfort. She lifted her chin to the nondescript door at the end of the hallway, ready to face the beasts in their den.

She cracked open her senses, and smells immediately crested over her in waves. The fresh scent of shifters, the spice of vampires and the sharp, overly sweet stench of an odd magic user were all added to the mix. Every time a practitioner used their craft, a splash of magic skittered along Raven's arms like she'd brushed against cobwebs.

The knot in her stomach clenched. She called it excitement, refusing to admit she could've made a mistake coming inside. The last time she'd been around this many people, it hadn't gone well. At the slightest threat, her power took control and did whatever it had to in order to protect her.

The harsh reminder soothed her ragged emotions, and she shoved them into the vault from which they'd escaped. Emotions meant loss of control, meant someone would suffer. Closing her eyes, she searched every nook and cranny of her shields for cracks.

When she found none, the last of the knots holding her muscles hostage faded. No one would attack her here. No one would be able to break her shields and discover the horrible truth.

"In or out?"

"Excuse me?" Raven whirled, her gaze unerringly finding those of a man...no, a wolf in human form who stood a little over six feet. He towered over her by at least half a foot, forcing her to take a step back in order to meet his gaze without cricking her neck.

Damn touchy-feely shifters. They didn't have any boundaries or understand the concept of personal space, especially between unclaimed men and women.

Fresh air clung to him, relaxing some of her initial surprise at finding him so close. Though handsome, there was something a little too masculine about him, a little too purposeful in his actions that left her unsettled. She resisted the urge to fidget, glad she took care to make herself as forgettable as possible. Dressed in black, her distinctive, silver-tipped hair pinned back like a prim schoolmarm, she little resembled the carefree, underdressed partygoers who frequented the place.

"I said are you going in or out?" Dark brows lowered in annoyance, and those deep brown eyes shone brightly in the hallway, revealing his animal nature. Power wrapped around him, barely leashed, rubbing against her. It didn't hurt, though it wasn't quite pleasant either. More of a brusque probe to find out if she was a threat. The taste of his magic revealed he had no interest in her.

She stepped aside to let him pass, refusing to shrink in front of him, taking care to ensure they didn't touch. He didn't seem to notice, not even sparing her a glance. He just grunted, gliding by on silent feet. The noise of the club rose as he entered the room beyond.

Raven pried open her clenched fingers, finding them reluctant to obey. Though she should be pleased, his dismissive attitude annoyed her. Despite having a very small portion of the shifter genetic make-up, her mind blared a warning that all males inside would have the same reaction. Like was attracted to like, and she most definitely was not one of them, not really, despite all the tests conducted on her as a child. Tests the labs performed to find out how much control she had over the animal counterparts locked away at her core. The same core that now gave a low rumble at his easy dismissal.

"Don't mind him. He can be an ass."

Raven jerked at the masculine voice, surprised to find herself not alone. She'd shut herself down so hard she'd inadvertently blocked some of her senses. A costly mistake, especially since her animals liked to come out to play when she shut out the very electricity she used to keep them at bay.

"My fault." She pushed the words past her constricted throat. From now on, she would stick to business and shove the personal nonsense the girls always spouted into the garbage where it belonged. She could deal with her gift by herself, like she had all her life. Plans were in place if the worst came to pass. "I should go."

When she went to retreat, the boy, who had to be no more than eighteen, stepped in front of the exit, barring her way. "Don't. Please."

The tremble in his voice drew her attention. Instincts sharpened. Then she noticed the slave collar clamped around his throat.

The delicate threads of metal, a combination of silver and gold, marked him as a slave to the shifter community. Welts beaded on his skin where the silver encircled his neck, and she couldn't prevent her lips from curling in disgust.

She understood the aching need to belong, but she couldn't condone the process. How could a person permit another to use them just to earn a place in the pack?

"Why do you do it?" The question slipped out without thinking of the consequences.

No retaliation came. More surprising, he didn't appear angered at her question. Pack always held their business close to their chest. Unless you were a fur-and-claw-carrying member of the club, you didn't need to know.

A sad look passed over the boy's face. "The collar protects me more than if I remained rogue. Without it, I'd be bottom to everyone. If I'm accepted into a pack, they'll protect me."

"Unless they kill you first." Rogues don't last long past their prime out in the open.

The lean man who stood so proudly before her didn't look to be the threatening monster everyone claimed about rogues, the reason for their unspoken, kill-first law for unregistered rogues.

He shrugged. "Those are the rules. Unless you're born into the pack or challenge and kill for your place, you have to earn your spot." An uncertain smile tipped the corner of his lips, an expression that didn't settle easily on his face. An almost indistinguishable sheen of sweat clung to him.

The people inside were like animals in the way that if they sensed fear or weakness, they singled you out. After years of practice, she made an art out of blending into the background. The boy had no such protection.

"Maybe you'll find me inside." Without waiting for her response, he disappeared into the club, leaving the scent of defeat, anxiety, and more damning…hope.

Raven debated the wisdom of leaving against all that she could gain. If the boy could face the crowd, then so could she. Five minutes, then she would yank her friends' asses out. Squaring her shoulders, she opened the door, her fingers steady only from years of practice.

Blue and red lasers flashed through the club. Black material clung to the walls, giving the impression of space. Drapes hung around the booths, adding a false sense of intimacy. She avoided peering too closely into the shadows and gazed over the crowd.

At twenty-eight, she was older than most. The elders of the pack usually didn't stray from the meeting rooms upstairs. It wasn't too long ago that packs had decimated other packs for territory. Not to mention the tenuous three hundred year peace between wolves and vampires was shaky at best. Only in the last ten years, when the paranormal world became exposed, did they start doing business with one another to present a united front to the humans.

Most of the shifters she saw in the club were male. Although female shifters weren't rare, very few pure bloods remained. Those selected few were treasured, rarely permitted to leave the protection of the den, and never alone.

The women trolling here were mostly donors for the vampires, while others were available for a more amorous relationship with the pack members, men who could control their shift and not accidentally change during heightened emotions.

Gazes slid over her, judging, testing. She pretended not to notice the cloud of vampires in the back or the gaggle of witches at the bar, not wanting them to misunderstand and take it as an invitation for more. The shifters' gazes swept over her like she wasn't there. She scanned the room for her friends, noting about a third of the crowd were scantily clad slaves with a cloud of desperation hovering over more than a few of them.

The press of people ate away at her shields. She needed a few minutes to settle the energy swamping her before she dug further into the crowd. She seated herself at a far table tucked in the corner. Not wanting company, she manipulated the energy that saturated the air, pulled the darkness around herself, merging into the shadows like an old lover. A trick she learned from a vampire. Most wouldn't see her unless they were purposely searching for her.

Once on the vinyl stool, she realized her mistake, realized why there were so many slaves present—an auction. She'd thought they'd been abolished when paranormals gained their citizenship. Since her friends held the same attitude as she did, they wouldn't have stayed to watch this debacle.

Any thought of lovers disappeared, replaced by concern for her friends. She needed to contact them and find out what the hell had happened. They wouldn't have abandoned her unless there was trouble. She groped for her phone when she spotted him.

The boy she'd met outside had since lost his shirt, revealing more muscle than she would've expected for one so slim, though it shouldn't have been surprising since most shifters were built sturdy. He carried a serving tray. Then he turned. Even at this distance, clearly defined marks crisscrossed his back, wounds days old.

The table under her hand groaned, plastic crunched, her fingers leaving behind impressions in the fake wood veneer. A slither of current escaped her control, and the phone in the other hand gave a puff of smoke as the circuits fried. "Damn it."

Flashes of images from the labs slammed against her mind, the wails of pain and terror, the fanatical need to escape the torture. She wouldn't allow that to happen here.

The kid should've been able to shift and heal but hadn't.

A curl of unease increased the sense of wrongness she picked up when she entered. She'd blamed it on nerves. Inhaling deeply, she couldn't detect a threat, couldn't see any overt danger from the crowd. She wished she could believe she saw trouble where none existed.

A commotion at the other end of the room erupted. The boy. She knew it even before she saw his face. Five women surrounded him, heckling and caressing him. He stood there, a frozen smile plastered in place, tolerating their touches. Tolerating, but not enjoying.

Then he flinched. His smile became strained, the women's laughter more wild. The boy's eyes hardened, but he kept still, enduring the obscene fondling and cruel taunts.

She scanned the crowd. A few people snickered at his discomfort, a few looked away, pity leeching the life from their eyes, but no one protested.

Then the man who had accompanied the boy stood to his full height. The muscles of her back loosened, and she eased back into her seat, unaware she'd half risen to her feet. The big man would keep him safe. But instead of rescuing the boy, the Ogre turned his back and pushed his way to the bar.

A lump grew in her throat at the unwanted attention the boy endured. Memories of similar situations from her past cut into her mind, blurring reason until fury burned along her veins.

Stillness settled inside her, burying everything but the need to do something, the need to prevent the past from repeating itself. Before she knew what she was doing, she moved.

The closer she came, the more she sensed his unwillingness and his resignation. She stopped outside the circle of women. Their gazes collided. Recognition sparked, and his gaze latched onto hers.

Pleaded.

It was a mistake coming here tonight, but she couldn't leave without knowing he'd be safe. Couldn't stop herself from rescuing him.

"He's mine." She reached through the circle of women, clamped down on his wrist and pulled him to her side. He came without a word of complaint, his head lowered, a small smile on his lips that barely lasted a second. His body trembled slightly before he controlled himself.

"What do you think you're doing?" A blonde in strappy, three-inch heels stepped forward, drink in hand and a determined expression on her face. The type of woman who always got what she wanted.

Raven wasn't impressed. "We're leaving."

As she turned, herding the boy in front of her, the woman's talons dug into her arm.

Reacting on instinct, Raven spun and thrust out her palm, slamming her hand into the blonde's chest, releasing some of the pent-up power that swirled inside in response to her anger.

The impact lifted the woman off her feet. She sailed over the table, one heel flying. Her mouth dropped open in moue of surprise, while her drink spun and sprayed her friends.

Conversation slowed, people turned. No one touched the woman as she staggered to her feet. Raven braced herself and scanned the crowd.

No one stepped forward to detain her or the boy.

"Is there a problem?"

Tiger.

He broke through the wall of people who circled the small group. Broad shouldered, lean but roped with muscles, he easily drew attention to him and it had nothing to do with the elegant clothes or wildly untamed mane of hair. The combination should've looked ridiculous but only succeeded in making him appear all the more dominant. It gave him a dangerous air.

An aura of bored arrogance seeped from him, but Raven knew differently. Power thrummed beneath his skin, annoyed at being disturbed, his beast roaming close to the surface even in his human form.

"No, sir. The lady here claimed me, and Miss Jackie objected."

"A challenge?" The tiger's eyes sharpened in the muted light, his attention never once leaving her face. He brushed against her shields, then shoved against them as if surprised to find resistance. The intensity increased, seeking a weakness, and her eyes narrowed.

Usually only vampires or very powerful alphas had such strong mental ability.

Protocol dictated certain rules, and he broke them by probing her without permission—and he knew it, too, if his sudden, impudent smile was anything to go by. If he pushed harder, she would retaliate. She refused to let him enter her mind, refused to let him harvest all her secrets. It was too dangerous for either of them.

When he persisted, she twisted a strand of energy around his shields, using tremendous control to surround him instead of breaking through, then slowly tightened her hold. She let it rest there, let him feel her perusal, the silent threat. Her fingers trembled under the strain, and it took everything she had to hold back the sudden deluge of power and ignore the dangerous lure to crush the threat.

Then his aura fluctuated, rubbed against her own shield in a way that sent a shiver down her spine in a very pleasant way. Her blood heated, and she could almost swear she felt a purr from her core. From the startled look and the aroused flush to his face, the reaction wasn't something he'd anticipated either.

Then he relented and retreated, bowing slightly in deference. "Please forgive my rudeness. I'm Jeffrey Durant, manager of Talon's."

She reeled in the string of energy, suppressing the unholy need to curse at the formal greeting. Rules of the pack dictated she reply in kind, supply her name at the very least, and the bastard knew it. She had to work with shifters. She couldn't piss in the pond just because she didn't want to do something. "Raven—"

"Do you know who I am?" Like a yippy little dog, the blonde charged forward, red blotches of anger coloring her face. Her eyes shimmered a yellowish-green with her emotions, but quickly reverted back to mud brown.

Part shifter.

A weak one.

Most males could shift no matter what percentage of animal DNA they possessed, but the women had to be at least half shifter for their animal to take form. That meant Raven could take this little dog.

Raven adjusted her stance, keeping the kid at her back, and met the threat, damning herself for being a sucker. "I don't give a shit. I know all I need."

"Oh, do tell." The rumpled blonde crossed her arms and smirked. "This should be good."

"You're too weak to be a pure blood. Not even quarter, if I had to guess. You surround yourself with people who are weaker so you have someone who looks up to you. You enjoy abusing the very people you're supposed to be protecting."

A fist flew at her face, and Raven caught it mid-air. Anger allowed her to easily lower the blonde's arm. She lifted her chin, relieved to know she'd guessed right. If the woman had been a true shifter, her jaw would've been crushed. "Are you issuing a challenge?"

A slight murmur went through the crowd. It was the only thing she could think of to get them out of there fast. A challenge meant more than possession of the boy, it meant pack position and a fight to the death. Jackie would die. Raven would see to it. Although she relished a certain poetic justice if she let the little wolf live. It would force the bimbo to the bottom of the pack, where she'd have to earn her place in the hierarchy. And something told Raven it wouldn't be so easy to step over the very people she'd been treating like servants.

Fury darkened the woman's eyes, the brown splintered and specks of yellow appeared, then vanished as fast as they came.

"No." She spit out the one word, a promise of retribution for this humiliation dancing in her eyes.

Giddiness trickled through Raven. Her unique gift remained secret. She'd been foolish to risk discovery over a boy. The need for fresh air pressed heavily against her, effectively caging her without the use of bars. She faced the tiger and raised a brow, doing her damnedest to exude a calm she wasn't feeling. "Then I believe I'm free to leave?"

A charming smile curled his lips, but the intent stare reminded her of his animal form. He was hunting.

And she was his prey.

"There's no rush." He edged closer.

Raven countered quickly, pulling the boy close to her back. "Nor is there a reason to stay."

The beautiful way he moved drew her gaze, hypnotic and beguiling.

"Except to get to know one another." The tone of his voice was deep and soothing. So inviting. The beasts at her core inched forward in curiosity.

A movement in the crowd snapped her to attention. The Ogre. Then the tiger's words registered, leaving a trail of cold in its wake. Clever kitty. She'd bet he lulled many people the same way, using that luscious voice, subtle movements, and just the lick of wildness to lure them to him.

"I think not." Though she tried to rein it in, power burned along her arms at the thought of being held against her will. The beasts retreated, leaving all that power behind, along with the dangerous urge to release it. The leather gloves she wore usually protected those nearest her, but even her gloves couldn't mute the effects of her touch when her dander was up.

The boy sucked in a sharp breath, and she quickly yanked her hand from him. She refused to look behind her, but there was no need when she could see everything in the tiger's reaction. The way he tensed slightly, the way his eyes flickered back and forth between her and the boy.

The crowd drew closer, pressing in on her from all sides, stealing the air around her.

She needed to leave.

The music grew louder, the lights brighter.

A bulb popped, glass shattered. Three more blew in rapid succession.

She took off at a run, dodging through the crowd, ignoring the shouts. The tiger quickly closed the gap between them. She could feel his breath against the back of her neck. Desperate for space, she thrust a burst of current into the crowd. A mass of confusion ensued as everyone received a nasty shock and started shoving one another. Lights flickered, plunging them in darkness. Electricity lashed out of the floor and up into her feet, the charge filling her with power.

She slammed out the door, escaping into the night and took off at a dead run. She should've known better than to be seduced into entering a slave auction by some innocent needing her help. She had a hard enough time staying out of trouble without the need to borrow someone else's. She just prayed no one could tie this whole, rotten evening back to her, or there would be no end of trouble that would land on her doorstep.

Chapter Two

"*W*ait. Please!" The boy's urgent shout pierced the blind panic consuming her, and Raven's steps faltered. Logical thoughts returned in fits and starts. The charge that danced up and down her skin fizzled, soaked into her body and bit angrily along her bones in retaliation for not being allowed freedom.

The labs had discovered she'd been born a conduit within days of being imprisoned. After a slew of painful tests, including shock treatments, she'd adapted, learned to manipulate that energy, and began storing large amounts of it at her core. Now, her body automatically absorbed electricity whatever it could, whenever it could. The only blessing was that when the energy was in control, the beasts at her core were leashed. It's the only thing that kept her safe all these years.

She couldn't detect that anyone else had followed them, but she needed to know for sure. She sent out a pulse of electricity, deflecting the energy that sought shelter in her body and used it to boost the distance she could read. Like a ripple in a pond, the wave reached out, passing through buildings and people. Anything with a heartbeat registered on her scale. To others, it was invisible. To her, an eerie, light blue wave expanded out from her.

Besides the boy, only the Ogre had followed so far.

She could hold off, control the itch to release all that lovely power long enough to set the boy straight.

"Go home, kid." She sucked in much needed air, trying to stop siphoning electricity. Her chest burned with indecision. Instinct shouted to run and not get involved further.

"Send him away, and they'll kill him."

The Ogre stepped out of the shadows, anger and disgust radiating from him like some age old god from Olympus who had judged and found her lacking. Her hackles rose at his animosity.

If she were closer, she didn't doubt he'd take a swing at her. "He's done nothing wrong."

"You claimed him in front of witnesses. He's under your protection and considered your pack now." He stepped off the curb and stalked toward her, his muscular legs eating up the distance between them far too fast for her liking.

She stood her ground on shaky legs. Never run from a shifter wasn't just hype. They loved the chase. A person just didn't always enjoy being caught.

"The others won't take him now."

"There was no ceremony, sponsors, or proof of pack status to support my claim." Proof she couldn't provide. Her gaze flicked to the boy. The pleasant expression stamped on his face belied the tension in his lanky frame. Shit.

"Those rules don't apply at a slave auction. Durant allowed you to leave. His permission was all you needed. Shifters receive five years on the market. If not claimed at the end of that time, they must head to a new territory or die. It was a last chance for those men. If anyone spoke a claim, they have thirty days to prove legitimacy in order to keep him or proof of the rogues' unsuitability and death." His too perceptive eyes remained locked on hers, silently demanding she do right. He jerked his head at the boy. "Taggert's yours for thirty days."

"That's barbaric." Raven was appalled. She couldn't take him home, and sure as hell couldn't guarantee his safety if she did. She grasped frantically for any excuse. "Suitable or not, what's to keep anyone from killing the slaves they claimed once they leave then lying about it?"

"Me." The growl in his voice bit into her skin. His teeth flashed, more a bearing of fangs than a smile.

"What?" All the blood drained from her head so fast the world tilted. In that one second of inattention, her control snapped. A low hum of electricity filled the air. Streetlights flickered and dimmed as energy danced closer.

Seeking freedom to cause mischief.

Seeking her.

She needed to calm down. She couldn't absorb more electricity, even if her body cried out for it, the craving so strong that she ached. She could only absorb so much before it seeped from her and infected others.

Fear blossomed, took root, and memories rose.

Some people had a natural talent to absorb a little energy without any ill effect. But with one little slip, she'd been known to blow pacemakers. Shifters were especially sensitive, transforming into their animal forms if they received an unexpected boost. Then there were the vampires. Like an exquisite brand of drug, the extra spike gave them a delicious illusion of life.

No one could know what she could do to either species. A spark in just the right place could even wake the dead, pulling them right from their graves. Images of decomposing corpses shuffling toward her flashed in her mind, and her throat closed tight.

A shadow fell over her, blocking the light. "You haven't heard a word I said, have you?"

She jumped, and the streetlamps burst like fireworks, raining sparks and glass over them. The big Ogre arched over her, pushing her low, covering her. She scrambled away, unfeeling of the glass digging into her flesh.

Beneath the pavement, the dirt rippled as current worked its way through the packed ground. Energy arched into her body. Fire burned along her nerve endings. Electricity funneled into her system faster than she could control the burn, preparing her body to fight.

"What the hell."

The world around them went dark. Not gradually, not one light at a time, but completely black from one second to the next. When she glanced up, the big man was searching the shadows for a threat. The boy was on all fours, balanced on the tips of his hands and feet, his eyes neon green, his whole focus centered on her.

Knowledge danced in his eyes.

She didn't know how, but he knew she'd caused this.

Tires squealed, headlights raced toward them, gaining speed. The Ogre moved, and she scuttled backwards on her ass like a crab. The car swerved around her, slid sideways, settling between her and the beast of a man and the boy.

The back door popped open. "Get in."

Chapter Three

*D*ominic. "Thank God."

Her car forgotten, Raven scrambled forward and dove inside. Even before her butt hit the seat, he took off. One glance out the rear window showed the boy sprinting after them, his face illuminated in the red taillights. There was no fear, no anger or pain, just sheer determination to follow her.

"I see you've made some friends." Humor danced in Dominic's dark green eyes when their gazes clashed in the rearview mirror.

"Shut up." The voice in the back of her head urged her to turn around. If she left without the boy, they'd kill him.

Fool that she was, she couldn't do it. She'd seen too much death to leave him to his fate. She would find a way to keep him safe.

"Stop."

When the car continued, she cursed Dominic and his protectiveness. She yanked up the corner of the carpeting, revealing loose gravel and scuffed sheet metal. The floorboard quickly warmed under her hand. She closed her eyes, allowed her mind to stretch along the frame of the car, seeking the source of the power.

A spark danced at her touch as she located the cable between the alternator and the battery. She drew down hard. Current jumped at her command, streaking through the metal. Her fingers eagerly soaked up the charge.

The engine clunked ominously, then died altogether when the battery drained.

The car instantly slowed, fishtailing as it rolled to an abrupt stop. "What the hell do you think you're doing?"

She pushed the door open and stepped out. Even with the distance between them, the kid continued to run at a steady pace toward her. A little part of her wondered if he wouldn't have eventually found her anyway if they hadn't stopped. When he drew abreast, he didn't say a word, but slipped inside the car.

In the distance, a truck took the corner on two wheels and jumped the curb, the engine screaming. The Ogre. Damn, but the man was relentless. Without another word, she jumped into the backseat.

"A little help here." Dominic's fingers were wrapped around the steering wheel, his focus centered on the mirror and the truck rapidly closing the distance between them.

Her hand settled against the metal. Electricity leapt from her body, slithering along the frame and hit the cable, feeding it just enough to turn over the engine. "Now."

The car revved to life, gears shifted, then leapt forward. She hit the back seat hard enough to knock the air from her lungs. Headlights grew brighter, lighting up the interior of the car. When she worried the Ogre would force them off the road, the car pulled away.

"How'd you know where to find me?"

He didn't spare her a glance, his dark head bent as he concentrated on navigating the streets. "Trish and Dina returned without you, muttering something about a slave auction. They assumed you would return home. When you didn't, I grew worried."

Raven tossed her trashed cell on the front seat in silent explanation and resisted the urge to roll her eyes at his overprotectiveness. "You were the one who ordered me to go out in the first place."

"Not with some ridiculous plan they concocted."

Ouch, that stung, but hindsight proved to be true. "So you came to rescue me."

"Let's just say you have a way of attracting trouble. I grew concerned."

A small frown twisted his lips, all the emotion he permitted himself. His gaze flickered to the boy in the back seat, and he dropped the subject despite the obvious desire to take her to task. He didn't have to say a word. Endangering others just to pick out a lover didn't seem like such a brilliant idea anymore.

A look out the back window showed the truck keeping pace.

"We won't be able to outdistance him. If we can find a working power grid, I should be able to lose him in traffic." Dominic took the next corner with a chirp of the tires.

Her ass slid across the seat, plastering her against the boy. Despite her graceless sprawl across his lap, he braced them both. Though not built with bulging muscles like the Ogre, he was no weakling, supporting her without effort, the steady strength very solid under her touch. Instead of worrying, he focused solely on protecting her, seemingly pleased at the attention.

Being so close reminded her that he was practically naked.

Uncomfortable with the picture, she untangled herself and scooted to the other side of the car. The temperature inside seemed to have risen. The scent of woods, his scent, followed her, wrapped around her and wouldn't let her mind shuffle him away. He had to be eight to ten years younger than herself. The Ogre said she was supposed to be his protector. In spite of her mental protests, delicious heat at the touch of his skin continued to lick over her body, inviting her to explore further.

Dominic met her gaze in the mirror. "We can take care of the threat back at the house."

A public confrontation would only draw attention, something she needed to avoid if she wanted to remain hidden. Trapped, Raven gave a subtle nod, hating the feeling of being cornered. They would take them both home.

God help them all.

The large house they pulled up to was technically not hers, but the great white monstrosity welcomed her with a little hum of energy it stored within its walls ever since she moved into the place…proof that nothing was safe in her life without her power trying to hijack whatever it touched. With the house, she didn't mind too much. It felt like home.

When she and a group of misfits escaped the labs, they also took whatever they could with them. Computer data, information on the experiments, background on the organization, financial accounts, deeds to houses, stocks, whatever they could grab.

They were trained to be fast, efficient, and deadly. In one day, they had almost everything of value transferred over to a holding company, then sold and filtered through a half a dozen other companies. This house was one of the properties. She claimed it as her own. Her refuge. It wasn't stealing, not really, since the property had been taken from its paranormal owner when they were inducted into the program.

It seemed fitting somehow.

Angry voices from the house drifted to them when Dominic cut the engine.

The gang.

Dominic exited the car, and she followed suit, the boy not far behind.

After escaping the program, they'd agreed the best survival method would be to stick together and work to protect others of their kind. They met once a month and worked through potential threats that endangered the tenuous peace between paranormals and humans. It worked in theory, not so much in actual practice. She usually stayed for the debriefing and then did her best to disappear until they left.

Dominic's face hardened, his shoulders drew back then fell as he sighed. Bristles lined his jaw, giving him a haggard appearance. "Are you going to be all right with them?" He jerked his head in the direction of the two men standing next to the truck. The Ogre was talking, gesturing, while the boy shook his head and pulled a bag and a case from the back of the truck.

"I'll be fine." She tried to smile, but feared it emerged more of a grimace.

"I'll expect a report when I return." He hesitated and studied the guys through narrowed eyes. Without another word, Dominic turned and disappeared inside the house. She didn't envy him his job of leader.

As the men continued to argue, Raven kept her back turned in a false sense of privacy. She didn't care what they said. She had more pressing concerns—like what the hell she was going to do with the both of them, before she could allow herself the luxury to relax her guard.

While she had time alone, rare in the last week and she had a feeling even more so now, she allowed a little of the excess current stored at her center to dissipate harmlessly into the ground. When finished, her muscles had the consistency of rubber, her body instantly missing the loss of spark. She shivered as every ounce of heat vanished.

When she'd settled into the house, the first order of business had been to remove any dead remains from the property within a mile radius. The last thing she needed was to accidentally re-animate a corpse when excess energy infiltrated the ground.

So far there had been no mistakes, nothing dead trying to sneak into her house, or hysterical calls from the neighbors. Small mercies. At least the dead were easy to control. The living...not so much. Objects were simple to manipulate, but people were often too fragile to handle any extra energy without suffering serious consequences.

She resisted the urge to rub her arms. Revealing weakness meant exploitation in the labs.

"We need to get your hand bandaged."

The boy. She blinked at him, surprised at his absolute silent approach. She followed his gaze to find tiny slivers of glass imbedded in the palms of her gloves. The excess energy had kept her from feeling the pain. She wiggled her fingers and felt a slight pull. Her body had healed with the slivers still inside her flesh instead of pushing them out.

When she reached to jerk the glass out, he caught her wrist. "We need better light. If you pull it out now, you might leave pieces behind. Show me where you store the medical supplies, and I'll do it."

Over his head, she caught the Ogre clenching his fists. Not removing her gaze from him, she answered. "I'm fine. Let's get inside and figure out where we go from here."

The old place had a Victorian feel, grand open spaces, large rambling hallways, and a staircase that curved along the wall to the second floor and opened up to a balcony. The acoustics were spectacular, as they could attest to by the heated argument from the office to her left. Hunching her shoulders, she hurried to the back of the house.

She pushed open the swinging door to the kitchen. Tall, wide windows dominated half of the room to the left. Their images gleamed back at her from the darkened glass. Ignoring the guys, she turned on the faucet and ran her hands under the water.

She sucked in a breath then yanked out a large shard, then two of the smaller ones in rapid succession. Sharp pain stung her palms as flesh tore and blood filled the fingers of her gloves.

"Here." When the boy reached for her hand, she jerked back.

"Stay away." The tightness in her throat pitched the words harsher than she intended. The light in his eyes dimmed, but he obediently stepped back. Ashamed of her behavior, she worked the zipper of her gloves and yanked the leather down her arms and then off. "I'm sorry. I—"

"I overstepped my bounds." He bowed his head, gazing down at his feet, so damned submissive her teeth ached.

"It's the blood." Heat filled her face when she blurted out the words. "You can't touch the blood. I'm not sure what would happen if you did."

Compassion softened his features. "Shifters can't catch human diseases."

"Not exactly." She turned her back on them and fished out the last bit of the glass, watching the pink water disappear down the drain.

Warmth burned her palms, and the gouges drew closed, sealing themselves. Turning off the water, she picked up a towel and dried her hands, avoiding their gazes.

"You're a shifter?" Wonder and excitement filled the kid's voice. "I didn't sense it at all."

"Yes. No." She tightened her lips and pressed her hands against the counter, bracing herself. "Right now, I'm more concerned about what to do with the both of you."

"But you healed yourself." The Ogre lumbered closer, a deep, puzzled frown between his brows. He leaned over and inhaled slowly, deeply, dragging in her scent, his thick, dark brown hair sliding over his forehead. "You don't reek like the stench of a vampire, but I don't smell even a hint of shifter on you either."

A shiver crept down her spine. Her stomach somersaulted at his nearness and the deep, vibrant sound of his voice so close to her ear. Something in her very much liked his closeness. The beasts at her center shifted restlessly, but thankfully remained hidden. She gingerly stepped away, uncomfortable with her swinging emotions.

"Jackson has some medical training. Maybe he can—"

"You're a healer?" Confusion swirled inside her. "Then why haven't you healed his back?"

The men stilled, studying her again. Something in their expressions drew on old suspicions that had kept her alive in the labs long after those around her had died.

She took another step back, facing both of them. "Why doesn't your animal heal your wounds or clear your system of the drug coursing through you?"

They exchanged a silent glance and dread tightened her gut. The boy turned to her, his head bowed both in submission and curiosity. "Shifters can't be drugged. Our metabolism acts too fast for anything to affect our system."

Raven shook her head. "At first I thought it was the necklace that wouldn't allow your beast to heal, but it's not." If what they said was true, it was her duty to protect the kid. Until she could find a safer place for him, she was stuck with the job. That meant she had to own up to her responsibilities.

"Continual dosing over a long period of time can lead to drugs lingering in your system." They did it to her and others often enough in the labs. She stepped forward, maintaining her distance from the Ogre...er, Jackson. "May I?"

When she stretched out her arm, the boy flinched, and she immediately pulled away. "I need to check something. You have my word I won't touch you."

A dusky rose filled his cheeks. "I'm yours to command."

Horror sliced through her at his soft refrain. "I'm no one's master." She almost lost her courage, almost left him to his own devices, but there was something shattered in his eyes that she recognized.

She lifted her hand again, palms outward, her heart stuttering at being so close and having all that naked male chest on display. "Don't move." She pressed closer, narrowing the space separating them to a few inches. Heat poured off his skin. She closed her eyes to concentrate, searching for the energy field that surrounded the living. Most people labeled it an aura. It bowed under her touch, fluctuating wildly at the intrusion.

Sparks snapped around her, melding with his shield, testing, judging and finding the source of the sickness ravishing his beast. Any attraction vanished, replaced by concern. To heal him completely would take more out of both of them than she was willing to risk at the moment, revealing more of herself than she was comfortable. The drugs would have to sweat out of his system the normal way.

With a little more push, she focused on the opened wounds on his back, forcing them to mend by redirecting the energy in his body to the injuries.

An abrupt, half growl made her jerk back. Her eyes snapped wide to find Jackson pulling the kid away. When both men looked at her, their eyes had gone neon yellow.

"What did you do?"

The guttural question stung like a reprimand. She curled her fingers into fists and lifted her chin, refusing to back down. She had done nothing wrong. Jackson had no right to judge her, when he demanded that she take responsibility for the kid in the first place. "He was injured. I healed him."

She shook off her irritation and faced the kid. "Your metabolism should drive the drugs out of your system in the next day or so. You'll be hungry, queasy, but you should start feeling normal."

They stared at her like she was a freak. Their perusal needled her pride, and she stiffened her spine. Maybe it was better this way. She spent her life keeping her distance from others. She didn't know what it was about the boy that had her forgetting her own rules.

"Food's in the kitchen, take any open room upstairs. We'll talk in the morning about other arrangements."

Chapter Four

DAY TWO: MORNING

*T*he smell of hickory coffee penetrated Raven's preoccupation, and she stretched at the computer, the long night leaving her exhausted. Her mouth watered, and she gazed longingly at the empty counter space.

Damn Dominic and his rules. His first order of business had been to remove her coffeemaker and place it upstairs, spouting such claptrap that she'd never emerge from her cave otherwise.

He wasn't wrong.

With a sigh of disgust, she lifted her fingers off the keyboard and watched her computer power down. One way to maintain security was to build a computer that only she could run. Who else in this world would be able to power the machine just by touch? Any tampering would melt the hard drive.

Another whiff of dark brew invaded her senses. She pushed back the chair and rose, tugging on her gloves, feeling more herself with the added protection. The vampire case would have to wait, the prep work, a must when dealing with the paranormal, was mostly done. The meeting to see if she would accept the job wasn't until ten tonight.

Vampire hours, you got to love them.

The lights flickered and turned off as she walked by, the basement suite built for convenience, sustained by her power. The reinforced cinder walls were able to withstand whatever she could throw at them without harming anyone else. In theory. She hadn't had to put it to the test yet.

Her knuckles whitened on the knob. A quick scan confirmed she had all her power locked down tight, leaving her feeling strangely vulnerable not to have the threads of energy at her beck and call. Maybe today she could have a normal conversation without running away like a coward.

She pulled the door open and promptly tripped over the body sprawled at the base of the door. With a yelp, she stumbled, nearly taking a digger on the floor before catching her balance.

Crouching, she pressed one hand against the wall and dropped the shields that took hours to prepare. Energy immediately leapt at her touch as if starved for the very taste of her. She drank the current from the wires like a glutton and forced her body to take more as she scanned the room for any threat. Static crackled across her skin, the hair on her arms stood to attention.

"Morning."

The boy pushed himself up from where he rested, turning until he had his back to the wall so they were eye level.

When no danger lashed out at her, she jerked her touch away from the wall. Energy slithered over her skin, luring her to attack and not wait for a fight. She inhaled carefully but found no stench of an intruder or coppery scent of blood. "Are you injured?"

"No."

Sleep left his voice husky, drawing her attention back to him. A bashful smile brightened his face. He ran a hand through his shaggy, sun-streaked mop of hair, only to have the straight strands fall back carelessly around his shoulders. A warm flush crept into her cheeks and her heart tripped at the sexy, rumpled look of him.

"Why were you on the floor?" Disgruntled by the array of emotions that flickered through her in the space of five seconds, she dropped her gaze, rose, and brushed off her pants.

"I must've fallen asleep."

She eyed him critically, searching for the lie. "On the floor?"

"I was waiting for you."

"Me?" Her voice squeaked on the word. "What on earth for?"

"Because he doesn't like being alone. Nor was he going to give you a chance to slip away."

The Ogre sauntered down the stairs, comfortable with his body and her house in a way that had her swallowing hard. His dark brown hair was still damp from his shower, a slight curl that softened his face despite the thunderous expression he directed at her.

She gritted her teeth, reminding herself that despite all that masculinity, an ass still lived beneath the surface.

"I gave my word." Raven straightened to face him and even managed not to wince, because she *had* intended to find a new place for them.

The boy stood gracefully, no worse for wear, and she craned her neck back to meet his gaze. She didn't remember him being so tall yesterday.

All he did was stare at her, unmoving, not breathing. Feeling self-conscious and flustered at the deep curiosity, she gathered up her hair, pinning it at the nape of her neck to cover the distinctive silver that continued to eat away at the tips of the black strands as a side effect from using her powers.

At her movement, his expression blanked. He picked up his small duffle bag, a guitar case and nodded to her. "Where would you like me to store my things?"

The bag couldn't hold more than a few shirts and an extra pair of pants. "Where's the rest?"

She received a shrug in answer. The silence frustrated her, reminded her of the prison, where you learned to stay quiet, don't bring attention to yourself, and draw their focus.

The memories left her stomach with knots the size of boulders. "I need coffee." She needed space. Turning away, she headed toward the kitchen. "Just find a room and throw your stuff in there."

Thankfully, they didn't follow her, and she had the kitchen to herself for the moment. She didn't know where the others were and was grateful for the time alone. Dumping those two and moving on was becoming a lot more complicated than she had anticipated.

She grabbed three donuts, hungry for the calories, and devoured them in less than a minute. Shifters needed nearly double the calories in a day to be able to keep dominance over their animal form. If she didn't eat, her body looked elsewhere for the energy, ready to cannibalize whatever or whoever was near. She grabbed a fourth when the door whooshed open.

London walked into the room, dropped the morning paper on the table, and prowled around without a sound. She would've said he lumbered like his animal counterpart, but he was more graceful than any bear she'd ever seen. Everything about him was blunt, from his short, cropped black hair to his attitude to the scent of leaves that always seemed to cling to him. There was an underlying violence in him waiting to erupt. She suspected he was a hybrid, but had never asked. Crossbreeds were a sore subject with him.

She and London had an unsteady truce. She kept her distance, and he pretended she didn't exist. Communication between them was kept to any mention of security for the team. The arrangement worked.

She poured her first cup of coffee, taking a sip when he spoke. "They'll cause problems."

And promptly burnt her tongue at his words. When she found his dark eyes pinned to hers, she bit back the curse that rose to her lips. "I know."

He sighed and shook his head. "I'll beef up security." He slapped an inch thick piece of ham between two slices of bread and was gone.

"Making friends with the big boy?" Trish sauntered in the room, her robe barely covering the small negligee she sported, her waist-length, long black hair swishing at her back like a tail. She poured herself a cup of coffee and rested her hip casually against the counter. Stiffness lined her movements, revealing how uncomfortable she was being alone with Raven.

Mockery darkened Trish's eyes, animosity pouring off the sleek little panther, but Raven refrained from saying anything. No fighting. Rule one of the house. Though Trish couldn't have known the outcome, Raven suspected the woman had set up last night's debacle. She just couldn't figure out why. As far as she knew, she'd never insulted the panther.

She was saved from actually asking the question when the boy and his protector entered.

"And who do we have here?" The honey purr of Trish's voice froze the kid mid-step, only his eyes moving as he located the source of the threat.

His heartbeat pounded at the base of his neck as his anxiety climbed. And in all that, he didn't so much as twitch. Raven glanced between the boy and Trish, wondering if they knew each other, feeling oddly jealous and protective of him.

"They're off limits."

An unbecoming flush filled Trish's face, and she laughed nastily. "Of course they are. Your wish is our command." With those bitter words, she disappeared out the door, but not without brushing close enough to the boy that their clothes touched.

His nostrils flared at the ripe scent of Trish's desire and the flood of cloying perfume she left in her wake.

Instead of pleasure, the boy shuddered, his shoulders hunched, almost curling into himself.

"Keep the cat away from him." Jackson issued the order, violence dancing in his eyes.

For some odd reason, she had the impression he held himself back from attacking Trish for Raven's benefit.

Raven nodded carefully, promising herself to talk to Jackson later and find out if there was going to be a problem. She could ask the woman to leave, they were only to stay for the rest of the week, but those five days would be an insult, one Trish would make her pay for in small ways for a long time.

The door whooshed open. Dina bounded in, bright and chipper as always. Cherry blossoms filled the room. "Good morning, everyone. I heard that we have company." The fox darted around the room, a ball of energy, her mouse brown hair tangled up in a sloppy knot at the back of her head that bobbed with her movements. She had an apron on and pans out in seconds. Within the minute, breakfast was under way.

Raven straightened and hurried toward the door.

"Don't even think about going anywhere. You have to eat first." Even though her back was turned, Dina was always aware of everyone in the room.

Raven grimaced, plunked down her coffee and sat at the table. "You might as well sit. She won't let you leave without tasting everything." Too bad Dina couldn't cook and no one had the heart to tell her otherwise. Usually, everyone snuck in before she rose or after she cleaned the dishes to see if she'd left anything untouched.

When in residence, most stashed food around the house. Raven sometimes found it days after they'd departed.

The boy slipped into a seat across from her and relaxed a little. His eyes monitored her every move, which left her unnerved and more than a bit paranoid. "What are you doing?"

"Watching you."

The simple answer made her uncomfortable. Attention of any kind always had her hackles rising. She'd learned the hard way that observation meant danger.

She turned to Jackson. "What is he doing?"

The muscles of his shoulders bunched then loosened as he shrugged. "He's assimilating himself into your house. He's trying to gauge what you like and don't like."

"What?" Raven was taken aback and completely baffled.

Dina laughed, her face shining with amusement. "What's your name?"

"Taggert." He answered Dina without removing his gaze from Raven.

"Raven doesn't understand people unless they're dead, so you're just going to confuse the hell out of her. My advice is to be yourself, and let her get used to you."

The phone rang. Thank God.

"I'll get it." Raven bolted to her feet. She rushed to the other side of the room, feeling their attention following her every step like a scratch between her shoulder blades.

"Raven."

"We have a new case." Cool, reserved, Scotts gave nothing away. He was a member of the police force that used her as a resource on unusual crimes. He was also one of the few people who knew about the labs, how the scientists had dissected both vampires and shifters in order to create enhanced soldiers to protect the humans against the monsters.

Scotts kept a special eye on the paranormal community and listened to rumors on the street. More than once, he'd directed clients to her that didn't fit inside the bounds of human law.

"Specifics?" Her heart thudded in her chest, and her appetite vanished. He only called her if it was something bad.

"A body. What we could find of one, anyway."

"Give me the address." She didn't bother to write it down; she knew the park area he mentioned.

"I'll be there in twenty."

"Bring waders." He hung up when she would've asked for more information.

The phone touched the cradle without a sound. The line of windows exposed the dawn as it crested over the trees and crept across the lawn. All she saw were mass graves dug for the paranormals the labs had destroyed before a rescue could be arranged.

She pocketed the keys to her car that London had so thoughtfully retrieved from the club. Squaring her shoulders, she walked toward the door, her mind already gearing itself for the outside world, and she began the process of wrapping her shields around herself in preparation to face both the living and the dead.

Only to find her way blocked by a pair of shoes.

She followed the line of legs, up past a lean, muscular packed body, and found the kid staring at her.

Taggert.

"If there's danger, you shouldn't go alone."

A trickle of humor curled through her. He was...sweet. "I appreciate the concern, but I can take care of myself." She waited expectantly for him to move. Instead, he gave her what she was beginning to understand as his patent blank smile.

Jackson snorted, whether at Taggert's actions or at her words, she couldn't tell. "I think he's worried about you."

She didn't spare him a glance, her humor dissipating. She needed to get to the site. The dead were waiting for justice.

Chapter Five

EARLY AFTERNOON

"*S*tay in the car." Raven slammed the door in their faces. Jackson was furious, waves of his anger beating at her despite her shields. Taggert lounged in the back seat, content that he'd gotten his way to come along.

Jackson, she understood. Rules. Laws. Duty. Taggert left her floundering. Maybe if she understood more about pack business, she could figure him out. Something about his total peace with the situation left her at a loss on how to deal with him.

"I'm glad you came."

She ducked under the tapeline and shook Scotts' hand. His jacket was gone, his pants soaked from the crotch down, and his arms dripped water with his every move. Though detective grade, Scotts trained under a man who insisted on being in the thick of things. Scotts subscribed to the same attitude.

"What did you find?" She snapped on the gloves he provided, walking toward the overgrown, man-made pond. The ground was soggy after days of continuous rain, the pond no better than muddy soup.

"A lot of muck and bones. Divers are still fishing out pieces of the body."

"The recent storms must have dragged the corpse to the surface." A lump filled her throat at the smell of rotten blood and stagnant water. She ignored the bones resting on the tarp like puzzle pieces and stared over the water at the two grim divers struggling to carry a water-logged torso to the edge. Even at the distance, she could tell the corpse had been gutted. "You don't think a human could've done this?"

"Not the way the bones were taken apart, rented in places and chewed in others. The ME examined the remains. There aren't any traces of knife or weapon marks." Dark, hooded eyes met hers, silently warning her to be prepared. "But he could identify teeth marks."

"Who's the ME?"

"Ross."

She gave a jerky nod. The man knew his business. "Show me." At thirty-four, Scotts kept in good shape and covered the ground quickly, his sweat and tobacco scent trailing behind him. The other officers either avoided her completely, grimness etching lines on their faces, or watched her with suspicion as if they expected her to sprout fangs and fur just because she hung out with the paranormals.

Ignoring them, she followed Scotts to the map of bones and mysterious body parts that were spread out near where the cadaverously skinny ME stooped over his work.

"Hey, Ross."

"Hello, pretty lady."

Raven gave him a distracted smile, and the sharp chemical smell she associated with him filled her nostrils. She pulled away to study what he'd set out already.

Stark white bones and raw flesh leeched of blood riveted her. Her mind stumbled, then pushed past the horror to methodically categorize what she saw. The torso lay exposed on the ground, oddly vulnerable and relatively unharmed—that was if you discounted the decomposition that made the skin resemble waxy, misshapen bread dough left too long in the heat.

One arm appeared torn from its socket. It was hard to tell from the tissue damage, but she saw no obvious blade marks. The head had been removed before the body entered the pond, and she could only be grateful not to take that image home with her. With one last glance, she switched her attention to the bones Ross labored over.

"There are two bodies, one old and one new. Both are shifters."

Which was odd in itself. She would've said a shifter fight, but shifters didn't leave one of their own behind.

She crouched, examining the smaller, exposed femur in closer detail. Grooves were gouged into one of the bones. "The tool marks are some sort of animal bites, but I would say there are two of them."

"How do you know?"

"The size." She pointed to the shattered femur bone with muscle tissue still dangling from it by strings that had once been tendons. Decay had the bones dripping with slime, turning the smell putrid. "See here? The bridge of this bite is wider."

Scotts scribbled in his notebook. "So we're looking for a pair."

Raven slowly shook her head, swallowing the bile that threatened to rise. "I don't think so."

Alerted to her tone, Scotts lowered his book and hunkered down next to her. "Why do you say that? You just said there were two different set of marks."

One was a shifter, but there was something off about the width on the second set of the teeth marks that didn't quite match any wild animal.

"One is human, the other is animal."

Raven jerked when Jackson spoke, her head snapping up. "What the hell are you doing? I told you to stay in the car." Raven leapt to her feet, putting herself between him and the evidence to prevent any contamination. Nor did he need to see the macabre scene.

She had to help the police like a compulsion. Needed to do some good in the world and catch the bad guys to make up for all the lives she hadn't been able to save when the labs collapsed and the compound was destroyed. No way was he going to ruin this for her.

"I told them I was your assistant, and they let me pass." Jackson tucked his hands under his arms.

"Raven, do you know this man?" Scotts gripped the handle of his service revolver.

She gritted her teeth, the muscles in her jaw bunching. She thought about refusing to answer, but that would only cause her more trouble in the end. She pried her lips apart and spit out one word. "Yes."

Scotts didn't stand down and Jackson refused to budge. They were about the same height. Though Scotts was thicker in the torso, Jackson had more bulk on him overall.

"I think it's best if we left." Raven paused, waiting for Jackson to leave, but the bastard wore a stubborn look that said he wouldn't budge without her. Her fingers clenched, eager to get her hands on him. Raven nodded to Scotts. "I'll do some digging and call you when I learn more." She'd return tonight when everyone was gone and visit the morgue to catch up on what she missed. The privacy would allow her to get a closer look without others watching, and she'd be able to see what her gift could pick up.

Those bodies were put in the pond, but she didn't think they were there to conceal a murder. They were placed there very deliberately, and she would find out why.

She stalked back toward the car, Jackson's silent tread following, her anger mounting with each step. She slammed the car door, revved the engine and took off just as Jackson shut his door. Taggert remained a silent presence in the back of the car.

As she turned onto the main road, Jackson retrieved his phone from his pocket and an ugly suspicion crept into her mind.

"Who do you think you're calling?" She didn't bother to look away from the road.

"There are people on the squad who will help bury this case."

Affronted by his lack of belief that she could do her job, she tightened her grip on the steering wheel. "You can't do that. Someone is murdering people. If you sweep everything away, he'll continue his rampage." Even with what little she knew of him, she couldn't believe he would allow a killer to go free.

When he continued to dial, Raven coaxed a strand of current to rise to the surface. The voltage flared in response to her anger, lashing at his phone. The plastic gave a warning beep and a trail of smoke rose from the keypad.

"What the hell!" He tried to turn the phone back on but without success, then glared at her as if he somehow suspected her involvement.

"This is my case." She flexed her hands on the steering wheel, taking the turn a little too fast. Tires squealed in protest, but no one said a word.

"If the truth of this gets out, the humans will panic again." The hard mask he always wore sharpened with his conviction. He ran a distracted hand through his hair.

She didn't think he directed his comment at her, it was more talking out loud, but it hit her anyway. Memories of the horror of the paranormal conflict ten years ago filled the car with tension. People hunting the paranormal community. The police unable to control either paranormals or the humans. The skirmishes and slaughter of innocents on both sides. It only stopped when the government issued a new law that made paranormals legal citizens, their deaths punishable by law.

At least that was what the citizens led to believe.

"Scotts knows what he's doing."

"That human?" The emotions on his face shut down, and he snorted.

Anger roared back to life. "Do you really think this is the first case we've come across?" She gave him a cynical look. "You're a fool."

"Must be nice coming from someone who doesn't understand what it's like to live inside the pack. Things are different. Rules have to be maintained. You've never had to watch people you know gunned down and murdered, never knowing who'd be next."

A bubble of laughter worked its way up her throat. "You pompous ass. Do you actually believe the wolves have it worse than anyone else?" She cast him a cynical glance, then focused on the road again. "Funny, but I saw bodies from both sides of the war. Wolves were very few and far between."

The animosity in the air made it difficult to breathe. "The pack takes care of their own. We'll find the killer. It won't happen again."

"That's why you said an animal and human tore them apart when you know damn well a shifter was responsible." Her shoulders slumped. That mentality only made it harder on the paranormal community. It raised suspicions and created a dangerous situation. Vigilante justice wasn't the answer. If the public learned of it, a rift would form and all the races would suffer. The dunderhead either didn't understand or was too stubborn to care. "Scotts is a good man. He's trained for these types of situations. He knows when he's over his head."

"And he calls you? What the hell good will that do?"

His harsh laugh grated on her nerves.

"I bet you're even in favor of the new paranormal unit the government is trying to enforce. What a joke."

And just like that, any connection she felt to him was severed. "Maybe if you got rid of that chip on your shoulder and paid attention to the world outside your pack, you'd know that something needs to be done before everything blows up in our faces." She would not allow them to fall back into war between the races.

"It's a last-ditch pity attempt to appease the breeds."

She grimaced when he used the slur humans flung at them. "So what. Who cares, if it actually works." If Jackson wanted to play cop, he was more than welcome, but she would not allow him to jeopardize everything she'd worked so hard to achieve. If he thought he would be able to step all over her case, he'd quickly find out why she was so good at her job.

Chapter Six

"*T*his isn't working. One call and I know I can convince them to make an exception. There are a few days left of the auction."

Raven drew up short outside her room at Jackson's comment. She was surprised to feel the pinch of betrayal, even though she knew it would be the best decision for all of them, especially after the scene at the park just an hour ago.

"I want to stay."

There was only a calmness in that voice. She didn't understand it.

"She won't be able to keep you. She's not registered. If the council demands proof of her suitability, she won't be able to pass the tests."

The soft tone revealed a compassion for the boy she hadn't expected.

He cared.

It created a picture of a man determined to protect. Despite his low opinion of her, she couldn't fault him for that…then the rest of his comment prodded her curiosity. Tests? What tests? She crept closer.

"You're wrong." Taggert seemed equally convinced.

She took the last two steps and entered the doorway. Taggert stood in front of her dresser, touching the few possessions that she'd left out, but otherwise avoiding Jackson. His submissive nature made her feel protective of him. It was a carefully crafted illusion. No matter how weak, shifters were deadly. Both men had their backs to her. In comparing them, she was shocked to realize Taggert wasn't much smaller in stature than Jackson.

As if sensing her regard, Taggert lifted his head and their eyes met in the mirror. He instantly dropped his hand, but didn't release her gaze. She could detect nothing in his expression that indicated any type of emotion.

"You said I was allowed to choose any room."

His empty bag rested near the bay window. When she looked back at him, he'd turned to face her. She would bet her life he'd known this was her room, but he still chose it anyway. Not that she used it often, as sleep was a rarity for her, but what little possessions she'd accumulated were here. She didn't believe he picked her room to start a fight, and it left her even more curious.

"Yet you selected mine." She saw the slight flexing of his fingers and stepped closer, unwilling to back down without him giving her something. Everything about him was so controlled she doubted he even knew how to be spontaneous. Maybe if she pushed and broke through his shell, he'd drop the act.

Taggert's eyes flickered and little crow marks appeared at the corners. Then his expression cleared, leaving her with a pleasant man with no personality. "I'll move if it displeases you."

Jackson stepped between them, blocking her view. "Pack members usually bunk together as a rule."

"A rule?" She studied his face closely, but couldn't see or smell a lie on him. The thought of sleeping with two attractive men within touching distance, did weird things to her body.

She wished she could say it was fear, but she knew that for a lie.

Normally dormant, she was surprised when the beasts around her core crept closer to the surface. Though she'd never been able to tell the animals apart, they were becoming bolder since Taggert and Jackson had moved into the house. She shivered at the thought and what it could mean.

"Yes."

Jackson kept changing his mind about her as it suited him, and it irritated the snot out of her. "Am I pack now?"

A muscle ticked in his jaw. "To be pack, the alpha has to petition the council or take a pledge of blood. For Taggert, there's no reversing that but death. Are you ready for that step?"

His blunt comment took her aback.

"She doesn't have to decide yet."

Raven peered around Jackson's shoulder at Taggert, admiring the way he stood up to Jackson. She had to wonder if it was fear of her turning him away that prompted him to speak, or if he was defending her.

"I don't spend much time in this room. If I sleep at all, it's usually on a cot in the basement between work. I'm not sure—"

"I promise not to get in your way."

His earnest answer hurt. Her heart thudded in her chest, a heavy, pounding rhythm as she debated the wisdom of allowing them to stay. Her control wavered when she slept. Dreams of the dead haunted her sleep, ghosts of people long gone begging her to save them.

What if she accidently hurt them?

"He's not use to sleeping alone," Jackson prodded her. "Touch for a shifter is an important part of building trust. Denying him is also considered a punishment."

It irritated her that he kept stepping between them, almost like he was afraid to have her focus on Taggert.

Or he was jealous, which was preposterous.

She felt herself weakening. What he said matched too closely to what she'd learned in the labs for him to be pulling one over on her. A little spurt of fear at even contemplating such an action couldn't keep her damn curiosity at bay. "No funny business?"

They both solemnly shook their heads.

"And you? Are you fine to sleep alone?" His only reaction was a slight flinch around his eyes.

"I will be within calling distance."

His answer gave her pause. Though she didn't want him in her bed, she liked it even less knowing he'd be watching, listening, and free to wander.

And a tiny part of her wanted him there with her. His presence irritated the hell out of her, but she could relate to him.

"I'll bring in a cot or a couch." He bristled, and Raven raised a brow. "You said it yourself, you're here to protect him. I doubt he'd raise any alarm if I tried anything."

Safety in numbers. Neither would try anything with the other in the room and maybe she could work on her control. If anything happened, Jackson would protect Taggert.

Taggert smiled slightly, his bland persona once more firmly in place. She couldn't help narrow her eyes a little. There was something beneath the surface, something she couldn't put her finger on that plagued her.

Then it hit her. It was the way he watched her, picked up small clues about her that she'd tried so hard to eradicate. It left her feeling very exposed.

"Fine." Jackson bit off the one-word answer.

She wondered if he agreed just to distract her from her line of thought. Then a muscle ticked in his jaw, and his Adam's apple bobbed. The big fraud was as nervous about sharing a room as her.

The second she opened her mouth, the fire alarm blared. Raven closed her eyes and sighed. "Gentlemen, dinner is ready." The comical looks of dismay on their faces had her smiling. Shifters loved their food, burning through calories at an amazing rate. This was going to be an unforgettable stay for them.

Both men followed her down the stairs. Though she couldn't hear them, she could sense them crowding close to her back. Even before they reached the kitchen, the smell of caramelized, burnt food clogged the air.

The odor grew worse when they opened the door. Everyone was seated, waiting for them. Raven swallowed hard at all the food. Jackson sat, but Raven couldn't make herself move. Taggert remained glued close to her side, his distress barely contained.

"Dina, I hope you don't mind, but Taggert wanted to show me some home-style recipes." Taggert instantly nodded, his eyes fixated on the scorched food in wide-eyed horror.

"Another cook in the house? I don't mind at all. Maybe later we can trade recipes." She gave a sunny smile and continued to pile what was supposed to be food on everyone's plate.

Taggert instantly went to the fridge and started taking out supplies. Raven grabbed an apple and shoved it in her mouth.

Jackson narrowed his eyes, but he didn't refute the lie. After one bite, his chewing slowed and his throat bobbed painfully as he swallowed, gazing at her, silently asking her to get him out of there.

The malicious side of her said leave him, while her compassionate side argued to rescue him. When she remained silent, his eyes narrowed. She'd no doubt pay for her rebellion later, but a little vengeance felt good.

A tiny smile played about Dominic's mouth as he watched the interaction. "While we eat, let's catch you up on the case we're running down."

Raven hesitated, surprised at the laid-back comment from Mr. Super-Secret. "Now?"

He spared the two men a brief glance and shrugged. "From the way I understand it, they're yours for the next month. If anything leaks, we'll know the source."

"If she came to the meeting like everyone else, we wouldn't have to re-hash everything." Trish took a sip of the ever-present wine at her side, while the food on her plate remained untouched.

"She had other things to attend." Dominic kept his tone firm but even.

Trish stood abruptly, the chair scraping loudly in the room. She slapped the table with enough force that everything clattered. Jackson stopped moving, the predator in him rising to the surface. One wrong step and he'd be at her throat. Taggert didn't react at all to the violence as he continued to make food, which surprised Raven the most. He trusted her to protect him.

"Why does she deserve special treatment all the time? You always come after one of us if we're late or don't show. Even in the compound, they treated her better than us. Why?"

Heart pounding, Raven slowly faced Trish and her accusation. "I was treated no differently."

"I didn't hear the guards enter your cell, then brag about their conquest. How many times a day did they visit you?" Fury rolled through her, and her voice raised.

"None." They did something much worse.

Trish snarled, shoving away from the table and stalked forward. "They made me their whore, while you, their little princess, were safely tucked away from it all."

Dominic stood and carefully placed his napkin on the table in a very exact manner as he battled his temper. "Trish, you will want to sit down and shut up."

She whirled on him. "Even now, he protects you. You're everyone's little darling. My God," she struck her arms out and slowly turned, "doesn't anyone else see this?"

Years of festering had taken its toll, bitterness and hatred flooding through the room.

Dominic opened his mouth to speak, but Raven forestalled him. "Tell me, Trish, how many times did they take you to the labs for tests?"

She rolled her eyes. "You think a few tests equals what we went through?"

Raven ignored her. "How many times did they torture you?" When Trish opened her mouth to speak, Raven stepped closer. Energy curled around her feet, lashing upward around her legs like roots, sinking deep into her bones.

"Each time they raped me instead of you."

Raven closed her eyes. "You want to know why they didn't breed me?"

"Oh, this should be good." Trish crossed her arms and tapped her foot.

"I'd been a prisoner at the compound for nearly twenty years." The confession startled Trish, but didn't ease her anger one bit. "They played the same games with me a few years after I was admitted. As soon as they deemed me old enough to breed." Memories long buried rose to the surface. A little spark at her core wrapped around her in response as if to protect her, but with it came the delicious urge to lash out at the cause of the pain. She took a shallow breath, fighting the need to make everything go away.

Trish flinched, and Raven didn't need a mirror to know her eyes had changed from pewter to a vivid blue. It happened whenever the current rode her hard. "They stopped the games the same day I fought back and killed everyone who came near me."

Trisha blanched. She leaned forward, balled her hands into fists, and planted them on the table. "And do you think I just let them do what they wanted without fighting?" She whirled and left without another word.

The room remained a frozen tableau. She hadn't suspected the group treated her any different, but she knew that for a lie. She was an outsider, even with the people closest to her.

Afraid to look at anyone for fear they'd see the hurt, Raven gazed out the window. She suspected that many of them knew about her past. She thought she'd made her peace with it, until Trish dredged it all back to life.

She should've left well enough alone instead of playing one-upmanship with Trish.

"Raven—"

"No," she cut Dominic off. He had nothing to say that she hadn't already said to herself a thousand times. And she sure as hell didn't need anyone's sympathies. "I shouldn't have said anything. I knew she hated me. I just didn't know why. That's no excuse for the way I acted." Energy spiked, pulling from the room to wallow in her body, building with the pain.

"You have the right to defend yourself." London's gruff voice only made it worse.

She needed to leave before she did anything else she'd regret. "We'll discuss the meeting later. If you'll excuse me."

Raven left by the back door and quickly lost herself in the woods, aware of the faint outline of blue that swarmed over her skin and now extended up past her wrists. It was getting worse. The blue lines were darker, more pronounced.

Her greatest fear was losing control, and no matter how she tried to stop it, her control continued to weaken more each day. She couldn't live with herself if she hurt someone she cared for.

Not again.

Chapter Seven

SUNSET

"*How* many shifters are missing?" Raven directed her question at Dominic, not lifting her gaze from her computer as she methodically entered data into the system. Thankfully, no one mentioned her blow-up earlier that afternoon, and she wanted to keep it that way. She shoved the last of her sandwich in her mouth and waited for his answer.

"Seventeen."

The large number snapped any other thoughts out of her head. Her hands hesitated over the keyboard as her gaze shot to his. "And we're only *now* learning about it?"

"There have been no police reports, no calls from concerned relatives—nothing to hint at foul play." Frustration rippled through his voice until it resembled nothing more than a rumbled growl.

"Then how do you know there's anything wrong?" Jackson and Taggert hovered behind her, observing every move she made over her shoulder. The study seemed to shrink in size. Their scents wrapped around her, tearing down the wall she was desperately trying to build between them. She wanted to shove back her chair and demand they give her space to breathe.

Instead, she suffered in silence, unwilling to admit, even to herself, how their nearness affected her, tempting her to relax her shields and be herself. That could never happen.

"Instinct. Experience."

Dominic leaned over her desk, his face inches from hers, his autumn scent helping to drag her attention back to business. She grabbed onto the excuse with both hands, discretely scooting the chair closer to the desk and away from all the men crowding around her.

"It's their MO."

It meaning the scientists. She couldn't dispute his claim, but not everything evil was spawned by the labs. "Do you have any proof?"

He straightened, running his hand through his wavy hair in a rare show of emotion. "Nothing yet."

He retreated across the room and propped himself against the window frame, his green eyes calculating as he studied her. The pose put her on edge. He was up to something. She braced herself, knowing she wouldn't like it. "Speak."

"That's why I want to pull you in for this one."

She was right. The thought of entering the labs again sent a flash of ice through her veins, rooting her to her chair when she wanted to bolt.

"This is unnecessary. The wolves would've been notified of any large scale disappearance and taken action." Jackson bristled.

The heat of his anger lapping at her back as he unobtrusively inched closer to her. She was half convinced his protest stemmed more from Dominic upsetting her than taking issue with the missing shifters.

The confrontation and sudden tension forced her mind into action. Both wolves locked eyes and refused to back down. She took a deep, steady breath, breaking the stalemate by relenting on her rule to never get involved in the labs again.

"Get me a list of names." That's the best she could do. She'd stopped hunting labs years ago, unable to bear witnessing the remnants of failed experiments and wade through all the pain that saturated the walls. Not if she wanted to remain sane. She'd delegated the hunt to Dominic and his crew, but there was one thing she could do. She could find these missing people.

Jackson turned to her, thunder in his eyes. "If there was something happening in the community, everyone would know. You can't hide that many missing shifters."

The insight into pack life snagged her attention, and she swiveled in her seat, pinning him with a look. Only to find his attention solely on her. There was just something sexy about a man when he focused on you so intently that no one else in the room existed for him. She swallowed hard, trying to gather her scattering thoughts. "You have a network."

He hesitated, and the moment shattered. Back came the imperial Ogre. "Each pack has an enforcer. They pass information along from one to another."

"And if one is corrupt?"

"No."

"No?" Raven gave a half smile, enjoying baiting him. "What do you mean no? Are they incorruptible?"

"We are when it comes to the safety of the community." The answer was straight and honest. He truly believed it.

She didn't. Power can easily be bought regardless of the race. "Tell me, Jackson, if you had the choice to have your whole clan slaughtered or give up a few members, what would you chose?"

"Neither. There's always a way—"

"Not always." She dropped her gaze, turning back toward the computer and pulled up a program that provided a back way into police records without leaving a trace. "If one pack was in trouble, would they go to another for help?"

He answered more slowly this time. "Pack business stays within the pack. Concerns are brought to the Council of Five, the governing body for all paranormals."

"So you truly don't know the workings of all the packs. One might not be as honorable as another." The image of him shaking his head reflected in her monitor as she worked her way deeper into the system to the paranormal files officials denied existed.

"An enforcer wouldn't let anything happen to the pack."

"Then you should check that all the enforcers are alive. Or maybe they were ordered to cull the pack and decided to earn an extra buck in the process." She envied him the strength of his convictions and the absolute protection offered by the enforcers, no matter how illusory.

He crossed his arms, the line of his jaw uncompromising. "We don't work that way. We're there to protect, we're not assassins." He quickly switched subjects. "If I can see the list of names, I might be able to learn something."

"No." She didn't want him caught up in this business. She wouldn't allow him to interfere.

He continued as if he hadn't heard her. "My guess is that the missing shifters are unregistered rogues who've since traveled to a new territory or died."

The answer was plausible, but it didn't take away the niggling at the back of her mind that something wasn't right. The way the corner of Dominic's eyes tightened said he felt it, too.

They'd both learned to sense things in the compound. It'd kept them alive long past when they were slated for death. "How can you tell the difference between a pack member and a rogue?"

"If you're in person, you can smell the difference. Some can mask it, but only to a certain extent. Rogues are loners and usually have a wild scent that marks them as different."

"Then the list of names wouldn't help. What can you do with pictures?" With a few clicks, mug shots of three people on her list filled the screen. She squinted, trying to see if she could pick out subtle differences that would betray them as a rogue.

Jackson leaned over her shoulder, much too close for her peace of mind and ability to breathe.

"The look in their eyes gives them away. Wild. Dangerous. Eager for violence," Jackson said, appearing lost in thought.

"That describes half the shifters I know." Raven gave him a slanted smile, ignoring the skip in her heart and the flare of heat under her skin.

Jackson rubbed his jaw, a stall tactic if she ever saw one as he debated whether to tell her the truth or not.

"Rogues have a harder time controlling their beasts. It's why pack is so important. Most rogues have been away so long they can't pass for normal anymore. A light color encircles their pupils as their animal gains dominance. It's the main reason why they're put down whenever possible."

Jackson's explanation made a sick sort of sense. If they turned feral and killed, they posed a threat to both humans and pack. No one could afford to have the wars return.

Whether beast or man, the human always remained dominant, the animal portion just an extension of that person. Memories from the labs surfaced. Of how she could tell when shifters lost control when caged or tortured too long. After a while, she sensed wild energy pouring off them as their human side receded more and more. There was usually no coming back from that. "But if they join a pack, doesn't that help?"

"Most of the time it's already too late." Jackson shook his head, completely convinced that death was the best option.

She just wished she could be as sure. She glanced at Taggert, her own rogue, curious at his reaction to what could easily have been his fate, but his face gave nothing away.

The clock chimed ten, startling her out of her first, long overdue lesson in pack law. Though reluctant, Jackson had finally opened up a little. The rest of the discussion had to wait. She closed the laptop. "If you'll excuse me, my appointment is about to arrive."

Anger darkened Jackson's face at being dismissed. The leather chair squeaked slightly as she stiffened, waiting to see what form of attack he'd take to get around her. She suspected he opposed her on purpose just to needle her.

Dominic nodded, pushing away from the wall.

"I'll stay." Jackson continued to stare at her, daring her to argue.

She didn't intimidate that easily. "That's not wise."

He drew up at her answer, using every inch of his body to appear larger. He did an impressive job of it.

"Why?"

His calm question came as a surprise. She expected a bully, not reason.

"Because I'm a vampire." A hint of old world accent colored that smooth voice.

Jackson's whole posture stiffened. Claws burst from his fingers. Fangs descended. Between one instant and the next, Jackson and Taggert leapt in front of the desk, snarling at the trio near the door.

The thin veil of humanity dropped away as their eyes gleamed yellow, the animal in them determined to protect.

Two of the vampire's entourage leaned forward, fangs bared, their eyes awash in black.

Raven met Lester's gaze, the lead vampire, and smiled at his serenity. Though she knew the elderly man exterior was a lie, his old way charm put her at ease. "I'm sorry for their behavior. If you would, please, have a seat."

He gave her a courtly bow and did as directed. Spice lightly scented the air, sharp and bold, but she couldn't place it. A breeze shifted around her, and Lester looked at his two guards. Without a word exchanged, they pulled back but remained standing between the shifters and their master.

"Jackson. Taggert. Either resume your positions or leave." Dominic, blessedly, remained by the door and in control of his beast.

"You can't—"

"I won't ask again." Raven sent a quick charge, zapping Jackson on the ass, using low enough voltage the vampire would assume it was alpha control. They had no reason to assume otherwise. A muscle bunched in Jackson's jaw, and he thankfully fell silent.

Though he hadn't shifted completely, she could all but see Jackson's fur ruffle. Without removing his gaze from the threat, he retreated to stand at her side. Hovering. Almost protective of her. She must be reading him wrong, seeing what she wanted to be there.

"You've acquired bookends." Humor danced in the vampire's voice, but there was none of it in his eyes.

Jackson's growl rumbled deep in his throat. Raven ignored him and focused on the bigger threat. "A trial only, I assure you."

The vampire nodded. "Understandable. We must take care to protect ourselves."

Raven released the breath clogging her chest. Although the vampire's approval didn't mean anything to her, she was grateful he understood that she hadn't brought the shifters there with the intention of offending him.

"You want to hire me."

"My son is missing." He gestured to one of his guards by lifting two fingers. The man carefully placed a folder on her desk and resumed his position. She gave him points for not flinching as the energy in the room swirled around her.

A missing person complicated matters considerably, considering the other case she was working on with the police and Dominic. She didn't believe in coincidences.

She made no move to touch the folder. She'd done her research on this master vampire and his iron fist. There were questions she needed answered first. "May I ask how you became aware of my unique services?"

A small smile crooked his lips, revealing a hint of fangs. "You were highly recommended as someone who knows how to get things done and when to keep her mouth shut."

"Of course." The fear that he came there to pry into her past eased, and she reluctantly pulled the folder closer, flipping it open. "What information do you have for me that's not in the file?"

"Jason's been missing for two months."

"And you suspect kidnapping?"

He tipped his head slightly. "No. Someone murdered him. I want you to find out whom and tell me."

Raven tapped her pencil on the desk, the rhythm breaking into the little haze the vampire exuded like a fragrance, a haze that could easily wrap around a person and put them under their control.

"Mr. Lester." Her lips tightened. She wasn't amused.

The haze instantly disappeared, and he dipped his head. "My apologies."

"Think nothing of it." The creature was too old not to be precisely aware of his every action, the calculating old goat. He was testing her.

"I would think you'd have more contacts to find answers than I would. Why come to me? And why do you believe he's dead?"

The stillness of his face finally broke, small lines and wrinkles melted away revealing the cold, intimidating man beneath. "All vampires have a connection to the ones they created, their protégés. Ours was severed three weeks ago."

"But you said he's been missing for two months?"

"Yes." Heat filled his eyes, his pupils dilated as anger wrestled for control.

The vampire spice in the air became so thick with his rage, she nearly sneezed.

"It wasn't done by one of mine. I checked personally." No doubt those he suspected were no longer available for questioning. "I need your resources to research other...venues." Lester's open-ended accusations, delivered in a bland voice, left no doubt whom he suspected.

"We don't stoop to your level." Jackson shot forward, his yellow eyes hard and intimidating. "This stinks of some underhanded vampire trick."

Lester rose, only a few feet separating them. "And I wouldn't put it past a breed to be ignorant enough to start a war by murdering my son. Miss Raven, I suggest you leash your pet or I will."

Raven stood slowly, uncertain where she lost control of the meeting. "Mr. Lester, I'm sorry for the loss of your son. I apologize for my companions, and ask that you stay."

Only when he seated himself did the current building in the air gradually dissipate, though it didn't disappear completely. She could feel the pull under her skin like an addiction, urging her to take all their energy and drink it down. The need had sneaked up on her, caught her unawares. It shouldn't have, if she wanted her gift to remain hidden. The last thing she needed was for the wolves and vampires to view her as a threat.

Both sides slowly pulled back from the edge, but she could tell it was only for her benefit. If given a choice, they'd rip each other to shreds.

"Thank you. Mr. Lester, please gather a list of people you've...contacted, and I'll research this matter further."

"You'll take the job." It wasn't a question.

Raven hesitated, thinking about the animosity between the two races. If she said no, it would only be a matter of time before a confrontation between the two came to a head. All the work promoting to the public that the paranormals were like everyone else would go to shit. "Yes."

"Very good." The man's appearance slowly rippled, his frame bowed, his jowls sagged, and his face loosened into that of an old man once more. He picked up his cane, barely touching it to the floor as he shuffled to the door. "You'll be amply rewarded for your time."

As soon as the door shut, Jackson stalked toward her with a decidedly unfriendly expression. Taggert inserted himself between them.

"You sell yourself to the highest bidder like a whore." The cruel gleam in his eyes convinced her he truly believed what he said.

Raven shrugged, but couldn't brush away the sharp sting of hurt this time. Pride refused to let it show. "I provide a service to the paranormal community that others cannot. I don't discriminate between the races."

"I won't allow you to dig into pack business on the say so of one of his kind." He jabbed a figure at the door.

Her patience grew thin with his damn holier than thou attitude. "Then I'll make sure you're not aware of my business in the future." His expression looked like she'd asked him to chew glass.

"There are other possibilities besides pack." Dominic's voice floated from her right.

Did he say that for Jackson's benefit or hers? She couldn't tell and it bothered her more than she cared to admit. Could the presence of other wolves be reminding him of everything he'd been denied by staying with her? A little part of her trembled at the thought of losing him.

"I've never doubted it, but it's my job to research all the angles. I don't choose sides; I find the problem and fix it." When Jackson didn't say a word, she glanced at Dominic and knew she'd been had. "I know what you're thinking. Stay out of my business."

"They could be connected." He pushed away from the wall, running a hand through his thick mop of wavy hair. "It wasn't too long ago that this very thing happened. People missing from both pack and clan communities and each race too stubborn to work together. So much could've been prevented if the scientists had been stopped."

"Now you're jumping to conclusions." She gave up on men. Needing a little peace from the testosterone in the room, she strode toward the door. "Just because it was a vampire doesn't mean I shouldn't take the case. It doesn't mean shifters are automatically the perpetrator. It doesn't mean that humans are stealing people to do testing. If I want your help, I'll ask for it."

"What if it's a trap?"

Taggert's question pulled her up short; there was something in his tone that made the back of her skull tingle. When she turned, she only found concern on his face.

"I'll find out the truth. I won't accuse the wolves or anyone else until I have proof."

Taggert shook his head, his gaze unrelenting. "A trap for you."

He didn't seem to care about the argument. His first concern had been her. That took her aback. "Why would they come after me?"

"You're unique. Something about you draws attention. I noticed it last night at the club. Though he might not admit it, Jackson noticed. So did Durant. Do you have the same appeal to vampires?"

A dangerous question that. One she didn't know how to answer truthfully.

Dominic's gaze on her sharpened. "It's worse around the dead, isn't it?"

Unnerved at how close he was to the actual truth about her lack of control, Raven lifted her chin, prepared to be just as stubborn. "Leave it be, Dominic."

"What did they do to you that makes you so dangerous?" Jackson's soft question did nothing to alleviate the anger that vibrated in the air.

Though the anger wasn't directed at her, she jumped under the lash of it anyway. The force of it left her little doubt why Jackson made such a fantastic enforcer for his people. No, neither of them could be allowed to know the truth about her birth, or the injections forced on her in the labs that made her a crossbreed. It was too dangerous for everyone. "I'm not something you can fix."

"No, but I can try to protect you if you'd let me."

Her throat tightened at Jackson's softly spoken words. She could see him shuffling through his thoughts, categorizing her, and adding up the facts, concluding that she was a lot more than human.

But if he knew, why was he being so nice to her now? What changed?

She gathered up her laptop and hugged it to her chest. "It would only get you killed." With deliberate steps, she turned and left. She had research to do without being distracted by the people invading her life.

The desire to slip out the front door taunted her. Escape whispered in her ears. But she wouldn't walk blindly into this mess without the proper research.

The basement door opened on silent hinges and lights flickered on at her movements. As she flipped the computer open, she lost herself in the world of reports and statistics.

She didn't know how long she sat there reviewing the photos Scotts had sent of mutilated victims, when her senses picked up on the intruder.

Jerking to her feet, she yanked the power from the room and dumped them in darkness.

"Please don't leave."

"Taggert?" Relief made her control waver, and the lights flickered then brightened. She picked up the gloves by the computer and tugged them over her naked hands, feeling very exposed. "What are you doing down here?" She closed her eyes and severed the connection to her core as hard as possible and all that lovely energy slowly melted back into her bones.

"It's late. You aren't sleeping."

He sounded hesitant, clearly expecting to be reprimanded for daring to voice an opinion. It was the only reason she didn't snap at him to mind his own business.

"I don't sleep often. Go on to bed. I'll come later."

He didn't move. "You need to rest."

She tipped her head to the side, confused at his actions. He appeared pale. A light sheen coated his skin, and a slight tremor passed through his frame. "What's wrong?"

"It's worse at night." There was no fear in his voice, only acceptance. Those strange eyes, like warm chocolate, focused on her.

"What is?"

"Taggert, go to bed." Jackson's harsh voice echoed in the cement room. He stepped out of the shadows wearing a pair of shorts and nothing else. His skin gleamed in the fractured light.

When she didn't say anything, Taggert turned and headed past Jackson and toward the stairs.

"Maybe it's about time you tell me what the hell's going on." Raven leaned against the table and crossed her arms. "He's going through drug withdrawal, but there is something else neither of you are telling me."

A stubborn look settled on Jackson's face. "It's pack business."

A disgusted sigh resonated in her chest. "Either I'm allowed to adopt him and treat him as pack, or I'm not. Make up your mind. Which is it?"

She didn't think he would answer. When he did, she wished she'd kept her mouth shut.

"Once you accept your duties, you're pack. Stop trying to find ways to get rid of him. You can't take him now then reject him later. Neither of you will survive if you don't decide soon."

Without saying anything else, he turned and left. She watched the muscles play across his back, but it was the near silent slap of his bare feet that made him appear vulnerable.

The image jarred the picture she had of him from a hard-ass to a man just doing his duty. But why would an enforcer care about the life of one rogue? Something didn't add up.

She was supposed to visit the morgue, but maybe it was time to dig a bit deeper into what exactly these two men expected from her instead. It was apparent that they weren't going anywhere. She closed the lid on her computer and tucked it under her arm, trying to avoid thinking about them waiting for her in her bedroom.

Chapter Eight

DAY THREE: PREDAWN

*B*y the time she entered the bedroom, Jackson was ensconced on the couch, his broad back toward her. Taggert lay in the center of her bed. Neither were asleep. Her heart thumped heavily in her chest at their invasion.

The image of them there made everything all too real.

She hovered near the desk nestled against the wall by the door. She set the computer down, then hesitated, uncertain what to do next. Nerves hummed under her skin, too tightly strung for her to pretend to be normal.

"The bed smells like you."

The muscles of her shoulders tightened as she straightened her already neat desktop. She worked hard to keep her scent hidden. She hadn't known her body betrayed her in sleep, but she should've. A little spark of curiosity zinged through her at his contentment at such a small thing. "What does it smell like?"

"The air right after a fresh rain. Ozone. Clean."

She turned and saw him gazing at her quizzically. "It upsets you that I can pick up your smell."

"It's not always in my best interest to be noticed."

A delicious smile appeared, brightening his eyes in a sexy, confident way that reminded her that he was all man when she desperately needed to see him as the boy she rescued. "You're good. I'm just better."

"Because you're a wolf?" She tucked her hands behind her back, toying with her fingers to cover her awkwardness.

He shook his head, a bashful expression on his face. "No, it's my talent."

Raven nodded, wandering closer, drawn as much by the lure of knowledge as by the invitation in his eyes. "I'd think that would be a valuable trait."

The smile slowly faded, his eyes dropped to his hands, and he shrugged.

"Why were you at the auction? Why didn't they snatch you up?" Raven wished she never spoke when an air of shame rose from him, and he wouldn't meet her gaze.

"Lights out."

Jackson's voice boomed in the room. She hadn't forgotten him, that would be impossible, but she'd thought he'd remain silent. She should've known better.

Raven didn't remove her gaze from Taggert. When he leaned back, the chain around his neck drew her attention. A scowl crossed her face at what that hideous necklace represented. "Why are you still wearing that?" She nodded to the delicate thread of metal, a twisted combination of silver and gold. Something so beautiful shouldn't be allowed to represent something so horrible as slave status.

"Once the council agrees to the match, they'll unlock it."

"This Council of Five."

"Yes."

The area around the neck appeared an angry red and sore to the touch, pissing her off all the more. Shifters wanted to be treated as equals to the rest of the population, but then they go and do something so asinine.

"Is it allowed to be taken off sooner?" She examined the metal, easing onto the bed when she didn't see the clasp. Time stretched, and she grew uncomfortably aware of her knee pressed against his hip, his heat temptingly close.

"They're unbreakable." Jackson rolled over and studied her so intently her insides quivered.

Would he trust her with information about his pack? It surprised her how badly she wanted that trust. When he spoke again, a breath of relief eased out of her lungs.

"If the slave is not selected and the chain not removed in five years, it kills them."

Five years. It was incomprehensible. Raven didn't meet their gazes, though she could feel theirs alive against her skin. The thought of Taggert dying didn't sit well with her. "What say you we give it a closer look?" She winked at Taggert to give him a sense of calm she wasn't feeling.

He gave a nod.

She picked up the delicate metal, turning it around, spotting iron underneath the silver and gold lines.

"The chain is unbreakable." Jackson stood, but didn't interfere.

"I don't need to break it." She twisted the metal, drawing closer for a better view when her nose filled with the smell of woods. Wild. Untamed. Tempting her to touch and take. The energy around her core sputtered. The animals stretched as if awakening, urging her to get closer to all that warmth.

She pulled back, a flush of heat stinging her cheeks. God, what was she thinking? Taggert was under her protection. She coaxed out a current, relieved when the animals seem to roll over and go back to sleep as she locked the cage door holding them back.

When the men didn't appear to notice, she released a painful breath. In the time she'd spent in Jackson and Taggert's company, her animals had reacted more times than they had in the last five months. Their waking frightened her. She couldn't allow that. Shifting to an animal form would kill her.

She cleared her throat, uncertain how to broach the subject, uncertain if she really wanted to know the answers. But to help Taggert, she took the plunge.

"Tell me what you've learned about me since you've been here." She had to be more cautious about using her power around them. Before she jumped into the fire so to speak, she needed to learn how much they knew. She had to ensure her secrets remained safe.

Taggert's gaze caressed her face. He didn't hesitate to answer. "You're not human."

She jerked a little at the charge, surprised by the bite of pain. As if he sensed her retreat, he hurried to continue.

"You're not a shifter, and you're not a vampire. You have the strength of a human, but you threw someone across the room without breaking a sweat." A smile came and went. "You always wear gloves. You tried and nearly succeeded to eliminate your scent, unheard of for anyone, normal or not. You have no last name."

"My name is Raven." Nothing more existed for her except a few vague memories of when she'd been sold to the labs; the records had been destroyed before she ever laid eyes on them. Everyone who'd known about her past had long since been eliminated. He hesitated, and a chill encased her heart. There was more. "And?"

"You healed me." His breath brushed her cheek, and she pulled away, uncomfortable at the attention, and cursing the small part of her that relished it. "You called the wolf in me. I felt him."

Her brows knitted at the awe in his voice. "Healers and pack leaders can call your wolf. I don't understand."

"Myths." Jackson broke into the conversation with one word guaranteed to capture her attention.

Raven shook her head. "But I've read the books. I've talked to people who told me of the old tales."

"Wives tales. Sure, a powerful enough alpha can call the wolf to the surface, but there are no such thing as healers."

"That's not possible." Shaken at the bald truth Jackson so casually offered, Raven retreated, perched at the edge of the bed, frantically shoring up the walls between them that somehow had thinned when she hadn't been paying attention.

"They say every few generations a healer is born, but the last hundred years or so, no one has been found. They're myths." Jackson leaned against the wall, a stillness to him that warned he was watching her closely. Too closely.

Hunting.

"But Taggert said he was born with a special gift."

Jackson nodded. "Some believe they're the offspring of those people."

"But you can't have it both ways. They're either a myth or they're real."

"It's an old legend. I believe Taggert's gift is a genetic mutation. An adaptation. He can't shift, so he's given an extra sense of smell for protection. It happens to the real old shifters as well sometimes. They adapt to their surroundings, learn a little something extra to help them survive. It's rare for the young ones."

If true, that meant she revealed more of herself than she'd intended. She felt their gazes on her, probing, questioning. The lab had believed those old tales and trained her in accordance to them, demanded the impossible if she wanted to save herself and others the pain of failure. A wild urge to laugh bubbled up in her throat. After everything she'd endured, it had all been a lie.

Jackson sat at the opposite edge of the bed, Taggert lying between them, a certain gleam in his expression that didn't bode well for her. "What do you say we play a little game of tit for tat?"

The smug bastard. She wanted to say screw him, but bit her lip against saying anything she might regret. She met his whiskey brown gaze. "I don't trust you."

"Then we're even."

That stung, too. She stood, pulling away.

This was a bad idea.

Taggert sat up, and the blanket pooled in his lap. Her retreat faltered, her gaze drifted lower. She couldn't help admire the image they presented sitting side by side. The normal cynicism in Jackson's eyes was absent. She couldn't tell if the men were playing her or not, but she couldn't deny the shiver that passed through her at seeing them in her bed.

A ray of light caught the chain, and any fantasy of having more fractured. He was a slave. Property to protect.

She gazed at Jackson and shook her head. "I'm not ready for that kind of exchange. For all I know, this whole thing could be a trap."

"Why would anyone want to trap you?" The low pitch of his voice was soothing, comforting.

A lie. She felt invaded by them and their damn curiosity. "Like you said, lights out." She reached for the light switch.

"Why bother with the switch?" Jackson rose, his eyes on her in challenge as he sat back down on his makeshift bed. Daring her, teasing her with the knowledge of how much he knew.

He never once looked away.

Plunging the room into darkness without so much as a twitch, Raven turned her back on them and went over to her desk. She should just leave. She didn't understand why she didn't.

The bed creaked, and she tensed. Risking a quick glance, she saw Taggert lying on his side, staring at her. "Don't leave."

Jackson's heavy sigh forestalled any questions she might have posed. Her eyes narrowed. She had to get Taggert by himself. He'd tell her what she wanted to know, and maybe she could find a way to pry Jackson's ass out of her business. She ignored the little niggle of worry that spending more time alone with either of them would only draw them tighter into her life.

The phone rang, saving her from forming an answer.

She rose, but Taggert was faster. "Raven Investigation. One moment, please." Taggert extended the phone. "Detective Scotts for you."

Raven winced and took the phone. Maybe Scotts wouldn't assume they were sleeping together. "Scotts?"

He spoke without preamble. "I have another body at the morgue."

She hesitated, cringing at the number of dead bodies in the vicinity of the morgue. She'd planned to sneak in later, but only after she had more time to lock her powers down tight.

She glanced at the men in the dark, their postures way too alert for her liking. She had a choice. More painful conversation or the small probability of accidently raising the dead. "I'm on my way."

Even before she hung up the phone, Jackson stood, groping for his pants. Part of her logical brain stuttered at all that flesh on display. She blinked and shook her head, ignoring the way her hand shook at the urge to touch him.

"You're staying." She didn't need company, especially if the place overwhelmed her, and she needed to detox.

"You can't go to the morgue by yourself in the middle of the night." He slipped socks over his feet, the boots came next.

"Stupid wolf hearing." Raven shut down the computer from sleep mode and locked it in the desk. "You're not trained for these cases or welcomed. You'll get us both kicked out again."

"You've tried to convince me that your detective is a reasonable normal. Prove it. He'd understand if I came with you as protection."

Protection? Wasn't that a laugh. Who would protect him from her if she lost control? "Not happening." She nodded toward Taggert. "You were sent to keep an eye on him. You're staying."

"Get up." Jackson slapped the bed, and Taggert immediately complied. "I was also sent to make sure you were a suitable candidate." His smile was all teeth. "Since you refuse to share the information, I have no choice but monitor you myself."

She wondered if she could reach the car ahead of them, then sighed. They were wolves. Her feet would never touch the grass before they caught up with her.

Moonlight gleamed off Taggert's backside as he bent over, and heat filled her face. She whirled around, flustered at the knowledge he slept nude. The fact that she'd sat within inches of him and had a conversation only made her cheeks burn more.

Raven clenched her fists and headed toward the door, running from the enticing images of them in her room and her life. If she had any hope of solving the cases on docket without more bodies piling up, she had to keep a clear head. That meant keeping her distance from them.

That didn't explain why the prospect of not seeing them sent her stomach dropping to her knees or caused an ache in her throat that wouldn't go away.

She had more to worry about than her personal life. The cases were too important to mess up. This new body could tell her if the same person perpetrated both crimes. Scotts could get her the information, but if she didn't go, she'd risk missing something important. She was supposed to be the expert. That meant bucking up and doing her job.

"Ready?"

Jackson's voice near her ear made her jump. The power grid in the house leapt at her spurt of fear, eager to give her whatever her body craved. Electricity crackled painfully up her legs. She resisted the lure to take what it offered, only to feel the tentacles burn against her shins in retaliation. The more current she carried, the more dangerous she was to those around her, and she couldn't risk either of them being near her if she couldn't keep everything under wraps.

Taggert opened the door. Moonlight and fresh air from the hallway spilled into the room. Her chest relaxed marginally.

As she passed, she saw the narrowed look he gave Jackson and realized he was trying to help her. Those chocolate eyes of Taggert's followed her, but the way he watched her didn't put her on edge as it normally would. His gaze more of a caress.

She would've said Jackson was oblivious to the exchange, except for the way he shifted to stand between them. What was it that he didn't want her to know? Something about Taggert or himself? Or something far worse?

They entered the morgue as silently as the ride over. "Hey, Chuck, I'm here to see Detective Scotts."

"Observation room three, Miss Raven." The slightly balding, overweight man gave her a welcoming smile, but eyed the two men trailing her, clearly expecting trouble.

"Thank you."

The vents were on full as they turned the corner, meaning that the body would be a bad one. Scotts straightened away from the wall at their approach, then gestured at the two men at her back. "They stay out here."

"Agreed." Scotts gave Raven a suspicious look at her easy capitulation, but his normal cocoa complexion seemed pale, his comforting tobacco scent a bit sour. She turned to Jackson and Taggert. "Behave."

She swept open the doors and nearly doubled over at the smell. She heard Taggert gag, and even Jackson swore. It was all she could do to force herself further into the room. Breathing through her mouth didn't help, as it made her feel as if something foul crawled over her tongue and died.

She pulled up the collar of her shirt to cover her nose.

"Here." Ross held out a medical mask.

The chemical smell from the paper material was so overpowering, she almost handed it back. "What did you douse this in? Lye?"

"My own concoction." The corners of his eyes crinkled, his smile hidden behind his own mask. "The putrid smell won't leak through the chemicals. It shouldn't hurt you." He crossed the large room to the lit area in the back.

While following, a chill snaked around her ankles and twisted over her skin. She shivered, turned and saw that the large morgue refrigerator door gapped open. The blackness beyond was so thick, she shivered again but not with cold this time. The three-inch metal was torn and ragged, hanging drunkenly on its hinges.

"We suspect shifters."

Raven jumped, not sensing Ross's approach.

"They did this?" Something appeared out of order, but she couldn't place her finger on what bothered her, the answer scratching at the back of her mind.

"They have the same motto as soldiers...never leave anyone behind." He turned and shuffled back toward the lights.

It was so similar to what Jackson said that she nodded and dismissed the part of her that wanted to explore further. She had two paying cases. She didn't have time to investigate anything else, especially just out of curiosity.

"Usually shifters are neater when they come and retrieve their own. Vampires are the tricky bastards, popping up and tearing through whatever stands in their way to freedom." He picked up a tool and looked at her questioningly. "Coming?"

Raven shook off the vague unease and turned to finish the job she came to do. Even from the distance, she could see pieces of the body dripped off the table to splotch on the floor. After a few steps, a wave of dizziness staggered her. She blinked a few times to clear her vision and pulled the mask away from her face.

And gagged, struggling to keep her breath. "Have you called in a hazmat team?"

Ross chuckled at her lame joke, politely continuing to work and allow her time to recover. "Not for this one. The chem panel revealed nothing toxic except for natural decomposition."

The only way to describe the person on the slab was as a lump of flesh. Raven squinted, unable to tell the species. "Did you test to make sure it wasn't human?"

More than half the bones were missing. Or taken. The killer was becoming more adept. No bite marks were discernible. Hell, she could barely tell what body parts lay on the slab. The tissue appeared pale. Bloodless. She would've said vampire except they don't tear and eat flesh this way.

Ross handed over the chart in answer to her question. She scanned the pages. "Another water victim?" She didn't look up as she flipped through the rest.

Ross grunted. "They basically had to strain the stream to find what pieces they could. This is the bulk of it here."

"The report says the enzymes are from a were. Do we know what kind?" Humans insisted on calling shifters were, short for the horrible movies that showed werewolves as two-legged monsters. It didn't matter that shifters only transformed to the four-legged variety. The name stuck.

The doctor picked up his scalpel and sliced cleanly through the outer layer of what she assumed was the chest. By the thickness, she would guess male.

"Not, yet. The lab was backed up, so I could only run the quick stick test. I'm assuming feline."

"Why?"

"Because of this." He lifted up a portion of the body on his side of the table hidden from view by the torso. Inch long claws dangled from what appeared to be human fingers. Partial transition. Which meant a very strong shifter, as it took years of practice for a shifter to be able to call upon their animal in human form without shifting completely.

At least half of the nails were jagged. Not a lot could destroy the hard enamel of shifter claws created to cleave down to the bone.

But what drew her gaze was the set of industrial shackles clamped onto his forearm. Her own wrists throbbed with memories. The feel of cold metal. The heavy weight. Her pulse sped up. Her breathing grew shallow.

If not for the chem panel in front of her, she would've sworn this poor creature came from the labs. But there were no drugs or toxins on the report, nothing to indicate any of the abnormalities the labs inflicted on shifters. "The other bodies were all shifters as well?"

"Yes." Ross didn't bother to look up from his examination of the cavity he cracked open.

"Can you show me the results when you receive them?" She needed to get out of there, needed to think rationally. She had to follow her own advice to Dominic and not jump to conclusions.

"Hum-huh," Ross didn't pause as he started to pull out and weigh the organs. A piece of pond scum and a congealed lump of blood oozed down the side of the body. Time to leave.

The air grew thin. The concrete floor felt soggy like sand under her weight. She kept her pace measured, her expression unchanged as she trudged toward the door.

Not here. She'd fall apart when she got home. Energy crackled along her bones, her body burning with the need to expel all the pent-up current. It would go for the bodies first. There was no way she could explain to anyone how she could make a corpse breathe and yearn for life.

Damn zombies.

Chapter
Nine

DAY FOUR: MORNING

*L*ondon handed Raven the local newspaper without a word. The sun dimmed on the path as she walked, dread balling in her stomach. She shoved the last bite of food in her mouth, needing to replace all the calories she'd burned recently, the once tasty bread like sawdust.

Taking a deep breath, she unfolded the paper to the front page. The headlines blared: *Police Hire Specialist to Catch Killer; Is It Doing More Harm than Good?* Underneath was a picture of Jackson and Scotts' standoff, capturing the back of her head in the process.

"Shit." The peace she managed to eke out after a few hours of sleep vanished. The nip in the air didn't feel refreshing anymore, the chill burrowing under her skin.

London fell into step beside her. "They're trying to raise an outcry so the legislature will pass the new law for the Regional Paranormal Liaison."

"Legalizing RPL gives a gun and badge to anyone who's approved." Groups would accuse each other of petty crimes. Despite what she said to Jackson, she wasn't sure this was the right route to take either. "It'd be an all-out war."

"Maybe, but it would also give you the right to view any crime scene that involved the paranormal without waiting for an invitation."

His comment surprised her. "Do you agree with what they're trying to do?"

He shrugged. "Whether I agree or not doesn't matter. It's a ploy to calm the outraged protesters raising a stink. I doubt it will ever pass. There are too many normals who'd object to giving the animals more rights, let alone arming them."

"But if it passed, would you apply?" She could see him doing a job like that. Or joining the special task force, a SWAT team for paranormals.

The big man shook his head. "Too many people. Too many orders. I like my place here. You should think closely about it before dismissing it."

That surprised her, but she ultimately rejected the idea. "If I apply, they'd require a blood test. I'd be forced to register." There was nothing either of them could say to that.

The last thing she needed was to be labeled as a conduit in a public database, not to mention her blood would reveal the mutations in her genes that made her a crossbreed. She wasn't prepared for the consequences of either, especially if the very people who infected her with the various shifter DNA increased their search to locate her. She was safe right now, hidden in plain view. If she applied, she couldn't guarantee a public position would protect her.

She pushed away those dark thoughts, along with the insidious fear at the mention of discovery. Thunder rumbled in the distance when the house came into view. Her feet quickened, eager to escape. London opened the front door and disappeared down the hallway to the section of the house he'd claimed as his own. Security central. She suspected he had a fridge in there as well and was tempted to follow when she heard voices.

"Where is she?"

Jackson's growl carried easily through the kitchen door and shivered through her. The heat of his anger struck her even through the flimsy panel separating them. No doubt she was the person he wanted; he reserved that rough voice strictly for her.

She hadn't seen or spoken to either wolf since they'd returned from the morgue yesterday. Until Jackson decided to share information about the pack with her, she really had nothing to say to him. She and Dina had spent most of the day yesterday out on the streets, questioning all the rogues they could find about missing shifters. Surprisingly, they responded to Dina, while watching Raven as if she would attack. Funny, since the rogues were supposedly the dangerous ones.

She cautiously stepped away from the kitchen, placing her feet with care. No sound. No trail.

The door opened before she'd taken two steps. She froze, hunching her shoulders as if she'd become invisible if she were small enough. Instead of the confrontation she expected, Taggert slipped into the room.

When she would've spoken, he held his finger to his lips. She smiled in relief, the knots in her stomach relaxing. Taggert she could manage. Alone without Jackson to interrupt them, he'd give her answers to a few pesky riddles that continued to nag her about shifters.

Taggert trusted her. Knowing that weakened her resolve to use him to get answers. Strangely enough, she wanted to prove his trust was well placed. He'd treated her as one of them since they'd first met. She wanted that so badly, she refused to consider that he'd be in the perfect position to betray her.

The instant she straightened, his eyes widened. He rushed forward, his arms spread wide in an attempt to herd her. Then she heard it.

Footsteps.

She would know that tread anywhere. Not needing any prompting, she sprinted to the nearest escape with the knowledge they'd never make it in time.

The closet.

She barely snagged the door open when Taggert shoved her from behind. A flash of light was the last thing she saw when the door snicked shut, plunging them into darkness. The lack of light gave her a false sense of anonymity, but any pretense of being a naughty child caught up in a game quickly disappeared in the tight space.

Junk crammed along the walls from the previous owner, jabbing her every time she twitched to put space between them. Plastered against him closer than fur on a cat, every inclination that said Taggert needed protection vanished. All her body understood was the warm male so close and so damn willing.

She swallowed hard, acutely aware of every inch of him pressed up against her, her breasts against the hard wall of his chest, his legs tangling with hers. Taggert didn't struggle, realizing the futility of it long before her.

"My scent. Can you cover my scent like yours?"

The whispered caress of his words against her ear sent a shiver of delight through her gut. His cheek brushed lightly against hers, almost nuzzling her.

Panic skittered down her spine. He didn't know what he was asking. To mask him, she'd have to take him into her shields. Open herself up to him. It'd leave her vulnerable. It would also make it impossible for her to pretend their attraction didn't exist.

"Raven?"

"Right." She was an adult. She could control her baser instincts. She had to swallow twice before she found her courage. "You might get shocked a bit."

Without hesitation, he wrapped his arms securely around her. She jumped at the contact, resisting the automatic response to jerk away. The full press of his body set her on fire, amplifying the burning need to touch him back. To arch into him and take what he offered, and damn the consequences.

"Hurry."

When she took a deep breath, his scent infused her, setting off another wave of craving. A delicious heat sank deep in her gut, and she shook her head to clear her mind, desperately trying to remember her purpose.

She grabbed that ephemeral thought and shoved all those delicious sensations away. She refused to examine them, refused to admit to any attraction. She couldn't allow herself to care for anyone. Not like that. Not again. "You'll feel something like a curtain of static surround your body."

"Do it." His whispered words sent a shiver of doubt tearing down her spine about the sanity of their plan. Then she took a leap of faith and did it.

She opened herself, allowing just a fraction of energy to wrap around him. That was her intent anyway. An electrical storm swept through her, leaving her with one thought. To make him hers. It would be so easy. He was so willing. Her knees shook as she resisted the command.

A rough, animalistic growl vibrated from his chest. The tone hit her body hard. She instantly responded to it with a wave of desire that obliterated any thought but to plunder. The side of his face brushed her cheek, then her neck as if he couldn't stand not touching every inch of her. A puff of breath on her pulse was all it took to break her damaged resolve.

The muscles of her legs weakened, and she sagged against him, delighted in the way he hardened under her touch, the ease in which he supported her weight. He didn't feel like the boy she mistook him for on their first meeting. He was at least five inches taller than her, broad in the shoulders, lean in the waist and definitely old enough to know what he wanted if his body was any indication.

He dipped his head, lightly brushed his lips against hers, and she couldn't find any air left in the closet to protest. A second passed. Two. Then breathing stopped being important when his mouth claimed hers again in a sweet kiss that left her insides a pile of mush. Trembling, she leaned back, embarrassed by her need.

What the hell did they think they were doing? But all that fled when he brushed his body against hers in just the right way to hit all her nerve endings at once. Imagining them both naked, him inside of her while he did that again, nearly had her growling at him to not stop.

He rested his forehead against hers, his body shuddering with restraint. When he gently and inextricably drew her closer, she didn't resist, wrapping her arms around him in turn.

His lips brushed her parted ones, lingering, tasting, testing, oh so temptingly within reach. He pulled the binding holding her hair until the strands spilled around her face. He inhaled deeply. In a rush of need, his hands slid over her ass then lower. She thought he was going to kneel when he straightened abruptly. With his hands behind her thighs, she found herself straddling his waist. Her back slammed against the wall of boxes, and the little rumble of hunger from him came so close to her neck that hot desire pooled between her legs.

Sharp teeth raked lightly down her throat, and her body hummed at such a simple but erotic gesture. She could barely open her eyes, but when she did, she instantly spotted the yellow bleeding the brown out of his gaze.

Not good. Not good at all. Reason reinserted itself. "I don't think this is such a good idea."

She pushed at his shoulders, and he immediately released her. Her feet touched the floor, and she trembled in an embarrassing weak-kneed way that threatened to topple her on her ass. His chest heaved, each breath brushed his body against her.

Lightly.

Teasingly.

Ratcheting her need higher, making her wonder why she thought halting was a good idea.

A few kisses couldn't be bad. Not when they tasted so good.

He pressed his palms on either side of her head and ducked so they were eye to eye. "Please."

The door flew wide, wood groaned, splintering. An animalistic roar rang in her ears. Light seared her eyes, and when she could see next, Taggert had vanished. Raven slid a few inches down the wall of boxes, fighting for composure and against the whimper working its way up her throat, waiting for her head to stop spinning.

The slam of flesh on flesh jerked her upright. She shot out of the closet in time to see Jackson slam his fist into Taggert's stomach. The man didn't go down, but came up swinging, clocking Jackson on the jaw. They went back and forth, exchanging blows, the bruises and cuts healing nearly as fast as the punches landed when she finally got her wits together.

"Stop." She pushed between them and received snarls from them both that raised the hair on the back of her neck. Yellow eyes gleamed, watching as if waiting for her to choose.

"Stay still." Dominic's voice was low and unthreatening as he approached. "You move and they'll pounce."

"What the hell is happening?" The energy from the two men swamped the room. She'd never felt anything like it. All she wanted to do was soak it up and roll around in it.

Dominic latched onto her arm, his grip unbreakable, jerking her away. Both men kept their gazes cemented to hers. But when Taggert took a step to follow, Jackson leapt. They skidded across the floor, fists pummeling with a force that had her wincing.

"Let me go. They're going to kill each other." She struggled against Dominic's grip. He wrapped his arm so tightly across her chest she could barely hold the panic at bay. The autumn scent she normally found so soothing now felt suffocating.

"This is pack." He shook her hard, forcing her to watch each blow. "This is how they settle disputes. We're brutal. We're vicious. And we're unbending when someone tries to take what's ours."

"What?" The words took the starch out of her, calmed some of the panic licking through her at being confined. The uncontrollable craving to suck in the energy waned the greater the distance she put between her and the wolves. She looked at Dominic, saw his yellow-green gaze, and swallowed hard.

Her mind cleared slowly from the lust-induced euphoria that had invaded her, the one that told her to do what she wanted without care for the consequences.

She had to get away from them. She was going to crash and crash hard. "Let me go." She spat the words. When nothing happened, renewed panic wrestled her for control.

A zap of static crackled through the room. Energy hummed in the walls, getting louder as her agitation grew. All other noise faded. All her senses lay in resisting the urge to sink her fingers into the juice, and just let go.

"Raven. Snap out of it." Dominic's words lashed at her, and she came to herself with a start.

Dominic stood three feet from her, his arms held out at his sides, trying to appear as unthreatening as possible. His head was bowed to the side in submission, his throat bared. It shook her to see him like that with her, a tough, proud fighter bowing to her in submission.

Shame gutted her. The lack of recrimination as he cautiously peered at her only made it worse. He just accepted it.

"Your hands." Taggert stepped closer, no fear in him.

"Stay back." She felt fear enough for both of them. A light glow surrounded her skin. She saw it. Now Taggert saw it. Could her gift be infecting him like it did the house? The others didn't notice anything, and she was pitifully grateful for that small mercy.

She retreated a step. Jackson circled, countering the move, boxing her in until her back hit the wall. At the contact, energy from the house poured into her.

"Ground yourself."

Dominic's yell sounded small in her ears, her senses overloading with the charge. To ground herself, she needed to connect to something solid. She needed bare earth beneath her feet, but she didn't think any of the men would allow her to leave, and she couldn't guarantee their safety if they followed.

Pain swelled in her head, eating along her bones the longer she held herself in check. Her body craved more, building off her panic. She clenched her eyes shut, her fists balled tight at the thought of them seeing her helpless. She reached down into her center, burrowed deep for the last of her strength. The core had welled with power. Begged to be used.

The temptation to linger and play with it nearly distracted her. Only the fear of them witnessing everything brought back her sanity. She had to get rid of it. She forced the twisting blue and white strands of energy whipping through her insides down her body, past her legs and finally through the soles of her feet.

It pulsed along her skin in protest, wrapping along her shins, tugging at her like a child begging to stay.

With one last mental shove, the energy cracked into the floor. The voltage left her so abruptly that she staggered and slumped against the wall. Her insides felt stripped of flesh, crying out for her to call back the energy. She adamantly refused, but it did no good. The power swirled around her, more eager than ever to find a way back.

When she opened her eyes, the floor where she'd stood filled her vision. Electrical burns crisscrossed the wood, wrapping around one another in a five-foot radius from her feet. A harsh reminder that everything she touched became tainted. How much longer before she couldn't control it at all?

"It's growing." Dominic's soft voice confirmed her fear.

Her stomach churned violently. She lifted her head, ready to face judgment. Only to be confronted by compassion.

"How long has it been this way?"

Raven looked away, wishing she could crawl in a hole and hide. If only they'd stayed away. When she didn't say anything, he drew closer.

"Weeks? Months?"

"Months. Maybe longer." She faced Dominic and flinched to see him within touching distance. He gazed at her like she was one of his wild animals to trap and lock away if he thought it necessary to keep them safe.

"Why didn't you call me? I could've—"

"What?" Raven shook her head, meeting his gaze squarely, resisting the instinct to bolt if he took another step. "There's nothing you could've done. You deal with the rest of the team. You have enough on your plate."

He shook his head, lines bracketing his mouth. "I could stand beside you for support."

Raven swallowed painfully at his words. What she wouldn't give for the opportunity to pour out her fears to someone. But she couldn't burden him that way, not when there was nothing either of them could do. She had plans in place for when she finally lost control. "I'm working on a way to ground myself."

"It's not helping?"

"No."

Jackson crouched and rubbed a hand along the floor. "The wax is burned clear away. The wood isn't just stained, it's seared into the maple."

Thunder rumbled in the distance, strong enough to rock the house. His eyebrows shot up. Heat filled her cheeks as she fumbled through an explanation. "Wood can only hold so much before the charge seeps back through the air. The extra charge will wreak havoc on the brewing storm."

Everyone around her acted so fricken normal. She was a freak, but they treated what she could do like a fascinating discovery.

A wave of dizziness smashed through her at holding so much current and releasing it all in one big rush. In seconds, Taggert was at her side. She recoiled from his touch, afraid everything that happened in the closet would come rushing back.

Her knee-jerk response drew him up short. "You need to relax. I'll fix some tea."

She swallowed down a wild laugh. As if tea would fix everything. When she would've protested and escaped like a coward, Dominic narrowed his eyes and spoke. "And while you compose yourself, we'll explain a few things about pack."

The muscles of Jackson's back tensed, and he purposely kept his face averted so she couldn't read him. She hesitated, desperate to know at least some of their secrets when so many of hers lay exposed.

No one moved until she gave a hesitant nod. She suspected her agreement was only a formality. Once in the kitchen, Taggert seated her and went about preparing her a cup of tea. She watched his hands, unable to face him after what happened.

"Don't worry about me." Raven waved him off, hating to be waited on by anyone.

He didn't bother to turn around. "The tea will help calm you."

A nervous laugh bubbled up from her chest. "What you have to tell me can't be worse than what you've just seen me do." The slight hitch in his smooth movements made her swallow hard.

She ignored Jackson as he sulked across from her and stared at Dominic, seated to her left at the head of the table. He gazed at his hands, so silent, as if dredging up the past was a physical ache.

"I was part of a pack for a few months before the labs. From what I remember, there are two ways to induct members into a pack. The most common is by gaining council approval. Though hardly used anymore, the other is by mating. Mating or breeding had always been survival of the fittest, until the last hundred years. Things grew lax. Technology, the fear of human discovery, and the Paranormal conflict ten years ago—"

Jackson snorted. "You mean the slaughter."

Dominic continued as if not interrupted, his intense gaze fastened on her. "—the population of the paranormal community began to suffer. Low birth rates. Hard pregnancies. Infertility. Pack members unable to shift. So the council took over. Mating became political for some and survival for others.

"Shifters now must have approval from their alpha to breed. Alphas are the exception, required to mate with as many as they choose, in hope of producing the best and strongest shifters."

Some of the information wasn't anything new. "I've read about the decline, but hadn't realized the extent."

"Try living it every damn day, watching your pack crumble as fewer offspring are born each year."

A knot of anxiety formed in her chest. She flicked a glance at Jackson's stern face, not liking where this was going.

"What have you read?"

She blinked, caught off guard at Dominic's simple question. "Just what you said. The males in the community are having trouble finding a mate. It's worse for some breeds. They're dying out because they can't find compatible females that can carry to term."

Dominic cleared his throat. "That's not exactly true."

Her brows wrinkled in confusion. "Which part?"

"Leave it alone," Jackson snarled.

His heated words took her aback. You'd think she'd be used to his rudeness by now.

"She needs to know." The snap in Dominic's voice sent a tremor through her gut. "Breeding between other races isn't a sure thing. If carried to term, the newborn isn't guaranteed to have the gifts of their shifter parent. Jackson reacted to you and Taggert because you awakened his wolf."

"Beg pardon?" Raven blinked, completely baffled.

"Jackson's wolf wants you."

She looked at Jackson, his animosity vibrating around him, and laughed. "How can you be serious? He wants nothing to do with me."

A growl rumbled out of him, and her amusement died quickly. Those eyes darkened, splinters of yellow interrupting the brown. The stare dried the spit from her mouth. Power boiled out of him, cresting over her. It was rough, untamed and delicious to touch.

He broke the stare first, dropping her back into the conversation with a rude plop. She was missing something important. "Okay, what does that mean exactly?"

"Females choose their mates. The more alpha the female, the more males she attracts." Dominic fell silent, staring at her.

"So?"

Taggert set the mug in front of her. She took a sip when Dominic spoke again. "His wolf is jealous."

The liquid sprayed the table. "What?" She glared at him for his cruelty and wiped her mouth with the back of her hand. "You must be mistaken. I'm not a wolf. I don't count."

"Sometimes men must find other avenues."

Raven felt her eyes widen to saucers. She looked between Taggert and Jackson and blinked once in understanding. So it wasn't her that set Jackson off. It also explained why he was so protective of the boy. "You mean they—"

"Oh, hell no." Jackson snorted. "He meant humans."

"Okay. So your wolf chose a human." That was a little better, wasn't it?

Dominic shook his head, his green eyes dark. "Wolves never awaken to anyone but potential mates. One of their own kind. Once awakened, they don't care about anyone else. Men can select a human if they don't believe they'll ever find a mate, or if they're too weak no wolf would take them. No great loss. With the shortage of female shifters, most wolves never awaken."

There was an awkward pause when Dominic spoke again. "His wolf is jealous you chose Taggert as mate material and not him."

"But I'm not a shifter. I was born with no animal connections at all." Raven chose her words carefully. "And from my reading, it's the female that locks the match into place. There's some sort of blood ritual." Her brows wrinkled as she fought to pull the facts from her memories. She fiddled with the cup as all eyes focused on her.

Dominic took a deep breath, rubbing a tired hand over his eyes and down his face. "Mating is a duty, not a human partnership, not dating. They're looking for the best genetic materials to produce cubs.

"For the men, they'll parade and show off their skills and wait for the female to indicate interest, but it's up to the breeding woman to initiate contact. An alpha female will choose the best and the strongest. Everyone else is expected to make do." He cleared his throat uncomfortably. "Only an alpha female or committed, pre-approved couples mate by taking blood. Once the connection is in place, the enzymes in the blood ensure the male will only want her."

"And if they exchange blood?" Tension spiked in the room at her innocent question.

"No."

There was a slight waver in his voice that caught her attention. "No?"

A gusty sigh escaped. "There's a romantic fairytale whispered amongst kids about Consorts. It's rare, a privilege granted to alphas and only if the council approves the union. Not only does it take two alphas out of the gene pool, it would bring about alliances between the packs involved."

"And if two shifters fall in love?"

"They'd be fine as long as they don't breed. A death sentence can be enforced if they breed without approval. The cubs could be inducted in the pack or labeled rogue and kicked out."

"What happens to the Consort's previous mates at this bond?" Dominic's eyes hardened, and any resemblance to her friend was replaced with the uncompromising leader. Her heart hiccupped in her chest.

"It depends on the strength of the alpha. Prior bonds should break at the exchange of blood. The fully bonded alpha male usually kills any who show signs of too much possessiveness. The rest will be ordered to breed again or, more often than not, the men become the female's protective guard. True Consort bonds cannot be broken once formed." He blew out a breath, avoiding her gaze.

Dominic wasn't finished. An awful feeling that he saved the worst for last crept over her. Nerves jangled to life, and she settled herself firmly back in her chair, bracing herself. "Just spit it out."

"I've read the reports of what they did to you in the program. They injected you with a number of different shifters' DNA. I'm guessing you have enough wolf to bring it out in them. Your innate gift boosts the impact." He paused meaningfully. "That's why shifters and vampires are so drawn to you."

"That's not possible." The chair screeched across the floor when Jackson stood. Betrayal lined his face when he glared at her. "A person can't survive an infection with multiple shifters. Not only does it take a major blood transfusion to infect a person, most don't survive one animal much less multiple."

A buzz filled her ears, her lips felt numb when she replied. "I didn't survive."

Chapter Ten

$\mathcal{P}$ounding on the front door interrupted the taboo discussion in the kitchen. Raven bolted from the room, eager to escape Jackson and the bomb she'd just dropped.

"What the hell does she mean?" Jackson's words were drowned out when something heavy smashed against the threshold. The reinforced wood shook but held under the strain, and Raven rushed toward it like a lifeline.

"Raven, wait." Dominic's footsteps thundered after her. The closer she drew to the entrance, the greater a sense of urgency swamped her. The only thing that mattered was opening the door. She disengaged the bolts and threw the door wide.

In poured Jeffrey Durant with a bundle of muddy rags in his arms. His clothes were soaked, his wild hair plastered to his head. Mud splattered the hard granite lines of his face. His normal green eyes were molten gold in his agitation. Her heart thudded in her chest at finding a man like him in such disarray.

When Raven tore his gaze away from him, she glimpsed pale flesh peeking out from the burden he carried.

"I need your help."

The roughness of his voice scraped against her soul, his anguish a living thing.

"This way." She didn't hesitate, ushering him into the study and pointing to the chaise in the corner. Something about his desolateness made her unable to turn him away. His pallor concerned her, and she searched him for injury, seeing nothing under the coat of mud. "What happened?"

"Rumor says you're the one to go to if you want the impossible done. She won't wake up." With infinite care, he set the bundle he cradled on the couch.

His voice was so baffled and lost, her breath caught. Focusing on the bundle, all she could tell was female. Young. Barely clinging to life. "I'll need you to step back so I can examine her." Wild, golden eyes met hers, so dangerous and threatening, but neither could hide the plea underneath.

If she took this final step, all her secrets would be exposed. She'd have nowhere else to hide. Some of her hesitation must've shown.

"Her name is Cassie, an orphan I've adopted into my pack. My cub." He cradled the girl's small hand in his, her nails torn and dirty.

The chit had the courage to fight back. That small detail shredded Raven's resolve to remain unaffected. Raven edged closer, and he allowed her to draw back the rags. A frown pulled at her brows. "I don't sense her animal. She's not healing."

"She's pack by courtesy. Human. I'm teaching her to run errands and take care of the business portion of the club when I'm called away to deal with the non-human clientele."

The girl couldn't be more than twenty-five. Slight figure but not delicate. A cold sweat covered her form. Tattered clothing stuck to her body. Her heart beat erratically, her breathing shallow.

"I smell blood." Peeling back Cassie's sleeve, she saw congealed blood from a two-inch swath of missing skin at her wrists. Gorilla tape, not manacles like the other victims. Bruises dotted up her arm.

Dreading what she'd find, Raven twisted the girl's arm up, startled at the searing heat. When the veins appeared clean, part of her anxiety eased. No IV or needle marks. Not the labs. Her mind began functioning again. "What happened?"

"I found her outside of town, thrown away at the side of the road like trash." Rage coated every word, batting against her like a big cat's paw, his control held by strings. "Someone called to say the club was in danger. They wanted a meeting. It was urgent. Since I wasn't there, she went in my place." Guilt thickened his voice.

"You suspect paranormals?"

"Yes."

Working on instinct, Raven lifted the pant legs. Her ankles were treated the same, the left leg so battered it appeared blackened by infection. "The wounds have been allowed to fester." The fever was worrisome, but Raven saw no other wounds, nothing that would prevent her from waking. Nothing that would kill her so slowly.

She wasn't a doctor; she didn't know what the hell to do to help. But she could scan the body to find the source of injury. Logically, she knew calling more power tonight would be foolish. The storms wreaked havoc with her system, not to mention her body ached from the abuse she'd just put it through.

Each time she overreached, she risked burning out or frying herself completely. Vulnerable while she healed. Her gaze came to rest on Durant. Loneliness clung to him in a way that felt so familiar her throat ached, convincing her to act when self-preservation said run. "I need to touch her."

Durant released his hold, gently folding Cassie's hands over her stomach before retreating.

Raven reluctantly removed her gloves and placed her hands on Cassie's arm, very aware of all eyes on her, studying her as she reached for her gift.

A spark pulsed through her, answering sluggishly to her call. A twinge of nausea squeezed the breath from her lungs. Her skin tingled as the spark burned along her arms and pooled into her palms.

Cassie's body bowed as current swept through her system, speeding along her veins and muscles, seeping into her flesh. All except for her upper shoulder and the blackness eating away her flesh, like bacteria.

Raven retreated, balling her hands into fists to hide the way they shook. She'd seen that bacteria before. She swallowed hard, dousing the current seething under her skin. "Roll her on her side."

Durant immediately complied. Then froze. His shoulders drooped and a huge shudder swept through him.

Raven caught a glimpse and swallowed around the grapefruit-sized lump in her throat. The bite looked like something tried to strip the flesh from her back by using teeth.

Vampire teeth.

Crimson streaks blazed against her pale skin.

"Dominic, take Mr. Durant and the boys to the kitchen. Bring me the med kit."

Durant snarled with such ferocity when Dominic neared, Raven tensed to step between them. Hopefully, they'd leave enough of her in one piece to heal.

"Mr. Durant." His gaze swung toward her, all parts human stripped away. "I need to examine Cassie without you in the way. She wouldn't want you to be here while I fix her up. It will be painful for her. How will your beast react to her agony? I can't watch my back and help her at the same time." He didn't blink, and Raven softened her voice. "You came to me for help. You must have trusted me for some reason. Trust me a little more."

A great shudder passed through him. "There is no coming back from a vampire bite once infected."

"She's the same girl you adore. She's dying, going through severe transition sickness. Most don't survive without large amounts of blood." Doubt dug its mitts into her, but she couldn't repress her next words. "I can't stop it, but I might be able to make sure she wakes up again." She met his gaze. "Can you live with that, if she was one of the undead?"

When he didn't answer, her heart dropped. She didn't know the man, so she didn't know why his lack of response disappointed her. Shifters and vampires were complete opposites. One vividly alive, the other craving life by drinking blood. Their opposite natures put them at odds.

"Try." The scratchy sound of his voice broke through her chaotic thoughts. Durant's eyes had partially turned back to human, the green splinters quelling her doubts. "Do what you can for her. Whatever happens, I won't forget what you've tried to do."

He loomed over her and the solemn, bleak expression gave her emotions another vicious twist. He turned, his shoulders back, his posture brittle. She sensed he let very few people close to him. If she let this wisp of a girl die, there would be even fewer.

Dominic followed the large cat at a cautious distance. Taggert and Jackson lingered, but she waved them off. "Go. I'll call you if I need anything."

Taggert nodded, but Jackson's brows lowered ominously.

To forestall any protest, she turned her back on them and offered the only incentive she had. "We'll finish our conversation later." If she lived long enough.

After three hours, she admitted defeat, struggling to fit her gloves on fingers shaky from overexertion. The pounding on the door had long since ceased. The wound had mostly healed into a rough scar, but no amount of energy she poured into the girl could animate her dying flesh. If Raven pushed harder, Cassie would not come back as a vampire, but a mindless zombie instead. Raven couldn't risk that.

Exhaustion pressed heavily on her shoulders, the current burning her from the inside out. As she opened the door, she braced herself to face the men in the hall.

Without a word, Raven shook her head.

Durant swallowed hard, his throat working. He slipped by her into the study, avoiding her eyes. He collected Cassie's body, cradling her against his chest, his devastation a private thing hard to witness.

"How long?" The gravelly words were barely audible. The tiger in him prowled its confines, searching for something to fight.

Raven bit her lip, indecision battling what was right. "There might be another way."

Darkness had fallen an hour ago. If there was a hope for survival, Cassie's transition should've started on its own. Instead, her condition grew increasingly worse. She was dying. Durant's golden gaze locked on hers, the grief consuming him.

"There's a man I met a few years ago who might be willing to help."

Dominic's brow wrinkled, and Raven swallowed hard at the can of worms she was about to spring on them.

"Who." The tension in the room escalated at the terse demand.

"Rylan."

"Hell, no." Dominic shot away from the wall, crossing the floor in a blur.

Jackson and Taggert stepped in front of her, their broad backs a wall blocking the enraged wolf prowling toward her.

"Do it." Durant's red-rimmed eyes didn't hold any hope.

"You don't understand." Dominic swiveled to him, shaking his dark head.

"I don't care."

"He's demented." A vampire driven insane from bloodlust.

The room stilled. She doubted anyone even dared breathe. "That's not fair. No one was sane while imprisoned."

He whirled, but kept his distance when her two protectors tensed. "You heard his victims scream as he tore them apart just as I did. When they released him, he was covered in blood." Bitterness tightened his face. "Shifter blood."

Raven blanched, but stood her ground. "You would've done the same."

"Never." Dominic spit the word at her.

That enraged her. How dare he judge someone for what they had to do to survive in that place. She crossed her arms. "How long did they starve you?"

"What?"

"Vampires have to eat once a day. They can skip a few days, maybe a week at most, but only if they're old and strong."

Dominic scratched his jaw. "So?"

"They starved him, fed him sour blood once a week."

"Shifter blood."

"Damn it, you're not listening." Power stuttered at her core, flaring along her skin as she struggled with her emotions. She prayed for patience and took a steady breath. "For months on end, they starved him. The regimen they created was specifically designed to see how long it would take to drive him insane. They wanted to document its effects."

Understanding darkened his eyes. "That doesn't excuse what he did to our people."

"You hardly know him. I was in a room with him for three days, watching him pace and go insane with hunger. He was so weak he couldn't break the chains that bound me." A tremor took up in her muscles. "Even when I offered him blood, he refused."

"Are you insane?"

A bitter smile crossed her face. "They had to drag his body out of the room when he collapsed from hunger." The desolation in his eyes still haunted her at night. The program pushed them, found a specific sore spot with each occupant, and did everything they could to break them. Once they got what they wanted, their test subjects were the perfect puppets.

"What happens when you don't have enough food?" She focused on Dominic, refusing to let him hide.

"We become more aggressive."

Raven shook her head. "No, your wolf fights for dominance." The next words thickened in her throat. "Now imagine what would happen to you and your control if you were starved for months with only a taste of rotten food every few days."

He spoke through stiff lips. "It's not the same."

"Why not? The more primitive side of his vampire self was exposed. They pushed him too far." Memories battled to surface. Panic beat its wings against the inside of her chest as she fought to forget. "They cut the victims and shoved him in the room. They nearly decapitated them."

She rubbed her face. "What would you do to protect one of your pack?"

"Anything." The one world held complete conviction.

"Even if it would destroy you?" She knew the answer. Everyone who survived the program answered the same. You protect the pack. "I'm going to call him. If you don't want to see him, I suggest you leave."

"What can he do that you can't?" Jackson appeared curious instead of his normal, doubtful self.

"All I'm doing is keeping her alive, but the sickness is spreading. I can't prevent her death. I can't cure her. If he's willing to finish bringing her over, I think she has a good chance at survival." She prayed no one asked for specifics. They might believe they understood her little peculiarity with electricity, but they didn't understand the full effects it could have on others.

"Find another way." Durant's words cracked in the room. Decisions became harder when you had to agree to change someone into a vampire rather than just allow it to happen.

All her anger and frustration bubbled over. She pointed to Cassie. "Is your pride worth more than her life?" When he didn't answer, she rubbed her arms, static crackling as she did so. She couldn't believe she'd so misjudged him, that he'd let his prejudice claim the girl's life. "If you don't want my help, I suggest you take her and leave."

Durant remained seated, unable to say no, but unable to agree to a pact with the very creature he'd fought a war against. Vampires craved the powerful shifter blood, high octane compared to humans. The danger came in when some vampires ensnared their donors and forced them to obey.

"Call him." Taggert handed her the phone. "You wouldn't have suggested it if there were any other choice."

Now that the decision was made, she hesitated. Vampires weren't much better than shifters. Their hatred ran just as deep. Prophecies said the wolves were created to protect the vampires while they slept. Until they rebelled and killed those they were sworn to protect.

A few vampires still believed shifters should either be called to heel and put back into service, or decommissioned. The shifters believed vampires should be made dead permanently before things reverted back to the dark ages.

"Your promise first." She looked at each man, daring them to glance away from her. "I want your word that you'll leave him in peace."

"Raven—"

"No. We escaped the lab together. We promised to stick together for protection. But the first instant, you turn your back on him." Anxiety tightened the muscles of her back. She had to find a way to make him understand. "He's my pack. I won't have him vulnerable to attack in my own home."

"No, Raven. *You* pulled our asses out of that hellish hole. If not for you, we'd still be there."

Taggert didn't seem surprised, but Jackson's all too curious gaze made her gulp. He'd demand answers she wasn't ready to reveal, the horrible truth about her childhood that she tried to bury deep inside where it'd be lost.

Part of her knew she was only moving through the steps, trying to find a cure where there was none. But she couldn't give up that slim hope. And she couldn't not give Durant that same hope.

She picked up the phone and dialed the number she prayed she would never have to use. Rylan knew her fears. Before he disappeared, he'd promised that if she lost control, all she had to do was call and he'd come for her.

He answered immediately, the low, honey sound of his voice soothing after all this time. Fear beat a heavy rhythm in her chest and silence stretched as she fought to force words past the painful memories.

"Raven." One word breathed a wealth of emotion.

"I need your help."

Chapter Eleven

DAY FIVE: JUST AFTER MIDNIGHT

*R*aven felt Rylan's arrival before she saw him. The air hummed with his arrival, power tickling along her skin. Unlike shifters, vampires gained power through what they consumed. Though Rylan wasn't ancient, he had a hell of a lot of power to call on, thanks to the labs. Now that he was here, nerves struck, doubts rose, along with a thrill at finally being able to see him again.

"Rylan." The men ranged close to her side as she whirled to face him.

"At your service, beautiful." The black haired vampire stepped out of the shadows, his lean body whipcord thin and immaculately dressed. But it was his haunted blue eyes that captured her attention and stole her breath.

"Thank you for coming." When she went to touch his arm, he deftly stepped out of reach. She swallowed thickly and accepted his choice, ignoring the stab of hurt at his rejection. She knew better than to touch anyone, especially him. "A person came, asking for help. I tried, but I fear my particular talent isn't enough."

Those sea blue eyes of his darkened in understanding. He knew her influence over the undead and how much danger it put her in if others found out she could raise them.

"Show me."

A relieved breath stuttered out of her body. She opened the door to the office and nodded toward the chaise. Cassie hadn't moved since she'd left. Her drying hair was clumped and snarled, the mahogany color limp. If anything, she appeared worse, her skin pasty and dull. Death hovered ever closer.

Rylan passed temptingly near, dancing with danger as Raven's power ached to leap into his body. She resisted reaching out to trail her hands down his back. Although they would both relish the contact, it wasn't healthy for either of them.

He knelt, and she found herself studying him and not the patient. There was something about him, the way he watched her that had Raven take notice and enjoy the attention. As if he could see below the surface and still liked her.

A corner of Rylan's mouth kicked up briefly. That one second told her he understood his effect on her. The slight tightening of his fists let her know that he enjoyed it, too.

"Well?" Durant's voice broke into the fantasy.

"The transition didn't take. She's dying. I can try to pull her over." He stood and gazed at Durant, unfazed by the cat ready to leap and take a swipe at his throat. "I can't guarantee it'll work."

"Why the hell not?" Durant took a threatening step forward, his fingers flexing as if claws were ready to burst from their tips. Raven grabbed the back of his shirt, surprised that he allowed her to stop him. The scent of leather rose from him.

"Because her body already rejected the vampire bite. If my blood is strong enough, it will clear out her system and re-start the change."

"You don't know?" Durant's voice was sharp.

Rylan shook his head, his face impassive. "I've never turned anyone. I also don't have a live blood source. If this works, she can use my blood for the transfusion, but she'll also need to use someone else for the subsequent donations."

"Why?" Jackson asked the question, but Raven knew the answer.

"He doesn't want to tie her to him. The initial transfusion will give them a connection, but each subsequent exchange strengthens that bond." She understood his reasoning. The less they tied themselves to others, the less it'd hurt later. People like them didn't maintain ties. Friendships didn't survive long.

It was safer for everyone.

"Do it." Durant turned his back, his hard gaze landing on her face. There was no grief there now. It was all suspicion and retribution. If anything happened to Cassie, she knew who'd be blamed.

The men exchanged a silent look that she couldn't interpret, one guaranteed to irritate a woman. She pretended she didn't see anything.

"She'll need to be fed a few times a night for the first couple of months if you want to keep her in check. If you miss a feeding, her control will falter. If she goes too long without food, her sanity will fade. The urge to search out prey will take control, until only the animal instinct to feed will take over. You don't want to see what a starved vampire can do."

Raven refused to face Dominic. They knew. They'd seen it firsthand.

"Do you wish me to continue?" Rylan kept his tone bland, not revealing even a hint of emotion.

A curl of disgust twisted Durant's lips, but he nodded. "Yes."

Rylan removed his jacket, placed it neatly on a nearby chair. He rolled up his sleeves in his precise way, met her gaze and nodded to the door.

Raven took the hint and cleared her throat. "Everyone out." Durant was the last to leave, and she had to prod him each step of the way.

She knew what to expect, but the others didn't. She planted herself in front of the door and waited. "Jackson, Dominic, would you stand by Mr. Durant? Taggert, please stand by me."

"What's going on?" Those tiger-eyes lifted to hers, suspicion heavy in his gaze, his power beating at her shields.

Before she could react, a scream of pain rent the air, riveting the men. The voice held such emotion, such devastation, they all flinched. When the second one came, louder, longer, they charged for the door.

"What the hell is he doing to her?"

"Hold him," she commanded.

Taggert instantly understood the danger, placing himself in front of her, bristling with enough energy that her own abused talent reared its ugly head and licked its lips. With a firm step, she backed away from temptation, nearly weak with relief when the hunger eased.

"Mr. Durant."

It was as if he didn't hear her. He slipped out of Dominic's hold and swung at Jackson. She winced in sympathy when the blow landed, splitting open his cheek, but the stubborn man didn't let go, didn't loosen his hold. Dominic quickly captured the other arm again, muscles flexing.

Each step closer was a struggle, Durant pulling the men along like dead weight. Taggert tensed, ready to launch himself into the fray if Durant so much as twitched.

"Mr. Durant, how did you think this would turn out? For the transformation to work, she has to die." She stepped closer, wishing there was another way, wishing she could offer him some sort of comfort that everything would work out all right. But she couldn't. She couldn't guarantee him anything.

Chest billowing under the strain, the big man finally halted. "She's still alive."

"Her body's been shutting down for the last hour. He's trying to turn her, but the process is painful. His blood will rejuvenate the cells. Since she's so far along in the process, it'll be agony as the change expels any drugs and toxins from her body."

"And how is it that you know so much about their kind?"

She felt the brush of his gift and nearly staggered when he slammed into her shields with the force of a jackhammer. Shards of pain shot through her skull. She pressed her palms against her temple in an effort to keep her mind from turning to mush.

"Stop." When he did it again, the walls around her control threatened to crumble. Electricity flared to life, eager to lash back.

Desperate to keep him safe, she yanked back hard on the raw energy as it sought a target. She was only partially successful. A strand escaped, wrapped around his body. If any more of her power infected his system, they'd have one very angry, determined tiger on their hands. Reacting without thinking, she drew down hard.

He gasped, but she couldn't open her eyes for the pain ricocheting through her skull. Despite her best intentions, he didn't stop, continuing to ram against her shields. She could almost swear his animal snarled. The voltage built again, burning along her skin. It grew, her core searing the inside of her chest. Breathing became difficult.

Then blessedly, everything went quiet. Her knees shook as the flare slowly dwindled. She was afraid to open her eyes, afraid to find out what she'd done.

"Raven, can you hear me?"

She blinked and found herself face to face with Taggert. Her gaze flickered toward the form spread out along the floor, and her throat ached at his absolute stillness.

"Did I kill him?"

Dominic snorted. "Nothing a little bump on the head won't cure. What the hell was he doing to you?"

She winced at his tone, rubbing her temples at the recent assault. "He wanted the truth, no matter how he got it."

"By ripping it from your mind? It could've killed you." Dominic looked ready to wake Durant so he could hit the man again.

Taggert cupped her elbow, nearly lifting her off her feet in his effort to help her stand. She noticed the bruised and bloodied knuckles and felt ashamed. "I was supposed to protect you."

"Things are a little more complicated than that. You take care of the pack, and they protect you from any threat." Dominic opened his mouth to continue when everything went ominously silent in the other room.

She staggered closer, using the wall for support and gently knocked on the door. "Rylan, is everything okay?" The door swung open in the middle of her question. She peered inside when she saw no one at the door.

Dominic brushed by her, entering first. Taggert hovered over her with Jackson bringing up the rear. She almost bumped into Dominic when he stopped abruptly.

From his ashen expression, she expected the worst. When she turned her head, the girl they once knew as Cassie greedily drew on Rylan's arm.

"Sleep."

Cassie instantly closed her eyes and slumped.

Rylan extracted his arm, then rolled down his sleeves. But not before she saw the chew marks that made his forearm nothing more than hamburger.

"Will you be all right?"

"I'll be fine." He avoided her gaze.

He didn't look fine. His energy was dangerously low, and she pushed when she would normally remain silent. "You need to eat."

He stilled completely at her comment, his back to her. "I'll be fine."

Raven shook her head. She stepped away from Taggert and stumbled. She would've fallen if Rylan hadn't whirled and caught her arm. As she met his gaze, she saw his fangs extend, saw his eyes darken to that wonderful blue that revealed his troubled soul.

"Don't touch her." Dominic's demand thundered through the room.

"I have no intention of hurting her. What happened?" As careful as a glass doll, he righted her, then pulled away, never removing his gaze from hers. His brows lowered. He raked his gaze over her, his hands curling into fists. "You're in pain."

She shrugged. "Like you, I'm fine. There was a little dispute. It's settled."

"That jackass tried to break her shields."

Jackson didn't even finish, and Rylan was already moving. Faster than humans could track, he crossed the room and disappeared out the door.

She hurried past the others, hauling ass, but not quick enough. Rylan had Durant by the throat, dangling the unconscious man off the floor. With his fangs fully extended, the vampire hissed in fury.

As if he understood the threat, Durant slowly opened his eyes, but otherwise, didn't move.

"Rylan." She shrugged off Dominic's arm when he tried to restrain her. "It's okay. He was worried about his friend."

"He wouldn't have a friend if it weren't for you. Is that the way he repays a favor?" The grip of his hand tightened. Beads of blood trickled down Durant's throat where Rylan's nails dug deep.

The big cat tensed, and his attention panned to her.

"My apologies. It won't happen again."

"You're right." Faster than she could blink, Rylan sliced his hand down Durant's chest. Blood gushed from the wound. Durant raised his arm to retaliate, and Rylan caught it mid swing.

"Don't." She didn't think he'd listen, but Durant stopped moving and allowed himself to be half dragged toward her.

"Take it." Rylan kicked Durant's legs out from beneath him. Grabbing his shoulders, Rylan righted Durant until he knelt at her feet.

Raven stared at Rylan in disbelief, shaking her head. "Don't do this."

He only stared at her, his eyes uncompromising. "Either you take his blood, or I kill him."

"What the hell's going on here?" Dominic stepped forward, and Rylan narrowed his gaze.

"He's trying to protect her." Taggert was the one who spoke. Then, surprisingly, he stepped in front of Dominic, blocking him.

What the hell was wrong with the men in her life?

"Get the hell off me." Durant jerked away and shifted to stand.

Rylan stooped, bringing his face next to Durant. A deep snarl rumbled from Durant's throat, but Rylan only bared his fangs. "I'd say we're even in our strength. We can tear into one another, possibly kill each other. But know this. Raven will not let me die, but your little girl in the other room has no such guarantee."

Durant's gaze met hers, and she tried not to flinch at the judgment there. He lifted his chin. "Do it."

"You don't understand."

Durant didn't move. "I understand. You're a vampire like him, just a different variety."

"That's not fair. I—"

"I don't care. Take what you need so I can get the hell away from you."

The callused words robbed her of breath. Durant winced when Rylan gouged his fingers into the tissue of his shoulder.

Pain funneled into rage at being forced into this situation infuriated her. "I refuse to let you die. I refuse to fight my friend for you. Tell me, Durant, where does that leave me?"

When he didn't answer, Jackson spoke. "What do you gain by taking his blood?"

Raven met his gaze, surprised not to see suspicion there. "I get an enemy."

She could feel Rylan's gaze on hers but refused his silent entreaty to understand his reasoning. Damn it, she didn't need anyone protecting her. They would only get hurt.

"A vampire's answer is always slavery." Durant shook off Rylan's restraining arm and rose.

Rylan tisked. "Not this tired argument. Let's not forget the benefits the breeds received. Things weren't as one-sided as they try to make you believe. Wolves were our daytime protection. Our blood strengthened them, creating faster, stronger, better shifters. They were virtually indestructible." He walked around and came to a stop at her side.

"You hear about the horrors we supposedly perpetrated on them. But do you hear about the other side? The stories of vampires drained of blood, where a group of wolves hunted and tracked vampires for sport, slaughtering them for the blood. But when the vampire dies, the power of their blood fades as well, so they have to do it again and again. They don't tell you how vampire blood can change a normal shifter into an alpha."

Awareness hovered at the edges of her mind, the bodies at the crime scenes drained of blood. Then she lost her train of thought when the men's argument increased in volume. Durant and Rylan circled one another. She stepped between them, praying neither man would take off her head. "Enough."

Taggert stepped next to her when the two men pressed closer. "I don't understand the problem. She's not a vampire, so she can't control him. The only benefit is to Raven. Protection from him. Could she control him?"

No one said anything. Raven cleared her throat. "No, his blood won't allow me to control him. I'm *not* a vampire."

"You hesitated. Why?" Durant crowded closer, but Rylan pushed against her back when she tried to retreat.

"I'm not exactly normal." She licked her lips, hating the way his scent curled around her, the way his heat invaded her body. She didn't want to give up her hurt that easily. "What should be a routine process usually backfires when I'm involved."

Durant relaxed slightly. "What do you think will happen?"

"I think it will connect us." Raven didn't need any more connections to anyone. Connections generally got her into trouble. She looked at each man in the room and realized she was the only one protesting anymore.

"Have you tasted anyone else's blood?"

"Not on purpose." That froze Durant. She could tell he didn't expect her answer. "I guess it all comes down to trust. I can't trust you. This is the second time you've tried to break my shields. After you asked for my help, been welcomed into my home, you attacked me. Tell me, Durant, if the situation were reversed, would we even be here talking? Or would you have killed me right out?"

A new, more horrifying idea came to her. She slowly stepped away from the men. She felt stupid for not realizing it sooner. "Dominic, I have tiger DNA. If I accept blood from him, we'd be pack."

Panic tightened her throat, and she looked at her friend for guidance. Did she have enough cat in her to be alpha? She was afraid that since her shields held against him that she did.

The expression on Dominic's face didn't change. "Yes."

Chapter Twelve

EARLY MORNING: 3AM

"*N*o. Hell, no." She shook her head and backed away, a deep sense of betrayal slicing through her. They were supposed to be her friends, the only family she had left.

Rylan swiftly blocked her exit. "It needs to be done." He gently brushed at her hair, always fascinated by the streaks and ragged silver-tipped ends. This time the gesture didn't offer her any calm. "If you were alpha, he wouldn't dare attack you."

"Unless he challenges me."

"A male can't replace a female leader. If he oversteps his bounds, you have the right to kill him." Rylan smiled, his fangs showing a little too much. "He can petition the council at the conclave to be released from your pack, and the council will cast judgment."

She didn't trust that smile, and her stomach somersaulted in her throat. "But?"

"The council has never reversed a female claim."

"But he's an alpha. Not only are you asking him to refute his ability to create his own pack, but also the possibly of finding his Consort." Raven had to talk sense into them. She looked at the others for support, but they just met her gaze without a word of protest.

"I believe what they're trying to tell you is, once we've mated, I won't care." Durant crossed his arms. "As for creating my own pack,

I won't. It's one of the concessions to owning my business within pack territory. Cassie doesn't count as she is human."

Raven blinked when his words registered, and she barely heard the rest of his explanation. "No one said anything about mating." Panic tightened her chest, breathing became difficult. "Why aren't you fighting them?"

"Are you saying you're a fate worse than death?" Durant shrugged, his focus unwavering and intense, seeing something in her that solidified his decision. "There are few of my kind living. The chances of me finding a Consort are slim." He shook his head. "And there's something about you that my beast wants. I noticed it at the club, and when I arrived here."

"Yeah, that's why you tried to kill me."

Rylan nodded, ignoring her as if everything made sense. "It's why he came to you for help."

The longer she stared at Durant, the more unsettled she grew. Something didn't fit. "You want this." The accusation erupted from her. Then she made the connection. He'd stopped protesting the instant her cat DNA was mentioned.

"I didn't plan it, but I'll accept it. It could be beneficial to us both." Durant stepped toward her while Rylan held her in place.

"Raven, the girl will wake shortly. She'll need to be fed. You have to decide. Either you take them or they die." Thunder rumbled in the distance, and her heart slammed hard against her ribs. The storm would be upon her within the hour, and then there would be hell to pay. She had to decide now.

If she accepted them, it would be her job to protect them. It would be her job to find out who attacked Cassie. The idea of escaping the house sounded good to her, even if she had to face the storm and a killer.

She felt Rylan's grip through her clothes, the slight shake in his fingers, the need in him. He ached. And she knew he'd never ask her for help. "Rylan—"

"You need to do this. This man can protect you when I'm not available."

Raven jerked away from him. The bastards were building a pack around her, whether she liked it or not. "That system is archaic. I'm not in danger. I don't need protection. I can take care of myself."

Rylan reached out for her, but dropped his arm without touching her. "The pack system works. You insist on working a dangerous job. Your powers are changing. You're vulnerable alone."

"What aren't you telling me?" What had she done to bring suspicion on herself?

Durant stepped forward, drew his nail across his palm, drawing a welt of blood. "I offer myself freely."

"It's all a lie." Her lips felt bloodless.

"It's what we make it." Those green eyes turned golden.

She could feel the pressure inside build as the storm worsened. The urge to hide, run away from the truth, and fight the cravings grew in her. If she did what they said, she could be free. Still she fought.

The blood slowed, the wound healing. "Why is claiming you different than claiming Taggert? Why—"

Durant smiled. "Tigers are a different breed from wolves. No one can make a tiger do something they don't desire. You claimed Taggert. This will be a mating that brings money and power to the pack."

The tone of his voice, the cadence, resonated in her.

Hypnotizing.

She shook her head to try and clear her thoughts. "You're doing it again, trying to influence me. You're trying to seduce me."

A small smile tugged at his lips. "It's a privilege of being packmates."

His face might have been smiling, but his eyes were dead serious.

"Never." Raven gulped, trying to find where the oxygen disappeared to when she desperately needed air. Durant bit his lip until blood welled.

Her heart slammed painfully against her ribs when he tipped his head toward hers. The warm scent of leather swirled between them.

"Taste." Durant murmured the words against her lips. "I can feel your hunger beat at me."

"I don't trust you." He'd changed his mind much too fast for her to be convinced he didn't want something. Then his lips brushed hers. When she pulled away, he cupped the back of her head and deepened the kiss.

Instead of blood, she tasted power. It curled through her, drugging her body. His aura fluctuated, melding a little with hers. His desire consumed her. The world fell away, and the threat of the storm vanished. Everything she needed was in this kiss.

His hands tightened painfully in her hair, dragging her back from the edge and the pool of power just beyond her touch. She wanted to reach deeper and brush up against the cat she sensed so near the surface.

When he pulled away, she met his gaze and licked her lips. The taste of blood broke through her euphoria. Durant's chest heaved with exertion, all the scheming she'd seen in his eyes had vanished.

He shuddered, looking as confused as her. "What happened?"

Rylan snorted. "Raven happened."

A movement in the other room jolted them into motion.

"Cassie's awake." Rylan nodded to Durant. "You're needed."

When Durant took a step, he staggered as if drunk. Surprise plastered his face as he quickly straightened. Those golden eyes of his met hers, and she knew he wouldn't forget what they'd shared. She just wished she knew what he planned on doing with the information.

She followed and watched him cradle Cassie. He winced when she grabbed his offered arm with two hands and pulled it toward her mouth. As his orphan fed, Durant's gaze locked on hers.

Raven turned away from the intimate moment, unable to bear the close exam from his too perceptive eyes. Only to find herself faced with four men. Jackson crossed his arms, a pinched look on his face. The fury in his eyes took her aback. "Jackson?"

"He might buy that excuse for now, but he's going to want the truth. What the hell happened?"

Rylan stepped between them. "Just what I said."

"I wasn't talking to you." Jackson closed the distance until the men stood toe to toe. "What did you do to them? What vampire tricks did you use?"

Suddenly tired, Raven rubbed her temple. "Jackson, he didn't do anything. I told you I was different. I accidentally reached inside the core where Durant holds his power. I'm not sure how it's possible, but he must have felt some of mine in exchange."

"Your hands glowed." Taggert stared at her hands, and she resisted the urge to hide them behind her back.

Rylan gazed at her, questions in his eyes. She wanted to ask if he saw anything, but couldn't open herself up to more scrutiny. Not when she didn't know the answers. "This whole thing wasn't necessary."

"We'll have to agree to disagree."

Though Rylan's expression was pleasant, she detected an underlying emotion in him that made her nervous. She couldn't help but feel she'd disappointed him in some way. That he needed something from her that she failed to understand.

"You need to feed." Rylan didn't move, just continued to gaze at her.

"You're going after them, aren't you?" He pursed his lips. "I think I'll accompany you."

"No." The last thing she wanted was to be in the company of a hungry vampire. Especially Rylan. He read her too well and would ask questions when she had no answers to give. She needed time and space to regroup. "She nearly drained you. You let her take too much."

"I could taste you on her." He murmured the last words. "It's enough."

Though it should've frightened her, the warmth in his words brought heat to her face.

"Until you crash in the middle of a fight." She wouldn't be responsible for his death.

"Then we'll split into two teams. One person has to stay here to watch over Durant and his charge. The rest of us will go."

Raven conceded defeat. If she left without him, he'd just follow. "Fine. Taggert will stay—"

"I have a better sense of smell than anyone here. If you have any hope of finding anything, you'll need me."

He had a point. Jackson was already shaking his head before she could speak. "He goes, I go."

"It looks like you take them all. Call me every twenty minutes and check in." Dominic grunted, watching her closely as if waiting for her to protest all the added protection.

"Thank you."

He nodded and walked away. She watched him a moment longer, sensing his concern. He was the leader of a group of elite fighters. He frequently maintained the command post, directing his little minions around like chess pieces. Today was the first time he appeared to chafe under his role. She hesitated, wanted to say something to appease him, but couldn't find the words. Or maybe she was too afraid to dig further. Her world was crumbling faster than she could gather the pieces, and it terrified her.

The storm swept closer, creeping up on her. Time pressed against her, slithering through her mind in a slow countdown. "We need to get there before the storm breaks." With a nod, she headed straight for the door and ignored the men. Especially Durant. If she were lucky, Dominic would have the house cleared out by the time she returned. She had other things to worry about than some delicious guy hunting her. And hopefully, he would forget all about this supposed mate garbage. She snorted silently, opened the door, and headed toward the car.

When thunder rumbled, she tucked her chin down and picked up her pace. A trickle of unease threaded through her. She should be in the basement, locked down while the storm blew over. While her body tried to recover from the last few hours of overuse of her gift, the lightning could prove dangerous. She wasn't sure if she could deflect all that voltage if it was called down close to her. Instead, she got into the car and did her best to ignore the way her body felt battered by all the current traveling in the wind, eagerly seeking the slightest opening in her shields.

Twisting the keys, the engine revved to life.

As she shifted the car into gear, the men were there. Rylan slipped through the passenger door Jackson had opened, the sneaky bastard using his talents to steal the front seat. After a slight hesitation,

Jackson glared at the man then slammed the door and got in back next to Taggert. Without a word, she took off.

Ten minutes passed in uncomfortable silence, the air thick with an argument waiting to erupt.

"Do you know where you're going?" Rylan broke the stalemate, thankfully choosing a topic she could answer.

"Strauss Forest near Overland Park." She flicked a glance at him. "Did you pick anything up from her?"

"Vague images. If she was there, I'll be able to tell. The rest of the memories were too jumbled. They chased her. If we cross the trail, your pet should be able to find them."

"Rylan, don't—"

Taggert leaned closer, apparently unoffended. "I caught the scent of her blood. If there's a drop anywhere in my vicinity, I'll be able to track her."

Jackson pressed forward and Taggert scooted over, his face close to her shoulders. The slight brush of his fingers against her hair almost made her pull away. She forced herself to remain still. Pack touched, she reminded herself, it was how they connected. If she pulled away, Taggert would see it as a rejection.

"Then we need to split into two teams; one of you with me and the other with Taggert." Rylan didn't say anything more.

She could tell Jackson wasn't pleased with the turn of events. She wasn't either, but she couldn't think of an alternative. "Taggert and I go one way while you two head the opposite direction." She pushed the gear into park, turned off the motor, and watched the storm draw ever closer, doing her best to clamp down on the seething core begging to be let out to play.

"I don't think we should split."

Raven ignored Jackson and opened the door. The darkness of the woods didn't look inviting. Shadows danced, but it was the lack of animals, the lack of sound, that had a chill creeping across her skin. "When you search, look for signs of any animals."

"Why?" Jackson sounded suspicious and belligerent.

Desire my ass. That was pure distrust in his question. Raven glanced at him and resisted the urge to sigh. "Call it a hunch."

Rylan narrowed his eyes. "Why do you think this is the right area?"

"Because I recognize that bite mark on Cassie from a couple of murder victims that were left here the day before last."

Two days seemed so long ago. Not waiting for any more protests, she headed forward. The darkness was oppressive, pushing against her as she walked. She blinked, and the shadows retreated, her eyes adjusting as the animals at her core woke from their slumber, allowing her to see through their keen vision.

Although she was grateful for the help, she hated acknowledging that she was losing control. Every aspect of her life was becoming blurred. All her careful controls were cracking. She wished she knew what would be left behind when everything finally broke loose.

"Rylan, head south at a forty-five degree angle from here. Taggert and I will head southwest. When you reach the stream, head toward my direction and we'll meet up in the middle."

Jackson stepped in front of her and refused to budge. "I don't trust him." He jerked his head toward Rylan, his eyes bleeding yellow.

Rylan shrugged, leaving it up to her to reveal as much as she wanted. "The storm's getting worse. I can't guarantee how long our phones will work. If Rylan is in the area, I can sense him and vice versa."

Jackson flipped open his new phone, and she winced at the reminder of what happened to his old one. "Service is—"

"She means that when she's around electrical devices, they tend to not hold a charge. It takes a conscious effort for her not to consume the energy around her. With the storm, it would be impossible. Since her phone is on her person, and Taggert will be near her, they'll be drained if they aren't already." Rylan turned and disappeared in the trees.

Vampire tricks. She shook her head. Then she jumped when his voice floated back to them.

"The sooner we leave, the faster we can get back."

In a blur of speed, Jackson streaked into the woods, disappearing just as fast. Relieved to be away from the tension between those two, she gave a wan smile to Taggert and took off.

The wind tugged at her, pulling at her clothes. Despite her animals' agitation, the power of the storm was exhilarating. She could almost taste the desire to reach out and pull down the lightning. Any fatigue vanished as the air literally recharged her. She'd worry about crashing after she did what needed to be done.

"Raven?" Taggert stepped in front of her and she blinked, unaware that she'd stopped.

She cleared her throat. "Do you sense anything?"

Taggert shook his head, his shoulder length hair framing his face, wild and untamed. His natural scent almost disappeared in the surrounding trees, but she could still pick him out. There was a subtle flavor to it that drew her, and she followed him as he scouted the area.

"I don't sense anything." He paused, but didn't turn to look at her. "Do you?"

She opened her mouth to answer when understanding hit. He'd seen the web she'd created at the club, knew what she'd done. Giving him a short nod, she closed her eyes. Energy easily answered her call, kicking up the air around them like a cyclone, building and growing with each second. In the distance, she heard a snarl, then the animals at her core fell silent and vanished.

The current crackled along her skin, seeking an outlet. The temptation to linger and play whispered to her along the wind. She let it build, felt it whip along her insides like writhing snakes. The longer she held it, the more agitated they grew until her bones turned molten.

With a short breath, she released everything in a giant pulse. A gasp from Taggert popped her eyes open. The energy had passed through him, but she could see he'd managed to absorb quite a bit.

That shouldn't have happened. It had to have hurt like hell. Yellow eyes glinted in the dark, their focus solely on her. Neither of them said a word.

After a moment, she registered Rylan and Jackson. She felt Rylan's discomfort, his hunger, and winced. She'd never sent such a powerful burst, never expected it to reach them. She wanted to blame it on the storm, but she didn't know if it was the truth and refused to hide behind a lie anymore.

"I sensed less than a handful of animals taking shelter from the storm. Nothing else." When she glanced at Taggert, she was startled to see him just inches from her, very much the predator.

She pushed at the hard wall of his chest, gasping when a shock zapped between them. Taggert flinched and stepped away, the look in his eyes clearing but not fading completely.

Taggert wandered a short distance away and knelt. "Here."

"Blood?" She crouched to see what he'd discovered.

"No, tracks. A lot of them."

Footprints, a couple of size ten and more, too trampled to see clearly. Definitely not kids. Ice wrapped around her heart. "A hunt. How old?" She needed to know if this was part of the murders, or if they were tracking Cassie.

"A day or less." Their eyes met, and they both knew the tracks would disappear in the oncoming storm.

"Follow them." The others would be furious that they deviated from the plan, but she couldn't lose this clue.

With a nod, he took off. His speed was incredible, and she knew he held back for her. She didn't allow herself to think of the miles she was putting between them and the rendezvous point. She unclipped her phone, but knew she'd drained it without having to look at it. She managed to fix a computer for her own use, but the power source was so slight on the phone that all the prototypes had melted.

The brush grew thicker with each step, snatching at her clothes. The air thickened as the storm worsened, the silence more ominous the further they went. Only when Taggert slowed did she swallow back her unease. "What is it?"

"Someone's watching us. I can smell them."

A shape streaked toward Taggert's unguarded back. "No." Without thinking, she threw a ball of energy. It surged out of her so strongly that her joints ached.

And missed. Vegetation shriveled in the wake of the heat.

Whoever it was had vanished.

Lightning struck nearby, and she could feel the current slice its way through the ground, arching toward her. "Move!"

Chapter Thirteen

PREDAWN

*R*aven made a quick decision. The lightning came from behind her, the killer was in front. She dodged around Taggert and ran toward where she last saw the figure, easily picking up the trail.

She sensed Taggert gaining on her and cursed her clumsiness. Sweat beaded her brow as the lightning threaded its way toward her like a juggernaut on a mission. She could only hold it at bay for so long before it consumed her.

The smell of fresh blood hit her first. The shape of a girl appeared out of the shadows. Only this girl moved oddly, her movements disjointed as if she'd been taken apart and put back together wrong. The air crackled around them as Raven fought to manage her fear. She couldn't fail, or Taggert would be left vulnerable.

The energy from the ground was too much for her to even attempt to regulate. Timed carefully, she might be able to funnel the massive voltage and take out the girl before the overload shut her down.

She held out her hand to Taggert, indicating he should keep his distance. Her movement triggered a reaction. The girl lunged forward, all awkwardness gone.

Flinging up her hands, Raven dropped her shields and allowed the torrent she'd held at bay to pass through her. Current surged up from her feet with enough strength to snap her spine straight.

The girl lunged, fangs bared, slashing out. Raven twisted, unable to dodge. Claws tore down her back. At the contact, the power roared out of her with the speed of a barreling train, scraping her insides raw as if taking chunks of her with it.

Burnt hair sizzled in the air. A sharp yelp almost shattered her eardrums and the creature disappeared through the trees. She staggered, then fell to her knees. Her vision wavered, but she refused to relent. Not when they were so vulnerable.

"Raven? I'm almost there."

"Rylan?" She blinked, unable to understand how communication reserved for vampires and their protégé worked between them without a large blood exchange.

"Hang on."

As abruptly as she felt the connection, it broke. Then the whole world went black.

The next thing she knew, she was being carried. Her body felt like she'd gone jousting without the tin can called a suit of armor. "Taggert?" Her jaw ached to even speak.

The strangle hold around her tightened. A whimper of pain caught in her throat and another wave of dizziness shot through her as the world spun. She breathed through it and concentrated on staying awake.

"Put me down." Every nerve ending felt fried. Partly overloaded. What little electricity she had was leaking like crazy. Her energy level would continue to sputter until she stabilized. He had to feel like he put his whole body in a socket.

Instead of listening, Taggert picked up his pace.

"Please. I can manage." At least she hoped she could. She hated being defenseless, hated relying on someone else.

When she tried to lean away from him, agony screeched through her body. Spots danced in front of her eyes. "Did she manage to leave any of my back intact?" She could barely form words, but she refused to be cowed by the pain.

When he didn't reply, Raven bit her lip. The first hint that something was dreadfully wrong pinged through her. "Taggert?"

Water splashed her back when he crossed the stream. Crippling agony ripped through her as droplets of water trickled into her wounds. She couldn't prevent herself from curling around him. "Please let me down."

Finally, Taggert stopped, somehow sensing she was at her limit.

It embarrassed her that she couldn't stop shaking. Five minutes. She needed five minutes to rebuild as much of her shields as she could to protect Taggert. She could survive an overload, but even a shifter could only take that kind of abuse for so long and not be damaged, especially since he couldn't take his animal form.

Though his chest heaved with exertion, he seemed reluctant to release her. He lowered her so gently that she didn't even feel the ground. When he made to stand, she grabbed the material of his shirt and held him in place.

The pure yellow gleam in his eyes should've repelled her, but the shattered, lost expression had her heart aching for him. "I'm all right. I'll be fine." She reached out to touch his face, halting when he flinched. His rejection shattered her.

She did that to him.

When she would've let her hand fall, he grabbed her fingers and pressed them to his check. His eyes slid shut, and some of the tension eased from his shoulders.

His skin pebbled at her touch, and she jerked back. "I'm hurting you."

Taggert slowly shook his head. When he opened his eyes, he appeared calmer. "Rylan and Jackson should be here soon. I can hear them, smell them. There about a mile away, moving fast."

He drew away, and Raven gasped at all the blood. "You're hurt."

Her heart gave a painful squeeze, and she couldn't find her breath. She tried to pull him back to inspect the wounds, but he refused her this time. If she didn't think she'd pass out, she'd damn the pain and follow.

Part of her anxiety eased when she saw the blood wash away. Then a new fear took root. Her blood. She gulped hard, her throat tight with a fear that wouldn't be banished.

"You have to get it all off." He was adapting to her and the current so fast it scared the shit out her. Infection would explain everything. Being around her was changing him into something else.

Something she could touch. She was ruining him, stealing his chance for an ordinary life.

A brooding expression crossed Taggert's face as if he sensed her turmoil, her withdrawal. He melted a little in the shadows. She didn't like the way he searched their surroundings, the way he refused to speak, or the way his eyes whirled when he looked at her. Thunder rumbled, and he flinched.

She cleared her throat, knowing that later...much later...they would have to address this issue. She just had to keep her distance until they found another solution for him.

"Your vampire just disappeared. Where the hell have you been?" Jackson pulled to a stop half way across the clearing. He had directed his question at Taggert then slowly turned toward her.

With incredible speed that made her flinch, he was beside her. "What the hell happened?"

"We've found the killer."

"What?" His roar rang in her ears.

Bile rose, her power fizzled and she fought to stay conscious. "Is there any way that we can take this conversation home before the storm breaks?" She wasn't proud the way her voice shook.

Rylan appeared out of the night from the direction of the fight, his clothes rumpled, his perfectly coiffed hair in disarray, his expression so stiff it frightened her. Without saying a word, he scooped her up and traveled with her back to the car. She closed her eyes and buried her face against the crook of his neck so as not to risk losing the contents of her stomach as the world blurred around them. The hot, spicy scent of him swirled around her. Like a trigger, she remembered that scent, remembered the way he cared for her whenever she became injured when in captivity.

He carefully placed her in the backseat, then brushed her hair gently behind her ear. When he straightened, she saw the knife. "No. You can't lose any more blood."

"Neither can you." He gripped the blade into his fist and pulled the knife clean. Blood welled and dripped from between his clenched fingers.

He opened his bloody hand and placed his palm directly over her wounds. She sucked in a breath at the touch, her stomach twisting up into her throat at the agony. Fire burned along her back and stole her breath.

"Damn you." She shoved him away with weak arms. Already, the blood had stopped dripping down her back.

Rylan stepped back, his all black eyes watching her with such emotion her heart ached. While she watched, he lifted his hand to his face and inhaled the scent of her blood. Then he was gone, circling the back of the vehicle.

Taggert was at her side, buckling her into the seat, cradling her hand in his. When she tried to draw away, he grumbled low in his throat in a not even remotely human sound, and tightened his grip.

Unable to focus on him and the pain at the same time, she turned to Rylan when he got in the car. Work. She had to focus on work for fear she'd cry at the way her messed up life was falling apart, taking her friends with it. "What did you find?"

"Nothing. Whoever it was had disappeared. I smelled lightning, burnt hair, and a lot of your blood." He gave her an accusing glare from the rearview mirror, his reflection didn't dim its potency. "The scent of whoever was there was so faint, I couldn't get a lock on them." He started the car and had it in gear when Jackson opened the door and jumped in.

"No one followed us."

They took off.

Both the men in the front faced straight ahead, their silence more stifling now than on the ride there. The trip home was vague as she wavered between full consciousness and the hazy lure of darkness. She came to herself when the engine rumbled to stop and someone opened her door.

She hadn't placed a foot on the ground when the front door burst open and Dominic and London were hurrying toward them. "Why the hell didn't you call?" His words trailed off when he caught sight of her. "What happened?"

Without waiting for the others, he clasped her arm and pulled her to her feet. The muscles in her back protested the abrupt movement. Ribbons of fire shot down her spine and into her legs. His grip flexed painfully on her hands when some of her energy splashed over on him, but he refused to release her.

"Attacked." She couldn't say anything more as she battled for breath. The muscles around her ribs protested each inhalation.

"Screw this." Jackson went to pick her up and found London blocking his way. Jackson was taller, but London had the weight of pure bulk to back him. "Get out of my way."

"Stop acting like boys." She didn't need this now. When the stand-down didn't break, she debated leaving them to slug it out. With a deep breath, she released Dominic's hand and took a staggering step toward the combatants. Anger shut out some of the pain, and she relished the feeling, embraced it.

Taggert stepped in front of her, blocking her way.

"Move." Her quarrel wasn't with him. She didn't want to hurt him more than she already had. Some of the energy began to build again, begging to be released. What better way than a fight?

"He's worried." He ducked his head a little to meet her gaze straight on, slightly baring his neck. "He has a right to be worried."

The hot air of her anger deflated a little and that only made her crankier. "Do you guys think we could take this inside? I need to call Scotts, not to mention I desperately need to wash up before heading back out."

All eyes latched onto her at her statement, stopping the argument dead. With one painful step, then another, she headed toward the house, waiting for the explosion from her troop of overprotective goons. They knew as well as she did that they needed to go back. Something was out there killing. Not to mention the issue of Cassie's missing informant still hadn't shown up.

Taggert drew near, and though it shouldn't, his presence easing the tightness in her chest. His touch was surprisingly comfortable when he scooped her up in his arms.

Skin touched skin.

A hiss escaped him, quickly drowned out by her groan of pain.

He instantly halted and lowered her. Once her feet touched the ground, her knees threatened to buckle, and she clung to his shoulders. Taggert's arms slipped around her hips, his hands cupping her ass. When she would've protested, he nudged her with his chin.

"Wrap your legs around my waist. I'll get you upstairs."

Raven hesitated then glanced at Rylan. "You'll stay?"

He nodded, his face like granite, his chest unmoving, every inch the vampire. She winced to see her blood liberally coating his shirtfront. The drive home had to have been torture.

As if he read her thoughts, he turned away. "I'll make a few phone calls. I'll see you after your shower."

Raven faced Taggert, looked at his young face, and felt a twinge of conscience, then shoved it aside for practicality. The instant he lifted, she wrapped her legs around him, and jerked, startled by the arousal she found pressed intimately against her.

When she loosened her legs, Taggert tightened his grip, avoiding her gaze. "Ignore it. That always happens around you."

Those were the last words he spoke as he mounted the steps. Raven bit her lip and thanked God for the pain to distract her. The last thing she needed was to feel desire for him. Worse, to have him guess how he made her feel. That way led to disaster.

Jackson strode past them. She heard the door to her room open, then water splash in the shower. She burrowed her face against Taggert's chest at the pain she knew would come.

"Phone call first."

There was only a small hiccup in Taggert's stride as they neared the bathroom. "After. We need to clean your wounds."

Raven swallowed hard and admitted the truth she wanted to hide from them. "I don't think I'll be conscious later."

Jackson's voice rose above the beat of water. "Dominic is handling Scotts."

No more stalling. She closed her eyes and took a deep breath...as much as her body allowed. "Lower me."

Jackson took control and spoke. "Your legs won't hold."

Something in his voice let her know that her back was worse than she'd imagined. It couldn't be a good sign that it had grown numb. "Cut my clothes off." The only sound in the room was their breathing and the shower as his claws make quick work of renting her clothes.

Although they tried to be gentle, blood had already sealed the material to her skin. "We're going to have to let the water soak the material. If we pull it off, the wounds will rip open."

Raven nodded, unable to speak above the knot in her throat. This would hurt like a son-of-a-bitch. She laid her forehead against Taggert's chest and braced herself. She would've protested Taggert's prolonged contact with her blood, but she feared the damage was already done to the both of them. He craved her touch a little too much; already saw her energy when she worked with her gift ever since that first unguarded touch at *Talons*. Even with her power burned away for the time being, the best thing for both of them would be to wash quickly.

The lukewarm spray hit Taggert's back, the water inching closer, sloshing over his shoulders as he tried to protect her. He turned slowly, the agony taking forever as it burrowed into each of her wounds. Fire erupted along her back, and the blessed numbness wore off.

Raven couldn't prevent the tears that fell and coated Taggert's shoulder. She gritted her teeth, refusing to bend, refusing to break and howl with the pain. By the time they turned the shower off, she was exhausted and barely clinging to consciousness.

Taggert lowered her legs slowly, each movement a new torture for her. Weaving on her feet, she felt Jackson cut away her pants. Both politely turned their heads when they tucked her into bed on her stomach. The cover rested low on her back, the last thing she felt was a brush of lips against her unmarred shoulder as she succumbed to darkness.

The sound of the shower turning off woke her a little bit later. Jackson rested awkwardly in the chair next to the bed, those whiskey eyes of his slitted, watching her as he pretended to sleep.

A shadow by the bathroom drew her gaze, and she nearly choked on her breath when Taggert strolled out with a towel so small it barely clung to his waist. She couldn't tear her gaze away, fearful that if she blinked, she'd miss seeing the towel slip.

His chest was lean and roped with muscles and so smooth she wanted to touch it to see if his skin was as hot as it looked. Though he didn't glance at her, she'd swear he knew she was watching. His movements slowed.

And he dropped his towel. Her eyes grew dry, and she blinked once. As he put on his clothes, he managed to turn so she saw every inch of him. Then she saw his back. Healed. Each scar, each mark, healed. The heat of a blush filled her cheeks, and she jerked her head away. And met Jackson's amused gaze. "Pack is very comfortable with each other and their own nakedness."

What an understatement. She distantly heard a drawer open, but refused to turn and be drawn in further. Jackson stood, his gaze locked on hers, and pulled his shirt over his head. The muscles of his body flexed and moved in such a sensual way, she could feel her body warm despite the throb of pain in her back.

She felt ambushed. She closed her eyes, released a shuttering breath and vowed not to open them again until she was alone.

"I'm going to take a shower. Watch over her."

The instant the door closed, Raven pushed herself up by her arms, dragging the blanket around to cover her nudity as she sat. "Help me dress." She couldn't do it on her own, and it galled her that she had to ask for help. It would be safer for everyone if she slept in the basement.

The bed dipped behind her as he got in beside her. She stiffened but didn't turn. When she tried to stand, she found the blankets trapped by his weight. Either she rose naked or she remained caught.

Trapped.

Tightness invaded her chest, her breathing grew ragged. She could almost feel the shackles click into place around her ankles and wrists. Dropping her arms, she let the blanket fall.

Raven straightened as much as she could, her pride wrapped around her as she shuffled to the dresser. The temperature in the room rose. She felt his eyes trace along her slim curves and tried her best to tell herself slow and steady and she'd be free.

Jeans were out of the question. She snagged a pair of shorts and slipped them over her feet. By the time she was done, sweat coated her body and rivulets of blood dripped down her back where her wounds had torn open.

The door to the bathroom opened again, the shower still running. "What are you doing?"

Raven didn't look at him, no need to when she could hear the lazy tone of his voice. Any movement would only aggravate the way the room was trying to twist itself about her. Her throat had gone dry.

With painful determination, she grabbed a shirt, pushed her arms through the sleeves, but couldn't force herself to lift it over her head. She needed another minute to guarantee she wouldn't pass out.

She sensed movement and, despite the pain, couldn't prevent herself from tensing. "Don't."

"Here."

Jackson held out one of his plain button-up shirts. When she glanced at his face, none of the humor or cruelty she expected to find was there. His face was respectfully averted from her body.

"The wounds would heal better if you left them open to air." Spoken from experience.

"They're already healing." The wounds itched as her body knitted itself together. Though the damage was extensive, she'd be healed by morning if she shut down. Instead, the slow healing racked her body with waves of pain she couldn't suppress. It left her vulnerable but conscious. No one could sneak up on her. "It would be safer if I slept alone."

By the time she managed to untangle herself from her shirt, she was panting. Admitting defeat, she allowed Jackson to slip the sleeves over her arms, wincing at the thought of leaving a trail of her blood on his clothes.

Not once did he touch her. Not once did he fumble or cause her pain. The ease with which he accomplished it, let her know this wasn't the first time he'd dressed a woman. She couldn't help wonder who she was, but ignored the bite of curiosity. And if she was honest, a little tug of jealousy came through.

Raven turned to the door and found it blocked by Taggert. "Move."

He shook his head, his gaze steady on hers. There was no way she could elude him. Without her usual control, any power she used could kill him. She couldn't take the risk.

"It's almost morning. Sleep. We'll stand guard. Our nearness should help accelerate the healing process." Jackson picked up a pair of pants from the floor and tugged them on. She quickly averted her gaze, but not before she saw all that God had given him. There was something about all the muscle, all that strength and knowing that every inch of him was there to protect and keep her safe.

They wanted her trust. Could she do it? Could she open herself up to them knowing that it would be more painful when they left her?

She looked at them, saw all the beauty and strength, saw the aching loneliness and the need to be needed.

They were worth the chance.

Allowing herself to be led back to bed, she gingerly settled herself on her side, closed her eyes, and coaxed the leftover energy snug around her body. A deep groan of pain escaped as her back muscles constricted, protesting the swiftness of the change. Power snapped along her skin, then sank deep, deeper, until her bones resonated with it.

Chapter Fourteen

AFTERNOON

*R*aven woke deliciously warm, the smell of sunshine and outdoors refreshing. Taking care to keep still, she cataloged her injuries. Her power level was dangerously low. The need for energy, like an addiction, twisted through her. Her body ached, but the open wounds on her back had closed, leaving deeply bruised tissue as a reminder of yesterday's events.

Her concentration broke when the bed beneath her swayed.

As in breathing.

Her eyes popped open to find herself face to face with Jackson. The beautiful whiskey brown color had bled completely from his eyes, leaving her with the brilliant yellow eyes of his beast. She didn't feel threatened, but she did sense its curiosity. Funny thing, she wasn't sure if that was much better.

"Ah, morning." She wiped her mouth with the back of her hand and wondered if she drooled on him when she used him for a pillow. How embarrassing. She must have rolled over to the closest source of heat and cuddled right up to him.

"They're healed." Taggert's words whispered against her skin. A cool hand trailed down her back. Nerves twitched. At some time during the night, her shirt had worked its way up. When she tried to ease away, she realized her legs were intertwined with Taggert's.

A rumbling growl, a vibration more than a sound, came from beneath her. Taggert didn't pull away, but he did stop moving. Raven slowly turned and found Taggert's gaze locked with Jackson's. The curious expression from Jackson was now replaced with a look of pure ownership. A hint of fang peaked from between his lips.

"Well, if you two are busy, maybe you'd both shove off and let me get out of bed." The heat that poured off them pooled in her until every joint ached. The urge to grab it and soak it all up trickled through her. Taking a deep breath for patience, she waited for Taggert to untangle his legs from hers. The instant she was free, she scooted down the bed. No way in hell she would try crawling over either of them. Not in their current mood.

What was she thinking? Not ever.

Just when she thought she was free, Jackson snagged her wrist and sat, pulling her up with him, dragging her along his body. A shiver raked her at the feel of him so close, pressed up against her so intimately.

"Don't." The really scary thought was that she wasn't sure if she was protesting or asking him not to stop.

"You're not leaving until I see your back."

In normal circumstances, she would challenge him for his audacity. But there was something in his eyes, something vulnerable. If she didn't allow this, he would tuck himself away and not open up to her again.

"Let go."

His grip tightened for a fraction, his eyes narrowed. His muscles bunched, preparing to wrestle with her to find out what he wanted to know.

She wasn't used to all this physical contact. The reactions flittering through her body confused her, and the urge to linger and brush against him and see if he tasted as yummy as he smelled grew. She wasn't sure she liked the change. She'd always been so focused on control; she never noticed how it felt to be so close to someone without having to worry about their safety first.

"Let me up. You can't see from this direction."

A startled squeak caught in her throat as she found herself pulled across his lap and draped over his legs. Cool air met her skin as he drew up the back of the shirt she wore.

"Hey, I said I'd show you." She tried to squirm around to glare at him, but stilled when she felt the hard press of his body's reaction against her. Whoa. Way too much information.

Her heart leapt in her throat as he ran his hand lightly across her back. His palm nearly covered her from side to side.

Pinned.

Goosebumps broke across her skin. A gurgle caught in the back of her throat.

She needed air.

In a space of seconds, she found herself crouched across the room with no idea how she got there, struggling to maintain her footing. Something surrounded her core where she kept her power. Something so bitterly cold, she lost her breath. The large beast blinked lazily, the creature so very different from her normal animals. It slowly twitched its large tail back and forth before curling it around herself again. When she'd let her guard down, the beast must have awakened.

"Raven?"

She didn't wait for a discussion. Dashing out of the room, Raven barreled down the hallway, her feet pounding on the hardwood. She grabbed the railing by the balcony on the way downstairs. The wood creaked ominously then broke under her grip.

Off balance, she tipped over the edge. Gravity took hold. A strangled scream gurgled in her throat as she caught the moldings. The railings plummeted below her. The loud smack made her jump. She glanced down to see jagged spikes of the wooden spindles pointed up as if waiting to impale her. Her grip slipped, and shards of pain erupted along her back, her muscles protesting the abuse as she dangled by one arm.

The power in her fluctuated wildly, dimmed, practically dissipating, leaving her power useless to help. She would've tapped into the house, but she couldn't risk accidentally ripping Rylan from his sleep. Vampires were vulnerable during daylight, their powers at their weakest. She refused to be responsible for putting him in danger. She witnessed too many vampires die when awakened from their slumber.

"Hold on." Taggert rounded the corner first, dressed only in pants.

She had to wonder why people always said hold on. Like anyone would let go on purpose. Sweat loosened her grip, and she worked to re-position her hold.

"You better hurry." The floorboards rumbled when Taggert and Jackson sprinted toward her.

Taggert reached her first and latched onto her wrists, drawing her upward. As she lifted her leg to boost herself up, Jackson reached out and grabbed her arm to help haul her back on solid ground. Jealousy winged through her at the ease in which they lifted her. They didn't even strain under her weight.

Her body brushed theirs when her feet finally touched the floor. Her knees trembled, and she took comfort from their touch and scent.

"What the hell were you thinking?" Jackson grabbed her jaw, angling her face up to his. Any gratitude melted away at his hard expression.

"You think I wanted to fall?" She jerked back from him, unnerved at the way the imprint of his touch lingered against her skin. The near miss must have scrambled her wits. To avoid his probing stare, she dropped her gaze and was confronted by the delicious gap in his pants where he'd zipped them but left them unbuttoned. The image shouldn't have been inviting, especially when he was angry, but somehow it didn't matter. A smattering of hair arrowed down his chest to disappear in his jeans, asking to be explored further.

Raven turned, cursing that her vaunted control had vanished. She was feeling more emotions. Desires. She couldn't allow that. The last time she tried to get close to someone, she'd nearly killed him. That day still haunted her, and Rylan had never forgiven her, forever maintaining his distance from her.

Her idea of taking a lover seemed foolish and further out of reach than ever. She'd been so desperate to find answers to her condition that she'd grabbed an impossible idea doomed to fail.

The sight of the railing drew her attention, and she tucked away her wayward emotions. She needed to focus on a mystery she could handle.

Smooth.

Her fists clenched as she peered over the edge. "The fall wouldn't have killed me, but a stake through a heart would've been another matter."

Fury tightened their bodies, their animals all but ready to pounce on anything that dared move. Though the death wouldn't have been permanent, it would've hurt like the dickens and put her out of commission for a while. Since she shut down to allow herself to heal, she hadn't monitored the house last night. Was this trap set by someone to stop her hunt? Or someone who wanted to hurt her specifically?

"London!" Uncaring if she woke the whole house, Raven bellowed his name again.

The man moved low to the ground in a blur of speed. When he detected no threat, he slowly approached the broken rail below, studied the ends. His brows drew together as he came to the same conclusion.

"The alarms were set. No one should've been able to enter without my knowledge." There was an apology in his voice and a boatload of anger. Those massive arms of his flexed as if holding back his animal counterpart. If he ever caught the person, she doubted anyone would find the remains. He was good at that type of thing, and she didn't ask questions. Better not to know.

Jackson ran a hand over the end of the railing, testing the smooth cut, his mouth tightening into a frown. Taggert's hand tangled in the back of her shirt, and a slight shudder passed through him. Without looking back, she reached for his hand and gave it a squeeze.

"Why don't you both go and change." It wasn't a suggestion. She needed to talk to London about security.

Taggert left, reluctance showing in the way he lingered. Jackson didn't twitch from his spot. "We didn't do it. Don't let your fear put distance between us. We're here to keep you safe. Taggert won't return to the auction. If you throw him out, you'll be signing his death sentence."

There was no plea in his voice. He wouldn't beg, but the tension in his frame told her enough. He was afraid she would send them packing.

"Was there anyone else determined to claim Taggert?" It seemed unlikely since Taggert had remained unclaimed for nearly five years.

"No." Jackson turned and walked back to her room at a slow and steady pace.

The stiff set to his shoulders, the clenched fists said he was lying. Or at least he wasn't telling her the whole truth. "Come to the study when you're done."

Another look at the railing below made her swallow, then she pushed it away and spoke to London, her determination hardening. "Gather everyone for a meeting. Study. Five minutes. And get that railing fixed."

"I'll review the exterior tapes." London jerked his head absently in what she thought must've been agreement and disappeared into the security lair. There was no incrimination in his voice about the lack of internal cameras. She hadn't refused his advice, but told him flat out that the first power surge, the electronics would be shot. He'd accepted the inevitable and did what he could, mumbling something about a security nightmare.

Raven hesitated at the top of the stairs, staring down the dark corridor leading to the safe room she'd constructed for Rylan. She placed one foot on the stairs and hurried to the study before she did something stupid like go to Rylan and question him about last night and the secrets he was keeping from her. Could her proximity be making their bond stronger?

She pushed open the door, her gaze automatically flashing toward the chaise.

Empty.

Durant and Cassie were gone.

A little of the tension left her shoulders. A short reprieve. It wouldn't be long before Durant came knocking. He'd changed his mind too fast for him not to want something.

She slipped into the chair behind her desk and picked up the phone. Three messages from Scotts about the case, telling her to call him as soon as she got them, each more urgent than the last. And one awkward message from Durant, thanking her for her assistance and to make sure that she'd returned home safe.

The time of the call had the hair on her arms standing on end. Five minutes after the lightning strike. Could their new bond have a bigger aftereffect than anyone expected? The thought left a chill in her heart that burned down to her soul. Taggert was already changing by just being near her, and she hadn't even claimed him fully. What would he become if he remained in her care?

Not surprising, Taggert and Jackson were the first to arrive. Taggert handed her a pair of pants, and she took them gratefully. She was tucking in the shirt when Dominic entered. She avoided his eyes and the assessing look he gave her.

"What did you tell Scotts?" She tapped her pen against the desk in annoyance. "He seems awfully anxious to talk to me this morning."

"The truth. That you followed a lead on one of your cases and you ran into his killer." Dominic didn't look away as he continued. "I sent him the approximate location Rylan gave me."

Anger narrowed her eyes. "You purposely sent them into danger."

He stalked forward and planted his hands on her desk. "It's their job."

"And it's my case. You had no right to interfere."

"I have every right to protect you."

Raven pushed back her chair and matched his pose. "So what? Better them than me?"

"Yes."

The muscles in her jaw ached as she gritted her teeth, trying to stem the flow of words. "I can take care of myself."

"It was your body they carried in the house last night. Your back was shredded to ribbons. Chunks of your flesh were missing." Dark eyes met hers, and she knew he blamed himself for not being there.

"And I'm fine." She reached out to touch him, needing to ease that flinty look he hid behind.

He jerked away, his animal giving him the ability to be there one minute and across the room in the next without appearing to have rushed.

"All better." His voice was flat. He didn't believe her.

"Dominic, this is what I do."

"You take suicidal missions and too many chances. You have others relying on you now. What happens to them if you die?"

Something behind his words disturbed her, some hidden emotion she didn't know how to name. There was nothing she could do to make him trust her. He was close to twice her age, still in the prime of his life, and he treated her like a young cub.

Heart aching, she hardened her spirit and accepted it would always be so. "I'm good at what I do. I'm one of the best in this area, and that includes you and yours. Don't try to shut me out of this investigation. You won't win."

God, she couldn't stand to do nothing. She'd go insane. She desperately wanted to be like everyone else and walk the street without fear, without searching for danger. To dare touch someone without having them look at her with terror. That would never happen for her, but she could make sure others were safe by doing her job.

Dominic's stance softened. "Raven—"

"What did I miss?" Trish sauntered in the room, dressed in clothes that had to cost a fortune, and doused in her normal bottle of perfume. Her gaze landed on Taggert, and her expression softened as she seated herself next to him with barely an inch separating them. "Thanks for saving me a seat."

Taggert's breath hitched. Every muscle in his body tightened, but he didn't move.

A hint of woods came to her, and Raven smelled his distress. Brow furrowed, she watched his agitation mount when Trisha smiled his way.

Raven didn't understand it. Trisha wasn't being malicious, but the attention froze Taggert to his seat. "Taggert, could you please go to the kitchen and tell Dina we're waiting for her? She can finish breakfast after."

His movements were slow, measured, but she could tell it was an act to prevent himself from bolting.

Trish sighed when he stood to leave, her eyes glued to his backside. Once he disappeared from the door, she turned and gave Raven a dirty look.

"While we wait, why don't you tell me what you found out about the group." Raven resumed her seat and aimed her attention on Dominic to get her mind off Taggert.

"Like you care. You're too wrapped up in your little life to give a damn about anyone else."

"Trish." Dominic's sharp rebuke shut her up but didn't take away the hatred burning in her eyes.

Raven's chest stalled at being forced into a corner. It was time to stop hiding. She could do what he asked, help them search for the lab he believed was in the area, and finally prove she was capable once and for all.

"You say the word, Dominic, and I'll be there." She didn't see the flash of triumph from him she'd expected. Cold fear twisted through her at the thought of going back into the system and being at the mercy of those sick bastards. Some humans thought they were animals without a soul, thinking there was nothing wrong with torturing and killing others who were different.

There was a long pause when he finally answered. "No, we can use you better later when the lab is found. We'll need your contacts then. You'll be too visible in the field. If even one person recognizes you, your safety will be compromised."

Relief trickled through her, and she slowly sucked in a breath of much needed air. She was the one who'd destroyed the last lab, the one who'd broken everyone out. The scientists had created her and would do anything to get their hands on her again in order to study and dissect her. They would create killing machines modeled after her, but ones that would obey.

"Did the virus work?"

A small smile tipped his lips. "We slipped your computer program into their system, piggybacking it through the security feed. Within minutes, it allowed us access into the building."

Relief edged through her, easing some of her tension. "When do you go?"

Dominic grunted. "London convinced me that he and Trisha should go in alone. Dina, Jenkins and I will go as backup and wait."

"Jenkins? Are you sure?" A chameleon could come in handy. He'd been near death when removed from the facility. It was a miracle he survived all the damage they'd done, extracting his bone marrow in hope of transferring his ability to others. The man desperately wanted to join the operations. Even though she knew it was best to stay away from anything to do with labs, she couldn't ignored the twinge at being excluded, easily understanding Jenkins' need to be a part of something.

Color bleached from Dominic's lips, no doubt gritting his teeth as he waited for her to protest. She didn't. "When do you leave?"

She needed to question a few vampires. Without him, she'd be able to focus more on finding answers and not on protecting his back. Shifter blood, especially purebloods, gave vampires a high when consumed directly from the source. The last time they went into a vampire setting, Dominic had been propositioned three times in as many minutes.

His green eyes narrowed dangerously at her easy capitulation. Raven stood her ground, keeping her face impassive. He had his job, and she had hers.

"Sorry I'm late." Dina bounced into the room, and the standoff broke.

Dominic relaxed, and the muscles of her shoulders eased a fraction. Dina took a seat next to Trish, completely missing the panther's scowl.

Taggert's gaze immediately locked with Raven's when he entered the room, like no one else existed. He sauntered to her side, trying to appear inconspicuous and failing. He leaned against the bookshelves behind her, and it took everything she could do not to twitch. She hated not being able to see everyone in the room.

When she opened her mouth to tell him, his desperate need to remain at her side swamped her. That shut her up. She promised herself to talk to him later and find out what the hell was going on with him and the cat.

"We'll start without London." Raven leaned back in her seat and studied each person in the room, feeling silly dressed in Jackson's oversized shirt. "You're here until the end of the week. I propose we cut it short."

Dominic slowly shook his head once. "No."

She only spared him a glance. "Someone broke into the house last night. If my guess is correct, London will find nothing. I can't guarantee you'll be safe."

Dina snorted. "We're not safe wherever we go."

"We're staying." London lumbered into the room with those words and shook his head at her unanswered question. "Nothing on the tapes."

"We'll do rotations at night, two person details, one inside, one out." Dominic's order drifted through the room. "I'll bring Jenkins back with us tonight to even up the numbers."

"There's no need. You'll be gone by the weekend anyway." The room fell silent at Raven's announcement.

"Not until the killer's caught."

Raven hadn't expected that, though she should've guessed. "This is a police matter—"

"That's somehow caught up in one if not both of your cases." Dominic crossed his arms, doing a pretty fair job of intimidation.

Though he might be alpha, she didn't care, and opened her mouth to tell him so when he beat her to the crux of the problem.

"You might be able to take care of yourself, but you now have others to watch over as well."

Raven winced at the way Jackson scowled at Dominic's words.

"We take care of our own."

Dominic slowly turned, his autumn scent wrapping a wall of protection around her. "Until she makes her choice, she's not yours."

A backlash of tension flooded the room as both of their animals flared at the challenge. Energy swirled around her body and every second that passed stole her breath. No one so much as twitched at the palpable threat.

"And until she either makes a choice to cement the pack or cut you lose, I don't go anywhere." Jackson's resolve was unbending.

This was getting out of hand. She refused to be a bone between the two men. Without saying a word, Raven rose and walked toward the door. Taggert followed her, but everyone else remained seated. "Let me know when you're done with your pissing match, and we'll talk business."

Raven silently closed the door after them and hurried up the stairs. Maybe if she was quick, she could escape before the others realized they'd been duped.

Conscious of Taggert's gaze on her, she quickly grabbed the first things in her closet and disappeared into the bathroom. In less than five minutes, she was ready to go. Instead of heading back downstairs, she opened the balcony window and greedily inhaled the fresh air. She swung her legs over the railing and jumped over the edge.

The impact jarred her bruised back. By the time she straightened, Taggert had landed silently next to her on the spongy lawn in a graceful way she envied. "I don't suppose I could talk you into staying?"

Those dark eyes met hers. "Where're we going?"

"To help the police find a killer."

Chapter Fifteen

"Where the hell have you been? I've left messages all morning." Scotts held up the yellow police tape for her to duck under. He appeared haggard, deep grooves of stress cutting lines in his face. His shoes and pants were splattered with mud. "Not you." He dropped the tapeline in front of Taggert, moving his bulk to block him from crossing. "You stay here."

Raven nodded, and Taggert dipped his head ever so slightly.

She scanned the tree line as he headed toward the scene, hardly recognizing the area of attack in daylight. "I got here as quick as I could. What'd you find?"

"Another body."

She missed a step, then increased her pace to catch up. She'd been afraid of that. She wondered if it would be Cassie's friend or the mysterious woman she'd encountered last night. She didn't doubt that she could kill, but Raven didn't think her hit had been strong enough to take down whatever or whoever she'd seen. The shadowy figure had been too fast, too strong. "Where?"

"The stream. We couldn't wait for you any longer and pulled him from the water." Scotts led the way past the other officers, and they stepped back, giving her a wide berth. Scotts, Ross and those who didn't know better, treated her with respect. The others waited for her to fail, hating that an outsider had to be brought in on their case. She couldn't blame them. She'd feel the same in their place.

Ross straightened when she drew near. "Here." He held out a pair of gloves. She snapped them on and coughed at the plume of powder that gusted back in her face. The burn of chemicals filled her nose, and she resisted the urge to sneeze. She recognized Ross's special blend of chemicals to stop the decomp smell and blanched. Nausea dropped her gut to between her ankles.

She gave a stilted nod, and he lifted the plastic sheet. The corpse was relatively whole. Relative being the choice word. Gnaw marks dotted his body, while sections of the legs had chunks of flesh ripped from them.

One fact riveted her.

The cadaver was pinkish.

Still fresh. They'd killed him about the same time that she was running around in the forest.

She swallowed hard at the black, gaping hole in his torso. They'd gutted him. The line on the stomach was clean. Her brows furrowed. Too precise. No animal, either shifter or wild, could have done that with claws. "Knife?"

Ross nodded. "One clean slice. No hesitation marks."

Raven paused, but she needed to know. "Dead or alive?"

"He was sliced open while alive."

Scotts crouched at her side. "I recognize that expression on your face. What?"

Raven looked to the stream, then back at Scotts. "All the bodies we found were in fresh water at least four feet from the surface."

"Yes."

"Someone killed them, but the bodies were left in the water on purpose." She turned away from his baffled gaze, knelt by the stream and trailed her hand across the surface of the shockingly cold water. "What do you notice about this water?"

"It's ass cold from the mountains."

"Right."

Things clicked, and Scotts swore. "They're keeping the bodies refrigerated, storing them. What the hell can do this, Raven?"

She bit her lip, debating the wisdom of sharing her knowledge. This case was entwined with hers. The last thing she wanted was him involved.

"Scotts—"

"Don't give me this paranormal bullshit. Tell me what you know."

She hesitated, but had no choice to put her client's confidentiality first. "I'll share what I can, but I suspect this is part of a case I've been hired to solve."

Scotts drew himself to his full height, his shoulders straining his cheap suit. "Murder trumps PI business."

A wiry smile crossed her lips. "I'll share, but I can't divulge my client or pertinent information."

"I could have you arrested for obstruction." The words weren't heated. They both knew he could, and they both knew he wouldn't. They needed her on this case.

"Tell me."

In the space of a breath, her knees weakened and all the strength poured out of her. The next instant, she landed on her hands and knees, unsure who cut the strings holding her upright. Every bit of current she carried vanished. The hollowness left behind felt like part of her had been amputated. She heard shouting but didn't look, having a hard enough time keeping her head from slamming face first into the slimy mud.

"Don't." She flinched when Scotts reached to help her stand. Her arms quivered under the strain of her weight. Mud squished between her fingers when she tried to force them to work.

Taggert appeared out of nowhere, knocking Scotts to the ground. The sound of guns leaving holsters rent the air.

"Taggert!" In an instant, he was at her side. When he reached for her arm, she pulled back. The lack of support tilted her balance, and she twisted to land on her ass.

"Raven?"

"That's it." Scotts hauled Taggert to his feet and shoved him away. "I should arrest you for assault. If you ever do anything like that again, I will."

The people around them tittered nervously, holstering their weapons and turning away. She could hear them snicker, believing she finally broke at the sight of a dead body. Not likely, but she'd accept the excuse if it kept them from asking questions.

It wasn't like she could explain that she was recovering from an attack when her wounds had miraculously healed. Like a flame, her gift flickered on and off. The electrical storm must have messed with her power more than she expected, taking her system longer to get back online.

"You okay?"

Scotts' soft question reverberated in her head, and she gave him a tight smile as she fought not to suck in all the energy around her. "Peachy."

"Liar."

"Empty stomach."

Doubt lingered for a moment on his face, then his eyes narrowed. "In return for not pressing assault charges, you'll share all your information on the case with me."

His smugness itched her the wrong way. "Blackmail, Scotts? I thought you were above that."

A tight smile tipped his lips. "I want answers."

Chapter Sixteen

SUNSET

*T*aggert's gaze bore into Raven as she slowly rose to her feet, his broad shoulders giving her some privacy. She used the tree for a prop, the bark gouging into her spine. She couldn't get over the feeling he was humoring her. One wrong move and Taggert would scoop her up and rescue her. Even if her touch killed him.

She gingerly shuffled to the car. Taggert opened the door, and she all but collapsed onto the seat. Snapping off both layers of gloves, she propped her elbows on her thighs and dropped her head between her knees, waiting for the world to stop tilting. Blood rushed to her temples. Everything around her dimmed until she feared she might pass out.

"Raven?"

She swallowed twice before she had enough spit to speak. "Give me a second. Watch the area. Make sure no one touches me."

"Were you attacked?" The vengeance in his voice was unmistakable, but she didn't raise her head. The last thing she needed right now was an overprotective shifter.

She ignored his question. Keeping her eyes closed, she allowed the world to drop away. When only her mind and the chaos within surrounded her, she reached out for the current that always swarmed through her. She'd thought she'd wanted to be normal. Now, without the current, she felt vulnerable and exposed, and only half a person.

The same ball of energy rested at her core, but wrapped around it was a dark shadow that blocked anything from escaping. When she probed the foggy layer, a deep cold slithered through her, stealing an inch of her heat at a time.

The shape moved, and Raven sensed she was under observation. The creature felt alien and wrong. She froze, unwilling to draw more attention to herself. The thing evidently found her lacking and curled up on itself, going back to its slumber.

Heart pounding in her ears, she scrambled for answers.

It was trying to stay warm.

She didn't know where the idea came from, but once formed, she knew it was true. When she would've backed out, she saw another shape in the shadows. Then another.

Something warm and furry brushed against her mind. Her chest hurt at the contact. Understanding slammed into her and a rush of air escaped her lungs. Something was making her various animals manifest themselves.

Her eyes snapped open, and she gasped to see Taggert crouched inches from her face. The concern and pure fear she saw didn't reassure her.

"We need to get you home."

The tremble in his usually placid voice raised her hackles. "What did you see?"

Taggert stood, turned away, and shook his head. "We need to go."

Before she could demand more information, he walked back toward the crime scene. She saw him talk to Scotts, purposely keeping his back to her so she couldn't read his lips. The way Scotts spun to watch her turned her displeasure to anger.

She picked up her gloves and pushed to her feet. She staggered, then gained her footing and thought better of stalking over there. Instead, she slammed the door. It felt good, but it didn't ease her anger. It curled around her, demanding retaliation. Each minute that passed, her rage grew.

She embraced the change. Anything was better than feeling weak. She couldn't allow herself to be helpless. Business was scheduled for tonight. A tour of Bloodhouses, local clubs marked by red doors that catered to vampire clientele and their blood donors. She clenched her hands into fists, relishing the prospect of a fight.

Though some clubs followed the rave circuit to avoid being targeted by vigilantes, the Bloodhouses were created with the safety of both parties in mind. Everyone walking in with a tag was free game for the vampires and couldn't cry foul.

She gazed at Taggert and Scotts. They must have recognized something in her look for they both took off running toward her. She snagged the door handle. The temptation to leave wrapped around her, but some part of her mind recognized that her actions weren't rational.

The need to hunt swelled. She opened the door and slipped behind the wheel, tossing her gloves in the passenger seat. Scotts waved, yelling something, but it was the determination on Taggert's face that made a thrill go through her. The engine turned over, and she slipped the car in gear, eager for the chase. Excitement had a mischievous smile tilting her lips.

Jackson would understand. She wished he was here.

Warmth brushed against her mind, and a sliver of reason battled against the urge to slam on the gas. She peeled her fingers off the wheel, and curled them into fists, relishing the pain as her short nails dug into her palm and drew blood.

The door ripped open. It was too late to change her mind now. An angry howl ripped through her mind. She leaned back against the seat, her whole body shaking. She shoved the car in park and turned off the engine. "We should go home."

They ended up in Scotts' car. It shouldn't have surprised her, but Taggert didn't have a valid license. Apparently very few slaves were granted the privilege. And the darn fool, Scotts, refused to let her drive. Courtesy of a rookie, her own vehicle would arrive later.

Once they pulled up to the house, she knew she wouldn't be able to leave again if the others found out what had happened. She couldn't allow that. "How old was the last victim?"

"Male, age eighteen to twenty-five." Scotts didn't take his eyes off the road. "What did you see?"

"This one was different." This victim was healthy. Possibly the informant who had called Cassie. But she couldn't say more for fear the police would demand to question Cassie. Turning a human into a vampire wasn't exactly against the law, not yet anyway, but Cassie was in no condition to answer questions, her moods too volatile to handle any additional stress. "That was a fresh kill. Did Ross give you a timeline?"

Silence crowded the car, and she looked away from the passing scenery to meet Scotts' gaze in the rear view mirror.

"You were hired to help the police. So why does it seem you get all your questions answered and mine get ignored?" He slowed to take a curve, dodging traffic in a way that would make a New York taxi driver proud. "Remember our deal."

Raven grunted. He was right. He deserved better. "I've been hired to find a missing person, but the further I dig, the more people I find have disappeared."

"Nothing out of the ordinary has hit the board." If it wasn't on the board, the police didn't know about it.

The slight distrust in his voice warned her that she walked a fine line. He needed more. "You wouldn't. Shifters and vampires are the targets."

Scotts scratched the stubble of his chin with his thumb. "I can ask around."

Raven waved him away. "You won't find anything. Nothing has been reported. They're targeting loners."

He took another turn that slid her across the seat, and she braced herself. A few more minutes, and she'd be home. She needed to talk fast. "I'm not sure your case and my missing persons are connected."

"But you think they are." It wasn't a question.

"Members of my team are checking other avenues."

"While you go it alone." Scotts shook his head. "I don't like it. You take too many chances. You need backup."

"I can't take you. You're too..."

"Human." Taggert finished and turned toward her. "But I'm not."

"I was going to say too much of a cop. And no, out of the question. Neither of you are going." The men shared a silent look of understanding that drove her crazy. She stared down at the kid, hoping to intimidate him. She contemplated shocking him into reason, but didn't think it'd change his stubborn hide. "I need to visit a Bloodhouse for answers." When he only blinked, unconcerned, she sighed. "You'd be a liability. I'd be spending so much time protecting you that I won't get any answers."

"I've been there before. I'll be fine."

The way Taggert's eyes darkened with memories sent a shiver through her. The wood scent around him sharpened and soured. Something horrible had happened to him, yet he was determined to go anyway.

"Why the hell would any shifter go there willingly?" The question escaped before she could think better of it.

"A test. You pass the test, you live."

A part of her heart thumped painfully. "Please tell me you didn't go alone."

"I passed." Horror sickened her at his carefully bland voice. How could they treat one another like that? Less than even an animal? Even Scotts looked enraged.

Wrath funneled into protectiveness. "I won't put you in danger." She couldn't.

"I'll just follow you. With the collar, they'll view me as prey." He hesitated.

"Or?" She didn't think she wanted to know.

"Or you can mate me. Show ownership. They won't pick on a shifter who's been mated for fear of retaliation from the pack."

She wanted to save his life, not condemn it. If she took his blood, there would be no going back. He'd be bound to her in a life she had little control over, and if her unruly powers continued to grow, she didn't want to take him down with her. The noose tightened around her neck and all the time she thought she had to find an alternate solution besides claiming him evaporated.

As if he sensed her resistance, Taggert spoke with a ruthlessness that surprised her. "I go, or I tell the others what happened today and your plans for tonight."

Chapter Seventeen

As soon as they returned, Raven pleaded exhaustion and took refuge in her room. Taggert's sharp look crawled under her skin long after she'd disappeared, and any secret hope of escaping the house without notice vanished. He'd found the spine he'd been missing when she needed it the least. Damn it.

As the dancing rays of the sun disappeared over the horizon, she couldn't believe that in the last five days, her whole life had changed.

Though the room was large, her restlessness made it feel cramped. She wanted the wide-open spaces of outside, but knew there would be no running from her problems. They'd just follow her and multiply when she wasn't looking. To shake away the nerves threatening to cripple her, she focused on what she could do well. Her job.

Stripping her clothes, she glanced at her closet, then quickly pulled out her outfit for tonight. Hoping for a little anonymity, she chose black clothes and boots. She scraped her hair back, securing it in a twist to hide the distinct silver swatch.

A knock like a gunshot filled the room. She jumped and the last pin she shoved home dug into her skull. Jitters ate away her calm. She'd been avoiding the subject, but there was no way around her half-unspoken promise to claim Taggert without her case falling apart and more people dying.

How could she have promised something so stupid? There had to be a way around it, but she couldn't think of anything. That it would ultimately save his life helped, but not a lot.

The gulp of air she took lodged in her throat as she shuffled toward the door. She'd expected Taggert and couldn't have been more astonished to find Jackson.

He shifted uncomfortably, and she instantly went on guard. "What's wrong?" God, please don't let there be another emergency. She didn't have enough time to figure out her problems, let alone others.

"May I come in?"

Dread filled her at the polite request. That couldn't be good. She opened the door wider and stepped away so his body wouldn't brush hers.

The expression on his face let her know he recognized her reaction, but surprisingly, he took pity on her and didn't goad her as she expected.

"You're going out tonight." He walked to the balcony glass doors, his back toward hers.

"Yes."

He turned slightly, giving her a side view of his face. "With Taggert." The curt response shouldn't have surprised her, but he always caught her off guard.

The attitude pissed her off, and she answered instead of evading. "Yes."

"When do we leave?"

Raven hesitated at the carefully controlled voice. Something was wrong.

She stepped closer, opened her senses and blew out a relieved breath to have them respond so readily. Then she saw his eyes, alive with such restless need, that her breath lodged in her throat. "*Taggert* and *I* won't be leaving for a while." She maintained her distance from the maelstrom of confusion swirling around him, tried to use the space to pinpoint her unease. "If you want to take a run, I promise we won't leave until you return."

Jackson opened the French doors and stepped onto the balcony. Energy swamped him, but underneath seethed a layer of rage that threatened to consume her. She didn't understand. The curtains rippled in the breeze. She debated the wisdom of following him, noted the stiff set of his shoulders, the tension ready to explode, the potential of being caught up in another crisis, and decided it was a bad move.

Then stepped out after him anyway.

"Want to talk about it?" He must miss his pack. Maybe he even had a girlfriend, and she was keeping him from her. A bitter taste soured her mouth.

"No." The gruff tone was devoid of its usual anger.

It sounded like pain.

She risked another step closer, reached out for him, but quickly dropped her hand. No contact. No matter how many times she told herself she could never touch others without hurting them, she could never pound home the fact. "You haven't contacted anyone since you arrived. I haven't seen you take advantage of the country space to run." Something didn't feel right, hovering ever so temptingly out of reach.

His wolf fluctuated wildly, nipping against her shields, but she sensed he didn't do it on purpose.

"My job is to monitor the situation and watch out for Taggert."

"I won't tell if you won't." She gave him a small smile, not expecting him to curse and whirl toward her.

Anger devastated his face. Her breathing hiccupped in her chest as the primitive look sent her knees quivering. She tensed to retreat, then carefully planted her foot in the same place. She knew not to run. Running would make her prey and give the beast more control. But the knowledge didn't lessen the urge to do just that.

"Jackson?"

He halted inches from her. His power didn't. It drowned her, pressed on her lungs. When he stooped over her, she flinched but stood her ground. Then he inhaled slowly.

"You smell like Taggert." Jackson didn't retreat, just turned his head to meet her gaze with those yellow eyes. Displeasure twisted his lips, his words pulled from deep within. The slow rumble trickling from his chest raised the hairs on her neck. The kind that either froze one in their tracks or made them run in the opposite direction.

The low tone only increased her awareness of him. "He was helping me." She bit back the rest of her words, afraid to say more lest he guess how his nearness scrambled her thoughts.

He inhaled deeply. "Truth."

Raven blinked, his shocking revelation eased the awkward tension that hovered between violence and the urge to touch him. "You can scent the truth?"

A devilish smile tipped his mouth, twisting that tension firmly on the pleasure side once more. "My gift as an enforcer." He straightened so swiftly she stifled her gasp. "Touch me."

"Huh?" Raven slowly shook her head. She couldn't. Not when there was a chance her gift could touch him as well. No matter how tempted. A whisper at the back of her mind begged her to take the jump. Not only would he guarantee her untold pleasure, she could finally learn about shifters phenomenal control up close and personal.

As long as she didn't kill both of them in the process.

"You touched him." The words growled from his throat, a tone he seemed to use strictly for her alone, and he crowded closer. "You allowed him to touch you." It was an accusation.

What the hell? This was not the Jackson she'd come to know. Raven searched for the ball of power and realized it had grown in order to compensate for the shadow.

Grew so much that she was leaking everywhere, threatening to swallow everything whole.

Oh, crap.

She slowly pulled the power to her core. Her heartbeat raced, sweat beaded her hairline as the energy fought to stay free. The power called his wolf, drew him to the surface, making Jackson more aggressive as the beast slipped its human's hold. No wonder he was playing with her.

Her skin prickled. Heaviness grew in the air. Her hair moved and crackled with energy as she methodically locked all the power down tight. She hadn't realized she closed her eyes until she opened them to find Jackson exactly where she left him. Only human this time, staring at her with suspicion and more than a bit of curiosity.

Her life could do without his curiosity.

"What did you do?" All his vaunted control was back.

Time for retreat. "I should get ready." She whirled and entered the bathroom. She shored up her core, but that didn't fix the problem. She couldn't let it spill over again, especially not tonight in front of a room full of vampires. She would not become a snack.

"I can't shift." His words halted her on the threshold.

Then the full implication of his words struck her.

Their attraction.

That meant she actually wanted him for the ass that he was and not the stupid idea she'd concocted to use a shifter to find control over her growing power.

She whirled to face him, so shocked that she blurted the first thing that came to her mind. "But your wolf almost broke free from your control. I saw your fangs and claws."

Jackson shook his head once, his eyes never leaving hers. "Only when I'm near you and never a full shift. My alpha sent me to the club, gave me official leave from the pack to avoid being challenged. I'm an enforcer. I can't enforce without being able to go wolf."

"So Taggert—"

"Babysitting." A derisive curl twisted his lips. "Shuffled away like an old wolf with no teeth."

"But you'll die if challenged." Her heartbeat stuttered at the thought.

He gave her a steady look and shrugged. "Can't shift, can't be an enforcer. You need to be strong enough to protect the pack."

The matter of fact way he said it gutted her. "Your wolf can heal—"

"There's nothing wrong with my wolf. He healed the spinal injury that laid me up, but we haven't been able to change since. The strain to allow me to walk drained us too much."

The thought of him injured so badly sent her head spinning. "But, eventually, you'll be able to go wolf." The tightness in her chest eased. She couldn't imagine a world without him in it, bossing around some poor, unsuspecting girl. She gazed over the expanse of lawn, trying to bury the quick spurt of jealousy that stabbed at her at the thought.

"I'll never live that long," he said it firmly, without pity.

Her head snapped up at his reply, the tone of his voice. Her eyes narrowed, and her anger built like a wave. The sneaky bastard was up to something. "Why tell me now?"

A smug smile curled his lips. "Your choice is to either mate me or release me back to my pack." He edged closer but didn't touch her.

Her lips tightened. "And your death."

He shrugged, watching her closely. "Eventually. My alpha can only protect me so long. I'm an enforcer. If I'm challenged for position, I will lose."

"Why tell me? Shouldn't you be too proud to ask for help?" Spite made her ask. Instead of insulted, his smile hardened.

"You're not going anywhere without me tonight. If you bite him, you bite me." Without another word, he left the room.

Raven slumped, her ass landing on the bed. Great, just what she needed, another complication. They were playing her, each of them. And they did it so well she couldn't see a way out of it that didn't lead to their death. Unless...

Raven shot to her feet and scrambled for the door. "Dominic!"

She halted on the landing and waited. Then she saw his head pop out of the study, his wavy hair standing on end from running his hands through it.

"You bellowed?"

A blush filled her face. She ignored the others as they came at the commotion and hurried down the stairs. "I need to speak with you."

The skin of his face tightened, and he gave a nod, stepping back into the room to let her enter. "After you."

Raven paced, watching him calmly take a seat. She noticed the brittle set to his shoulders. Some of the chaos in her mind quieted, and she stilled to stare at him. "What's wrong?"

Dominic raised a brow. "I thought you wanted to talk."

She waved a hand, trying to pin-point her unease. "You first."

"Just working through the plans for tonight."

He sounded sincere, but his eyes tightened at the corners. Yes, he was worried about the upcoming mission, but that wasn't what was bothering him. She knew better than to try to force the issue. He'd only shut her out. "I'm there if you need me."

He gave her a steady look then shook his head after a lengthy pause. "No, it's best you remain behind."

Wrapped up like a china doll. She shoved off her disgruntled thoughts. Contrary to her earlier protests, she'd do what needed to be done if they found an operational lab.

"Why don't you tell me what has you all fired up."

"I want you to claim the boys."

"No." He leaned back in his chair, his posture anything but casual.

The air in her lungs left in a rush. "But you didn't even think about it."

"Jackson is already part of a pack. The only way another can claim him is if his current alpha released him or a female sought approval and mated him," Dominic said, giving her a cryptic look from those green eyes that she couldn't decipher. "As for Taggert, only a woman or an established alpha male can claim a slave."

She ignored Jackson's situation for now. "But you're an alpha."

He snorted. "Not by half. I'm not established. I have no territory. I have no mate, and I haven't proven myself. If I did this, I'd have so many challengers, I would be fighting for the rest of my very short life." He gave her a smile to soften the blow. "I'd try if I thought it would help."

"No." She cleared her throat, uncomfortable with the understanding in his eyes. "I don't want to put you in that position."

Son of a bitch. She didn't like being cornered.

"You could give them back."

Raven shook her head, her gut clenching at the suggestion, the visceral response surprising even her. "I'd be signing their death warrant."

"Not your problem."

She stared at him, taken aback by his brusque statement. "The whole problem started because of me."

"Not true. Taggert knew he was facing a death sentence. You're just the Hail Mary pass. Jackson will go back to his pack. Neither will fault you for denying them."

They might not, but she would fault herself. She couldn't do it. Dominic leaned over the desk. Something in his demeanor riveted her.

"Be careful. Weres are tricky. Don't let them guilt you into something you don't want. Once you take this step, it's irrevocable."

The hard bite to his words made her question her decision, doubt the fragile trust growing between her and the men under her care. "You think it's a mistake."

"I think you need to worry about yourself first. But it's ultimately your decision."

The guarded answer gave her nothing, yet said everything.

She nodded. "Stay safe. I'll wait up."

Dominic straightened, rubbed his jaw, and gave a tired smile. "Go to sleep. We'll call you if you're needed. We'll meet in the morning to discuss."

Raven watched the team leave, not feeling an ounce of guilt for her slight subterfuge. They had their mission, she had hers. When she entered the kitchen, she met Taggert's chocolate brown eyes and jerked to a halt, afraid to enter the room, wishing she could turn around and pretend nothing had happened.

Until she saw the emotions he tried so hard to bury.

The hope within the depths of his eyes reminded her of what it felt like to be in the labs, looking for any scrap of kindness, but knowing better to expect any.

How could she do any less? Panic wedged in her chest, and she swallowed it down. Her fear wasn't worth his death. If anything happened to her, at least he'd be safe. Clenching her fists behind her back, she cleared her throat, wincing at the painful tightness. She croaked out the words that would seal their fate and tie them together for the rest of their lives.

"How do you want to do this?"

Chapter Eighteen

Sweat dampened Raven's hairline. This was really going to happen. As Taggert's smile blossomed to a full out grin, energy snaked along her nerves, rising as the control over her emotions weakened. "Before we go any further, explain each step of the process and what I can expect."

She wasn't stalling. She was being analytical. Cautious.

And maybe stalling just a little.

The door slammed against the wall. Startled out of her own worry, the spark building under her skin dissipated, burning as it reabsorbed back into her body. Jackson loomed in the opening, chest heaving and ready for battle. Something about his stiff posture and tight expression relaxed the brutal grip on her throat.

A deep rumble rolled up from Jackson's gut as he faced Taggert across the room. "Back off."

Raven winced. Though things would be so much harder with him there to watch, part of her was relieved to have someone present in case things went wrong.

He was dependable.

Reliable.

He would give his life to save Taggert. Even from her. "Taggert, go upstairs and get ready for tonight."

Taggert practically bounded out of his chair, muscles flexing in a beautiful grace that drew the eyes. Silence lengthened after he left, and Raven finally turned to face the glowering Jackson.

"You agreed to do it, didn't you?" The accusation lashed through her.

Frustration boiled over, and she snapped back. "Isn't that what you wanted?"

"Yes." He spit out the one word between clenched teeth.

A deep sigh for patience escaped her at his contrary attitude. Funny enough, his disgruntlement firmed her resolve. "I won't let him die a slave because I have a few reservations."

But that didn't stop her stomach from churning with dread at the prospect of her abilities interfering with what was normally a commonplace procedure. She and commonplace didn't get along all that often.

"I know." The low voice held no emotions, the fury died, only the splintered yellow in his eyes remained alive with his vitriolic emotions.

When he didn't offer further protest, she couldn't delay the inevitable and stepped toward the door. When he backed out of the way without a word, she paused. "Will that mean your duty has been satisfied?"

The drum of her heart beat loud in her ears, and she hardly dared to breathe, memorizing the details of his rugged face as she waited for his answer.

"Sorry to disappoint, but I'm here until the end of the month and they remove the collar." A cruel twist to his lips tripped her heart in her throat. A spike of excitement tingled across her skin at the promise in his eyes. "And I'll be watching closer than ever."

Raven licked her lips and turned away, ignoring the way the knots eased from her gut at his promise. It was ridiculous. His threat should've angered her. She doubted he intended his comments to give her a strange sense of peace. It also gave her time to figure out an alternative way to help without putting him in more danger by mating him. He deserved a chance at a normal life, not trapped in her chaotic version of hell.

The house was quiet as she climbed the stairs. She entered her room, then pulled up short at the sight of Taggert, gloriously naked on her bed, every inch of him on display. Her mouth watered, and the heat of desire burned through her body. She knew she should turn away, but she couldn't make herself move and deny herself the view of all that flesh just waiting for her touch.

The dread came back in a rush, along with the inescapable feeling that fate wouldn't let her escape this unscathed. Jackson stepped in behind her with barely a space between them. His delicious heat soaked into her skin, easing the cold stealing down her spine.

Worry fell away. Muscles relaxed. A brush of fur rolled through her. The need to run, the urge to hunt, increased.

"Cover up." Jackson snapped out the order, pushing against her back.

The contact worsened her condition. The smell of fresh cut grass filled her nose. She turned toward Jackson, her ache morphing into pure physical need to touch him. To take what she needed. She didn't have to think anymore.

Desire thickened her blood when she saw passion reflected in his eyes. He wasn't unaffected. His fist clenched, his muscles shook as they locked into place. She suspected that at the slightest hint from her, he would pounce. When she met his gaze again, he very deliberately tipped his head to the side, offering his throat.

She shuffled closer when Taggert stuck his arm between them. Jackson snapped his teeth in warning, but Raven caught the smell of forest and freedom, breaking the spell Jackson wove.

"What's happening?" This couldn't be right. She shouldn't feel this uncontrollable lust that spiraled through her body.

She was so screwed. She hadn't even touched them.

Taggert pressed closer to her back, forcing her into Jackson's warmth. "Our wolves are showing their pleasure."

A shiver shook her whole body at his bald explanation. Good Lord, no wonder shifters wanted to touch so much. When he lowered his head next to hers, she tipped her head to watch him, fascinated by the way he licked his lips. The way his gaze zeroed in on her mouth as if he wanted to taste her again.

He nudged his wrist to her chin. "Bite."

Her lips tingled at his hunger. He brushed his wrist against her mouth and the urge to taste him so intimately bucked through her, along with a deep fear what would happen to them if she went through with this. "Jackson?"

His jaw flexed, teeth bared as he grunted. "Do it." He followed Taggert's lead and pressed closer. All she felt was them and the need to stake her claim.

She opened her mouth and laid her lips against the warm skin of Taggert's wrist. Desire swelled through her body. The clothes between them became an annoyance when all she wanted was to touch flesh. He groaned, urging her on by pressing closer, sliding his hand down her side.

"Please." The word was spoken on a breath of air.

When she would have turned to face Taggert, Jackson grabbed her hips, and she moaned at the feel of him snug against her, so ready that she throbbed with need.

Taggert whimpered at her arousal. Jackson grunted and both men pressed closer. The grip on her hips turned brutal. "You have to call your wolf and bite. I can't hold back much longer."

Raven met his gaze, saw the strain on his face as he held their animals in check. Her job as an alpha she realized, something she failed to do while she allowed the novelty of the emotions to overwhelm her. Giving up the inevitable, she parted her lips and bit.

"Harder." Taggert's mouth brushed her ear, a plea and demand all in one word.

The skin broke, and she resisted the urge to pull away as the coppery taste of blood spilled in her mouth. Taggert bent and brushed his lips along the back of her neck.

The first swallow spilled down her throat. Taggert's aura bent, melding with hers. The power of his wolf brushed against her, the warmth and smell so similar to Taggert, she couldn't resist trailing her fingers over him.

Then the dark shadow at her core uncurled, stealing the warmth of the joining. The feel of Taggert's wolf retreated as the beast woke. The greedy darkness begged her to take more, demanded she bite harder, sink her teeth deeper.

Blood flooded her mouth. It felt wrong, the taste sour. Then she understood.

Only a wolf could claim a wolf.

"Call the wolf."

At Jackson's command, the wolf at her core charged at the shadow, snarling with rage at being denied. Pain rippled through her with each slash of the wolf's claws, each gouge of the fangs. The touch of Jackson and Taggert's wolves made hers stronger, more determined to claim what was hers. The darkness retreated as if pleased to have stolen a taste.

The wolf brushed against her mind then stalked off in victory. Rational thought was slow to return, the throb in her skull a dull ache. Raven ignored the pain and snapped open her eyes to find herself pinned to the floor under the combined weight of both Taggert and Jackson, unable to move.

"Is everyone all right?" The husky scratch of her voice made her wince.

"The better question would be what the hell were you thinking." Rylan's blue eyes zeroed in on hers, a hardness in them that didn't allow her to guess at his thoughts. Every inch of him was perfectly in order, as if finding her on the floor with two men wrapped around her didn't ruffle him.

"It's my fault. I didn't realize the mating process was so delicate, that I needed my wolf to complete the exchange." When she struggled to sit, snarls erupted from both of the men holding her, their anger directed at Rylan, pure wolf boldly glaring from their eyes. "Rylan, I think you should leave."

"No." The one word was implacable, and she was helpless to make him obey, the bastard, and he knew it.

Careful to keep any fear out of her voice, Raven nudged Taggert. "Release me."

The rumble in his chest died. He cocked his head at the sound of her voice, then slowly turned toward her.

She expected ferocity.

She expected fear.

It unnerved her to see utter devotion in his gaze. "We were going to go out tonight. Remember? If you still want to go, you need to release me and get ready."

He hesitated a second before he finally did as told. Instead of standing, he crawled over her in a loose way no human could duplicate. Jackson bared his teeth, but Taggert ignored everything as he came closer. Balanced on his hands and feet in an amazing display of muscles, he bent down without touching and inhaled deeply.

The energy around him dimmed and the part of him that was human slowly emerged. Then she saw the mess she'd made of his wrist and blanched. "What did I do?"

Taggert gazed at her calmly, clearly pleased by her concern. "It doesn't hurt."

She reached out to stop the bleeding when Rylan spoke. "Not while you're touching both of them. Bite marks become very erotic when touched by their alpha."

Color rose in her cheeks at what a picture they presented. "Taggert, go with Rylan and bind your wound."

Rylan gave her a dirty look but nodded. "You have ten minutes." He gave Jackson a hard glare and disappeared.

Taggert didn't object, and she found herself alone with the undivided attention of a wolf.

"Jackson?" Those yellow-green eyes met hers. When she shifted, his hold loosened, but didn't release her. If she so much as twitched, she had no doubt he'd drag her under him and take what his body demanded. And she wasn't sure she'd protest. If anything happened between them, she wanted the human in him to decide he wanted her, not some primitive animal instinct.

She slowly lifted a shaky hand to his face. Those eyes followed her every gesture. She laid her hand against his cheek. Instead of retreating, he leaned into her touch. "Jackson." His eyes slid closed, and he inhaled her scent. When she would've pulled away, he grabbed her wrist.

"You need to get away from me." The guttural demand took her by surprise.

"What?"

"The wolf is fighting me." He panted, each word torn from him. "And I don't think he has any plans on letting you go."

A chill swept through her gut despite the warmth of his embrace. "What do you need me to do?"

A fine tremor shook his frame as his body fought itself. A grunt of pain escaped his clamped lips, and a hint of fangs protruded from his mouth. Part of her screamed to run. The sensible part told her to trust him and wait for his signal.

She placed her hand over the wild beat of his heart. A swirl of energy battered his insides. She tried to drop her shields and pull it away from him, but her animals were in full charge.

"When I let go, run."

"But—"

"Now."

The warm arms she'd found so comforting peeled away, leaving her feeling naked and exposed. Before she had a chance to move, he scrambled backwards so fast he was on the other side of the room in less than a second, the dresser he cracked into rocking at the impact.

"Run!"

Raven ignored the most basic rule of shifters and darted out the door, slamming it behind her. She hesitated, her hand on the knob, pressing her forehead against the cool wood, her body itchy with need to touch him. She swore she felt him on the other side of the door, pressed against the wood as if seeking her.

"I can still smell your need." A sharp, pain-filled chuckle cut off abruptly. "Go!"

Could she leave him in there to suffer alone? She could help him, she knew she could, but damn it, she just didn't know how.

When something battered against the heavy oak wood, she slowly drew away. Another blow landed on the door, shaking the frame. Giving into his plea, she dashed down the stairs and ran straight into Rylan. A scream strangled in her throat at his unexpected appearance. For a second, she'd thought it had been Jackson.

"Did he hurt you?" He gripped her arms, his eyes whirling slightly as he searched every inch of her for an injury.

It did nothing to stop the pounding of her heart. Hell yes, she was afraid, but part of her liked the chase and that frightened her the most.

"I'm fine. Jackson—" She hadn't even finished when Rylan streaked up the stairs in a blur of black. "He didn't hurt me."

Rylan didn't stop. She went to follow him when Taggert stepped out of the kitchen wearing only a low slung pair of jeans and snagged her arm. "Leave them.

"But they'll tear each other apart—"

"They're just blowing off steam. Neither would do anything that would upset you. If you want to leave without them following, now's the time."

Raven hesitated, studying his face, uncertain what to make of his comment, but more certain she wasn't ready to face Jackson anytime soon. "You're sure?"

He understood her unspoken question. "They'll both be alive when we get home."

That sounded more ominous than comforting.

The balcony doors in her room shattered in a crack of wood and a tinkle of glass. Her eyes narrowed at their childish attitude to strike first, and any residual concern for their wellbeing vanished. "Let's go."

Raven quickly collected her keys. They were down the road in under five minutes. The constant battering of emotions was exhausting. She didn't know how people stayed sane under the constant bombardment. Diligently, methodically, she built her walls back into place. It was harder this time.

If she could just treat the men like a job, then maybe she could prevent the episode back at the house from happening again. She feared it'd be a lot easier said than done.

But the best place to start was now. "First thing we need to do is stop to get you some clothes."

Taggert's eyes glittered in the darkness. "Have you ever been to a bloodhouse?"

"No." The silent amusement in his question made her uneasy, and she shifted in her seat. Being alone with him after what happened only made her feel more awkward. She wasn't sure how she was supposed to react after what happened between them. Part of her wanted to inspect his injury and the horrible mess she made of his arm, but she was afraid to touch him. Afraid how she would react to his touch. Could claiming him have made her craving for his touch worse?

"Then you'll be in for a surprise. And believe me, for where we're going, I'm overdressed."

Chapter Nineteen

A LITTLE BEFORE MIDNIGHT

*R*aven parked the car a discreet distance and walked the rest of the way to the club, ignoring the urine and rotten cabbage smell of garbage wafting from the alley. When they reached the door, the bouncer, a huge vampire who must have been a Viking in a past life, spoke.

"Donor or visitor?"

Raven grimaced at the thought of donating her blood and what it would do to a vampire. "Visitor."

"You sure?" The giant tossed a disbelieving look at Taggert and his collar that raised her hackles.

"Yes." She narrowed her eyes, and resisted the urge to step in front of Taggert. The bouncer just grunted and heaved a sigh.

Once inside the darkened entryway, she glared at Taggert. "You could've warned me it'd be so expensive." One hundred fifty dollars each, triple the normal fee for bringing a shifter as a visitor instead of donor. No wonder vampires were rich. Blood suckers, ha! More like the visitors were the suckers.

"You would've come anyway."

True. She turned away without giving him the satisfaction of agreeing out loud. She didn't bother to bring a picture of Jason. Being Lester's son made him a celebrity in the vampire world.

"Stay close." Anxiety wrestled away the calm she fought to maintain, and she wondered if this was such a bright idea with their bond so new and her emotions so shaky. She didn't know if she could analyze the situation clearly if Taggert was threatened.

She needed muscle, not food. And Taggert was food. He was too far down the dominance pole to be anything but subservient. Shifters had an allure to vampires. They were like liquor, some more potent than others, but all tasty and all very addicting.

"Are you sure you want to do this?" Fear clung to her. What if she couldn't protect him?

"You're not going in alone." He gave a simple shrug. "I know what to expect."

That didn't reassure her. She debated ordering him home.

Something must have alerted him to her thoughts. He lifted his chin mutinously, clearly not going to let her get away with it, and stepped closer.

"Don't." She immediately countered and drew away. She wasn't falling for that trap. No touching. No emotion. She wouldn't be persuaded or seduced by his touch.

At her retreat, all expression smoothed away. "I have no qualms about telling the others your plan."

She hadn't noticed how much he'd begun to relax around her until she saw the blank mask he used when they first met descend over his face. That he'd use it on her stung. She hadn't realized how much she relied on him to always be on her side. The least she could do was return the favor. She took a steady breath. "Fine."

"Fine?" Taggert's face slowly softened. "You won't regret it."

Maybe not, but she had a feeling she'd pay for it later.

When she opened the door, Raven blinked, taken aback by the club scene. She couldn't tell what surprised her more, the near naked bodies twisted on the dance floor, or the slap of power that bit along her skin. For some reason, she never expected to have so many vampires probe her mind at once. They adhered to protocol, not pushing but waiting to see what she was: visitor or shifter, food or rival.

"It's not what it appears." The velvet voice to her left thrummed with power.

The man who spoke wasn't conventionally handsome, but he had that magnetic quality that drew humans. Brown, curly hair tumbled around his shoulders, softening his appearance, a trick that made him appear less like a vampire and more approachable. All the more dangerous to the unexpecting human.

Taggert crowded her back, hampering her movements and she resisted the urge to take a step away in case she needed the space to defend them.

"What do you mean?" She blinked at the stranger's comment then turned to study the dance floor again, ignoring the sharp burst of sweat and spice from the bodies as human and vampires mingled.

"Sexual favors are prohibited on the premises." He came to stand by her side as if invited. "This exhibition is to titillate the visitors and keep them coming back."

Raven watched the vampires in the room, easily picking them out from the crowd, even the ones that pretended to be human, and saw what he meant. The vampires were putting on an act. Suspicious of their oh-so-helpful vampire guide, she twisted to keep an eye on him. "So it's all show?"

A deep chuckle escaped and a charming twinkle sparkled in his eyes as he studied her face. "Not all. We give them what they expect."

He nodded to a couple in the corner. Two skinny socialite girls who looked as if they were expecting to be munched on at any moment sat huddled nearly under their table, unable to stop gawking as they snapped pictures to show they had survived. "They come for the excitement. Some come for the danger."

Very aware of his critical gaze on her, judging her, Raven purposefully kept her eyes averted to avoid any mind tricks. "And you give it to them." The words were barely audible, but he took it as a rebuke.

"We take their money, a sip of their blood, and give them the thrill of danger without the threat." There had to be less than ten vampires present.

"So the Bloodhouses are all a ruse." She studied the vampire next to her, suspicious at all the free information. "Why tell me the truth?"

"Not a ruse. They have their purposes. It lets the humans think that they're safe and we're regulated." He gave her a slight bow. "I'm one of Lester's people."

"Ah." That explained everything. "So he assigned you to keep an eye on me." Or to ensure that she didn't probe too deeply into the dark shadows the vampires were famous for using to protect their secrets.

The man's smile never wavered. "He told us to be useful to you in any way we can." She didn't miss the way his eyes fanned her body, the way his eyes lit in invitation.

A growl rumbled up Taggert's throat. Despite the warning, the vampire never looked away from her. When their guide brushed against her without lifting a finger, her eyes narrowed.

"Don't. You won't like the consequences."

The prospect of a tussle lightened his eyes, but then the mischievousness in him died. "You should leave."

She couldn't be sure if he was issuing an order or giving them a warning. "Can't. I need information on Jason, and the only way to do that is by talking to his peers."

"Lester *questioned* everyone. No one here will be able to give you answers." He didn't bother to scan the room. "I doubt there's anyone left still standing that would be of help to you." His expression hardened a little. "Your breed has a fresh wound. Not a wise choice in a bloodhouse."

Something in his voice tightened the muscles of her spine. In a casual scan of the room, she noticed the not so subtle glances cast their way by the vampires, the light swirl in their gazes as the color bled away. Every vampire eye was on them. One thought was clear. Lunch.

When she wanted to grab for the current at her core, she hesitated. If she fought back, her gift would be exposed. If she killed them, she'd make enemies.

"Go."

She didn't move. Not without answers. "I'll not let them have him. I don't wish to fight." She met his gaze, ignoring the buzz at the back of her mind as the vampires communicated with one another. She didn't have to listen to their conversations to know whom they were discussing. "If they start something, I'll finish it."

"I'll handle them."

Raven hesitated, but she couldn't help but believe him. "And Jason?"

"Try his girlfriend."

That caught her attention. "Girlfriend? I'm sure Lester already checked that route."

The man shook his head. "She was a shifter. She's food. He'd never believe his son dated the likes of her." He stood in front of them, blocking the rest of the room from view. "Go." His voice grew more insistent, harder, the cheer and helpfulness gone.

Taggert caught her hand and tugged. She kept her feet, refusing to budge and leave their informant alone to face the half dozen or so hungry vampires.

"Come with us." The vampire stilled completely, his humanity stripped from him.

She either startled or surprised him, an unnerving experience to say the least. Then a dazzling smile danced across his face.

"Don't worry about me. We'll meet again." The promise throbbed in his voice, the intimate tone heating her face.

Taggert jerked on her arm, hauled her away. She couldn't compete with his strength. When she would've protested, she saw that the other vampires had closed the distance without her sensing them. "The longer you stay, the more danger you put him in."

The vampire they'd spoken to had already turned to block them from being followed, a warning against the others. Taggert was right. On the way out the door, Raven stopped by the bouncer.

"The vampires are growing restless."

The big man cursed, casting her a dark look that clearly stated he thought it was her fault. "Damn breeds, I knew you'd be trouble."

He puffed up and charged inside the doors. Shouts rent the air as people poured out the doors. The humans.

"Come. You did everything you could. We have to go or everything he's done to let us leave will be for nothing."

With one last glance at the club, Raven nodded and took off at a jog, Taggert easily keeping pace. When she reached the car, she was slightly out of breath, while Taggert didn't even appear winded. She really needed to start working out.

ELECTRIC STORM

The car turned over immediately. She weaved through the traffic, avoiding Taggert's searching gaze lest her anger slip its leash. "You knew that would happen."

"No shifter goes to the houses without being a donor." His voice took on the careful tone of not revealing anything.

"Son of a bitch. Why didn't you tell me?"

"You would've left without me." The answer was simple and true.

"Why did the bouncer let you enter?"

When silence filled the car, she risked a glance at him. With an acceptance that pissed her off, he lifted his collar. "Slaves go where they are ordered."

"They sent you in there without protection before." Her heart skipped a beat. The implications shocked her. She understood the need to regulate the pack and their numbers, but she couldn't get over the cruelty. There had to be a better way than to kill the most vulnerable. Especially if your numbers were already dwindling.

Taggert shrugged. "If you don't listen to the orders, you don't get selected."

"But if the vampires had gotten their hands on you, they would've bled you. I saw the intent in their eyes." She gripped the wheel hard, battling her anger and her own stupidity.

"They usually send us in twos or threes to increase our chances of getting out alive. Most vampires know better than to take too much blood. The auction takes place every few years. It starts on a full moon, lasts for a month until the council meets. We have no choice but to prove ourselves. You only get so many seasons before you're labeled undesirable."

This all sounded so much like the labs that bile rose in her throat. Obey without question. Break your spirit by any means available until you're willing to sacrifice your own kind to please them.

"Jackson warned me about the auction, told me what to expect. This was my last chance. I have nothing special to offer. If I survived all the tests, proved myself, I could find a sponsor." His posture unbent. "Then you came."

"And shoved you in the same barbaric situation." Gods be damned. Her ignorance kept putting them in harm's way. How was she supposed to keep them safe when she didn't know the dangers?

~ 165 ~

Her face hardened with determination. "When we get home, we're removing that collar."

He stilled, his eyes tracking her. "Only the council has the power."

Her lips curled back in a snarl. "I'll do it." Damn them if she didn't. She wouldn't let them rule what was hers.

"No one has successfully removed a collar. If the seal is tampered with, the bearer will die."

Her grip tightened on the steering wheel. She could see others trying it like some animal desperate to break free from a trap, willing to die to be free.

"You won't die. I won't let you." And she had the power to back up her claim.

Chapter Twenty

DAY SIX: AFTER MIDNIGHT

She sped down the driveway, trepidation thickening around her as they drew near the house. Jackson and Rylan were going to kill her for sneaking out. The clock showed a few minutes to three.

Raven glanced up in time to see a shadow take shape out of the fog directly in front of the car. She slammed on the breaks and jerked the wheel. The tires caught gravel, spun them around, throwing up a cloud of rock and dust. When they came to an abrupt stop, her head cracked against the side window with a resounding thud.

She probed her bruised temple, flinching at the sensitive area. "You all right?"

She caught Taggert's nod from the corner of her eye. Dropping her hand, she scanned the driveway, half expecting to find a crumbled body slumped across the road.

Nothing.

Silver moonlight peeked through the mist. The darkness had an eerie quiet that sounded deafening, almost expectant. She peeled her hands away from the wheel and reached for the power that pooled in her core, absently swirling the strands around her fingers as she studied the shadows for any sign of movement.

Even knowing she could defend herself did nothing to soothe the shaking that persisted at the near miss. That had been too close. Not willing to wait for the fight, she grabbed the door handle. "Stay here."

"Don't."

Annoyed at his over-protectiveness, she tried to leave, only to find her arm captured.

"It's Jackson, and I don't think he's happy."

Raven whipped around and squinted out the window, searching for any sign of him. Some of the uncertainty settled, changing into pure anger at him for risking his life so needlessly. "What the hell was he thinking? I could've hit him."

As the words left her mouth, his familiar form took shape out of the darkness, big and low to the ground, coming toward them with incredible speed. If she blinked, she would've missed him. The door handle ripped out of her grasp as he flung it open. Metal crunched, and she found herself face to face with one furious man.

His anger fueled her own. Rage burned along her mind, eager for the match. "What the hell do you think you're doing? I could've killed you." The energy she'd tapped rebelled at being shoved away, wanting to fight, wanting freedom as it burned along her skin. She shoved his shoulder and stood, unwilling to have him tower over her. A spark arched between them at the touch, and he backed away with a snarl. Little of the man remained.

He scanned her from head to booted-foot. His detached gaze felt cold, and she was surprised at how she'd become used to expecting the hint of heat from him. Calm slowly crept over Jackson, the stiff set of his shoulders relaxed a fraction.

"Where the hell have you been?" The words were guttural, forced past clenched teeth, a hint of fang flashing.

"Doing my job." She stomped away, knowing she couldn't get back in the car while her anger had a hold of her. She'd fry the computer. Damn his control. She wanted to fight, confront him and get everything out in the open.

She sensed Taggert more than heard him as he followed, but she didn't turn, afraid to draw attention to him. Jackson bristled as he stalked at her side, but remained quiet.

Rylan met them at the door, a carefully blank expression on his face. Until she got closer. His nostrils flared. Color bled from his eyes. "What were you thinking?"

She clicked her tongue in disgust. Rylan backed away, allowing her entry, though he did so grudgingly and followed close enough to be mistaken for her shadow.

"I can smell them on you."

"Them?" Jackson growled, shuffling closer to catch a whiff of what lingered in her hair and clothes.

"Vampires." Two sets of eyes pinned her, bonding over taking her to task.

She liked them better when they were at odds. "I'm working on a case. I go where the answers are."

"And damn the consequences?"

She winced at the betrayal that edged into Jackson's eyes. A look she deserved. When he didn't throw any accusations, guilt dug in its claws. She'd all but promised to bite him, then vanished. She'd run. She didn't like that picture of herself and lashed out. "What am I supposed to do? Wait for the killer to fall in my lap?"

Rylan's jaw bunched in anger. "You're supposed to protect yourself and those in your care."

She'd had enough. Raven tipped up her chin and faced her accusers. Three faces, one impassive, two furious, met her gaze. "I survived long before any of you had come along. How is it that I'm so inept I need three bodyguards wherever I go?"

"You have more to lose now."

Faster than her eyes could track, Rylan came to stand in front of her and it annoyed her to no end. She could feel the impotent anger in him, the need to reach out and shake sense into her. Didn't he understand?

"People are dying."

His face hardened further. "And I won't have you be one, too."

"Are you mad that I went there without you? Or just mad I didn't need you to protect me?" It was a low blow, but she wouldn't take back the question. "You treat me like a child. I'm a lot stronger than you give me credit."

Rylan reached out, almost touched her, then dropped his hand. He spoke softly, his voice devoid of emotion. "You are also a lot more vulnerable than you want to believe. You're not indestructible." He relented with a small smile that twisted her heart. "You called me to you to help. Let me. Tell me what you've learned. Maybe I can be of assistance."

"That's it?" She didn't relax at his easy acceptance. He kept his distance from others of his kind for a reason. No way would he concede this easily.

He shrugged. "For now." He didn't bother to look over his shoulders. "But I'm not the only one who wants answers."

Taggert kept his thoughts hidden as always, but Jackson held his fury close to his chest, all bottled up and ready to explode. They wanted to protect her. She was so used to being alone, she didn't know how to deal with them.

Could she really keep them ignorant when staying with her put them at risk? Inhaling deeply, she admitted defeat. "Let's go downstairs, and I'll explain what I can."

She reached for the door handle only to find Taggert already there, opening it for her. His continued subservience disturbed her, reminded her of the labs and the way they conditioned some of the shifters to serve. Though his spirit wasn't broken, she knew he wasn't whole either, and she didn't know a damn thing about how to fix him. But she did know one thing that would help. She needed to get that collar off him. He wasn't a slave any longer.

The lights flickered and turned on when she walked into the room. "Taggert. Sit." She pointed to a stool by her lab. At his hesitant expression, she amended her statement. "Please." She opened a drawer, riffled through the tools then slammed it shut when nothing appealed to her. "Let's see this thing."

He bowed a little so she could reach. The slave collar left a red ring around his neck, but didn't break skin. Her power affected it last time. She wasn't sure how, but she was going to find out. "Let me know if you feel any pain."

"Raven." Rylan said her name very softly.

She lifted her chin, daring him to stop her. "I won't hurt him, but he can't wear the collar anymore. It puts him in too much danger. They saw him at the club and thought he was there to play. They didn't see anything but that damn collar." She refused to look at Jackson and was surprised when she received no objection from him.

She kept her gaze on Rylan, silently asking him to be ready. He gave a subtle nod. If something went wrong, he'd stand between her and Jackson until she could fix it.

Taking a deep breath, she centered herself and reached into the recesses of her body where she stored energy. That thing was still wrapped around the source, nearly swallowing it whole. Her core compensated by growing still larger. She wasn't reassured, but pushed away her concern in order to do what needed to be done.

She carefully dipped into the pool and gathered a few strands, weaving them together. The power felt incredibly good to touch, eager to be used. She needed to leave enough that if this went ass-backwards, she'd be able to call Taggert back.

He was so alive, so different from the dead she'd accidently called back. If anything happened, she had to be quick in order to bring him back whole with his body and soul still intact. A shimmer of doubt rose.

She looked at his young face, saw the harsh past reflected in his eyes, the uncertainty, and a shiny new hope for the future.

And silently cursed. She had to try.

When the power burned along her hands, she gripped the strands, twining them through her fingers despite the way her skin sizzled. She held the collar with care, ensuring none of the metal touched his skin.

Slowly, steadily, she wrapped the strands of power around the silver, iron and gold. The necklace absorbed all of it without change. She did the process twice more when she noticed a difference. "The damn thing is protecting itself. The iron beneath carries a spell."

She slowly withdrew and let the power settle in the piece and cool. When she lifted her gaze, she saw Taggert's eyes had turned completely yellow. Though she hadn't moved, she sensed that he wouldn't allow her to retreat. He inhaled her scent, and that seemed to be enough to keep him docile. For now.

She didn't look away from Taggert as she spoke. "I need one of you on each side to grab the collar and pull when I give you the signal." She hoped the magic hadn't had time to compensate for the influx of extra energy and would thus be brittle.

When Jackson came to stand beside Taggert, she realized he wasn't in much better condition, but he seemed to have better control. Rylan slipped on her other side. She gave them a nod then touched the warm band. All the power she dropped in it was seething at being trapped, fighting the magic trying to tame it. Taking a deep breath, she jerked all the energy she could out of it, fast and dirty and with no finesse.

It came so readily to her call that she staggered under the onslaught, fighting to swallow it all down. She had one chance at this. Magic had a hand in creating this piece. If she let go now, the next time that very magic would fight her and do everything it could to wound Taggert.

"What are you doing? I smell magic."

"Magic wielders work by controlling energy. They take a little of that power, harness it and then mold it to do what the user demands."

She panted as the strain continued to grow. "A magic user needs spells to practice their craft. Their spells are like needles, the energy, the string, and they sew very carefully, very delicately to create a pattern in order to get the energy to do what they want.

"For me, magic's like trying to sew with a railway pike. What I'm trying to do is destroy that pattern. If I can disturb it for just a second..." Her voice trailed off as the energy threatened to drown her. Her eyeballs felt as if they were floating in acid.

Then she felt it.

A faint waver.

"Now," she shouted, hoping they had enough time to break it before the magic ricocheted inside her, desperate to be absorbed back into the necklace.

Neither man questioned her. They grabbed hold of the blisteringly cold metal and pulled.

A crack like ice breaking rang in her ears. When they continued to pull, the necklace split in two, throwing both men backwards.

The energy inside her went wild, tearing her up in order to get out. She doubled over, unable to gasp for breath.

"Drop them. Get out of the way." The metal clanged to the floor, the pieces appearing tarnished and old. When all three men stepped away, she allowed her hold to slip. The magic slammed out of her and funneled into the metal. The pieces clanked together. The crack melded, the polish shining once more as the magic forced the energy back into the pattern of the spell.

Raven gasped, desperate for air, falling to her knees when everything quieted. The lights flickered then dulled but remained stable. When she looked up, it was to find all three men staring at her with varying degrees of shock.

"That's not possible." Jackson's eyes had reverted to their whiskey brown color.

Rylan snorted. "Of course not."

"Did I hurt you?" Taggert gingerly touched his throat, and her heart pounded at his silence. Raven groaned as she tried to find her feet. Even her hair protested moving.

Taggert didn't move but to stare at her. Then he slowly shook his head.

Some of the tension that kept her back straight seeped out of her. "Then go upstairs and take a shower. It's been a long night, and I have a full day of work tomorrow searching for Jason's girlfriend."

A noise bubbled up the back of Jackson's throat. He looked at the necklace and nudged it with his foot. Nothing happened. "If people found out..."

"They won't." Steel underlined Rylan's word, a warning to both the shifters and her.

But she knew someone would eventually. She had to prepare for that time. Just not now, not when her brain felt scrambled.

Rylan bent and retrieved the necklace, touching it carefully. "I think you just defeated the boogieman." A cynical smile passed his lips then quickly died as he studied her. His eyes crinkled a little at the corners as his gaze narrowed.

"You have a couple of messages in the study. While they're getting ready for bed, why don't I show you?"

He was giving her an out from the questions building in everyone's minds, time to recuperate and settle the fluctuating power that sloshed in her like a drunken sailor on shore leave.

As soon as the others left the room, Rylan dropped the necklace on the table and pulled out a chair. "Sit."

She collapsed onto the hard stool and groaned, grateful for the support and Rylan's instinctive understanding of her need to hide her weaknesses from the others.

"How bad is it?"

Raven shrugged. "I held a spark too long. When I took the magic and poured it back into the necklace, it took everything. I don't know how they bear the price magic demands. If I didn't have so much stored, I don't think it would've worked."

"Damn the necklace. What the hell were you thinking, taking chances like that? I've seen witches die for less. Rule one is never touch an active spell you haven't cast yourself."

Raven gaped at him, a little shocked at his display of emotions. He always kept them tightly under wraps for fear someone would sense he was different. With his wavy hair and wild emotions, he could pass for human. Except for the hint of fangs peeking between his lips.

"If he continued to wear it, he would've remained a target."

"Then leave him here with his guard." Agitated, he ran a hand through his hair, messing it up further before the strands obediently fell back into place. Not even his hair or clothes dared defy his control for long.

That's when she noticed the little tears in his jacket and pants. "What the hell happened to you?"

He stilled complete as if caught, his back toward her. "Rylan?"

"Jackson and I had a few things to settle."

Flashes back to Jackson's darkening jaw and ragged clothes came back to her, and she groaned. "At least you didn't kill each other."

Rylan turned slowly. "You don't get it. You don't even know how close to danger you were when you were alone with him."

His accusation left her completely flabbergasted. "What do you mean? He would've never hurt me." At least she didn't think he would, not without her giving as good as she got. He couldn't risk being separated from Taggert or sent back to his pack with the threat of a challenge hanging over his head.

Rylan shook his head and gave a bitter chuckle. "You don't understand, and they're too much of a coward to tell you. The female is the one who decides to mate, but the male can bind a female as well. He almost bit you. I saw the possessive look in his eyes. He wanted it so badly he barely held himself in check."

Raven licked her lips, her mouth going dry at the thought of being bound. "They said only a female can bind a male."

It was one thing to have others attached to her. She could protect them, do what needed to be done to keep them safe, but she refused to be under anyone else's control.

"A male can't force a true mating because they don't have the enzymes found in the woman's blood that are needed to hold the connection. The bond fades. The man would have to bite her over and over to keep her craving him." Rylan glided closer, his feet seemingly to hover over the floor. "And there is the matter of your blood. What do you think would've happened to him if he'd swallowed your blood? Do you think he could go back to his normal life after you?"

Chapter Twenty-one

PREDAWN

*R*ylan's question haunted her all the way to her room. She came to herself when Jenkins trailed downstairs, a sleepy yawn cracking his jaw. He gave her a bleary wave and shuffled past to the kitchen. Another member added to the *Addams Family*.

Rylan cleared his throat. "You actually do have messages in the study."

"Of course." She promptly turned around.

Both of them were subdued. She refused to push Rylan out of her life, but she knew he wouldn't hesitate to leave her if he thought it best. He'd already done it once.

Unwilling to rock the boat further, she settled for a mundane topic. "Have you heard if the others were able to infiltrate the compound?"

Rylan shrugged. "They returned an hour ago. We didn't speak."

She couldn't help notice the careful lack of emotions. Even though he gave no indication, the tick in his jaw gave away his annoyance.

Heartbreaking loneliness clung to him, but she understood his fear. Rylan was a powerful vampire. When he lost control, he did it in a big way. She'd witnessed it happen once, and Rylan had never forgiven himself.

She rounded the desk to find the morning paper London had left by the phone. The headlines immediately captured her attention.

Police Are No Closer To Cracking The Case, Tax Payers' Money Being Spent On Specialists. Skimming the article, she read the plug for RPL representatives being lobbied, and tossed the paper aside with a sigh.

She listened to the messages. One from the team saying the mission was successful, the building cleared of suspicion. The other message was from Jeffrey Durant.

Unable to curb her curiosity about him, or her unease, she played his message. Just the sound of his voice over the phone lingered like a caress against her skin. She hated the helpless shiver that twisted her insides into mush. He was playing with her, and she couldn't help wonder if claiming him made her more vulnerable to the chemistry between them. She hoped not as she wasn't sure she would survive if he turned up the charm.

The cryptic message just left her more confused. "Durant called, but he didn't say what he wanted."

"There's one way to find out." Rylan nodded to the number she jotted down at the time. "He does work at a nightclub."

He smirked at her hesitation. It gave her the courage to dial.

"Talon's. What's your pleasure?"

Raven snorted. The greeting suited him. "I'm looking for Durant."

"I'm sorry, but he's busy right now. Can I take a message?"

A shot of disappointment pierced her, and that made her more disgruntled. "This is Raven. I'm retur—"

"Of course. One moment please. I'll get him."

Before she had a chance to protest that she didn't want him disturbed, his voice filled the line. Despite the distance, the seductive tenor made her feel like a schoolgirl with her first crush.

"I'd like to request your presence at my club tonight."

The carefully phrased invitation immediately put her on alert, any awkwardness dissipated. But was he warning her away or formally inviting her because of her status?

"What time?" Either way it didn't matter. She was his alpha. If he was in trouble, she'd go.

"Say eleven?"

Raven agreed, ending the call. She replaced the receiver, but let her hand rest there as she sorted out what bothered her exactly.

Rylan's teasing smile faded, his earlier amusement at her discomfort forgotten. "Do you expect a trap?"

"I have no idea." With that, she rose. She should be able to manage a few hours sleep before she had to be up. She paused in the doorway. "Thank you."

Rylan blinked, but otherwise didn't look up or move away from the desk. "For what?"

"For being here." His start of surprise told her just how bad of a friend she was that she hadn't told him sooner. Not waiting for his response, she left the room feeling his speculative gaze following her.

She walked into her room, uncertain what to expect. Her gaze caught on the shattered window and the very obvious lack of balcony doors. She'd have that fixed tomorrow. Jackson wasn't anywhere, but the sound of the shower spilled out of the bathroom. Taggert lay curled up on the bed.

Naked. Again.

Heat burned her cheeks, but more out of curiosity now than shyness. "Don't you have any pajamas?"

She went to her desk when she heard the bed creak.

"No."

She turned and breathed a little easier to see he'd slipped on his jeans, then felt petty for making him wear them. They couldn't be comfortable to sleep in, especially since shifters hated to be confined. "You really don't have anything else?"

"You don't need much when you're a slave."

The answer was simple and heart wrenching.

"You're not one anymore." She was pleased to see all signs of the collar had already vanished.

Taggert cocked his head and stared at her. "You're angry."

"No. Yes." Raven sighed and grabbed a pair of shorts and a tank top from the drawers. "No one should be treated as a slave."

"Where do we go tomorrow?" He looked at the clock. "Today?"

Taggert slid back into bed, his eyes tracking her every movement, seemingly fascinated just watching her. It still unnerved her to be the center of attention, but she was coming to understand his need to make sure she didn't disappear.

"You and Jackson will go shopping." She had more than enough wealth to share. She never spent any of the money that had been given to her when they'd left the labs, reinvesting or donating it. It was time to put it to some use. "I'm going to ask around and see what I can find on Jason's girlfriend."

"No."

She didn't know Jackson had entered the room until he spoke. She turned, uncertain what to expect, a bit relieved to see him dressed in a pair of shorts. Okay, if she was truthful with herself, a little disappointed as well, but she quickly shoved that horrifying thought to the back of her mind where it belonged. "You were sent to protect him. I don't want him to go by himself."

He crossed his arms. "We can help you."

"You can help by keeping him safe." She walked to the bathroom, her clothes tucked close to her chest like they could shield her from him.

She quickly shut the door, and immediately heard the men's low voices in the other room as they plotted. When she exited a few minutes later, she breathed a sigh of relief to find the room dark.

As soon as her head hit the pillows, she was out.

It was the lack of warmth that woke her early that afternoon. Raven opened her eyes. Jackson lay on the couch, looking very relaxed and unlike himself while he slept, but she was alone in bed. Rolling over, she saw Taggert on the floor, his guitar in his hands. Besides his clothes, the instrument was the only other possession he had with him.

"Play something."

All movements ceased. Then Taggert lifted the instrument, twisting it so she could see the face. The strings were ruined. That they would destroy something so precious to him infuriated her. "You'll buy new strings today. Or get a whole new guitar for that matter."

She sat up, pulling the blankets up with her, and touched his shoulder. He slowly leaned against her thigh. When she didn't move away, he relaxed.

"I'm sorry." It was so little to offer, she felt awkward. She gingerly lifted her hand and then touched his hair, running her fingers through the shaggy strands, the softness encouraging her to linger. "You're no longer a slave. If anyone ever treats you like one, speak up."

He hunched his shoulders then laid his cheek against her leg as if he expected her to reject his tentative touch. Though she knew it was dangerous, she let the power dance close to the surface. The energy seeped into his pores, offering the only comfort she knew how to give. A connection he craved. His breath stuttered out of him, and he hesitantly set his hand on her foot.

She glanced at the clock, reluctant to leave, but they had too much to accomplish to stay. It took her ten minutes to dress and get her hair up into a twist to cover all the streaks. And another ten minutes to get off the phone with her credit card company and repair man. By the time she turned around, Taggert was dressed, and Jackson had just stepped out of the bathroom.

"Here." She held out a card. "Charge whatever you want." When neither man grabbed it, her brows wrinkled. "What?"

"Pack members usually work and give a portion of their earnings to the alpha to keep things running." Jackson appeared confused.

Raven shrugged. "You both need things. I have the money." She stared at them and didn't understand the look that passed between them.

Jackson took the card, his fingers brushing hers. The touch caught her breath in the back of her throat, and she quickly jerked back her hand. But not soon enough to cover her reaction. Damn shifters saw everything.

"Make sure you both sign up for phones under my plan." She handed over a business card, careful to keep her fingers free this time. "Tell him I sent you, and he'll set you up with something sturdy."

Jackson pocketed the paper, and an awkward silence filled the room.

"I better go." When she strode to the door, Taggert followed. She drew up short. "What?"

"Be careful."

Raven blinked at his concern, all the awkwardness rushing back. "You, too."

Before she could leave, he hugged her. As abruptly as he embraced her, he let go and darted out the door. Raven lifted a brow at Jackson, baffled at the behavior, her heart beating just a little too hard.

Jackson met her gaze and heaved a sigh big enough to hear across the room. "You really don't understand." He chuckled, shaking his head.

She couldn't tell if he was laughing at her or not.

"You're family and family is a big deal to shifters. You were able to release the slave collar and that raised your status even more in his eyes."

Raven flinched. That was the last thing she wanted. Jackson saw her reaction, and his expression shut down. Well, hell. "I just did what you told me to do. Protected him."

"And danger will come when others find out about what you can do. Are you willing to kill for him?" Jackson spoke the stark words softly.

Raven glanced down at her hands, hands that could wield so much power, but that also put everyone near her in danger.

Jackson snorted at her lack of response.

She'd killed. The faces of the men and women haunted her dreams. She just didn't know if she could do it again and keep the last bit of herself that had survived the labs sane. "Call me if you run into any trouble."

Without waiting for his reply, she slipped out the door. She couldn't handle any recriminations with her emotions so close to the surface. Thankfully, the rest of the house remained quiet, and she escaped without detection.

In two hours, she'd only found three pieces of information. Jason's girlfriend's name was Sarah No Last Name. She'd lived with Jason and went missing the same day Jason had disappeared. When Raven arrived at their house, everything that might have been Jason's had been cleared out. Anything of Sarah's had been destroyed. In the rubbish, the only clue Raven found was a torn picture of a laughing woman. Possibly Sarah?

It was too much of a coincidence that no one claimed to know the woman. There were no hospital records and no missing persons report filed.

Which led her nowhere except the last resort for missing persons.

The morgue.

The phone rang, startling her out of her thoughts. She glanced at the name displayed and smiled. Jackson. "Hel—"

"There's trouble at the Diago. Jackie and a few others have cornered Taggert outside the store. Unless they cause violence, I can't touch them. No matter where we go, they're following." The frustration in his voice raised her own.

He wasn't telling her everything. "What's holding you back?"

"My job of protector changed the moment Taggert became pack." As abruptly as that, the connection died.

Changed? Changed how?

She pulled the phone away, disgusted to realize she'd sucked every drop of juice out of it when her emotions rose. "Damn it."

She pulled the car out into traffic and did a quick u-turn, ignoring the symphony of blaring horns. Then Jackson's statement struck her. He wasn't her pack. Now that she'd mated Taggert, Jackson couldn't interfere in any dispute with another pack.

Jackson sounded furious, and she couldn't say she blamed him. She wanted to believe it was because of his inability to shift, but she had an unsettling feeling that it was because she hadn't mated him. Nor could she get rid of Rylan's disturbing conviction that if she didn't do something about it, Jackson would. Not on purpose. But if his control ever slipped, he'd come for her. Part of her was thrilled at the prospect.

She was ten minutes away. By the time she pulled up, a crowd of people loitered at the entryway of the alley. Humans watched the scene but did nothing to intercede. Typical.

"Stand back." She pushed her way into the crowd. When they didn't seem to hear her, she pulled at the energy rumbling beneath her feet, wrapping it around her like a shield.

When she pushed her way into the crowd this time, her shield slapped against the bystanders just watching and doing nothing.

People gasped at the nasty shock they received and scrambled to get out of her way.

She saw Jackson first, his muscles bulging, ready to pounce. He noticed her almost immediately, and some of the tension pouring off him eased.

Then she spotted Jackie in the group, her sharp citrus smell clogging in her throat. She ran her fake, ruby tipped nails down the front of Taggert's ripped shirt. Something about seeing her touch Taggert so intimately had Raven's power flaring to life. She acted quickly, pushing it through the earth. Instead of zapping Jackie, though, she aimed for Taggert.

The bitch snarled and jerked her hand back as a bit of the current transferred to her. Taggert eyes splintered to yellow. The absolute stillness in which he'd held himself changed when he turned his head toward her. A smile lit his face.

A few of the groupies backed away at his relaxed demeanor, creating room for her to reach his side. "Taggert. You are no longer a slave. You no longer wear the collar." People gasped, and she could swear she heard Jackson groan. "If they touch you, you have my permission to touch back."

To prove a point, she sucked in a gust of energy and sent it out like a wave. A number of them went down, a whine like a dog's caught in their throats. A few hit the brick wall of the building and were out. The rest took off running.

Raven calmly walked over to Jackie and smiled. The woman flinched, but then stubbornly lifted her chin. Raven crossed her arms. "Be very careful of what you start. It may begin with you, but I will make sure that I end it, and anyone associated with you."

"I'll make sure my alpha knows." A smirk came to her lips, and with a pleased look in her eyes, she rose to her feet.

"Do that. Tell him I'll be at Talons tonight if he has anything to discuss with me."

"You're not going alone." Jackson sat in the front seat of the car, his gaze focused on the traffic around them.

She didn't need to see his eyes to know he was pissed.

So maybe she shouldn't have all but challenged another alpha, but she couldn't allow Taggert to be bullied. "No, I suppose not."

Taggert's hand barely brushed against her hair when the strands tumbled around her shoulders. "Hey." She tucked a piece behind her ear, self-conscious of the way her unique DNA turned part of her hair silver. He inhaled deeply then settled back against the seat.

His shirt gapped open, revealing a chest packed tight with muscles. He fingered a pack of guitar strings, and the hard knot inside her stomach since Jackson called finally softened.

"I still need to stop by the morgue and see if I can find any records on Sarah. I—" She stopped speaking when Jackson picked up his phone.

"Let me ask around first."

Raven hesitated. She didn't want them anywhere near her investigation. It was becoming too dangerous; too many shifters were coming up missing. When she paused too long, the angles of his face hardened. Against her better judgment, she relented. She understood the need to be useful and hated the way people tried to protect her. He must feel doubly so since the loss of his wolf. "Do it."

She swung by a local take out place and ordered while waiting for Jackson to finish his call, doing her best not to eavesdrop—or being too obvious about listening anyway. The cadence in his voice when he spoke to a girl changed him into a charming rogue. It was uncomfortable sitting next to him, knowing that he openly flirted with others while he snapped clipped answers at her.

He hung up just as she was being handed the bags. She sent the first bag to Taggert. He took it with a smile and dug in. She gave Jackson the second and claimed the third for herself. She pulled away and parked in the back of the lot, away from prying eyes. Shifters consumed double the calories, and she was no different. If she didn't eat, her body looked elsewhere for energy, cannibalizing anyone or anything that got too close.

She took her first bite of fries when Jackson spoke. "An EMT remembers bringing Sarah in as a result of a hit and run. She was

DOA." He opened his bag, his eyebrows rising at the quantity. He didn't say anything as he took out his food. "She had a copy of the records and remembered the vampire boyfriend. He had insisted Sarah be assigned a room and hooked up to a respirator."

"She has a good memory." She refused to admit she was curious about what type of woman would interest Jackson. It made sense that he'd go for the medical type, since Jackson had a passing interest in the field himself.

"Being threatened by a powerful vampire has a way of sticking out in your memory."

"True." Raven snorted. "What happened to Sarah?"

"She doesn't know. The next time she was on that floor, the room was empty."

When Jackson didn't say anything more, Raven gritted her teeth, a bit miffed that he forced her to ask. "Anything in the files?"

"Nothing useful. Only her own notes. When she went to fill out the hospital charts, they were gone."

She finished off half of her meal and noticed Taggert engulf the last bite of his third burger. "Here." She pushed hers at him.

He took it, but hesitated. "Aren't you going to eat?"

Raven shook her head and put the car into gear. "No. I don't need any more grease, not where I'm going. I'll drop you off at the house." When Jackson opened his mouth, she raised her hand. "I'm going to the morgue to find out what I can learn. You won't be any good to me there. Get your things put away and be ready for our meeting tonight."

"You mean your date?" Jackson kept his face and tone perfectly straight, but she detected something lurking beneath the surface.

"No. If it was a date, I wouldn't be bringing either of you. The way he phrased the request made me think something's wrong and he needed me at the club."

Jackson's jaw slowed, but he continued to eat. "He wouldn't set a trap for you."

"You sound awful sure." She could use some of that reassurance about now. She really wanted to know what Durant planned to throw at her so she could prepare herself. She didn't do well under stress. Things always seemed to go badly for others.

"Hello?" Raven knocked on the door to the morgue, noticing the dim lighting. "Ross?"

"Come on in." Ross stood in the corner, a mask over his mouth and nose, his face hidden behind a spatter guard. He picked up a bone saw. "You best put on that mask."

Raven covered her face just in time to see Ross open up some poor guy's skull. Her breathing became labored under the heavy chemical powder lining the paper material.

"What can I do for you?"

"A girl was brought in DOA a few weeks ago. A shifter. I can't find any records and hoped you might have more information. She was at the hospital, so she had to come through here eventually." The morgue was tied to the hospital. Even if the body didn't need to be autopsied, the cooler space was often used for storing bodies waiting for burial or pick up.

Ross chuckled. "Very few shifters actually pass through my gates. Most bodies are claimed by their pack long before they reach me."

"Are you sure?" The room felt absurdly warm, heat blasting along her skin like fire ants. Her lungs felt starved for air.

"Quite sure." The saw seemed louder. "I remember all the shifters that come through here. We have to take special precautions as shifter blood can react badly when it comes into contact with the wrong chemicals."

"That's right." Shifter blood turned toxic when it came into contact with formaldehyde. It's why they're claimed by their own instead of sent to a funeral home. Why didn't she remember that?

A wave of dizziness crept over her, and she widened her stance to keep upright. The image of the gurney wavered, the body undulating in a way that kicked her gag reflexes into overdrive. The room grew dark. She reached out and stumbled into a metal stand.

It didn't hold her weight and crashed to the floor with a resounding clang that sounded hollow to her ears. She felt herself falling and could do nothing but watch the ground rush up and greet her. The last thing she heard was Ross.

"Oh, dear."

She woke up swinging, barely missing Ross's face. He ducked faster than she would give him credit.

"My head." She settled her aching skull between her hands and tried to swallow down her nausea.

"You passed out when I opened up the guy." He shook his head. "By the time I stopped and looked up, you were sprawled out on the floor."

"I'll never live it down."

"Don't worry. If you don't say anything, I won't." Ross patted her awkwardly on the shoulder, and she jerked away.

Something in the way he said it, something in his touch, sent a shaft of revulsion through her. She rubbed her arms, trying to wipe away the chill that engulfed her. She needed to get away, needed air. She stood hastily and swayed. "I have to go. I have a meeting tonight."

"Sure. Sure. Sorry I couldn't be of more help." He studied her with his brown, near black eyes.

She knew that look. She'd seen it in the labs often enough. Beneath his smile, beneath his benign exterior, was a sharp mind that missed very little. Though she'd always respected Ross, something about him creeped her out. She assumed it was the dead bodies. She wasn't so sure anymore.

Once the open air hit her face, her mind cleared a little. She was being paranoid. He was concerned. She would be too in his place. She wasn't supposed to be there without prior approval. It could land them both into trouble.

As soon as she reached the sidewalk, she uncrossed her arms and winced, feeling like someone had tried to snap them off. She rolled up her sleeve.

Nothing.

She did the same for her other arm.

No bruises.

She healed fast, but she'd only been out for minutes. There'd be evidence if anything was done to her.

Being unconscious in the labs meant tests. With everything putting her on edge, it was no wonder she jumped at shadows. She tried to brush it off, but the image of him standing over her with a detached look stuck with her.

Chapter Twenty-two

SUNSET

*R*aven walked upstairs then paused when a noise from the kitchen raised the hairs on the back of her neck.

A whimper. Barely a breath of sound.

She slowly retraced her steps and pushed open the door, dreading what she'd find.

Trish had Taggert pushed up against the wall, her hands pinning him in place, her teeth at his throat. Terror swamped the room, drowning her senses. Without giving it thought, she crossed the room in a blink, gripped Trish by the back of her neck and tossed her away from Taggert. Glass shattered when she sailed out of the kitchen via the wall of windows. Rays of the dying sun spilled over the floor like fresh blood.

Aggression surged through her at the thought of Taggert being mauled by one of their own. When she would've followed, Taggert snagged her arm, wrapping himself around her. Red claw marks scorched his torso, shallow nips marred his neck. She carefully touched the wounds, wishing she could erase everything. She promised herself that she would later. "Are you all right?"

London and Dominic rushed in at the commotion, halting at the sight of them and the gap in the wall. Dina followed a second later.

"Get Trisha's ass in here." She growled the words, so infuriated she could barely hold back the tide of electricity eager to seek vengeance.

At her aggression, Taggert hugged her harder, nearly squeezing the air from her with his strength.

London and Dominic moved in unison to do as told when a dripping wet, gloriously naked Jackson burst into the room. He took in the situation at a glance and snarled.

"Here." She pushed Taggert at Jackson, quickly untangling her arms. She needed her hands free, and she needed him busy. If anyone got to rip apart Trish, it would be her.

Trish roared, and her animal form sailed through the hole in the glass. The black panther skidded on the smooth floor, but quickly gained her footing and charged. Acting on instinct, Raven reached into her core. The vat of boiling power sizzled as she drew the current down her arms to pool in her hands. She tossed it at the angry cat.

Energy exploded over the dark fur, stopping the panther short. The black hide rippled, and the animal whirled, nipping at her body, crazed with pain.

As if it understood the cause of the agony, the panther turned toward Raven and snarled, her fangs glistening with saliva.

"That was only a warning shot. Shift and accept the consequences of your actions." Her words set off the animal. Muscles bunched, and the cat launched herself in the air. Raven caught a movement from Jackson from the corner of her eye.

"Guard Taggert."

Right before impact, she located Trish's center, the place where her animal dwelled, and pulled down with all her strength. Raven cracked into the wall under the weight of the body plowing into her. Air whooshed out of her in a rush.

People shouted as they slid to the floor in a heap. Her vision dimmed. Unable to catch her breath, she shoved the weight off her chest, and greedily gulped air. Strong hands pulled her to her feet. She swayed and found herself wrapped in Jackson's arms.

"What the hell did you do?" The guttural growl came from Trish. She lay sprawled on the ground in her human form, naked and struggling to stand.

"You sold the boys out, told Jackie where they would be. You deliberately put them in danger." She didn't know it for sure, but it made a sick sort of sense. "You were practically raping him when I walked in the room. What did you think would happen?" Her throat closed a little at the end of her words, her question deadly quiet.

"Not you killing me over a consensual kiss." A snarl twitched Trisha's lips. "He never once protested. Maybe that's what really bothers you."

"You had him by the throat!" Raven shook her head, wishing she could let her anger reign and solve things like animals, instead of with reason. The thing that held her back was that Trish truly didn't understand she'd done anything wrong.

As a victim in the labs herself, she thought Trisha would be more sensitive to the subject, more careful of those around her.

"Did you think Jackie would've killed me and leave Taggert for you?" A horrible suspicion trickled through her mind. She dismissed it at first, but dread gathered in her gut and wouldn't let her shuffle it away. "You cut the banister."

Something hardened in Trish's eyes, and she raised her chin. "I don't know what you're talking about."

"What if someone else had fallen? You put everyone in danger for petty jealousy."

"Petty. Petty!" Trish jerked to her feet, unadulterated hatred giving her the strength. "Everyone bends over backwards to bow to your every wish. Everything comes to you so easy. You don't have to fight for a damn thing. What gives you the right to boss us around?"

"You're blind." London shook his head, the betrayal cracking his legendary stoicism. The smell of leaves she associated with him had turned musty and rotten. "I didn't even suspect her."

Those big dark eyes of his met Raven's in apology, the shattered expression in them rending a fissure in her heart for the indomitable man who risked so much for them only to be double-crossed by one of their own.

"I'm leaving your little cult." When a second passed and nothing happened, an enraged growl worked up Trish's throat. "Why can't I change?" She threw herself at Raven, screeching in impotent rage.

"Not so fast." Dominic snagged her arms and wrenched them behind her back. When she put up a fight, Dominic slammed her against the wall, uncaring of any pain he inflicted. "Did you think we were fools, and only you could see the truth? Did it never once cross your mind that there was a reason we stay with her of our own choosing?" He shoved her away from him as if unable to stand touching her. "Get her away from me."

"My pleasure," London rumbled, taking her arm none to gently, dragging her from the room.

"You're all fools. She's nothing but a pretender. She'll get you killed." Her frantic voice became unintelligible the further they drew away.

Raven pinched the bridge of her nose, her whole body throbbing from the body slam and the snap of power that felt like it'd pulled her guts inside out. "What are you going to do about her?"

Dominic remained quiet for a time. "You have to understand that we can't allow her to be free."

She nodded, but couldn't speak. With all the power she extended, she expected to feel weak or tired. Instead, she had too much. She shrugged out of Jackson's hold and began to pace. Energy tingled along her fingertips, ready to come at her call. Too ready. The damn thing was changing on her again.

"Raven?"

"What?" She snapped then drew to a halt, realizing Dominic had been speaking to her. "Sorry."

"Are you all right?"

"Yes, fine. It's been a long day."

He paused before speaking. "Then we'll discuss this later. Why don't you go upstairs and rest."

Without replying, she nodded. She was through the door when she realized the guys hadn't followed. She pivoted, ready to enter the room again when they spoke.

"Has she always been able to prevent a person from shifting? To be able to yank them from a shift?" That was Jackson, always suspicious. She stifled a grunt of disgust, determined to listen.

"No, but she very rarely shares anything personal. I don't know if this is new or not." Dominic's voice faded as if he moved further from the door.

She gave a second to consider if they could sense her then dismissed it.

She wasn't budging.

"Has she been acting out of character recently?" He sounded hesitant.

Taggert broke the silence first. "From what?"

Dominic snorted. "She doesn't allow anyone close to her." She could hear the growl of impatience in his voice and could picture him snarling. "I swear each time I see her, she's changed more, has less control."

"Or is growing stronger and having difficulty finding a balance." Jackson posed the question as a statement, and she heard nothing for a long time.

The words dropped her gut to her feet. Damn. She'd thought she'd been so careful to keep her growing powers and her inability to master them a secret. Obviously not. She'd been so desperate for contact, she'd stayed with the group longer than she knew was reasonable. A mistake. She refused to be a burden to them.

She either needed to gain control or cut them out of her life completely. Once she finished this job, she'd assess the situation, and take whatever steps were necessary.

She hurried upstairs, stripped down and stepped in the shower. The sharp sting of the cool water refreshed her somewhat. Her body healed sluggishly, begging for a few hours rest after the long day and the disturbing missing time at the morgue. Too bad it wasn't going to happen. She had to meet Durant tonight, and needed to keep on her toes.

A knock startled a little scream out of her. The door opened before she could comment, and Taggert peeked around the edge. She went to reach for a towel and opened her mouth to blast him when she saw his downcast eyes and the slump to his shoulders.

"Taggert?" She quickly turned off the water and wrapped the towel around her. "Are you okay?" She stepped carefully forward, noticing the flinch around his eyes at her approach.

"Will you send me away?"

His question threw her. "What do you mean?"

"I'll take your punishment, but I don't want to leave." He slipped to the floor, moving toward her on all fours.

"What are you doing? Get up." She went to him, determined to jerk him to his feet if she had to.

"Please." He rested his forehead against her foot. "Please."

When he said it a second time, the plea in his voice made the back of her throat catch.

Raven captured his chin and forced his head up. Her lips were tight when she spoke. "Let's get one thing straight here. I don't condone what she did to you. I don't blame you for anything. I have no intention of sending you anywhere. Are we clear?" The look in his eyes made her uncomfortable, especially since she barely covered. "Why didn't you fight back? Tell Trisha no?"

"Have you ever seen large cats in the wild?"

Jackson's voice snapped her head up. She wanted to tell him to get the hell out of her bathroom, but she needed answers more. "No."

"They like to play with their prey. He can't shift and defend himself." He kept his face carefully blank. "It's a game for them, the chase and struggle make it more enjoyable."

Raven closed her eyes, unwilling to see the message in his eyes. "Rape."

"It's not rape if you're willing."

"Bullshit." Her eyes snapped opened, and she glared at Taggert. "The choice of death or sex is rape."

Taggert settled heavier against her. "Some of the women weren't bad. It was the ones who liked pain that were the worst."

Raven glanced away briefly, horrified by what they accepted so casually.

As if reading her thoughts, Jackson shook his head. "You're thinking like a human. We're not human." Jackson grabbed the doorknob, turning to go. "If you have any hope of trying to keep him, you have to stop thinking of us as human with an extra ability."

She took a deep breath to argue, but Jackson had already disappeared. She hated when someone left before the argument was over. Her hair was drying, and the bathroom was growing colder with the door open. She shivered.

Taggert wrapped his arms around her legs, his head nestled against her thigh. She felt very self-conscious to notice his face so close to the end of the towel, then cursed herself. Jesus, Trish almost raped him, and she was worried about clothes.

She touched his back then drew away. "Get rid of those clothes and take a shower." She didn't want that woman's scent on him.

When he slowly straightened, she helped him off with the shirt. "Give me the pants, too. I'll have them burned."

He blinked then complied without a word.

She averted her gaze, her eyes still seeing the marks on his flesh and it infuriated her. She wanted to find Trish and mark her in kind. She'd insist on healing him if her emotions weren't so wild. The last thing she wanted to do was hurt him more.

"Taggert." She waited for him to meet her gaze. "If anyone tries that again, kill them."

Not waiting for him to reply, she left the room. "Burn these." She tossed the clothes at Jackson. He took one look at her expression and complied.

Once alone, she chose her most conservative clothes. Dark, slim, and as unrevealing as possible. She picked up her gloves and carefully put them on, fiddling with them when the shower turned off. She straightened, unaware she'd been waiting for the sound until she heard it. Now that she had, she was nervous as hell and desperate for a reprieve. "I'll wait downstairs for you."

The coward that she was, she escaped to the kitchen to eat. She was too jittery to remain still for long. She didn't know if it was because her power refused to settle or if she sensed something would happen tonight.

She feared it would be the latter. Jeffrey Durant wanted something from her, had agreed to become her pack for a reason. Like it or not, she had a feeling she was about to find out.

Chapter Twenty-three

EVENING: 11 PM

*R*aven saw the strained smile on Durant's face as soon as she entered the club, and her nerves fluttered to life. The tiny lines around his mouth eased when he spotted her, and she barely resisted the need to twitch under his regard. She didn't know how to react to him after their last encounter.

He stood and sauntered toward her, exuding sexiness with a single-mindedness that drew attention to his body. It also drew the admiration of every female in the room and that of a few males as well.

It took more time than it should've to work her eyes up to his face. At his expression, she gulped, repressing a shiver of lust as she struggled to focus on the unease she sensed behind his smile. The large meal she consumed congealed in her stomach.

Something was wrong.

"Whatever you do, don't react."

Taggert nodded at her order, while Jackson, the barbaric caveman, just grunted.

She scanned the crowd again as unobtrusively as possible, noting that the place was packed with shifters and vampires. More so than usual.

Their presence prevented her from being able to use her gift. She couldn't risk it being traced back to her. She locked down, shutting everything out. What felt like more than half her senses died when the door clanked shut, leaving her much more vulnerable than she'd ever wanted to feel again.

Durant stepped in front of her, stopping only inches from her in a way that seemed to suck up all the air. "Is there something wrong with the club?" She couldn't think what else would cause him such concern.

"Raven." Durant enveloped her in a tight hug, and she resisted the urge to stiffen. She was his alpha. If she refused his touch, she'd only cause more trouble. Gritting her teeth, she inhaled his scent of leather, absorbed his warmth and clumsily, wrapped her arms around him in return. And surprised herself by actually leaning into his touch.

Under the lighting, his golden hair appeared streaked. When she continued to stare, she identified what nagged at her...the barely there stripes were identical to his animal's namesake. Instead of looking foolish, it boosted his charm and added a hell of a lot more wildness to his sex appeal.

He brushed at her shields, not demanding entrance, more like knocking.

Polite.

That was so not a good sign.

With severe misgivings, she lowered her shield a fraction. *Be careful. The guy you're going to meet is dangerous. He's heard stories of you and was sent to investigate.*

When he pulled away, Raven nodded. "What's this about, Durant?"

"Follow me, but please...just be careful."

When she would have pulled away, Durant captured her hand and slowly intertwined their fingers together. If he was in his animal form, his tail would be twitching. What could possibly make a seven hundred pound tiger nervous?

"Ah, you must be Raven." A man of medium stature, with brown hair and nondescript features, rose then indicated she should take a seat across from him.

She hesitated. "And you are?"

"You may call me Randolph." The tone was congenial, almost mockingly polite, but the cold, penetrating gleam in his eyes put

Raven on alert. It wasn't that he was hiding something, there was just nothing behind his gaze at all.

She carefully lowered herself, half-expecting to hear the slam of cage doors. Taggert and Jackson sat at the next table. Both appeared unable to remove their gaze from the mystery man. Curious, she glanced at Durant and saw the same lull in his expression, though he fought it.

She reached across the table and took Durant's hand. A sharp pinch like that of a spider bite stung her fingertips when Durant blinked. His expression cleared and color replaced the pallor of his face. "You okay?" Whatever held Taggert and Jackson broke as well.

Randolph stopped scanning the club and slowly swung his head toward her. "I must say, I'm impressed."

Raven tensed and reluctantly met his gaze. "About what?"

"By touching him, you were able to break my hold over them." The smile on his face looked stiff. "And you were affected not at all. Very interesting."

She sensed more than saw Jackson bristle, but Taggert's reaction captured her attention when he stiffened. When she followed the direction of his gaze, she saw why. "Jackie."

"Excuse me?"

Raven very deliberately turned her back on the she-bitch. Randolph had lost his smile. Though he didn't appear disturbed, the clipped edge to his question said he didn't like the way her focus had shifted away from him.

"A person in the club attacked one of mine earlier today. I issued a warning to her about the consequences of doing it again, but apparently not strong enough." Even before she finished speaking, a waiter dropped off a drink, setting it in front of Taggert with a nod in Jackie's direction.

Raven tightened her lips. One wrong move could spike Randolph's annoyance, but she couldn't leave the challenge unanswered, especially as it threatened Taggert. "Randolph, I'm sorry for the interruption, but would you mind waiting a moment while I settle this?"

As much as she wanted to march across the room, she remained motionless for his answer, her muscles brittle as she waited for his decree.

"By all means. You have me curious."

Some of the tension eased, although she didn't care for the spark of curiosity that entered his eyes as he studied her. Something about his lack of expression stirred a memory at the back of her mind. A horrible suspicion of Randolph's identity kicked her heartbeat into overdrive, but she could do nothing without proof. "Taggert. Please hand me that glass."

He did as told in an instant, hovering by her side.

From the slight widening of Jackie's eyes, she knew her suspicions were true. "Randolph, would you say you are an excellent huntsman?"

If her suspicions were true, he was the best. A true huntsman trained by the labs to track paranormals. No one knew his identity, as those who lived after meeting him remembered only what he wanted them to recall.

Amusement darkened his gaze as if sharing a joke between them. "Yes."

"Would you care to tell me what's in this drink?" She slid the glass across the table with the tips of her fingers. Jackie edged toward the door. "Durant, please make sure no one leaves."

He rose and signaled the bouncers at the doors.

Randolph leaned over the glass, careful not to touch anything. "Liquor. Orange juice. Grenadine." Then his brow furrowed. He inched closer and picked up the glass, his face pinched tight. "There's something else."

He lifted the drink to his lips.

Raven raised her hand. "I wouldn't."

"Oh?" He very deliberately set the glass back to the original spot.

Durant led a very reluctant Jackie toward them. "When Taggert came to me, he was heavily drugged."

"Impossible." Randolph spoke the words but something malevolent took shape behind his eyes.

"It slowed down his healing by days. He wasn't as alert, less aggressive than he should've been, and he was submissive to everyone." She didn't spare a glance at Jackie. Something told her not to divide her attention. "He built up a tolerance and went through withdrawals after he came into my care."

"Your little wolf isn't very strong. You could be mistaken." Randolph met her gaze squarely as if her future depended on her next words. No doubt it did.

"No." She recognized the signs of being drugged all too well. Deep foreboding about Randolph's true purpose for being there sank claws in her gut. He was there for her. If she hesitated or backed down now, they were all dead.

"Designer drugs. How am I to know you aren't the perpetrator?" He nodded his head to Jackie. "That you are not using me to get rid of your little pest?"

Jackie struggled out of Durant's hold and came to Randolph's side. "She did it. I caught her drugging him the night she took him from me. She claimed him to prevent herself from being found out."

He stiffened imperceptibly, all the hardness rushed back in his face. Jackie must have sensed the change as well for she stopped short of touching him.

A slow awareness of Randolph's true purpose dawned. He had come for more than an investigation. A dart of fear kindled in her chest, and Raven resisted the urge to attack. Energy swirled around her like an angry cloud, sinking into her skin a little at a time, as much as she dared take without notice.

"You didn't know about the drugs." It wasn't a question. The corners of his lips tightened, and she didn't think he would answer.

"No."

"You came about the murders." Instead of talking, he bowed his head and another disturbing suspicion rose. "And you think I killed them."

"No." He seemed as surprised as she was by the answer.

"Then why all the questions?"

"To gauge your intent now that you are in possession of one of the very few known tigers and managers of one of the three approved clubs on pack territory." While he said the words, he continued to stare at her with those disturbingly dead eyes.

"He's pack."

"And you would die for them?" It wasn't an idle question.

"Yes." She didn't hesitate, even though Durant appeared ready to protest.

"It's his club peddling drugs. That's a killing offense." He reached out, but didn't touch the glass, his fingers hovering over the condensation that had collected.

"Kill him and the real perpetrator will only switch to a different venue. They already tried to take him. They stole the life of his employee when she showed up instead." Now that Randolph was here, everything made sense. Someone wanted to run drugs through the club, and the only way they could get to the shifters was through an approved club like *Talons*. They dumped Cassie's body in the killer's hunting ground to cover their crime.

She ignored the pounding of her heart, ignored the way everyone near them stilled as if they could taste the menace in the air. Power built beneath her skin.

"How do you propose to catch this dealer?" An uncompromising, hard look came into Randolph's expression. "How did you even learn about it?"

"They're pack. Are you saying you don't know everything about the people you live around?" She dodged the question, but she knew that it only delayed the inevitable.

He gave a slight nod of his head, relaxing a little. "True."

She could tell he was disturbed not to have known about the drugs, that he had to have been told. Some of that anger burning below the surface showed in the way he shifted slightly.

"But how did you find out? Unless you tasted it in his blood."

She shivered at the demand for the truth. He wouldn't be pawned off. If she wanted her pack to live, she couldn't hide. "I claimed him by blood."

Jackie gasped, but Randolph only nodded. "But you recognized the effects of the drugs before then, didn't you?"

"Let's say I've seen the effects."

Randolph's hand stilled. "When?"

"The labs." She bit the words out between stiff lips, audible to only those nearest them. She hated being forced to admit the painful truth in front of so many.

A snort of laughter escaped Jackie, her posture loosened and that bitchy smirk came back to her face. "She lies."

"Are you lying?" Randolph asked the question, his gaze trained on Raven as if dissecting her.

Something about his stillness triggered a buried memory.

Raven couldn't respond, finally recognizing what was different about him. He wasn't a shifter or a vampire. The energy lines she used to gauge a person's threat level wavered around him, hiding him from her. It took more than just the magic to do that.

"You've been inside one as well." A snarl worked its way up her throat as her hackles rose. "You're enhanced. A damn soldier they engineered to protect the humans from us monsters."

Power surged, tangling lines of blue down her arms. The shield she wore parted, and what made her such a killer in the labs peeked out.

Raven's chair scraped as she shoved back from the table. She didn't have to look to know that her eyes had changed to vivid blue. "How does it feel to be a real monster amongst the monsters?"

"Jesus, Raven. Be quiet." Durant barely got the words out when Randolph's power lashed against her skin, searching for an opening.

Raven snatched the strands, yanked them closer and wove them into a ball. The golden energy was different than her normal blue. It was more volatile and ice cold, scoring her wherever it touched. Instead of fighting it, she absorbed it throughout her system.

A mistake. The instant the strange power touched her core, her blood felt like it was boiling. The animals inside roared, slashing at the cages to get out, but what scared her the most was that the strange creature surrounding her core gave a lazy stretch as if awakening.

Randolph's eyes widened and as quickly as the attack came, the spike died. The energy she'd siphoned fought her as she tried to expel it. The gold lines wrestled with her every step of the way until her body screamed for mercy. She couldn't get rid of it, the strands clinging to her body like a leech.

Desperate for relief, she yanked the golden ball away from the animals. She shoved the explosive energy into a cage, pouring her energy around the vault to stop the golden lines from bleeding into her system. Though the pain instantly eased enough for her to breathe again, a slight buzz warned her that it wouldn't be satisfied for long.

Ignoring the vague sickness that lingered, she licked her parched lips and studied Randolph for any nuance. "What are you?"

"No soldier. I never volunteered." The mask he hid behind cracked. Something dark danced in his eyes, something that haunted him. Memories of what they made them do. Then like a switch, everything shut down. "When the main lab was destroyed, they abandoned a few of the smaller ones, fearing they'd be attacked next. They went through emergency protocol."

"They killed everyone." Her lips were numb when she said the words. They might as well have said they killed everyone because of her.

"But not all of us died." There was a tightening around his jaw, like he'd revealed more than he wanted to share. He quickly changed the subject before she could foolishly probe for more answers. "What do you plan to do about the drugs?"

It was a truce of sorts. A silent, tentative agreement that he would let her and her pack live.

"Murder comes first. Someone has been taking and killing shifters. Possibly vampires as well. Until I can find the killer, I can't divide my focus." Refusing to investigate was a gamble, but as far as she knew, no one had yet been killed from the drugs.

"Agreed. Would you mind if I did some digging?"

She stifled a snort at the polite inquiry. "Would I be able to stop you?"

The smile he returned didn't boost her confidence. "No."

"The only lead I have on the drugs is Jackie." She avoided looking at anyone but Randolph. "The other person who had any information was murdered yesterday."

"I don't have to stand for this." Jackie twisted away from the table.

She took a few steps when Randolph gave a signal. She soon found herself blocked on all sides. The twit paled and quieted.

"She's been using the drugs to gain status. And if I would have to guess, she's too stupid to cover her tracks."

"So she's not selling it?" He nodded toward the glass.

Raven paused to think about it. "I think someone gives it to her to play around. She tested it and found she liked to pretend she's alpha." The idea had merit. "If I had to guess, I'd say her alpha is suspicious and wants her gone as well or else he'd be here to protect her from the warning I issued this afternoon."

A little grunt escaped the hunter across from her. "A drug like that could be used as a weapon by anyone, rogues searching for power, vampires, or even humans who want to put shifters in their place. The drugged shifters would be vulnerable, which would leave the pack vulnerable to attack."

"Agreed." None of the options were good. "Be forewarned, the drug's addicting, so whoever has had a taste will want more."

Randolph reached into his pocket, and Raven resisted the urge to put him out of commission. As if sensing her unease, he carefully lifted one hand. "I found this." He tossed an envelope stuffed full of paper across the table. "You might find it useful in your investigation."

He stood and gave a light bow. "It's truly been a pleasure."

She thought he might have been sarcastic, but the hardness in his eyes softened. It was the first time she could tell the color. Winter green. That's when she realized his power rested in his gaze. He must have realized what she'd guessed for he straightened abruptly.

"We'll meet again."

The promise sounded more like a threat.

Some people adapted to their new life as one of the paranormal, others fought it tooth and nail. Randolph liked the killing, liked the thrill. If they met up again, he would push her to see what she could do, test himself against her. She didn't think he'd kill her, she was too much of an anomaly to destroy without probing for answers, but that was a gamble she wasn't willing to bet her life on.

When Randolph walked to the door, people didn't seem to notice him even as they moved out of his way. One of his lackeys pulled an unrestrained Jackie from the club.

Raven didn't take a deep breath until after they left. Before she could even relax, Durant snatched her wrist and hauled her toward the back of the club, nearly pulling her off her feet as he did so.

Jackson followed, Taggert a step behind, pausing just long enough to pick up the gift Randolph had left at the table. And Raven realized it was a favor, one that he expected her to repay.

How the hell did she keep digging herself deeper into other people's problems? What happened to all the easy cases where everyone minded their own business and stayed out of hers?

"Wait here." Durant didn't even pause to see if the men would listen to his demand when he dragged her into his office and slammed the door in their faces.

"Raven!" Cassie rushed forward, only to stumble to a halt at Durant's growl. But that didn't stop her from talking. "Did you find him?"

Her informant. Something on her face must have given her away. Cassie stilled, not even breathing. "I believe so."

"Dead." Cassie's voice went flat, the animation in her eyes dimmed and bled black for a second as emotions stormed through her.

"I'm sorry. He was already gone by the time we arrived."

"Yeah. I think I already knew that." Cassie nodded, and some of her control returned.

Remarkable for one so young.

For being dead, she was quite vibrant, her skin a healthy pink, her mahogany hair shiny even in the dim light. Death agreed with her. Shifter blood had advanced the change by a couple of weeks.

Cassie grabbed her jacket, avoiding their gaze as she walked to the door. A light ginger spice clung to her. "I think I'll take a walk."

"Take the guys with you." She didn't know why she said it, but she didn't want Cassie alone, not with Randolph in the neighborhood. When the door closed, Raven watched it for a moment longer.

"She's fed. Your pack's safe." The carefully restrained voice made her tense. He was furious, his anger battering her shields.

He had no right. He'd invited her into his business, so he must have wanted her to handle it. She's the one who should be angry. Now a hired killer, a trained hunter, knew about her. All her work to keep below the radar was fading fast. Soon, others would know as well.

"What the devil did you think you were doing?" Durant swung her around, the angry tiger right beneath the surface and ready to fight.

"You invited me. What was I supposed to do? Stand there and let him kill one or both of us?"

"I can take care of my own business." A hint of fangs peaked out from his mouth.

"Then why the hell did you call for me?" His eyes turned golden, his animal shredding his humanity.

Raven snapped her mouth shut, her fingers itching to reach for power and defend herself.

A growl sounded around the room. "How the fuck is the pack supposed to protect you if you throw yourself into danger?"

"What do you mean? It's my job to protect you." The volume increased with her frustration until it matched his. Every time she thought she knew what to expect from pack, they changed the damn rules.

"You protect us by ruling, not by endangering yourself." He calmed a little at her confusion. "The pack is there for your protection. If anything happened to you, everything would fall apart. Some other alpha could step in and take over.

"You have to make alliances, plans to have your pack absorbed by another. Unless they have some talent that makes them useful, your pack members will either be killed outright or revert to rogue status. That's why pack wars are a bloody, desperate fight to the death."

The dire future he painted didn't look so rosy. "Why would shifters set up the ruling structure that way?"

"To keep the pack strong. Weed out the weak."

"An alpha should be strong enough to protect everyone."

"You're only as strong as the weakest link in your group." Anger left Durant, and he gentled his voice, his comforting leather scent twirling about her. "We don't follow human rules for a reason. We're not always human; most of us enjoy the animal side of our life and revel in the lax laws."

To be able to rule the pack, she'd have to understand both shifters and their laws more. She thought she'd known what to expect but obviously, she'd underestimated what needed to be done to keep her pack alive.

"What do I need to know?"

"Trust us. Allow us to guide you. Don't push us away." He stepped closer, clasping her hand in his. "I—"

"Raven." The door flew open, and Taggert entered. "Dominic's on the phone. The police found another body and are asking for you."

Chapter Twenty-four

DAY 7: AFTER MIDNIGHT

*S*cotts' dour face peered at her over the police line. She plucked at the bright tape and raised a brow at the necessity. They were three miles into the forest with no one around but authorized personal.

"One body is torn apart and scattered through the woods like breadcrumbs." Scotts ran a hand over his head and blew out a heavy sigh. "We marked the area off. Easier to find and collect all the evidence."

The tape wound around a dozen trees, the space at least thirty feet across. There had to be only shreds remaining of that poor soul.

"The other body is for you."

"Me?" Raven almost got whiplash turning to look at him and nearly missed a step.

Those hard cop eyes of his watched her for any nuance, searching for answers...or guilt?

She very deliberately relaxed her posture. Scotts' stiff body language and all-cop attitude scraped her skin the wrong way. Something was very wrong. "Explain."

"This." He pulled out a plastic bag. Inside rested a letter, the surface half-matted with blood. One word jumped out at her. Her name. The letter was addressed to her specifically.

"The note was found pinned to the poor bastard's back with an eight inch blade." He hesitated before handing over the letter. "He'd been alive when it was done."

Evil saturated the note; she could feel it reaching for her, ready to drag her into hell. Dread clamped hard on her chest. The killers knew her name. Since she worked hard to keep her life private, it had to be those damned newspapers. "Body first, then the letter. Show me."

"Come."

The breeze sliced through her, stealing her breath. Floodlights barely fought back the invading darkness. People milled about, their sideways glances slamming into her back. She registered their looks then dismissed them. Though disturbing, they weren't the ones who sent that slice of unease deeper. There was a presence that lurked in the air that seemed to be stalking her.

The body lay sprawled face down under a pool of lights three yards away. Large. Male. Mid-thirties. Malnourished if the clear lines of his ribs were any indication. And not an inch of flesh remained free of mutilation. The police left the body untouched for her.

Raven drew up short. "Why do I have a feeling you've already decided my fate, and I'm being marched to the gallows?"

"Look at him. Read the letter." The gruff voice held no warmth.

The chill in the air wrapped around her skin and burrowed into her flesh. The branches smashed ominously against one another, the sinister sound like a clank of a skeleton as it dragged itself toward her. That haunting image of her past rose so vividly, she couldn't force herself closer, couldn't bear to see him try to speak, begging her for help.

Surprisingly, it was the stench of congealed blood clogging her nose that reassured her. With the vile taste coating her mouth, she pushed forward and breathed lightly in hopes of keeping her lunch. She needed to see everything. She didn't have time to be weak.

The pressure in her chest eased. The analytical part of her mind shoved aside the horror scattered across the forest floor. She had a killer to find. "What happened to the flesh?"

"They skinned part of the body, then cauterized it with a blow torch to prevented him from healing too quick." Scotts looked at the darkness as if unable to bear gazing at the ravaged body.

Raven tightened her lips and crouched, unwilling to miss anything because of her squeamishness. Pus and blood continued to ooze in spots while others were crusted over. Some areas appeared waxy. She shooed away the flies, noticing the recently hatched larvae busily eating away the evidence. "A shifter. You can tell by the new skin growth. He tried to heal." She shuffled closer, noticing the fingers. "Claws or nails were torn out of his body."

She picked up a stick and lifted his hand closer. Twigs and leaves stuck to his fingertips. She couldn't imagine the pain. "He was crawling toward something when they stuck the knife in his back." She glanced up to see Scotts looking at her. "He was heading north. Away from the road. Away from freedom." Toward the shredded body. Only one thing would make a shifter do that. Pack.

Without a word, Scotts stuck the letter in her face. The comforting tobacco scent she associated with him was sharper, more blunt, and anything but peaceful. She obediently read, knowing she wasn't going to like what she found. *"Let's play a game of cat and mouse. We skinned the kitty, see if you can catch us before we capture and devour your little mouse. We look forward to the chase."*

A tremor shook her hand, and she shoved the letter away, wishing she could push it out of her mind as well.

She cleared her throat. "They must have grabbed a weak shifter. If we don't catch the killer, they'll do this again." She nodded to the corpse. "From the pronouns in the note, there's more than one killer."

"And they also have your name."

She couldn't take her gaze off the body, the crushed bones and the collapsed side of his face that resembled nothing more than raw beef. His determination haunted the air as did his despair when he realized it was too late.

She looked north, the direction he'd been dragging himself, her eyes drawn to the scattered pieces of what remained of the other body. "If you can find his identity, you should be able to find out the name of his companion. My guess would be female. They pinned him, then forced him to watch as they tore her apart. Despite what they'd already done to him, he was trying to go back for her."

Scotts bent closer, his warm breath doing little to thaw her soul. "How did they know you were on the case?"

"Out of all of this, that's your question?" Raven pointedly locked gazes with half a dozen officers then raised a brow at Scotts, unable to keep the sneakiness out of her voice. "It's not exactly a secret."

"You're off the case." Scotts stood, stiff strides swiftly carrying him away from her.

"You can't do that." Raven bolted to her feet, struggling to calm the wild surge of emotions ricocheting through her skull.

Hostile energy poured off Scotts when he whirled, the power of it bombarding her defenses. "This is an official police investigation. If you stick your nose or any part of your body in my case, I'll have you arrested."

"What? Don't you even want me to see the second body before treating me like the suspect?"

Scotts stalked back to her, stopping when he was in her face. "The killer knows you. He made this personal. That means you're off the case. It's protocol."

"Bullshit. We both know it's at your discretion. How does taking me off the case help?" Then something clicked, something so horrible she pulled away from him even as she thought it. "You're not taking me off the case to help; you're taking me off the case because you think I'm connected somehow." Disbelief covered the well of pain that threatened to sink her. The truth glittered in his eyes, the way he flinched under her stare.

"Not you, but you've been hanging out with the wrong people. They—"

"You mean paranormals?" Disgust tightened her face. "When did you become so prejudiced?"

Scotts appeared tired all of the sudden, rubbing a hand down his face. "Your wolf, Jackson, has been asking questions."

Her gaze flew to the two men on the other side of the police tape. Jackson straightened abruptly under her regard, but he didn't turn away from the accusations. Damn him. "Fine." She gritted her teeth, keeping her gaze on the traitor. "But you're making the wrong decision. Whatever may or may not have been done was not brought on by my people."

"Raven."

She walked away, ignoring the rest of his speech. He didn't want her on the team, fine, but she didn't have to stay to be preached at either.

"Let's go."

They wisely followed without a sound of protest as she marched toward the car. Pissed at being steamrolled out of the investigation, she wrenched opened the door. But instead of getting inside where her anger would fester in the metal cage, she rested her arms across the top. With her volatile state, she couldn't risk being in the cramped space with two shifters.

She met Jackson's shuttered gaze.

The bastard knew.

"You went against my orders. I told you not to interfere."

Jackson lifted his chin, a mutinous look to his face. "Wolves investigate all shifter deaths."

A growl worked its way up her throat. "Investigating is fine. My problem was you went to them against my orders. You had no right to involve them in my case."

"We take care of our own."

"Pack mentality. It'll get you killed."

"It keeps our people safe."

"Tell that to the two people tortured and scattered over the ground."

"That's not fair." Jackson puffed up his chest, growing a couple of inches as he straightened.

"Instead of telling me to my face, you let me discover your perfidy by someone I work with, and was dressed down for it in public. Now, not only are the killers issuing me their own challenge to the hunt, but your questions get me kicked off the case."

"That was not my intent." His jaw bunched as if forcing himself to speak. "Did you ever think the cops are playing you? Using you as bait?"

"These are cops. It's illegal without my consent."

"Unless they believe that you had something to do with it."

She and Scotts had worked together for years. They were a team. Yet she couldn't refute Jackson's comment since the same thought had crossed her mind.

Regret darkened Jackson's expression, surprising her with his sincerity, but he didn't take anything back.

He could be right. But if Jackson thought she had something to do with the murders, he would've set the shifters on her without giving the police a chance to take her into custody. She needed to know if she could count on him. "Either you believe I'm capable of solving this investigation or you don't. Do your loyalties lie with the wolves or me?"

Jackson flinched, then scanned the tree line with hard eyes. He looked so torn, she almost felt bad for putting him on the spot. "Maybe it would be best if I met you back at the house."

Part of her shattered at his non-answer. Despite the hint of confusion in his voice, she bit her lip against offering him comfort. "Maybe."

He stayed still for a moment, waiting for her to relent. The silence felt heavy, and she battled herself. He nodded and turned away.

"Raven—"

"Get in the car." She wondered if Taggert would abandon her as well. A pit opened at her feet, ready to swallow her and suck her back to the lonely world that existed before they bounded into her life and shook up her staid existence.

Taggert gazed at her solemnly then obeyed. She hesitated, watching Jackson disappear in the darkness, and a jagged pang of regret bit her hard on the ass. How could she ask him to choose between his wolves, and a woman he barely knew?

Once behind the wheel, she turned over the engine and took off in a spray of dirt and gravel.

"Jackson was trying to protect you."

It took Taggert five minutes to speak up and defend Jackson. Longer than she'd thought it would take.

"How? By getting me kicked off the case? Now, instead of being able to use the police resources, I'll be out there on my own."

Taggert's large eyes landed on hers, a hesitance in them, yet he forged ahead. "I'm sure he didn't plan for you to get fired."

"He meddled."

"He did what he thought was right."

With that, she couldn't argue. She had to respect a person who thought they were doing what was right, though that didn't mean she had to like it.

Lights filled the mirrors.

Blinded by the dickheads who were following too close, she swore and slowed down so they would pass. When she hit forty and they slowed with her, unease had her tightening her grip on the wheel.

"Taggert, buckle your seatbelt." Shifters didn't like to be confined and since they were the devil to kill, they rarely wore seatbelts. Most walked away from accidents that would kill humans.

The engine in the big, boxy Dodge behind them roared in her ears. The solid wall of metal edged closer to her bumper. She hammered on the gas and increased the distance between them. But only for a heartbeat. They gunned the engine, and the lights made it impossible for her to see the road until they were too damn close.

Their bumper connected with hers, slamming her and Taggert forward. The seatbelt nearly strangled her. The car fishtailed, and she wrestled to keep it on the road. She managed to straighten them out, but the Dodge was relentless and gaining ground fast.

"Taggert. Call Jackson. Tell him our location." She ignored his nod, glad he did as told without arguing. His composure eased the ribbon of fear edging into her mind.

The lights grew blinding. She braced herself for another hit. The car threw her forward. The seatbelt cinched tight in a bear hug that threated to steal her breath. She controlled the skid and started to pull out of it when the car hit them again, smashing the fender and sending them spinning across the road.

She muscled her vehicle away from the ditch, but it had a mind of its own and veered to the opposite side of the road like a demented road runner caught in traffic. Taggert braced himself, and she gave one last wrench on the wheel so that her side of the car would take the brunt of the collision. She had a better chance at surviving the accident, while Taggert had the strength to protect himself and run if necessary.

Taggert cursed into the phone. The tires caught the gravel at the side of the road and spun them in a tight circle, then abruptly gripped the edge of the tar. The car twisted up on two wheels. She thought she managed to keep them out of the ditch, when the second vehicle tapped the rear edge of her car.

The car flipped once. Metal crunched. Glass shattered. A tree appeared out of nowhere, and the driver's side door took the brunt of the impact.

Metal bit into her body, tore her skin in one agony-inducing moment. Bark flew in the car, abrading her cheek. Then everything grew eerily quiet. Every inch of her was battered.

"Taggert?" When she twisted around to reach him, the car refused to release its hold on her body. Warm blood gushed down her side. Pain stole her breath for a precious few seconds.

"If you can hear me, get out and run. Don't let them take you." It was all in that damned letter, but she let her pride get in her way of seeing the danger to her people.

"Raven?" His voice sounded groggy. He ripped away his seatbelt, then leaned over to work on hers. Blood trickled down from a nasty gash on his forehead.

She tried to reach up, but realized she could only lift one arm. She grabbed his hand and shook him. "Leave. Run." The movement exhausted her. She coughed and winced when blood filled her mouth.

Car doors slammed, and her eyes widened. "Run."

Taggert disappeared from view. Relief made her lightheaded. Then she heard it. Fighting. Fists meeting flesh. Men swearing. Then gunshots.

"Taggert!" Damned fool. She tried to loosen the seatbelt but to no effect. Impotent rage tore a growl from her throat. She struggled to pull away from the metal's embrace. Flesh tore and warmth spread over her left side as her blood soaked through her clothes. Her body slumped over the console when she broke free from the metal talons.

"Stab her with the fucking needle and let's go."

She fumbled with the seatbelt. Her chest wheezed as each breath see-sawed out of her lungs, stealing the very air she fought to keep.

A flashlight's beam blinded her. A prick pinched her upper arm, and she struggled to keep out of reach. Too late. Her skin burned. Fire raced through her muscles.

A trunk slammed. Doors closed. An engine screamed, then faded into silence as she struggled to keep her eyes open and focus. North. They were circling the damn forest.

She fumbled with the stack of napkins on the floor and tried to stanch the flow of blood. It did no good, instantly soaking the meager bandage. The blood felt hot against her cold hands. Her blood-coated fingers grew numb.

"Raven!" Warm fingers touched her face.

It took her eyes a moment to adjust and recognize Jackson's face. The stark fear made her want to reassure him, but she couldn't find words.

She swallowed twice before she could speak. "They took Taggert." Her lips and tongue felt clumsy.

The seatbelt released and agony ripped away the lovely haze. Jackson's soothing voice faded. All she heard was her heartbeat as it slowed. Concern for Taggert and Jackson were the only things on her mind when her heart stopped.

Chapter Twenty-five

PREDAWN

*H*er back bowed as energy arced through her. Her heart thumped to life, and she gasped for air. Power sputtered and died as abruptly as it came. As she fell back on the bed, pain streaked through her body. Years of practice allowed her to work past it instead of succumbing to the waiting darkness. She muddled through her thoughts, desperately trying to piece together what happened.

Besides the fact that she'd died.

Again.

She pried open her eyes, dreading what she'd find, only to relax when she saw a normal room with windows and not the neglected kennels that were used in the labs. When the subtle scent of males reached her, some of the anxiety pounding away at the inside of her skull eased a fraction.

"Raven?"

She turned toward the deep, rumbled sound of her name. Whiskey brown eyes met hers. Recognition hovered at the back of her mind, something hauntingly familiar that lingered frustratingly out of reach. Smells of cut grass and fresh air swamped her senses. From him. The tanned face, thick brown hair and ruggedly handsome face gazed back, unblinking.

The intensity of his stare should've sent her running. Not from him though. She wanted to stretch and luxuriate at the heat building through her. The attraction should've scared her shitless, but it only felt right.

Or almost right. Something was missing. Something she was supposed to remember. Consuming large amounts of energy had a way of sucking away her memories.

Pain stabbed into her skull as she fought to reclaim the missing seconds. A whimper climbed out of her throat, and she pushed the heel of her hands into her eyes to relieve the pressure.

"You're trying too hard to remember." At Rylan's voice, she dropped her arms and some of the blackness clouding her mind funneled away.

"What the hell happened?" She struggled to sit, only to fall helplessly back onto the bed. Her body curled into itself as pain riddled every inch of her. It took an embarrassingly long time to get her breath back to speak. "Who ran me over?"

She meant it in jest, but silence greeted her. When she could crack open her eyes again, Rylan sat at the edge of the bed with a stoic expression that sent a shaft of alarm straight through her heart.

His dark hair fell over his forehead in unusual disarray. The slow tick in his jaw betrayed his emotions. "We don't know yet."

"Crap." Her throat clamped tight. The smell of gasoline and blood nearly gagged her. Fragmented pictures bombarded her.

Bright lights.

Shattering glass and the sickening crunch of metal.

Gunshots.

"Taggert!" She struggled to sit again, clenching her teeth against the fresh wave of agony and all-consuming rage. "They took him."

Jackson took pity on her and cradled her against his broad chest. She grabbed his wrist, his touch the only thing keeping her sane. Inviting heat poured from him, wrapping around her chilled flesh. She leaned heavily on him. It was either that or keel over.

"They headed north. If we leave now, we can track them." She swung her legs over the bed, ignoring the men's protests and the way the floor dipped under her feet.

"Dominic and London are tracking them. There is no trail."

"Don't say that. I can find one." She tried to shrug Jackson off, but his hold didn't budge. She shook her head, amazed that she'd found the infuriating male attractive for even a second. The comfort she drew from him changed subtly, the heat grew overwhelming and left her vaguely nauseous.

"You're not ready." Rylan kept his voice even and reasonable and it shot her irritation level higher.

"He was under my protection, and I let him get taken."

"You didn't let them do anything. You died trying to keep him safe."

"A fat lot of good that did. Tell that to Taggert when they hunt him down like some prize." Her speech left her exhausted, her side throbbed, and something inside her shoulder crunched when she moved. She pressed her lips together against the pain. She probed the area, only to be blocked by a thick wad of bandages.

"They'll wait for you. You said it yourself. They want you to hunt them."

"How long was I out?" She ignored Jackson and yanked the bandage obstructing her movement, wincing when a stubborn piece of tape refused to budge, and ripped off a layer of skin with it. She had to get back out there.

"The accident happened last night. Only a few hours ago."

Her head snapped up in time to watch as a rim of black slowly darkened the edges of Rylan's blue eyes. "You were dead one second and alive the next. No coma. No rest. You need time to heal. Your body went through a severe trauma, not to mention death. It has to have time to adjust."

"So that's why I feel like shit." She shook her head and gritted her teeth as she ripped off another bandage. Sweat beaded her hairline when the small action exhausted her.

"You won't do him any good when you can't even stand on your feet," Jackson chastised.

He grabbed her hand, stopping her from ripping off the thick cotton wrapped around her torso where the metal had bit into her ribs and side. The wound felt raw and exposed. She didn't struggle, unwilling to lose such a simple match and prove their point.

"I can't protect him from here. What good am I as an alpha if I can't keep my pack safe?"

"Protection was my job. I'm an enforcer, but I let my pride get in the way." Jackson refused to meet her gaze. He probably even believed that bullshit. "I should've been with you. If I had, none of this would've happen."

That wasn't right, but she found it hard to concentrate. She wiped her forehead with the back of her hand, cursing the way her muscles trembled. "If you were with us, they would've taken you, too."

Heat continued to pour into her, each injury stung then burned like hot oil was being poured over them. Her body no longer felt her own, and she had no idea how to appease the demands to make the pain go away. She probed the energy at her core and encountered a vast blackness of nothingness, so cold that she shivered. "Something's wrong."

"Step back." Rylan gestured Jackson away.

She'd forgotten he was holding her hand until he released her, leaving her cold, trembling and so alone it hurt to swallow.

"They injected me with something." Her parched throat made speaking difficult.

Rylan lips tightened. "You died shortly after the accident. It would've stopped the progress of any drug. Now that you're awake, your blood's pumping, speeding whatever they injected you with through your system. The only blessing is some of the drug should've broken down when you were not...living."

"Why drug me but take Taggert?" She rubbed her forehead when she found that the little bit of backup power she carried in her bones was gone like everything else, leaving her with nothing to burn away the poison. She couldn't risk sucking in energy from the house to heal, not if she couldn't control it. "They left before I died, so they had the opportunity."

To her surprise, Jackson spoke. "They didn't know you would die. They injected you with something to give them a head start. They expected a hunt."

Raven inhaled slowly. She'd be fine. She just had to wait it out. Then a horrible thought struck her, destroying the tiny foothold of comfort she scraped out. "That means I know the killers."

"They knew you were on the case," Rylan agreed. "It's a logical assumption that you'd be at the crime scene. They were probably waiting for you."

His reasoning did little to calm her building panic.

Her skin grew warm again, itching as the animals at her core roused.

Then she had the awful, sinking realization that she knew what they'd given her.

The symptoms fit.

If right, she'd have a lot more to worry about than just her injuries. "They injected me with a serum to jumpstart a shift. The animals are waking and want out. And I have no power left to hold them back."

She resisted the urge to scratch. She'd seen that reaction before...in the infected. Right before they died by scratching the skin and flesh from their bones.

Rylan swore, but Jackson narrowed his eyes as if dissecting her statement. "Shifting is either active or dormant. You either can shift or you can't. You don't know until you hit puberty."

"Even if you weren't born a shifter?" No one spoke. So not reassuring. She risked a glance up at him, uncertain how her beasts would react to seeing him in her territory.

"I don't believe they meant to kill me with the serum." Not again, she wanted to say. "I think someone grew suspicious, wanted to know what I am. If I'm human, I would pass an uncomfortable night. If I'm a shifter, my animal would gain dominance." She met their gazes, real fear stealing her breath. Shifting was one thing she didn't know if she could heal from. She always understood if she tried to shift, it would killer her permanently.

Jackson took a step toward her, and an animal in the darkness charged forward, slashing out with a claw. Each swipe tore her insides raw. She bent double at the agony, unable to stifle her whimper. "Don't. Your nearness is making it worse."

Jackson thankfully paused, then shook his head. "A full shifter should have a calming effect."

"You're forgetting she's an alpha. Her beast will want to fight for dominance." Rylan sounded grim. "She can't transition. She's infected with more than one strain of animal. If she shifts, we can't predict what will happen to the other animals."

She waited for the denial or derision, but Jackson appeared unconvinced.

"The closer contact to a dominant shifter, the calmer her animals." Jackson took one arrogant look at her and stepped closer.

"Don't." She glared at him from where she was sitting at the side of the bed, unable to find words as she reacted to his nearness with a need to both crawl closer to take what she wanted from his body, and conversely to rip out his throat for daring to approach her.

She fisted her hands, pressing them hard against the mattress. Her nails throbbed, the skin of her fingertips tight as if ready to split. Then she forgot everything, nearly swallowing her tongue when he stripped off his shirt. "Wha-at are you doing?"

"I can't change into a wolf, but the scent and touch should help." He slowly advanced, and she gulped.

Heat burned along her veins. Her body felt too small. She stretched, straightening her spine and her joints popped. She tried to settle inside herself, but her bones didn't seem to fit under her skin anymore. Despite the fear of the transition, her injuries slowly mended as the animals rose to the surface.

"You're making it worse."

In answer, the big doofus dropped the shirt he held. The urge to tear into him ignited. Her fingers curled into her palms, her nails gouged flesh, and drew blood. The rich scent of it caused her skin to prickle painfully, and her teeth ached. She probed her gums with her tongue, wincing at the sensitivity.

This couldn't be happening. A roar filled her head. Her center grew restless and shadows paced, checking the perimeter for weakness. As her control slipped further, those cages wavered. The temptation to let go danced seductively in her mind.

Not her thought.

One of the shadows detached from the group and trotted closer to the edge of where she confined them and laid down to wait.

A wolf.

For the first time, one of the animals in the menagerie became very real. Her senses sharpened. Scents became overwhelming, sounds made her ears ache. She could almost taste the air. Jackson's smell captivated her the most. Wonder washed away some of the pain, some of the worry. She didn't know if she should be thrilled or horrified. Did that mean she had more control over them or that they were closer to breaking free?

She couldn't afford to find out. Bolting upright, she scrambled to the bottom of the bed. She dropped to the floor, biting off a scream of pain when she jarred her injuries. Panting for air, she stumbled to her feet and headed toward the door.

As the distance from Jackson grew, the energy in the house woke and crackled at her touch, soaking into her bones in one deluge. All thoughts of animals retreated. She doubled over as her muscles convulsed. Her insides felt shredded, but it wasn't the animals ripping into her this time. Liquid heat burned along her skin, cauterizing the wounds in one vomit inducing second.

As if on the fritz, the overwhelming wave of power drained as suddenly as it came. She landed on her hands and knees hard enough for them to sting in protest. Air was a little harder to come by, her lungs taking a full minute to remember how to work.

The accelerated healing was worse than the injuries themselves. The brutal agony took its sweet time to fade. She wobbled, debating the wisdom of pushing herself upright when a pair of shoes came into view.

"Your injuries are almost healed." Rylan scanned her from head to toe again, as if to check over her injuries...or lack of them. "That type of rapid regeneration can have serious, long-term side effects."

She tipped her head back and met Rylan's concerned gaze. They both knew that this couldn't be a good sign. Part of her was relieved that her natural born power conquered the shifter DNA.

It meant those bastards didn't get what they wanted.

Bits of power continued to roll back to her core, much too slowly for her liking, securely locking the cages and keeping the beasts at bay. For now at least. She was close to burning out. The lockbox with the golden power was half the size, as if the power had faded when she died. Or maybe her body had consumed that energy, causing her to wake early without proper healing.

Rylan reached out to help her stand, but she shook her head, terrified to touch him after so much power had swept through her. It took another minute to get her feet under her.

"We have to get Taggert." She didn't need to tell him that they had to rescue him before her symptoms became worse. "I received a packet that should help us. Do you have it?" At his blank expression, she swore. "Please tell me you had the car towed back here."

"It's in the garage."

She took a staggering step when Rylan blocked her. "Let me get it. You need to rest."

"I need to stay busy. I'll grab the papers and meet you in the study." The last thing she needed was time to think about what could be happening to Taggert while she sat on her ass and did nothing.

Jackson's total lack of response to everything put her on edge. He lingered at her back, but she refused to face him, afraid of what she'd find in his eyes. That she had almost shifted scared the bejeezus out of her. She couldn't even imagine what he thought, and she escaped to the garage like a coward.

The envelope had lodged beneath the driver's seat. She wrestled with the package until the car finally gave up its hold. She gazed at the twisted wreckage that resembled a ball of steel. The left side of her body felt heavy, the not quite phantom ache throbbing in memory of the impact.

Blood coated the driver's seat. Glass glittered like diamonds under the light. She'd managed to maneuver the car to take the brunt of the impact. Taggert should've been able to walk away. Why the hell didn't he run when he had the chance?

The envelope crumpled in her grip, and she retreated to the study. He had to be alive, or she'd never forgive herself.

Instead of going to the desk, she sat in front of the coffee table and spilled the contents over the surface. Missing person's reports. Police reports. Hospital reports. Newspaper clippings. All within a fifty mile radius. There had to be forty people here. How could so many go missing and no one notice?

And none of them had ever returned. She wouldn't allow Taggert to be one of the statistics.

Chapter Twenty-six

LATE AFTERNOON

$\mathcal{V}$oices roused her from the dreams that stalked her. Dreams that evaporated without a memory, yet left a lingering unease that stuck with her after she woke. Even with her eyes closed, light slashed through the bay windows with blinding force.

She probed her wounds with her mind. Healed except for the deep tissue bruises that dotted her body like a checkerboard. They hurt like a bitch, but she was functional.

She reached for her core to test her strength only to find the energy dangerously close to empty, every lick of it tied up in healing. Gold flared around the edges of the lockbox holding Randolph's power.

Like roots, bits broke through and wrapped around the cage, grafting to her flesh, and spilling darkness through her system. She carefully peeled off one tentacle and shoved it back into the vault with the rest. It surrendered readily, but took its pound of flesh with it. A ribbon of darkness remained behind like a scar, leaving behind a lash of pain. Only half a dozen more to go.

The process only took seconds but left her exhausted. Though secure for now, the box left a hollow pit where it burned and sputtered in her gut. She had to find a way to rid her system of the power before it spread further. That meant using it. And she couldn't use it until she got Taggert back for fear that it would put her out of commission. Too bad there were no antibiotics to take for something like that.

She opened her eyes to see the files were gone. In their place, she spied yesterday's paper tucked under a plate of sandwiches. London must have put it there for her to see. The headlines screamed at her: *Dissent On The Police Force; Killer Gets Away While They Argue.*

"Where did she get this file?" She recognized Dominic's commanding voice, saw him standing behind the desk, palms flat as he leaned over and scanned the papers scattered across the surface.

"The guy at the club." Jackson rubbed the back of his head as if recalling the name hurt, which wouldn't surprise her. Deep lines dug grooves into his face, his thick brown hair stood on end in clumps, and his clothes were wrinkled as if he'd slept in them. He looked like shit. "Randolph something. I don't think he was a shifter, but there was something about him that warned everyone to keep their distance."

London slowly stood, his posture ramrod straight, his thick brows drawing down into a straight line. "Randolph?"

A deep chill settled in her bones at the mention of his name. She refused to allow any of her people near that man. She gingerly sat, her body struggling to remember how lungs should work.

"If he's after her, he'll be more trouble than we can handle." The rumble of London's words caused Dominic to shift his attention away from the scattered reports, but it was the flash of unrestrained fear she glimpsed in London that grabbed Raven by the throat. Even in the labs, nothing penetrated the thick shields he had erected. Until now.

"What do you know?" The vicious growl of Dominic's words jerked Raven's head up. The deep-seated rage that hovered in his voice brought home why he was the leader of the group. "Who's Randolph?"

Though he directed the question at the others, Raven answered, knowing that there was no way to explain it away. "He's the fabled killer from the labs rumored to have hunted down our own kind for sport and bring them in for testing."

"Damn it, Raven, you just can't do things the easy way, can you?" He ran a hand through his thick hair, his resigned expression making him look older than he had a few minutes ago.

"He was after bigger fish than me." She cut Dominic off when he would've said more. Randolph wouldn't be pleased that others were aware of his existence. The less everyone knew, the safer they'd be.

"But now he knows about you."

Score one point for London.

She met his hard stare with one of her own. "He already knew about me because of my claim on Durant. He came to the club to assess and possibly kill me if I happened to be a big enough threat."

She resisted the urge to rub the ache in her ribs that she got by just talking. She couldn't let them know how weak she remained, or they'd lock her up and prevent her from doing what needed to be done.

"You're still alive." London scanned her body from head to toe, looking at her like she was a ghost. His total disbelief made her want to pat herself down to make sure that she was solid. "Randolph never fails a mission."

"He was informed that I was a threat. I explained otherwise." She nodded to the papers. "He gave me those when I told him I was hunting the real killers."

Jackson neared and she hastily stood before he could get close. Though she ached for his touch, she was afraid of what it would do to both of them.

"I gave him something else to focus on other than me." Raven sat in the chair across from the desk, not only to see those papers but prevent herself from sprawling on the floor.

Jackson refused to retreat, but refrained from touching her. Without a word, he handed her a sandwich. She eyed the food, then ate without tasting, more out of need than any hunger. Her mind churned as she methodically chewed. There had to be a way to save Taggert without risking anyone else.

"Maybe you'd better explain what the hell you stepped into on this case." Dominic sat at the desk, his voice a command, not a request.

"You and the group leave by the end of the week. I've been trying to keep you out of my cases for this reason. Leave it be."

"Like hell." Dominic slammed his fist on the desk.

The vehemence response took her aback. He ensured everyone's safety in the group, evaluated the risks and decided what cases to take. His actions now didn't make sense. She wasn't one of his, not really.

"Don't be foolish," she chided, hoping he'd see things her way. She would not put them at risk.

A vein throbbed along his neck. "It was your decision to bring him into the pack. We don't leave one of our own behind."

"I recognize some of these shifters." Dina's soft voice broke through the argument, and Dominic's confusing comment about pack.

"What?"

Dina didn't lift her attention from the pictures. "Three of them were part of my Recovery Group."

Her words confused Raven more. "What group?"

Raven had pulled people out of the rubble when the labs were destroyed, doubling back to ensure that the guards wouldn't be able to track them, but she didn't recall any such recovery group after everyone scattered.

Dina's normally soft, doe eyes were hard when she glanced up. "Some of the shifters released from the labs weren't ready to be set free into society. I created a group to help them adjust to civilization."

Hurt flickered through Raven at being excluded. Though she wasn't a true shifter, she was desperately jealous of the pack Dina had created. After she'd destroyed the lab, she'd suffered severe burnout, her powers flickering on and off unchecked. Afraid that she'd actually hurt people if she lingered, she'd put all her concentration into pulling out every bit of technology from in the labs. People needed that money and those files to make a clean break.

She hadn't even realized they needed help in other areas as well.

Dina shook her head as if to deny her thoughts. "You had other things on your mind. You did enough by rescuing us all. I saw the toll it had on you." She touched the papers on the desk. "You brought us together, you made us a pack. These people didn't have anyone. Some of them were born behind those bars. They didn't know how to handle outside people or wide open spaces. I created a network where they could rely on each other to survive."

One word slammed into her mind.

Pack.

They considered her pack.

After years of always being on the fringes, afraid to get too close, hearing that they considered her one of them sent turmoil swirling.

"And as pack, we don't leave anyone behind." Dominic nodded to the desk. "Explain what this means. Something flickered in your eyes when you viewed the pictures."

Air in the room became thin. She couldn't allow them to stay. She couldn't allow anyone to hurt them. Without them, she had nothing.

Jackson's palm covered her shoulder. She jumped, tried to jerk away, only to have his grip tighten.

"Breathe."

The word was soft enough only she heard it. Fresh air that smelled of Jackson and wolf filled her lungs.

The phone rang, but no one moved, waiting for her to spill what she knew. The answering machine picked up.

A man nervously cleared his throat. "Uhm, Raven? I know you're not on the case anymore, but there's another body delivered this morning that you need to see." The man cleared his throat again. "This is Ross." The call cut off abruptly.

Raven ignored their stares as she rose.

"This isn't over." Dominic sounded resigned, but didn't object to her leaving.

Jackson ghosted her movements. When they reached her room, he shut the door carefully and advanced on her. She resisted the urge to back up.

"You have a plan." There was no question in his oh-too-casual voice. He crossed his arms over the large expanse of his chest.

She had to admit he was impressive...er...imposing. Neither meant he would get his way. "Working on one. Why don't you take a shower first?"

His smile was all teeth. "I think not."

Raven resisted the urge to roll her eyes. "I believe I can manage to find the morgue by myself."

Jackson grunted.

"You heard Ross' call. It's not like I'm trying to sneak out."

"Fine."

His easy acceptance threw her. She never expected him to relent, and it left her off-kilter. The bastard was up to something. She narrowed her eyes, wishing she'd listened to Dominic when he said shifters were tricky bastards. "Fine?"

"Promise to come right back."

She pursed her lips, but didn't answer.

"Promise or I'll follow you." It was a threat. He crowded near, his wolf so close to the surface that it splashed over her in waves. Delicious heat radiated from him. Inviting her to touch. She curled her hands into fists, unable to back away from the temptation. It was all she could do to remain still.

"I promise." She agreed more in hopes that he'd back away and give her room to breathe. Lord knew she didn't have enough strength to walk away from him and the need building inside her.

Only he didn't move.

"Jackson?"

He dropped his arms and stepped closer. Part of her mind went fuzzy, and it took her precious seconds to remember he wasn't hers.

But she could change that.

"Will you let me try to see if I can call your animal?" His face turned to granite, the heat doused, his reluctance clear. She just didn't know if it was because of her or a fear that no matter what she tried, she wouldn't be able to fix him.

At the back of her mind was hope. If she could pull his wolf forward, the death sentence hanging over his head would vanish, giving him choices again. But would he choose her or loyalty to his pack?

For wolf shifters, pack was everything.

"Do you trust me?" His whiskey brown eyes darkened, and she thought he wouldn't answer. She counted off the ticking second, her heart speeding as she waited, her palms growing sweaty.

"Yes."

She swallowed hard at his answer, then removed her gloves, noticing how little they helped anymore. He watched the action so intently, you'd think she just stripped to her underwear. She nodded behind him. "Sit on the bed."

He backed up and did so without taking his eyes off hers.

She licked her lips as nerves stormed through her. "You realize I've never done this with anyone else."

He nodded and the rest of the world dropped away until only the two of them remained. His energy wrapped around him, subtly different from humans, seductive in its strength. He didn't move, his shoulders tense as if bracing himself for her to strike.

"If you feel any pain, tell me and I'll stop."

"Do it."

Raven gazed into his eyes a moment longer, praying he wouldn't hate her if she failed.

She placed her hands on his shoulders, and jerked in surprise when they flexed under her touch. Goosebumps raced up her arms, and she shivered as desire nearly drowned her. The wolf at her core inched forward at the touch as if curious.

Blue eyes filled her vision.

The need for freedom, the need to run, bore down on her. It was all she could do to remain still. She inhaled deeply and the cut grass and fresh air smell that she associated with Jackson filled her head.

Could her own wolf help Jackson?

The last time she pulled her to the surface, Jackson's own animal had reacted. The unconscious urge to do just that built. If she tried hard enough, pushed hard enough, she knew they could help him.

Her hands slipped down to his chest, her fingers slightly stroking the hard lines of his muscles. A light growl resonated under her palms, and she cursed the shirt that separated them. Eagerness built as the wolf began to pace. When Jackson's hands settled on her waist, her eyes snapped open.

His eyes splintered to yellow with his wolf. She belatedly remembered Rylan's warning about Jackson's compulsion to bite her and froze. Sweat beaded on his brow, strain bracketing his eyes and lips.

As if sensing her hesitation, his hold tightened. "Don't you dare leave."

He leaned closer, his nose inches from her throat, and inhaled. Her breath caught, tingles swept over her skin as pure lust poured through her. The irresistible draw to him had her shuffling closer. All she wanted was to crawl into his lap and bask under his attention. She was coming to understand the compulsion shifters had to touch.

"Jackson."

They were so close his breath feathered her lips. His eyes dilated, but he didn't move, which was its own aphrodisiac. She couldn't help but wonder about his taste. If she just leaned forward...

Self-preservation screamed at her to pull back, but her senses said that this was the right path if she wanted to help him. Taking a leap of faith, she crushed her lips to his, praying she knew what the hell she was doing.

Chapter Twenty-seven

JUST AFTER SUNSET

Jackson's lust exploded through her with the first taste of his lips, spurring Raven to seek more. Everything around her vanished as sensations consumed her. All that mattered was him and the burning desire to take everything he offered.

His arms slid around her waist, and he fisted her shirt, whether to draw her forward or hold her in place, she didn't care. She had no intention of going anywhere. She locked her hands in his hair to slow him down, wanting to linger and enjoy every second of what he did to her.

When he sprawled backward, she eagerly crawled on his lap, nipped at his lips and luxuriated in the heat that seeped into her bones.

"Raven."

The husky, reverent sound of her name on his lips sent her heart pounding. The fog clouding her mind lifted a fraction. She had a job to do. It hurt to pull away from him.

She drew up short by his grip on her waist. Yellow eyes locked on hers. A growl thrummed in Jackson's chest, and an answering call rose in her. Power shimmered, growing brighter. Her skin grew tight, and the glow spilled over onto him.

Faster than she could register, his hand rose to cradle her head. His fingers sank into her hair, and she shivered at the demand as he angled her face down to his. He twisted until he lay over her, his hard body surrounding hers, and she lost her breath. Delicious heat enveloped her as he ravaged her mouth. The wolf at the center of her took that moment to charge.

Like on a rollercoaster, her stomach jumped in her throat, the beast ready to burst through her chest. Pain riveted her, searing her insides, tearing a groan from her.

"Raven!"

Her eyes snapped open to see him reach for her. "No!"

But it was too late. The instant his hand touched her skin, the power of her wolf raced up his arms. Seconds took an eternity to pass. Then his eyes rolled up in his head, and he collapsed.

His weight crushed her. Frantic with worry, she touched his back, running her hands over him, but couldn't detect any injuries. "Jackson?"

No response.

Terrified she'd really hurt him, she allowed what little power she managed to save to rise up in her. Strands crawled over every inch of him, wrapping around him as if picking up on her concern.

And found nothing wrong.

The connection abruptly died, taking the last of her power with it. She wiggled out from Jackson's weight. She paced, wondering if she should tell someone, but knew Jackson would hate to have their privacy exposed. And what could they do, anyway?

He looked so vulnerable she covered him with a blanket, unable to bear leaving him so exposed. When she went to smooth back his hair, a tremor shook her naked hand, and she pulled away, afraid the contact would hurt him worse. She backed up another step.

She knew better than to touch someone. She should count herself lucky that she hadn't actually killed him. Deeply buried doubts rose. Who's to say what would happen next time? They got off lucky.

What made her think she could ever be normal?

But there was one thing she could do.

Quickly opening the drawers, she grabbed the first set of gloves that met her fingers and yanked them on over her hands. She pocketed her cell and hurried across the room, giving the bed a wide berth. She stepped onto the balcony then leapt over the side, landing on the balls of her feet in the grass. She cradled her ribs as her bruised body protested. As she entered the woods, she dialed Ross.

"I'll be there in twenty minutes." Jackson would be fine, she assured herself, but she couldn't resist the urge to gaze back at the house one last time.

The morgue was empty when she arrived. The guard, Chuck, was nowhere to be found. Her steps slowed, but she didn't wait for him to return. Observation room one, two and three were glaringly empty.

"Ah, there you are." A voice said from behind her.

"Shit." She whirled to face Ross, unnerved not to have noticed him sneak up on her. Her heartbeat skyrocketed. Power hovered under her skin, eager for a confrontation.

"Ross." She tried to smile, but feared it came out as more of a grimace. There was no danger, but the power refused to dissipate back into her body, fighting her for control. Dying had a way of screwing with her system.

"Jumpy." Ross smiled pleasantly, already dressed in the paper scrubs. "This place has that effect on people."

He reached into his pocket and removed two masks. "Here, you'll need this. It's another bad one."

She hesitated, glancing at the door with a grimace of distaste and gingerly accepted his offer. "I hope you don't get into trouble with Scotts for bringing me down here." She slipped the mask over her face, coughing slightly at the dust of powder.

"Oh, I don't think we have to worry about him anymore."

The room spun, and it took her a while for his words to register.

"Excuse me?" She glanced at him, nearly dropping to her knees when dizziness assailed her. His expression appeared detached as he observed her. A horrible realization sank deep in her gut. Her gaze slid past his shoulder and landed on the empty autopsy table. She clawed at the powdery mask and threw it away, disgusted at being so stupid.

"It was you." The words were slurred, her lips growing numb. She should've connected it sooner. How he knew too much about the paranormal world, how things worked, how he called them shifters instead of weres like most normals. The strength went out of her legs, and her knees cracked against the tile floor when she fell. "You sell shifters to the hunters."

He took Taggert.

And she was next.

"Nothing so barbaric. I turn the shifters over to the hunters once I've learned everything I can from them. I couldn't let them free afterwards. They knew too much."

She took a deep, calming breath, hoping that the fresh air trickling into her lungs would clear her head. "You've been dosing me with poison." Chemicals had been rousing her animals, not Jackson or Taggert like she'd originally thought.

"Not poison. You're too important." Ross smiled as if enjoying the conversation. "At first, I wasn't sure if you were a *normal*, but you reacted to the powder. Not much, but it was enough to trigger my curiosity.

"You see, shifters react rather violently to it. Only alphas are able to withstand the chemicals without being forced to take their animal form. But not you. I had to inject you with the liquid form, and you're still not reacting as predicted. You're not human, but I can't place what type of breed you are."

Ross paused as if he were waiting for her to supply him with answers. Raven laughed, unable to help herself. "You fool. I can't change into any animal."

A smile broke across his face, and a deep 'oh, shit' passed through her. "That's what makes you such a superb specimen. You're the closest thing to a shifter and human that I've run across. You're the key to my research. Vampire blood can heal wounds, but did you know that shifter DNA can be extracted and used to slow some diseases?

"All the answers are in the blood, but shifter blood isn't compatible to humans. I need to do more tests. Though shifters can heal incredibly fast, their blood weakens after a few weeks of study.

When they have nothing else to offer me, I hand them over to the hunters. It's a win, win situation."

"Why?" Her voice rasped painfully, her numb throat fighting her.

Ross lost his smile. "My mother died after a prolonged hospital stay, rotting in a bed, hooked up to machines. She died for nothing. A shot, once a week, would've prolonged her life."

"You were trying to find a cure." Though his original intent had been noble, she didn't feel a twinge of compassion for him.

"I wasn't in time. I didn't have enough subjects to test. I found a way around that now."

"By draining people until they're near death to create the serum."

"Filthy animals." His lips curled in rage, his movements grew more agitated and violent as he spread out a tarp on the floor. "Scientists have always experimented on animals."

He actually believed it was no big deal. "They're people."

Images of Ross with a needle in his hand, holding her down and taking her blood exploded through her mind. "You did something to me when I collapsed."

He nodded as if talking to an associate and not someone he planned to kill. "I wanted a viable sample. By the time I was able to work with yours, the blood had degraded too much to profile it."

He shook his finger at her as if she were naughty. "But I know you're different. You're the key to perfecting my cure. This time I'll take tissue samples. You heal amazingly fast. I'll take care not to let you die."

Despite his words, malice gleamed in his eyes. He'd keep her alive, too, until he found his answers.

Ross puttered around the room, dragging out an old black doctor's bag. He whistled tunelessly, while pulling out a pair of heavy shackles. She tried to rise, but found her muscles unable to obey, as if her hands and knees were cemented to the floor.

"Don't try to run. You won't make it far. The shot last night at the crash has weakened you, leaving you susceptible. The second dose I just gave you will keep you docile for a few hours."

Her head snapped up at his mention of the crash. "Where's Taggert?"

Fear plummeted through her. She didn't know what was worse, the thought of Taggert being hunted or being the subject of an experiment.

Rage like she'd never known shimmered up her spine. Energy flared under her skin, sizzled, burning away the drug, but it faded too fast to completely flush it out of her system. The trauma over the last few days had taken its toll. If she could just hold him off for a little while longer, then she'd show him what it meant to be part of a pack.

"Your Taggert hasn't been harmed." He glanced at her with calculating eyes. "I wouldn't try anything. If I'm not at my laboratory to answer the phone at ten, they'll release him, and the hunt will begin. Obey me and he might live." He smiled slowly. "Who do you think will get him first? The hunters who'd paid for him, or the leashed shifter who craves the taste of flesh?"

Sickness lurched through her. The girl in the woods. The killer who eviscerated the bodies, then buried them to save to snack on later. Ross's experiments must have pushed her past the limits of her sanity if she'd eat the flesh of her own kind.

A cough racked her again. Her ribs protested but each exhale expelled the powder from her lungs. "You hunt them in the woods."

Ross pulled a shiny scalpel and small mallet out of his bag, so absorbed in his task that he didn't bother to face her. "The hunters feel that it evens the odds to let the shifters run in their natural environment. It increases the danger and adds to the adrenaline rush." He shook his head. "Fools."

Raven let him talk. If she could remove her gloves, she'd be able to access the energy grid teaming below her. Her clumsy fingers made the task difficult. Frustrated at the lack of progress, she finally just used her teeth to tug the leather over her hand.

Cold cement seared her palm.

Nothing happened. The grid hummed but remained dormant under her demand. She gritted her teeth as panic threatened to overwhelm her. Power fluctuated wildly at her emotions. She pushed past the pain, dug deeper, only to watch helplessly as any power drained back into the floor. No matter how hard she tried, she couldn't hold the charge worth a damn.

A kick to her ribs took her by surprise. Pain robbed her of breath, and she crashed to her side on the tarp. She glared at the man who caused all this. "Bastard."

"Hmmm." He glanced at her distractedly as he reached for his instruments.

It was now or never.

"You want to know what makes me different?" His eyes sharpened. She'd finally caught his attention. "This."

She grabbed his ankle. His pant leg did nothing to protect him. She might not be able to give him the jolt he deserved, but she sure as hell could take every bit of energy that made him human.

He gasped as his essence dribbled out of him. His heart slowed. The blade he held clattered to the floor. The urge to keep taking grew, but if she wanted to find Taggert, she needed Ross alive.

And for that insult, the bastard would pay.

Chapter Twenty-eight

"$\mathcal{H}$e sets up illegal hunts, using shifters as prey." Raven had debated long or hard whether or not to go home and get reinforcements. The deciding factor was her promise to Jackson. Also, though it galled her to admit it, she needed help if she had any hope of getting Taggert back. "And I'm afraid if they notice Ross's absence, they'll pull up stakes and slaughter those still captive." Her jaw clenched as she said those words.

"How do you know he's behind it?" London finished securing the last tie, elbowing Ross in the back of the head when he rose.

She understood his doubt. Ross was twenty pounds too skinny for his lanky frame, with thinning hair and an air of weakness around him. He didn't look capable of capturing a fly, let alone so many shifters.

"He bragged. Ross knew how packs ran, and avoided snatching anyone associated with them to avoid suspicion." She didn't go into how he tortured his captives for the information.

Dina walked in the room, not gazing at anyone as she paced, her cherry scent a little too sweet. Her words were slow in coming. "Jenkins isn't ready."

Raven didn't say anything at first, swallowing hard. She was determined that this plan would work despite everything that could go wrong. That meant she needed Jenkins. "No one ever is."

Dina sighed, a defeated slump to her shoulders. "He said he'd do it."

Raven never expected anything less, well understanding the need for revenge. The cold stone in her chest dissipated a fraction knowing that her friends stood behind her. "And the others?"

"Dominic took Jackson to check Ross's home as soon as you called." London peered at her over Ross's head; something in her expression had him narrowing his eyes. "They left you here to recover. They'll be pissed if you dare move from this house."

Relief nearly bent her double to learn that Jackson suffered no aftereffects from her. A large part of her was grateful to have him gone from the house when she'd returned. She didn't know how to face him after what happened. After failing him. "Do you believe we can wait? If Ross isn't there to answer that phone, Taggert will be the next body they pull from the water."

The superior attitude Ross had exuded at the morgue had annoyed and scared the shit out of her. For an intelligent guy, he honestly didn't understand the magnitude of his crimes. Or his punishment.

"What about him?" London nodded to Ross.

"Leave him here for Rylan. Dina can—"

"I'm going with you." Her voice was adamant. "If any of my people are still alive, they'll need me. You'll be too busy tracking down Taggert."

Raven tightened her lips at putting another defenseless shifter in danger. She ran the scenario through her head a thousand times, but couldn't fault Dina's logic. "Get Jenkins in here."

A skinny ghost of a man slipped into the room on soundless feet. The paleness of his skin reminded her of the prison they called the labs, the lack of sun, the exhausting tests that left a person so weak that they often didn't wake up for days, if at all. "Are you sure you're strong enough for this?"

He was so emaciated, one good wind could knock him down.

"I'm ready. Like you said, I won't be in any danger. I just have to answer the phone." A fierce need to be useful entered his eyes, a need she recognized. "Let me do this for you."

She flicked a glance at London, relaxing slightly at his subtle nod. He'd protect Jenkins if it came to it. "Thank you. What do you need to start the process?"

"I'll need to touch him." Distaste curled Jenkins' lips.

She knew the feeling, but she couldn't bring herself to tell him not to bother. She needed the abilities of a full chameleon who could manipulate both his vocal cords and his body. But what else could he pick up by touching someone, even in passing? She decided she didn't want to know.

"How long will it take? How long can you hold his form?"

"It usually takes twenty minutes to assimilate a shape. I can hold it for three hours before the integrity degrades. I won't be able to try again for at least a day." He appeared apologetic and spoke quickly. "But I'm getting stronger with each shift."

"It's a miracle you can do this for us at all. Thank you for being willing to even try." A chameleon was a rare thing, one of the most endangered creatures alive. So much so that most people thought them myths.

It took closer to an hour for the transformation. Jenkins' skin bubbled, melted and twisted into the new shape. Bile rose in Raven's throat. She couldn't imagine the pain and was thankful the doctors had never given her a transfusion of his blood.

Ross woke partway through the transition. Instead of panic, Ross calmly observed the process, cataloging everything in a way that sent her skin crawling. Her fist curled, and only her will prevented her from stalking over and cold-cocking him into oblivion. No matter what happened, she couldn't allow him to leave, or Jenkins would never be safe.

London steadied Jenkins when he rose. The first thing she noticed was the height.

He saw her stare and shrugged. "Nothing I can do about the proportions. I can manipulate my flesh like any shifter, but I only have my weight and height to work with."

Goosebumps crept over her to hear Ross's voice come out of Jenkins.

"God. That's uncanny." Dina summed it up exactly.

Very few shifters were born with the genes to shrink or gain mass, and those few who did were highly prized. It was a trait they'd tried to breed in the labs.

Tingling swept along her arms, and she lifted her face to the ceiling. "Rylan's awake."

Now all she had to do was convince him to take Ross's blood so they could find his lab.

She'd already searched the office at the morgue but to no end. She highly doubted the guys would find anything at his home. Ross was too smart for that. It could take her hours to pick up a paper trail, but that didn't guarantee she'd find anything in time to be of any use. Ross didn't strike her as a stupid man. He wouldn't hold anything in his name.

"I hear you've been stirring up trouble again." Rylan's amused voice flowed over her in a soothing wave.

He sauntered into the room, his elegant clothing neatly pressed with a style that could easily pass for a man a century ago. Charm twinkled in his blue eyes, making her heart pitter-patter pathetically. Every time she saw him, she wanted to mess him up. He exuded competence that she could rely on. After she explained what she needed, he'd help her make things right.

"No, absolutely not." Wounded betrayal darkened his eyes, and she didn't understand.

"You were able to tell where Cassie had been by taking her blood. We need to know where Ross keeps his lab."

His jaw stiffened with each word.

"What's wrong?"

"I don't take blood."

Raven hesitated, but couldn't let it rest, not when Taggert's life was at risk. "I don't understand."

"I don't take blood from people. Ever."

"But Cassie..."

"She was already dying. I only did it because you asked." He glanced at Ross, his every thought completely hidden. "Don't ask me again."

Then Raven understood. Her blood had changed him. "You see into their minds when you take blood as any normal vampire, but there's more, isn't there?"

Those battle-wounded eyes of his gave the answer.

"Because of me." Acid churned her stomach and nausea threatened. He'd lived with the affliction for years without a word of blame.

How many other lives had she ruined and just walked away from without a clue?

"Don't look like that. It's not your fault."

She met his gaze steadily, her heart shredded. "Isn't it?"

Dina broke the spell when she spoke. "What made Cassie so different?"

Rylan swallowed hard, never removing his focus from Raven. "Raven."

The pure lust in his expression slammed into her so hard, she couldn't catch her breath, let alone her run-away thoughts. She'd always thought Rylan kept his distance because he didn't care. That she'd destroyed things between them when she tried to get too close. Now she saw that he actually believed he was protecting her from himself. She was his addiction. He might care for her, but he feared his craving for her blood more.

"I never knew. I never understood." She was stupid, blinded by her own problems. Shame heated her cheeks.

"I couldn't let you see. I didn't want you to know." He ran a hand through his hair, dropping his gaze. But not before she saw the humiliation. They hadn't broken her in the labs, not the way that one devastated look did now.

"You should've told me." She couldn't prevent the way her lip trembled.

Sadness poured from him. "So that you would feel guilty and try to fix me?" He shook his head. "I've lived this way for years. I can manage my affliction."

"Where does that leave us?" London bared his teeth at Ross, cracking his knuckles. "Would you like me to take a turn at him? I'm sure he'll give up his secrets."

Raven wasn't so sure. The angle of Ross's chin showed his stubbornness, and his complete conviction that he would get out of this alive.

She looked at the people in the room as Jackson's words came back to haunt her. Shifters weren't human, they didn't think like them. She wasn't either, not really. Maybe it was time to put away her dreams, face the fact that she'd never be normal, and embrace the other side of her soul that few people knew existed.

"Leave the room." She'd think of something. She had no choice. She remembered the way Durant tried to crack her shields. It was possible. She just had to peel back the layers. She'd never exploited her gift that way, but it was worth the risk.

"I'll do it." Rylan's quick turnabout baffled her.

"No. If I'd known, I would've never asked—"

"I'm volunteering." His gaze was uncompromising.

"Why?" His actions confused her, especially now that she understood the cost would push him one step closer to the insanity of bloodlust.

"I know what you're planning. I'll survive. I'll get the information. They need you on this case. Taggert needs you."

"And damn the consequences?"

"I'll accept them all on my own. They won't involve you."

"Like hell." She snarled at the secrets he had no right to keep from her.

"Let's argue when your Taggert is home."

Suspicions darkened her thoughts. "And you'll be here when I get back?"

Before she could react, Rylan's eyes bled to black. His image blurred, and he struck.

Ross's struggle sickened her, but the least she could do was watch what she'd put into motion.

The fight slowly went out of Ross, his sharp expression grew dazed. When Raven thought Rylan would drain him, he withdrew his fangs. Blood trailed sluggishly down Ross's neck, but he lived.

Raven quickly turned her attention to Rylan. The tense set of his shoulders slowed her step, and she swallowed hard past the tightness of her throat. She hesitated, uncurled her clenched fists and reached out. "Rylan—"

He whirled, his extended fangs glistened, his eyes wild as he fought the lure of blood. The damned fool had waited too long to feed.

Raven didn't flinch under his regard, and he cocked his head as if curious. "What did you see? Where's the warehouse?" She wouldn't cry at what she'd forced upon Rylan. She couldn't let her emotions win or she'd lose both of them.

Those black orbs didn't show any recognition. The muscles of his body flexed to leap at the first sign of fear or weakness. Across the room, London shifted a step closer, ready to intervene.

She shook her head. At the movement, Rylan gripped her arm with vampiric strength. Energy rippled at the touch, surged up without her command, coursing under her skin and bubbling up to the surface. It splashed into Rylan, bowing his back. His gasp of air, the sound of deep pain had her skipping back out of range.

At the absence of his touch, she staggered, nearly falling to her knees. Everything inside her quieted. Rylan didn't fare any better. His body crashed to the floor and didn't move.

"Shit." Stumbling over Ross's feet, she knelt at Rylan's side. "Can you hear me?"

Rylan blinked lazily, his eyes dilated, but normal, thank God. The zap must have cleared the bloodlust.

"Baker Street. They call at ten sharp." Something dark moved in his gaze. A shadowy memory and a vengeance so strong she flinched. "Go quickly, but brace yourself. He set up his own labs."

She rose with reluctance and came face to face with Ross. The bastard was alive but barely. "I'll bring them back."

She spoke to Rylan, but the promise in her eyes was for Ross and he knew it. Fear shaded his face, and he seemed to understand the danger for the first time.

He wouldn't be leaving alive.

Maybe Jackson was right. This was a matter for shifter justice. Those in the labs deserved to see the bastard die by their own hands...or claws.

Chapter Twenty-nine

Though Raven expected the call, the shrill ringing of the phone sent her pulse galloping. She gazed up at the clock, her gut a ball of needles.

Ten sharp.

Jenkins hand rested on the cradle of the phone and waited for her nod. "Do it." Her eyes were drawn to the cramped cages on the cold cement floor. The thick metal enclosure wasn't large enough for anyone to stand, let alone stretch out

So many empty cages that her mind stumbled.

The congealed blood on the floor stood out like a reprimand, each stain a reminder of a life taken, a life lost.

Dina had evacuated the few refugees. London had painstakingly dismantled all the computers, readying them for transportation back to the house. Those files would tell her everything she needed to know about who'd died and what had been done to those who'd survived. It felt like too little, too late.

Again.

"Ross."

Her head snapped up, her gaze sharpening on Jenkins as he spoke into the phone. Ross's image reflected back at her, and she tightened her fists, nails digging into her palms to remind herself that the real Ross was not going anywhere.

"I have another body for your hunt."

A knot formed in her throat, quickly loosened by anger. This was the perfect way for her to get to Taggert. By using their own system against them.

"She's not a normal shifter, but I don't think you'll be disappointed." Ross's voice warbled, and he coughed. The transition was fading. They had to hurry. "I won't be able to stay tonight."

Jenkins bent over the desk and scribbled on a piece of paper. "I'll leave her there for you to pick up." Another long pause and beads of sweat dotted Jenkins' forehead. "I can try to find another female cat, but it's going to be harder. Since they began finding the bodies," he added just the right amount of reprimand to be realistic, "the shifters have become more protective. Women are the hardest to snatch. Too few of them are free to roam without protection."

Another long pause. "I'll do it, but it will cost you double." The hard, flat sound of his voice matched Ross's so exactly, a chill crept down her spine. "Fine."

Jenkins hung up without waiting, then sat heavily in the chair, his posture drooping. "Do you think he bought it?"

Guilt assailed her at the shake in his voice. She'd pushed him hard. She just hoped it was worth it. "We'll know if they show up at the dump site. You did well."

A grimace of pain crossed his face, his skin rippling like bugs were crawling beneath the surface. Pale splotches of skin appeared when his face settled.

"Are you all right?"

He waved away her concern. "This is normal. The transition back is gradual. You have more things to worry about than me. Go. Get ready." He tore off the paper with his scribbled note and handed it to her. "Be safe."

She gave him a nod and turned, wishing she could ignore the smell of blood and terror permeating the walls of the derelict warehouse. The need to get out crushed her chest, and she threw open the door. Fresh air buffeted her, and she eagerly sucked it down. Too bad she couldn't forget as easily.

"Raven."

Shit. She froze, and air wheezed out of her lungs. She'd forgotten about London.

"You were leaving."

His accusation struck at the heart of her plan. She wanted to keep everyone safe, didn't want to draw any more attention to anyone else. "Listen—"

A sound rumbled out of the darkness, raising the hair on the back of her neck, and she took an involuntary step backward. When she faced London, it was to find him gazing at her, unrepentant.

"Jackson?"

He nodded. "And my guess, Dominic's not too far behind."

Jackson's yellow eyes reflected in the dark, barely a block away and coming up fast.

"You told them we would be here." Of course he did.

"I had a feeling you'd try to leave by yourself if I didn't bring backup."

Something in his words gripped her insides hard. "What did you do?"

To give him credit, he didn't back down.

"I believe he means me." Durant's shape melted out of the darkness less than ten feet away, sauntering toward them with a lazy gait, an uncompromising glint in his golden eyes.

"Damn it, London." She fisted her hands, so angry she shook. The man had the gall to cross his arms and give her a hard stare.

"You would've gone alone."

She shrugged away the accusation. What could she say? It was true. Before she could respond, Jackson and Dominic muscled between them, disapproval radiating from them. It was the first good look at Jackson she had since she'd left him unconscious. He appeared fine, strong and uncompromising, but something about him had changed subtly. Power surrounded him, snapping at her with surprising strength.

"It didn't work." Disappointment pierced her.

Not only did she fail to fix him, she'd dragged his wolf so close to the surface that he had to be teetering on the edge. Such hyper-vigilance couldn't feel good. How long could he go on like that without breaking under the strain?

He didn't have to say a word of reprimand, though she felt it anyway, and his silence made it all the worse. He stepped closer, stalking her in a way that tightened her muscles in preparation to either fight or flee. She shifted her stance and found her back pressed up against Durant's chest.

"You aren't going without us."

Jackson's guttural words kicked up her heartbeat. She swallowed hard and nodded dumbly. It was too late anyway.

Durant placed his hands on her shoulders, dragged his fingers down her arms, and she leaned into him as her legs threatened to give out under the assault between the both of them. When his hands trailed over hers, he pulled the note from her nerveless fingers.

She jerked away, biting back a groan of protest at the loss of contact. The bastard had used the attraction between them to distract her. Although she should be angry, it faded quickly under the rush of arousal that flooded her body, and the gut wrenching compulsion to touch them both back.

"I know this location. It's five miles west of where I found Cassie."

"You're missing one important fact." She crossed her arms, feeling exposed and chilled as some of her reasoning returned. "They're expecting to find a woman waiting for them."

"We'll stay hidden."

"And if they have shifters on the hunt?" That was a hard fact to swallow, but she knew they had one. The markings on the bones proved that. Who's to say they didn't have more? "They'll be able to pick you out of the trees in seconds. I won't let them keep Taggert."

"Nobody else wants that either." Dominic tried to sound reasonable, but there was a harshness around him that wouldn't be compromised.

Those dark eyes of his locked on hers, and he leaned so close that their noses almost touched. All the excess energy and frustration pouring off him wrapped around her, peppering her fragile shields, choking her with its strength.

"You'll not leave here without us."

"Fine." She bit out between clenched teeth. She didn't really have a choice anymore, not when they knew the drop off location. "How do you want to do this?"

The silver and iron zip tie gouged into her wrists until her bones felt bruised. She resisted the urge to shift positions on the hard-packed ground, hating that she could barely feel her ass anymore. The lack of gloves made her more uncomfortable than her situation. And that said a lot, thanks to the light drizzle that left her clothes sopping wet and her skin clammy.

The sharp sting of the hunter's gaze bore into her. Assessing her, but he didn't make his move. The countdown to the pick-up time had come and gone twenty minutes ago. With each minute that passed, her chest tightened. This had to work. She didn't know any other way to stop the next killing, didn't know any other way to ensure Taggert's safety.

Bright lights flashed in the distance, and her heart rate accelerated into a pounding rhythm. Voices rose and fell, and her suspicions flared to life. She twisted to see the lights angle off in the wrong direction.

Crap. Those weren't her men or the hunters.

"Halt. This is the police. Don't move."

Scotts. Son of a bitch. For half a second, she debated the wisdom of showing herself. If she did, she'd lose Taggert. She didn't know if Scotts had found the hunters or her people, but she couldn't interfere. If the police caught one of her men, the worse they'd have to do was explain what they were doing in the woods.

But what nagged at the back of her mind was how the hell the police had known they were out in the middle of nowhere in the first place. Who took a stroll in the forest at night? Unless the bastard had her followed.

The underbrush crunched, the noise indicating the person headed in the opposite direction. "God dammit, don't shoot. We need him alive."

The lights and voices faded in the distance. She stretched, groaning as her body protested. A twig snapped behind her and she jerked, twisting to see who was there.

She craved to be able to use her senses, but she couldn't risk something going wrong while her powers were still on the fritz. The more time she had to heal, the more control she'd have when she needed it.

The air around her grew heavy. Everything fell ominously silent. She glanced up in time to see a shadowy face she didn't recognize looming over her. She tried to speak with the gag in her mouth, but the words came out mumbled.

"Don't worry, I got you." The deep, masculine voice sounded so concerned, she half-worried she was about to be rescued. Until he reached for her. She recognized the device in his hands. The large meal she ate for fuel lumped like coal in her gut. She twisted away, kicked out, but much too late.

The taser hit her high in the shoulder. She heard the zap, smelled the electricity when the jolt arced through her body. Her back bowed, her teeth clenched, and a muffled scream escaped her gag.

She closed her eyes and allowed the voltage to roll over her. Instead of absorbing it into her system, it snagged on the cage. Under the assault, the vault holding Randolph's stolen power cracked.

Forever passed until the pain finally faded enough to think clearly. When she became aware again, she found herself slung over a man's shoulder, her arms dangling down his back. Nausea pressed heavily against the back of her throat, each swaying step testing her control.

She had to get her bearings, but everything looked wrong when viewed upside down. She went with what she knew. There was no trail. The edges of his pant legs were damp, but the only stream was miles from the dumpsite.

His booted heels scraped rock as the dirt give way to stone. Blinking in surprise, she mentally viewed the maps London had gathered. None mentioned a cave system.

The outside world vanished, along with the light, as she was lugged lower and lower into the bowels of the earth. Cold air swirled around her, snaking through her clothes. Then she saw the tracks. The old gold mines. He must have carried her south through the stream to throw off the scent.

Her eyes took a while to adjust to the absolute darkness. Stale water made the air thick. Then, pinpricks of light glowed in the distance, and she could vaguely distinguish shapes in the tunnel.

A rumble of voices grew louder as they neared. She slammed her eyes shut and steadied her breathing.

And none too soon. A fist tangled in her hair, wrenching her neck back. A grunt sounded, and she felt a finger trace the angles of her face. It was all she could do to remain still under the cold touch. The brutal grip on her loosened, and her head dropped, smacking the small of her abductor's sweat-stained back.

"Put her in the cage with the others. Check on her every hour. I want to know when this one wakes."

The man turned, and she bit her lip against making any sound when her arm scraped along the narrow tunnel. Then she found herself falling. She struggled to keep herself from tensing when her head cracked against the unforgiving ground.

Air whooshed out of her lungs.

Stars danced, and she found herself drowning in darkness.

Chapter Thirty

DAY 8: SOMETIME AFTER MIDNIGHT

Coldness crept over her flesh and shivers racked her body. She groped for her blanket, cursing when she couldn't find it.

"Raven." The harsh whisper clanged loudly in her head. She rolled over and slapped the alarm.

Only to have her hand hit stone. She winced at the unforgiving surface and pried open an eyelid. Inky blackness greeted her. She blinked a few times and a faint light from the end of the room slowly brought everything into focus.

Reality came crashing back.

She rubbed the bracelet of bruises on her wrists, relieved to have those blasted ties removed. All she heard was dripping water, the sound lonely in the silence. A movement across the way drew her attention. She sat quickly, then sucked in a harsh breath when her battered body protested. "Taggert?"

"What did you do?" The guttural reprimand in his voice stung. Dirt smudged his face and matted his beautiful hair. His face appeared gaunt but unhurt.

He was alive.

Part of her had been terrified she wouldn't make it in time. The back of her throat ached with unshed tears, and she had to clear her throat twice to speak. "I came to get you out of here."

Here appeared to be an underground way station. The cages were nothing more than three by four foot boxes carved out of the stone walls with thin wires acting as bars.

"You shouldn't have come." Taggert shoved away from the edge of the kennel, disappearing into the shadows where she couldn't see him.

"You don't mean that." His sharp rebuke confused her. Raven expected relief, not the bitter, nearly uncontrollable rage. It left her floundering and a little unsure of herself.

Movement in another cage caught her eye, but she couldn't make out any shapes. Her determination hardened, and she shoved the hurt away to deal with later.

"How many are here?" She needed to factor their numbers into her plans.

"If they didn't kill Digger yet, there are four of us including you." The raspy male voice was from a stranger, his words giving away little information as to his identity. "They emptied the cage when they heard you were coming."

That they'd kill another to make room for her was devastating when so close to rescue. "Could he still be alive?"

No one spoke for nearly a minute, and she closed her eyes as guilt twisted through her.

"Not for long. They never come back after they go beyond this point." The voice hardened. "You should worry about yourself. It's always worse for the women."

Raven reached for the cage.

"Don't."

But it was too late. Her hand curled around the wire before she could pull back. Electricity sizzled up through her fingers and along every nerve ending. While her core remained dormant, fire spread along her muscles until her whole body spasmed. She lost her hold and slid bonelessly to the ground, every inch of her screaming in agony.

"Raven?"

The hoarse sound of her name from Taggert reached through the haze of pain. She had a feeling it wasn't the first time he called for her. She'd forgotten what it was like to be hit with raw energy, how evil it could feel. It was devastating to be close to all that power, taste it, feel it and be unable to access it when she needed it most.

"I'm fine." Though she knew she had never let out a whimper, she barely recognized her rough voice. She was good at swallowing the screams. "Are all the cages similarly charged?"

"Yes." There was a slight hesitation in the answer, and the mysterious man crept toward the edge of his cage.

Perfect. She scanned the room, stealing a bit of the raw electricity that saturated the air. Current singed her in retaliation for daring to touch it, but thankfully allowed her to direct it. Wires around the floor and ducts lit up like the Fourth of July to her eyes. Most of the cords were laid in haste, exposed and easily manipulated.

The back of her teeth ached at the prospect of working with live current without the filter of her core. It was unpredictable, unreliable, and hurt like the dickens to use in its raw form, but at least she wasn't at the mercy of her unstable gift. The only drawback was that she could only use it for so long before it killed her. Raven clenched her hands to control the tremor in her fingers, then inhaled deeply and reached for the cage again.

"Raven, don't do this."

The plea in Taggert's voice made her hesitate. She lifted her head to see him mimic her position across the way.

"I can do this. If I can bring down the generator, you can get everyone out." She licked her lips, noticing they were chapped and bleeding.

"Even if we can escape the cave, it won't work," the other man spoke. "There's still the girl. The four of us won't be able to overpower the guards with her standing watch."

"What's your name?"

Another lengthy pause and she thought he wouldn't answer. His shape appeared blurred by shadows, but she recognized the scars burned across the back of his left hand. A branded rogue.

"Griffin."

She swallowed hard and made the only decision she could. Rogue status or not, she had to trust him.

"I'm going to rig the bars to take down the generator. When they take me out to hunt, you should be able to break the lock and get the others out. Head north. My team and the cops are ready." She ignored Taggert's growl of rage. "Keep Taggert safe."

"Raven, don't." Taggert looked furious enough to rip apart the cage.

"Just hurry. I won't be able to evade them forever. I'll try to stall them long enough for you to bring backup." She very deliberately placed her hands back on the bars, whimpering when the energy slammed into her again, stronger than ever. She quickly manipulated the current in the wires, looping circuits away from the generator, knowing she didn't have much time.

The lights flickered. At the signal, she loosened her hold. Her arms dropped to her sides, and she groaned at the unexpected pain. Her arms felt like they would fall out of their sockets. The first part was done. A surge of relief left her giddy.

One more time should do it. The generator was unhooked. She just needed to bleed the system dry. She straightened, and it took nearly twice as long for her to rise to her knees. Fresh burns and blisters felt raw on her hands as she resolutely crawled toward the door. She swayed and swallowed hard, squinting when her eyes refused to focus. Just one more time, and Taggert would be free.

"Stop." Taggert's hissed whisper sounded more animal than human.

"I'm sorry." Raven braced herself for the charge, allowing it to roll over her. The voltage nearly dropped her on her ass. Only sheer determination locked her fingers on those searing hot wires.

She did her best to suck all the current from the system. Only it was too much. Breathing became a struggle. When her vision dimmed, she flung herself backwards. Spasms contorted her body, her hair stood on end like a cloud around her face. Then everything went black.

The sound of locks tumbling jerked her back to awareness.

"Up you go."

Hands grabbed her under the arms and dragged her out, uncaring that the bars abraded the flesh of her lower back and legs.

"You son of a bitch, leave her alone."

A dark chuckle came from the man above her. "Don't worry. Your time will come. We're just going to play with her for a bit."

Lights blinded her when they moved her, and it took precious seconds for the makeshift room to come into focus. The walls were stone, the floor swept clean and covered by a rug. The space had a kitchenette, a desk and fridge. They'd been here for a while. Then she turned her head and saw the waist-high table. It wasn't the table by itself that scared the shit out of her, but the metal cuffs dangling from the edges that struck terror in her heart.

She wouldn't go there meekly.

Brutal images of the labs rose to haunt her. Her heartbeat sped up, her skin tingled. She was seconds away from panic overtaking her. If she lost her reason, she'd ruin Taggert's chance at escape.

She needed to assess the situation rationally.

She tipped her head, straining to see her captor. Military haircut, strict dress code, sturdy boots. The scent of gun oil was so strong, she could almost taste it. A hunter for the thrill. Big, built, no-nonsense, do-your-duty man from the closed, almost bored expression on his face.

"If you want a better hunt, I can give it to you." The man cocked an eyebrow at her as if he'd heard it all before.

"Oh, you'll run." He hauled her on the table and reached for the cuffs.

"But what fun is the hunt where the prey is wounded. Women give a poor chase."

He didn't say anything as he latched one cuff around her wrist. The cold metal felt like a thousand pounds.

"What if I can guarantee you the hunt of your lifetime?"

Soldier Boy ignored her, but his movements slowed a fraction.

"I met that shifter you keep on a leash the other night. Did she come back a little fried?" She said it mockingly, but she definitely had his interest now. He stopped and drew back, leaving one arm, and her legs free. She considered it a small victory.

"How do I know that was you?"

"She's five six, brown hair and moves disjointedly until she gets the scent of her prey." The description rattled something that hovered in the back of her mind, something she should know. She ignored it and forced herself to smile at the interest in his eyes. "You keep the men off me, and I guarantee that I'll be able to escape your little pet. She makes it too easy for you, doesn't she?"

The burly man ran a distracted hand down the pommel of the blade at his side, judging her. "You don't look like much."

"I survived seventeen years in the labs." She leaned closer, ignoring the way he licked his lips. "I escaped there. You let me loose outside, and I can promise to give you a run for your money. You like to hunt, not chasing down half dead shifters. I bet your little pet kills a better part of them before you even get into the game. Do you miss the thrill of going after something that can kill you if you make a mistake?"

The heat in his eyes grew uncomfortable and only her self-control and the cuff kept her in place. "If they rape me in here, I'll fight back. People will die. They'll put me down before I even get off the table. You don't want that, do you?"

Raven tossed her head in the direction of the cavern. "I saw the men in there. They won't give you half the battle I can."

"Don't you have her stripped and tied down yet?" A skinny cowboy of a man strutted in the room, dressed in too tight black pants, cowboy boots, and a plaid, pearl-button down shirt topped with a string tie. The dark hair he sported was so greasy it appeared black enough to blend into the background and stank of gunky motor oil. A mustache, pitted skin, and cold eyes told of a man who liked women, but didn't have time to waste romancing them to get what he wanted.

This would be her rapist.

She eyed Soldier Boy and raised her brows in challenge.

"She's mine."

Cowboy just laughed. "Don't worry. There's more than enough to go around." He raised a hand, reaching to touch her face when Soldier Boy caught his wrist.

"No. You had the others. This one is all mine." Soldier Boy gazed at her when he spoke, his words a promise.

A wave of relief threatened to weaken her spine, but she didn't allow herself to show it. Talk about jumping from the frying pan into the fire, but she'd worry about that later.

"You can't do that." Cowboy jerked his hand away, narrowing his eyes when Soldier Boy took his time releasing him. Hatred thickened the air.

Soldier Boy straightened to his full height, his chest puffed up, his stare unwavering. "She's mine."

The man finally seemed to sense the danger. The vicious look tossed her way warned her that she'd better watch her back. As soon as Soldier Boy dropped his guard, she was meat for the taking.

"We'll see about that." Boots clumped out of the room. Soldier Boy nodded to her and left. Raised voices resounded in the small cavern, and she willed herself to remain calm. He'd keep his word; he needed the adrenaline rush too badly to let Cowboy win.

The cuff latched onto her wrist could be broken with time, but she wouldn't be able to sneak into the cavern and release the others before her absence was noticed.

She searched her core, noting that neither her animals nor her power seemed to be very interested in helping her out. Not that she could blame them after the abuse she'd put them through. It was the vault that drew her worry.

With nothing to hold it back, it was leaking like a sieve, spilling poison into her system. It wouldn't be much longer before it reached her core and put her out of commission. A few of the animals paced restlessly as the poison threatened their domain, and she felt helpless to do anything. Her hands were tied until her power came back online.

A small sound snapped her head around. She searched the room, but found nothing. "Who's there?"

A shadow moved. A dirty face leaned out of the darkness, intelligent, kind eyes looked at odds with the collar and chain strapped cruelly around his throat.

"Digger?"

"Smart girl to play them against one another."

The whisper barely reached her ears, the range so low she wondered if she'd imagined it.

Then he flinched. "They're coming back."

Then she heard the footsteps, too. She licked her lips and spoke quickly. "When they take me out, Griffin will come get you. Run like hell and don't look back."

He lifted a finger to his lips and vanished into the darkness, meshing with it so completely that even with her keen sight, she couldn't detect him. She quickly refocused her attention away from him and cleared all expression from her face.

"So you're the one who's put my boys at odds." An older, white haired man who could pass for anyone's good-natured grandfather entered the room. The light scent of peppermint candies rose from him. Even his voice sounded jovial.

Not his eyes though. Those snake cold eyes observed everything, dispassionately cataloged every weakness and strength he could ferret out.

"I can see why. There's something different about you." He rubbed his chin, the short, clean whiskers rasping dryly against his hand. It was all she could do not to flinch under his regard. "The police are closing in on us thanks to you. We'll have to close shop in this area."

She couldn't prevent a betraying twitch at his accusations.

A hard smile crossed his lips. "You didn't think I recognized you from your picture in the paper?"

Relief struck hard, and Raven bit down on the inside of her lips to prevent another tell. Grandpa didn't know that the police and her people were out searching for them this very moment. She could still make this work.

He continued as if he didn't expect a response. "Nah, you're the type of girl a guy doesn't forget. Too bad you're a filthy paranormal. Stink clings to your kind." His hand lashed out. Fingers cruelly gripped her chin, dug down to bone, before she even thought to twist away. "Ross usually doesn't send us his leftovers in such pristine condition. You must have been getting too close."

Raven carefully let her mind go blank, thankful for the cold metal on her ass to give her something else to concentrate on. She wasn't up to playing word games with this man. If there was any hint of trouble, he'd finish her now.

She suspected Grandpa had a bit of paranormal in him to be able to pick others like herself out of the crowd so well. Maybe that was why he hated them so fiercely.

"Police involvement gives us a little problem. A surplus of breeds. No sense taking them with us when there are so many of you." He dropped his hand and stepped away, his fingers looped into his belt buckle. "We're going to make things a good deal more interesting and shackle two of you together. We'll see if this pack business works, or if you'll gnaw off the other's arm to escape."

A malevolent glint hardened Grandpa's eyes, and a shiver crawled over her skin. Part of her confidence eroded under that glare.

"You and the little wolf who objected so vehemently when you were dragged in here will be paired."

The back of her throat dried, and she willed herself not to swallow, not to react. This man would sense any weakness and ruthlessly exploit it. He grunted, obviously disappointed in her lack of response.

The animals at her core began to pace and panic brutally grabbed her throat. Please not now. She desperately needed a boost of energy to keep them at bay. Hell, she'd even be grateful to be hit with that cursed taser.

"You escape, you're free." He shrugged, a little smile quirking his lips. "It's that easy."

With the image of freedom dangled in front of them, the animals calmed. She and Taggert were well matched. He might be faster, stronger, but she could disrupt their trail and track the others when they got too close. The only complications would be managing the burnout and her animals with him so close.

"Take her and get them ready. The hunt will begin at one."

She shot a quick glance at Solider Boy, who had entered behind Grandpa, willing him to protest the change in plans. A muscle jumped in his jaw, but he kept quiet. No help from that quarter. She debated making a play now, but stayed her hand. Everyone needed to be out of the cave. When she made her move, she had to be one hundred percent sure that whatever she did, she struck hard, fast, and with killing force.

Then she saw the taser.

"Shit." She gritted her teeth at the necessary evil, ready to swallow everything down in a faint hope that her core had recovered enough to restart.

The spark jumped from the gun to her before it even came into contact with her flesh. Pain rolled over her, the current snapping along her skin, seeking entrance. When denied, every muscle contracted in agony. She willed herself to remain conscious, desperately trying to clutch the electricity, cursing when the voltage dissipated without her being able to capture even a spark.

Darkness hovered over her awareness, and Soldier Boy pulled back when she would've succumbed. Not for humanitarian purposes. To preserve his precious hunt. She slumped on the table, helpless to do anything as her body continued to fight the painful effects.

The cuff snicked open, and she found herself thrown over his back, carried through a series of underground passages. He dumped her unceremoniously on the floor, knocking the breath from her lungs. While stunned, he efficiently latched an inch wide metal manacle around her wrist.

Cold bit into her ass when the man walked away, the temperature a relief after all the energy she'd handled in the last few hours. Her eyes traced the metal links to another cuff hooked to the wall just out of her reach. A light, pine filled breeze brushed against her face, and she knew the entrance had to be close. She struggled upright.

Shuffling feet drew her attention. She quickly scanned the cave for a weapon. No rocks or twigs were nearby. The stone walls were completely devoid of any power. There was nothing to use to defend herself. All she had left was the gold power Randolph left her.

Part of her hesitated to even touch it, but if it meant Taggert would go free, she'd take the risk. She carefully harvested a strand, sucking in a sharp breath when the cord nearly gutted her.

She wrapped up the unruly energy like a ball, prepared to throw it hard and fast, anything to get it out of her hold.

Sickening horror flashed through her when Taggert stumbled out of the darkness. She scrambled to swallow the current down, sucking in a sharp breath when everywhere it touched burned and became as sensitive as freshly broken blisters. Just when she thought it would kick her ass, it finally settled.

Her gaze shot to Taggert, half fearful she hadn't stopped her attack in time. Though severely bruised and battered, all the wounds were old. They also looked worse than she'd first estimated.

Then she noticed he was alone. "Run!"

The walkie-talkie clenched in his fists squawked. "I have a rifle aimed at her head. Shackle yourself to her."

She cursed herself for not seeing that this could happen. Those chocolate brown eyes locked on hers, and he resolutely walked toward her. Her heart slammed against her ribs as she watched him click the heavy weight to his own wrist, trapping them together. "Taggert."

"He would've killed you." He cradled his ribs when he settled at her side. He showed no remorse in his actions, running a hand lightly over her hair, fingering the strands with trembling fingers. The metal irritated his wrists, instantly turning his skin red.

An ungodly howl erupted, echoing in the caves, threatening to pierce her skull. A deep chill crept over her skin. Taggert bolted to his feet, jerking her up with him.

"Run!"

He pulled her along and some of his urgency washed over her. She stumbled over her own feet as she tried to keep up, cursing her clumsiness. Nothing had gone as planned. The burnout had scrambled her system more than she'd wanted to admit, the current coming and going in surges, but mostly going.

Her animals refused to settle as the gold power insidiously worked its way through her body, leaving black cinders in its wake as it consumed her from the inside out.

Another rage-filled howl spilled down the shadowy tunnel, washing over her, spreading goosebumps over her body.

Running sounded like a very good idea.

Chapter
Thirty-one

"*H*urry." Taggert jerked on her arm, nearly pulling her off her feet, half lifting, half carrying her as they shot out of the cave.

The hunt had begun.

She risked a glance at the cave entrance and saw nothing. That didn't stop her heartbeat from skyrocketing. Something was there in the darkness, something hungry and coming fast.

Adrenaline surged through her body. The fresh night air eased the tight band around her chest. Some of her coordination returned. She picked up speed despite the stitch growing in her side, but couldn't dodge the obstacles nearly as well as Taggert. A branch took her unawares, smacking her hard enough to draw blood.

"Stop." She tried to slow, but Taggert would have none of it. When he would've muscled her forward, she threw out her arm and snagged the trunk of a slim tree. The bark ripped off a few layers of skin from her tender underarm. Taggert barely halted in time to prevent her shoulder from dislocating.

"We have time before she catches up to us. It wouldn't do for her to be on us too fast. The hunt would be over too soon." She lifted her arm in the meager light to get a better angle on the locks.

Everything metal.

"We should run." But he stayed still, allowing her to pull him into a crouch, making them a much smaller target.

"Running blindly through the forest is what got the others killed." She scanned the surrounding area to gain her bearings. The wind swept low to the ground, shadows jumped as past chases haunted the area. She could almost see them running scared, panting in fear, their only intent to escape, knowing each step, each breath could be their last. She shook her head to rid herself of the images.

"I can't unlock these." She looked at him in the darkness, saw him trying to hide the pain so clearly etched on his face, and wondered how long he'd be able to keep going. She needed a plan and fast.

"They picked me up on the other side of the stream. That's where everyone else is waiting. With your heightened sense of smell, can you get us there?"

Taggert lifted his head and inhaled deeply, shuddering as air filled his chest. He cradled his ribs, but didn't stop scenting the air until he found it. "Follow me."

He shot to his feet in the graceful way of his kind. Raven cursed her clumsy body, doing her best to keep up. After ten minutes of running, she was more than a little embarrassed by her lack of endurance. The stitch in her side was a taunt.

Wounded and starved, Taggert wasn't in much better condition. The signs were there in the way his chest hiccupped with each breath, the way his stride hitched. He just hid it better.

"If we can get that far, we'll have backup." But she didn't hold out much hope of making that distance without a confrontation. With each footfall, she pulled raw energy from the earth to disperse tiny grains of current across the surface of the forest floor. The roots eagerly soaked up the extra boost. The grass sprang back, bent leaves straightened, snapped twigs mended. Each step took its toll. She wouldn't be able to cover them for long. Even now, a fever heated her body.

They needed help.

"I need to track the others." She swallowed hard as she said the words, her body already flinching at the pain to come.

A shudder ran through Taggert's frame, though he didn't slow or miss a step. "Do it."

Something in his reaction had her hesitating, sucking up precious moments. "Are you sure?"

"You won't hurt me."

His trust didn't reassure her. A strangled inflection in his voice had her guts clenching with unease. Weighed against the overwhelming need to protect him, there was no contest.

"Stop."

He instantly stilled and cocked his head to listen. His bloodshot eyes met hers, and he nodded to indicate they were alone.

To keep him safe, she imagined a five-foot circle surrounding them. Then with great care, she pulled energy from around them and fed her power to the circle. Built it. Like a leech, it devoured the charge, greedily pulling everything faster than she could gather it. Trees became brittle. Plants wilted and turned brown, then black. Grass withered. All the while, her temperature soared with each pull.

Once saturated with as much energy she could gather, she released her hold, nearly dropping to her knees at the strain of working with pure energy. Power shot out, blasting through the forest with impossible speed.

Taggert's growl rumbled through her as he was hit with backlash, but she kept her focus on the wave. The first hit captured her attention. "Shit."

She shoved Taggert down just as a shot sounded. A burn lashed along her arm. Before she could peel herself off him, Taggert rolled, dragging her into the shelter of the trees.

Crouched facing her, Taggert's eyes glowed. He no longer resembled the boy she knew but a warrior determined to kill.

She clutched her arm, warm blood spilling through her fingers. Her core still sputtered, remaining unusable. The raw energy around them was too unpredictable to manipulate into closing the wound. She felt exposed and useless without her gift there to save them.

"Here." Taggert tore off the bottom of his shirt and wrapped her arm. She gritted her teeth when he tightened the makeshift bandage to slow the bleeding.

"Sorry."

She grabbed his hand when he dropped his arm and squeezed. "Thank you." When Taggert tensed, she slapped her hand against his chest. "No you don't." She lifted her arm, and the chain clanked. "We do this together."

"We can't stay here. He'll kill you." He lifted his face to the wind. "I can smell him, the powder on his gun, the tar in his hair." Taggert turned slightly and nodded. "He's coming from that direction."

"He'd found us too damn fast. He's tracking us somehow."

Taggert stilled, not even breathing. "It's me."

Her lips tightened, anger burning bright as she imagined what they'd done to him. "Where?"

"There was a cut on my back when I woke. It never healed."

"Turn."

He growled as if furious with himself and turned. "There's not much time. He's closing fast."

She peeled up the shirt. The infected wound stood out against the corded muscles of his back. The skin looked partially healed over, but a bright, angry red.

Without giving either of them a chance to flinch, she probed the small incision. Warm blood and nothing else met her fingertip.

"Hurry." The light sound barely emerged through his gritted teeth. He had to be riddled with pain, but he didn't show it.

He was right. There was no time to be squeamish. She pressed deeper, ignoring the fresh dribble of blood that smeared his back. Her fingertip touched the edge of something hard. She grabbed and pulled it free, wincing as she tore the object from his flesh.

Iron. The bastards. Since he couldn't shift, the wound would leave a permanent scar. She dropped the tracker, relieved to see the dribble of blood down his back already slowing.

"The old man said that if we escaped, we'd be free." Tension spiraled through Taggert. "Do you believe him?"

She didn't have to think twice. "No."

"Then we run." They kept low to the ground, Taggert guiding them away from the hunter. Another shot whizzed in the dark from somewhere behind them.

A bellow of rage followed, and she couldn't prevent a hard smile. "Cowboy found the tracker." And he was close enough for her to smell the grease on him.

Taggert pulled her to a stop and crouched, facing her. "You were right. More of them are ahead. If we run, they'll take us."

"How many?"

Taggert shook his head. "The wind carried just a hint of scent. Three?"

"How many were there in total?" She cursed her inability to send out a probe. She poked at the gold power that steadily bled into her system, but let it be. She couldn't risk using it with Taggert so near without knowing the consequences.

Taggert shook his head. "They made sure we only dealt with one person in the cave. There were two others that dumped me in the woods. Also a big guy with the taser that picked me up."

"There's also the girl and the old man. Plus they must have at least one person to guard the prisoners at the cave." She nodded to the darkness. "The cowboy is a coward. If we can unarm him, he'll be easy to take. One is a hunter, a soldier. He's in it for the chase. Killing's become boring. He needs bigger prey to get his thrill. The leader is an old man who detests all paranormals with an unquenchable hatred. He feels it's his duty to keep the rest of the world safe. Neither of them will stop."

"So we fight." There was no fear in Taggert's voice.

Adrenaline surged, burning away the pain and exhaustion. The animals at her core perked up in interest, spurring her forward. A quick glance at Taggert revealed the same. No lust for the kill, just grim determination to get them out alive.

Narrowing her eyes, she stared in the darkness back the way they came. "We take Cowboy first and even the odds."

With a game plan in mind, they slipped through the forest with barely a sound. As she guessed, Cowboy couldn't find anything without his technology. He lingered within five feet of where they'd left the transmitter, stomping the ground, muttering to himself, slapping at a watch-like electronic box strapped to his forearm.

Taggert jerked his chin at Cowboy, and Raven nodded. They moved in unison. Cowboy heard them and brought up his rifle, the barrel of his gun pointed dead center of Taggert's chest, though the pervert didn't know it in the darkness.

Raven tugged on the chain that bound them, jerking Taggert out of range and behind her.

Cowboy dropped the night goggles over his eyes, instantly spotting them. A vicious smile curled his lips. "It doesn't matter to me if my women are dead or alive."

Even as he squeezed the trigger, Taggert swept her feet out from underneath her. The ground came up to smack her as the shot rang out. She felt more then saw Taggert's body jerk. He didn't go down, doing his best to protect her while pinned in place by the chains connecting them.

Rage stole all rational thought. She was on her feet without being aware of moving. Taggert mimicked her, and they rushed Cowboy. The chain caught the pervert around his neck. His back slammed against a tree trunk. The gun went off harmlessly into the ground. She found herself facing Taggert behind the tree when the sound of Cowboy's neck snapping calmed the volatile emotions that threatened her sanity.

Chapter Thirty-two

*T*he body lay slumped against the tree, sightless eyes staring up into the sky. "We have to leave. The noise will bring them right to us."

Raven ignored Taggert's pronouncement. "How bad are you hurt?" The rawness of her throat made the words difficult.

He marched directly in front of her and got right up into her face. "We need to leave."

Raven couldn't let it rest, not with her fingers still tacky with his blood. She eased away from him, her breath catching at all the sight of all that blood low on his abdomen. With her fear, her core flared to life for the first time since she had been taken. "We need to stop the bleeding. Your wolf should accelerate the healing process if we can cut out the bullet."

"It went through. The bleeding's already slowing. We have to go." His tone was calm, soothing, and very insistent.

Some of the panic crowding her mind subsided. The tightness choking her chest eased. He was right. They had to keep moving. "Can you scent anything?"

Taggert shook his head. "The gunpowder is too strong."

While she still had access to her core, she sent a burst of electricity into the forest. This time she didn't protect Taggert. Despite insisting he was fine, his movements were sluggish. The injuries were impacting him. The extra energy would help him heal. It would keep him on edge and bring his wolf closer to the surface.

As the energy gushed out of her core, her legs trembled, threatening to dump her on her ass. Her core dimmed to a fraction of its former self, but it didn't vanish completely. The burnout was fading.

Then her wave got a hit. Two. Three. Six. And they were all heading in their direction.

"We have to leave now." She shoved at Taggert's shoulder and spun him around to face the opposite direction. "Back toward the cave."

"They'll trap us there." Though his body cowed at the mention of the cave, he did as asked and hustled.

"We'll have to circle around or be caught up in their net." When the shadow of the cave came into view, she pulled up short.

The hair on the back of her neck rose. Taggert jerked to a halt, the cuffs stretched between them, peering at her in confusion. "There's an energy shield of some sort around the cave like an underground fence." She tipped her head to the side and held out her arms, walking blindly, her fingers brushing the edges.

"Here." She traced the path down. "There's an electric fence buried here." The fence sparked when her fingertips bumped over the line. The tip of her finger burned then grew numb. She quickly pulled back, rubbing at the blackened tip.

A shadow shifted to the right. A person lumbered out of the darkness, the gait awkward. Twigs were tangled in snarled hair. Something about the shape of her face, the placement of her eyes, nagged at her.

"Sarah?"

The shape turned toward her, and the truth rocked through Raven. The laughing picture. Jason's missing girlfriend. Childlike confusion clouded the dull eyes. A flicker of recognition flared as if she remembered Raven from their first meeting when she almost fried her. The girl pointed back toward the cave.

"The cave?"

The girl shuffled forward. She had one foot across the fence when her body jolted, and a scream of rage bubbled out of her throat. The total despair bled Raven's heart.

A snarl of frustration transformed Sarah's face, the consciousness in her eyes faded as she swung toward them.

"I don't think she's happy." Taggert retreated a step when Sarah bared her teeth. They were jagged, half human, half animal.

Her movements smoothed out, her joints became fluid. She was going to attack.

Fear for Taggert curled through her. She'd come too far to let anything happen to him now. "Freeze."

Taggert instantly stilled in the uncanny way that she normally associated with vampires.

Raven lifted her hands to draw Sarah's attention. "You want in there?" She pointed to the cave. Sarah halted and gazed at the cave. The killers had something in there, something they used to ensure that Sarah obeyed.

Raven knelt and dug her hands into the ground. Cords of power snaked through the earth, leaping at her touch, eager for release. "Taggert..."

"If you don't do this, she'll kill us both."

Raven still hesitated. Even with perfect control, those shackles would transfer at least some of the shock to him. "I don't know what it'll do to you."

"I see the way you channel energy." The wolf stared back at her when he spoke. "I felt you do it when your lips were on me and you took my blood."

A shudder went through him, and she didn't think it had anything to do with pain.

"I can't absorb it the way you do, but I believe the wolf can help channel it so it doesn't kill us."

Her heart leapt at his confession. She would've questioned him further when Sarah's pacing grew more erratic. Raven didn't know if Taggert was lying to protect her or not. His steady gaze held hers, and she took a leap of faith.

"If you're lying and you die on me, I'll bring your ass back just so I can kill you myself." Without giving him a chance to say anything, she curled her nails into the cold earth and sucked in the power with a hard, steady draw. Her core filled in fits and starts as it sputtered, making it harder to work.

An off-tune, jerky hum from Sarah sent chills down her spine. Her brain shut down as the voltage arched through her body. Her fingers burned, the muscles of her body twitched in protest. When she didn't think she could draw more, the power wavered below her.

Her heartbeat thundered in her ears, and every inch of her crackled with excess energy. She could barely breathe past the pain as her core grew brighter and pulsed. Acid burned through her veins, seeking escape, wanting freedom. But knowing Taggert stood connected to her made that impossible. The damned chain would ensure that if any slipped her control, too much would try for him first.

Just when she feared that her skin would burst from the strain, the darkness around her core shifted, curling tighter. Choking. Her breath left her in a rush. Then all the air was gone. Her lungs were starving. The world narrowed to the creature with the strangle hold on her guts and the bright core threatening to go nova.

A cool breeze brushed across her face as if in a caress, and the flare slowly died, scraped from her core. The creature stretched through her chest as if searching for more. When it found none, it curled up and stilled. Any extra boost she might have gained vanished, leaving her raw, edgy, and without an ounce of spark. The ground was nothing but cool, clean earth.

When she had enough courage to lift her head, she found herself sprawled in the grass, Taggert's yellow gaze no more than an inch from hers, and no sign of Sarah.

"You alive?" Dryness from controlling so much energy sucked the moisture from her, making her throat raspy.

A light hum rumbled in his throat, his beast too much in control to allow him to speak. The muscles of her arms trembled when she pushed herself upright, and a shot sounded in the night.

When she would've flattened herself, Taggert launched himself forward, caught her under the arms and hauled her upright. When they vaulted toward the cave, another shot echoed through the trees. Taggert threw them backwards. They took cover crouched behind another tree.

"Soldier Boy," she muttered under her breath, cursing their luck. No one could've been worse. He was a hunter who loved nothing better than running his prey to ground. Then she bit her lip. An idea sparked in her mind, daring enough to work if Taggert didn't kill her first.

"You want a fair fight," She yelled at the shadows. "How is tying me to a dying shifter fair?"

Taggert jerked on the chain, but she didn't take her attention away from Solider Boy's location. She reached out and brushed her hand down Taggert's arm, trying to convey that everything would be all right.

He narrowed his eyes, then nodded slightly. She licked her lips, praying that playing with Soldier Boy's pride wouldn't get them killed.

"Stay hidden." She hissed the words and struggled to her feet.

An animal at her center trotted out. As it drew near, Raven recognized her wolf. Fur brushed against her mind. The trembling faded, the fever abated slightly, and some of the damage done to her body began to mend ever so slowly. She didn't know whether to feel grateful or scared shitless.

"Why don't we even the fight?" She stepped out of hiding, raised her arm and pulled the chain taut between them. She could've kicked Taggert when he left the shelter of the tree with her, presenting another target. "Free me. Hunt me in the open without your gun like a man."

A bullet tore through the night. She braced herself for impact, only to feel the restraints jerk. The chains broke. Her arm fell to her side with a tinkle of metal. It took her precious seconds for her to realize she was free.

"Run!" She shoved Taggert and took off in the opposite direction. When his footsteps thundered after her, she cursed. "You're running in the wrong direction. Why can't you ever listen? Get to safety."

"Not without you."

"Damn it all to hell." She jerked to a halt, resisting the urge to hit him over the head. "I can take care of Soldier Boy better without worrying I'll injure you in the process."

Didn't he understand that nothing could happen to him or it would all be for nothing? Memories of another escape flowed through her mind. Of too many people who had died in her arms when she'd arrived too late.

Something didn't feel right.

She turned toward Taggert. A shadow rose from the ground from behind him. A blade flashed in the meager light. Something in her expression must have warned him. He threw himself forward but not quick enough.

The knife sliced through the flesh of his back in a large sweep. What was intended to be a killing blow carved down to bone instead. When she reached to drag him away, Soldier Boy stepped forward.

If she tried to help Taggert, Soldier Boy would deal him the death blow. She retreated slowly, aching with the knowledge that Taggert could bleed to death mere feet from her while she was unable to do anything to help.

When Taggert struggled to rise, Raven shook her head. She switched her focus to see Soldier Boy drop down in a fighter stance.

When he lashed out with the knife, Raven dodged and struck back. The chain at her wrist snapped out, catching him across the face. Instead of stunning him, he struck back, hitting her forearm. The smell of her blood scented the air. That she didn't feel anything warned her that the knife had cut deep.

Taggert growled as he got to his hands and knees.

A line between Soldier Boy's eyes drew her attention. The hunt was too easy. She couldn't wait for him to strike first. If she didn't do something, he'd stop playing and kill them outright.

Still unable to raise even a spark, she did the opposite, drew his energy toward her. Any extra strength she received from her animals vanished with the use of her power. She stumbled, but quickly gained her footing. Without touching, there was no finesse but brute determination.

Soldier Boy's gaze sharpened. He tightened his hold on the knife as if sensing a trap. The blade slashed through the air. She weaved, but he changed directions and hit her upper shoulder.

Her concentration faltered, and she lost her hold on the energy. Gritting her teeth, she swung around and faced him. His hand wove back and forth, the movement of the knife a distraction to draw her gaze. She studied the rest of his body, waiting for a slight tensing to tell when he would strike.

Breathing hard, she coiled her chain around her hand to make a metal fist, ignoring the twinge as the metal touched her still partially singed hands.

She dodged his next blow. Her ankle scraped against a fist-size rock.

When he swung again, she twisted and slammed her metal gauntlet against his face with an arm-jolting thud, then used the momentum and rolled, snatching the rock.

Not fast enough. He sliced through the flesh of her thigh. Pain streaked up her hip with every step. Damn, but she really needed to get London to train her on how to fight. She couldn't rely on her powers anymore, not when they were so erratic.

She hefted the baseball-sized granite. When he lunged again, she brought up the rock and swung. The knife snapped with a ping, leaving him a two-inch blade. He'd have to get closer to reach her. If she could get her hands on him, she could tear the power from him.

Her wounds slowly oozed blood down her arm, thigh and shoulder. Too many cuts, too many wounds, too much spent energy. Her body protested every small movement. If she didn't finish this soon, she wouldn't be good for anything.

She risked a glance at Taggert to see him awake, aware and waiting for the slightest signal to attack. Faint voices sounded behind her, too far away to be of any assistance.

Soldier Boy appeared to be distracted. She lunged forward, reaching for his aura. The instant her hand touched him, the shield around him bowed under her touch, met resistance, then popped like a balloon, and her power jabbed through. Energy danced through her fingers, and her core sparked, greedily gulping down everything within reach.

"Raven!"

Soldier Boy pulled back his arm and slammed his knife forward. Though she knew it was too late, she threw herself sideways.

The jagged edge meant for her heart sank into her upper shoulder. Her legs buckled. Taggert's devastated gaze locked on hers as he struggled to his feet.

She reached up, ready to yank the blade free, waiting for the last second in order to preserve her strength when a blurred shape erupted from the woods to her right.

Jackson. Coming low and fast.

He launched himself head first into danger. Just when she expected them to collide, Jackson shifted to his wolf mid-flight in an awe-inspiring display of power.

Shifting normally wasn't smooth, wasn't graceful. Jackson's shift to his animal form was different. There were no muscles popping, no bones snapping or rippling fur, no blood as flesh reformed. What should've taken minutes, he managed in seconds. Part of her wondered if she might have changed something by trying to fix him.

Then all thoughts vanished when Soldier Boy went down, arms locked around the wolf, a crazed smile on his face. The wolf yipped. Then there was a snap. A horrible sense of disbelief clenched her heart. The bodies were still. As each second passed with no movement, the vise around her throat tightened.

Regret staggered her. Regret for not taking the chance to mate Jackson when he'd wanted. But there was hope. He was still in wolf form. That meant he was still alive. She clung to her shaky reasoning as she crawled toward him. She groped for her core, but there wasn't enough power to try to bring him back from the dead, much less heal him.

Hands reached for her, and she struggled, determined to reach Jackson. Durant cupped her chin, forcing her to look up. His lips moved, but she couldn't hear anything past the buzzing in her ears.

"He's alive."

She followed Durant's nod. Fur rippled as the animal pulled free of the weight trapping him. Soldier Boy's arm flopped on the ground, and Jackson turned toward her, a savagely triumphant expression in his eyes. Eyes she recognized, fiercely proud and reveling being in his wolf form once again.

The big wolf was gorgeous, the lines of his body tightly packed with muscles, and easily twice his normal size. His fur was an amazing mix of tawny gold tinged with black instead of the normal black and white of his race.

Tears clouded her vision.

He took a hesitant step and whined when his foot refused to hold his weight. As he limped toward her, she couldn't grasp that they'd made it.

"You're alive." Her eyes caressed Jackson's form, looking for any sign of further injuries.

"And under arrest for murder." Scotts' voice broke through her shock. She turned from Jackson to face the resolute expression of the police.

Chapter Thirty-three

*T*he pain grew in waves as the numbness wore off, but if Raven could've reached Scotts, she would've smacked him. The worst thing was that she couldn't even catch her breath to curse him. Remorse darkened Scotts' gaze, but it wouldn't prevent him from doing his job. Jackson licked her face, distracting her from her anger almost like he was trying to tell her that he'd be all right.

"Taggert?" Her voice emerged as a rasp. She tried to turn, but Jackson had crawled in her lap, effectively pinning her in place.

"He's fine. A few nasty scratches, but he'll be as good as new after a few days." Dominic helped Taggert stand and eased him down next to her.

Only when he carefully leaned against her did she finally believe that everything might work out.

Dominic's laser-green gaze pierced hers. "I'm more worried about your wounds. Let me see your injuries before Scotts calls those medics he's been threatening to have trample through the forest and destroy evidence."

Raven stilled at Dominic's warning. That's the last thing she needed. She couldn't allow others to touch her blood and question how fast she healed. If someone got curious and ran her DNA, she'd be screwed.

"Fine." She gripped the knife, ready to jerk it out when Durant's large hand latched onto her wrist.

"Wait. Let me get a bandage first." With a serious flex of muscles, he slipped out of his shirt to reveal a close fitting tee that drew attention to his body. He ripped the material into strips. The men exchanged a look. Taggert slipped an arm around her waist and tightened his grip.

"I can do it." She wiggled, trying to break free. Durant couldn't touch her blood.

They ignored her. Durant nodded, lifted the makeshift pad, while Dominic gripped the knife handle. One jerk and the metal slipped free with a juicy sound. She struggled, but it did no good. Blood spilled down the front of her shirt. The pain spiked when fresh air hit, twisting through her chest as if the knife took a chunk of her shoulder with it.

Durant knocked away her hands when she grabbed for the pad and deftly applied enough pressure, stopping any protest she might have given by stealing her breath.

She gritted her teeth, cursing her weakness. Tears tore at her soul as blood soaked his hands. The fight drained out of her, and bitterness sought a target.

Unwilling for the police to see them in such a vulnerable position, she snarled. "There is a cave that way. Why don't you see if you can rescue someone there."

She jerked her head, indicating the vast darkness beyond the circle of trees. As soon as Scotts glanced away, Dominic pocketed the knife with her blood on it.

"Head south about two hundred yards. Why not try to catch the others before they escape." She didn't say instead of harassing us like she wanted, but it was a stretch.

Tact.

That was her.

A mask descended over Scotts' dusky, dark complexion and the hardnosed detective took over as he ordered his men about. What he didn't do was leave them alone. Raven gave a subtle nod to Dominic to oversee the police. He hesitated, gave her one last searching glance and melted into the surroundings like he'd never been there.

"Too many people saw your wolf kill. I have no choice but to haul him in to the station." Scotts paused, a bit resigned at her stiff attitude. Raven kept quiet lest she say something irrevocably damaging, and he finally relented. "I'll do my best to process him quickly. I don't see any issues with you being able to pick him up in the morning after we've cleared him. This is a clear case of self-defense."

Despite the turmoil, Scotts' statement was a huge concession.

For her.

Though she fought it, she was grateful. And that made her all the grumpier. Most shifters brought in on murder went through an inquisition that took months. By the time they gained their freedom, most went a little insane at being confined.

Only a very few packs had the political sway to reclaim their members from such a charge without huge fines and a lot of favors changing hands. Any law enforcement officials would say it doesn't happen at all.

"Thank you." Although she knew she was pushing him, she couldn't resist making a demand. "Will you allow me to see if I can get him to shift?" She couldn't stand to see him locked with chains and shoved in the metal wagon reserved for shifters in their animal form with only the bare minimum of padding to protect them.

Depending on the strength of the shifter, it could take hours to revert back to normal. Most didn't have a choice when their animal contorted back to their human shape. But she had a feeling that Jackson was different. And a sinking suspicion that she'd made it worse with her interference.

Now she'd possibly infected Durant as well. Guilt battled for dominance, and she quickly shoved it away. She'd deal with Durant later.

"Jackson—" Even as she spoke, his fur receded, flowing into him like water. His back arched, a hiss escaped as his muscles pulled tight, and his body settled back into itself. He blindly reached for her, and she grabbed his hand. "I'm here. I have you."

The whole process was very private, and she hated that Jackson had to go through it in such a public manner. She brought his hand up to her face and brushed her cheek against his fingers to soothe them both. Someone thoughtfully handed him a pair of shorts.

"Sir." The radio crackled to life, the static startling in the deep silence of the forest. "We have two bodies slaughtered here." In the background, you could hear someone retching. "They're bad."

"Shifter?" Scotts gave her a probing look. They both knew he wasn't asking if the victims were shifters.

"From the pieces we can find, it appears so."

Raven lifted her chin, daring him to even suggest that it was one of hers. When no other report came across the radio, the sour taste in the back of her throat dissipated. Digger and Griffin had escaped. The guards were dead. Somehow, she didn't think Grandpa was one of the casualties.

"Secure the scene and search the forest near the opening. See if you can find any tracks leading from the cave. Watch for both human and animal. I'll send the techs in with the crime kit. We should be there in twenty minutes."

"Yes, sir." The young voice wobbled a little, and she had to give the man credit for not backing down at the prospect of being alone in a forest full of shifters.

Scotts replaced his radio and nodded to rookie at his side. "Cuff him."

A deputy licked his lips and resolutely pulled out a set of cuffs from his belt.

Affronted on Jackson's behalf, Raven glared at Scotts. "Are those really necessary?"

Jackson sat up, taking her by surprise when he brushed his lips against hers. "I'll be fine."

A tremor shook her hands, and she reached for him. The feel of his arm beneath her fingers calmed some of the unease that insisted she not let him go. "Did I say thank you, yet?"

Jackson winked despite the fatigue that had to be dragging him down. The length of time shifters were in their animal form often left them asleep for hours, if not days as their system recovered from the trauma. The shorter the shift, the longer the recovery time. "You can thank me properly in the morning."

She knew what he wanted. Pack status.

She gave a hesitant nod, and Jackson allowed himself to be cuffed and led away with a limp and one last self-satisfied glance at her.

Darkness swallowed him, and she bit back the demand that he come back.

Scotts hesitated. "Go home. Rest. Take your friends with you." He stared at the trees where Dominic had disappeared. "All of them."

Raven complied without another word. They wouldn't find anything incriminating here, Dominic would make sure of it. The hunters were gone. Everyone was safe. It was time to close the case.

Too bad she feared it was much too late to keep the others safe from her.

"Will the police find the others?"

Durant snorted, not bothering to lift his gaze from the windshield. "They won't be searching for the right things, nor do they have the tracking skills that shifters do."

The agitation eating Durant alive wasn't revealed by any actions, but it grew beneath his surface, ready to tear through his skin if provoked. That was fine. His mood matched hers perfectly.

The pain of being moved to the car gradually faded as she concentrated on the feel of Durant's and Taggert's warm bodies pressed on either side of her. Her animals responded to their nearness, accelerating the healing process.

Raven agreed with Durant's assessment of the police. "I'll have London come back at dawn to track the few hunters that had managed to escape. They were planning to disappear after tonight. My guess is they've already moved onto the next hunting ground." But not if she could help it. She'd track them and ensure this never happened to others.

Right after she talked to Lester. She had most of the pieces of the puzzle. The biggest gap in the case was what had happened to Jason's body.

The road to the house loomed, and the occupants of the car fell silent. Part of her hadn't believed she would be returning with everyone relatively safe.

They had won.

"What about Sarah?" Taggert voiced the question that had been nagging at her. They limped together to the house, Durant doing his best to keep them both standing. "She's still out there."

"They were controlling her." To some extent.

"She might have killed at their command, but she's still a killer," Durant's voice rumbled with violence. "You nearly died from her first attack."

Though his words were harsh, his touch remained gentle as he eased her up the stairs. They followed Taggert's unsteady gait as he lead them to her room.

Raven didn't have the strength to shrug. "She's more animal than anything, squirreling away body parts for food stores. She wanted away from them."

"And now that the police removed her food supply," Taggert reminded her, "she'll hunt for more."

Raven shook her head. "They've been hunting in these woods for months. There were dozens missing, and we found only a fraction of them."

Neither man was satisfied with that answer. Hell, she wasn't either.

"Taggert, shower first, then food."

The glaze in his eyes told her he was at the end of his rope. The wolf had been too close to the surface for too long, taking a toll on his body. Seconds later, the shower thrummed to life.

"Let me clean you up." Durant guided her to the bathroom. He wasn't asking.

He prowled around her, always remaining within touching distance, always watching. The large tiled bathroom felt cramped with him in the room. No place to hide from the strong leather scent that always clung to him. It softened her edge when she needed it most.

Before she knew what to expect, Durant slipped his large hands over her hips and lifted her onto the counter. Cold granite sucked a gasp from her. When she opened her mouth to object, the tightness around his mouth had her rethinking her protest.

"The first aid kit is under the sink."

He bent, retrieved the cardboard box, inspected the healthy supply and grunted as if the abundance of products was barely adequate. He carefully unwound the makeshift bandages, his touch so light she barely felt it. The slice on her arm was a thin line, the wound already clotted and sealed thanks to her animals. The gunshot was the same but had more of a singed look. He wet a cloth and cleaned each area, edging closer until he was wedged between her thighs with her having no idea how he got there.

Under the light, with his head bowed, she could see faint stripes in his wild mane of hair. Something about it had a smile curling her lips, but she resisted the urge to pet him. She didn't think he'd appreciate the fact that she thought it was cute.

She shifted to give him better access, and the scab on her leg broke open in protest. She didn't say a word, but Durant stilled. He inhaled deeply, a line forming between his brows.

"You re-opened your wound." It was an accusation. He glanced down, peering through the jagged gap in the material where Solider Boy's knife struck her thigh. "I'll have to cut off your jeans."

"This is the second time that's happened this week. I'll be out of clothes soon if you guys keep it up." She meant it as a joke, but the lines around his mouth deepened.

"I'll replace them." As he spoke, he pulled out a large double-edged knife from a sheath at his back.

One she hadn't even known existed.

She jumped, expecting to feel cold steel, but he sliced the fabric with practiced ease. When she leaned back to give him room, he lifted the knife and sliced through the shredded fabric of her shirt.

"Hey!" The top gapped, revealing her chest down to her navel. Feeling very much exposed, she jerked up the corners to cover her bra. When he didn't move, she finally lifted her gaze, knowing the bastard's patience would outlast hers. "What?"

His focus zeroed on her injuries, a closed expression to his face made her feel lower than an insect. "You never called. You knew you were going into danger, and you never called."

"I—" She didn't know what to say. She didn't even think to give him a call and knew he wouldn't appreciate that fact if he ever found out. "Everything happened so fast. We had to move."

This time he wouldn't meet her eyes, busying himself by searching in the med box. She felt the need to explain further.

"I've been alone most of my life. I don't know anything about pack. I've never been in one and don't have the first clue of how one works," she said as he put a bandage on her leg, ripping the tape with his teeth. She grabbed his hand when he finished securing the last edge. "I don't know how to rely on anyone else."

The shower shut off. Durant pulled away without acknowledging her and inspected her shoulder. He picked up the cloth and dabbed the area. Like a damn cat, he wouldn't be appeased with an apology. He was going to make her work for it.

Taggert stepped out of the shower. The vicious cut slashed across his back from lower waist to mid back. The bullet wound still oozed blood. A patch of angry red marred his upper shoulder from where she had torn the tracker out of him. Skin stretched over each of his ribs as if he hadn't eaten in weeks.

She jumped down, ignoring the jarring pain that shot up her thigh. Testing her core, she cursed the dormant energy, unable to call upon even the tiniest thread to heal him. The meager supply was all locked up mending her own body, and not allowing her to gainsay it.

The house stored a lot of energy, but it was raw power. She'd have to funnel it through her body to make it usable for healing. She reached out to touch Taggert when Durant caught her wrist.

Taggert's gaze lifted, flickered past hers, and he gave a subtle nod. "I'll grab something to eat while Durant patches you up."

When she would've protested, Taggert trailed a finger down her hand, then left with only a towel around his waist. Her jaw snapped shut. Trust. He was asking her to trust the pack.

Turning to face Durant, she was startled to see the anger on his face. His fierce gaze fastened on the hand Taggert had touched. Then the look disappeared as if it'd never been there.

"You're so angry." Despite her own irritation, the need to understand and soothe him refused to go away.

"That boy has a higher standing in the pack than I do." And he was obviously infuriated by it.

"You and Taggert are the only ones in the pack." His statement baffled her. "What kind of standings could there be with only two of you?"

"Enforcer. Lover. Breeder. Healer. Soldier." He rattled off the names as he finished inspecting her shoulder. "You obviously don't think I fit in the first or last category. You placed yourself in danger with Randolph and again tonight when you didn't call me for help."

"You have a club to run, Cassie to protect. I assumed this whole pack thing was a way for you to get something from me. I just hadn't figured out what yet." She could've bitten her tongue when his hands flexed on her arm. She almost missed the pain that flickered behind his eyes.

"And lovers?" His tone became devoid of emotion as he continued his task.

"You don't need my permission to take a lover." That shifters had to ask permission for something so intimate repulsed her.

"If I do, you'll never select me."

"Huh?" His answer struck her dumb. She pointed back and forth between them. "As in you and me?" The last word ended on a squeak.

Some of her confusion must have finally pierced his anger. He crowded into her comfort space, not stopping until he had his body pressed up against hers.

His scent actually made her ache to touch him. Only sheer will prevented her from lifting up her hands to caress the hard lines of his chest. She detested being forced into a corner. She was almost grateful that her injuries stopped herself from doing something stupid.

"I don't know how pack works, but if I take a lover, it's my choice, not some pack business that needs to be handled." She sidestepped him, instantly missing the heat of his body. "I agree that you're pack. You're welcome in my house."

"Anytime?" He rummaged in the med box, retrieving ointment and a roll of gauze. He paused and gave her a too casual look, as if the answer mattered more than it should.

Her reply was slower in coming, trying to gauge his motives as he busily cut strips then dabbed her shoulder. She couldn't read him and that only made her more suspicious. "I can have a room prepared where you can leave your things if you'd like." Those words were hard to get past her lips, half expecting a trap. "But I have one rule."

The shifting moods that crossed his face froze. He nodded once, watching every nuance of her expression, as if her next words were vitally important to him.

"My cases are business. They don't involve pack. As long as you don't interfere, we should be fine." She'd make sure Jackson learned that, too.

"Only if it doesn't endanger your life." He quickly countered her offer, his concentration centered on bandaging her shoulder. Unless you looked closer and saw the tightly coiled muscles and the controlled way he held himself.

Raven paused, understanding that this negotiation could be pivotal. "Who gets to decide?"

"Pack votes." The reply was automatic. He taped the last edge, head ducked to hide a smug smile.

But that meant she got a vote, too. She hesitated a second more, then reluctantly agreed. "But Rylan is included in my pack. And Cassie gets a vote, too."

His brows lowered, clearly not happy, but he knew better than to push further. "The house is empty. I'll stay until you hear something from the others." There was no hesitation in his voice, nor was there a question, just a statement of fact. Bossy cat.

"I'm going to grab a shirt while you wash." Though he remained uninjured, mud dotted his chest and arms, along with splotches of her blood. The sight halted her in her tracks, and anger roared back into her at the reminder.

He slipped his shirt over his head, washing from the sink, pausing under her perusal. Concern immediately darkened his face, and he turned toward her, dripping wet. "What's wrong?"

"She's afraid her blood has infected you," Taggert said as he entered the room.

Raven stiffened, refusing to turn and face him and the truth that she'd already infected him.

"I'm a shifter, I can't get anything." Still half naked, Durant stepped closer, confident and cocky.

She skittered away from him. If he touched her now, she'd lose the last string on her temper. Anger burned along her skin, ready to ignite. As long has he kept his distance, there would be no spark.

"It's not a disease." Taggert wrapped his arms around her waist, fingers biting into her skin, holding her in place when she would've bolted. She didn't want to have this painful conversation. Not tonight. Not ever.

"You didn't harm him." Taggert forced her chin up to face Durant.

It pissed her off to be overpowered and weak.

"You can't know that." A tremor shook her, and she jerked away from them both. God, how she wanted to believe him, but there was no refuting the truth.

"Don't we? Your blood hasn't harmed me, and I've been exposed more than once."

"You're affected by my touch. Every time you're near, you absorb something from me that—"

"Allows me to help you." A very contented smile curled his lips.

Her throat felt thick at his confession. "You can't know what damage it'll do in the long run. A body is only capable of withstanding so much abuse."

"I heal fast."

She wanted to smack him for being so obstinate. "You have no idea what prolonged exposure could do."

He reached out to pull her back to him then winced, curling his arm around his ribs. "And maybe it's making me strong enough to be with you."

Horror thickened the back of her throat. The labs had managed to alter her in ways to ensure her survival. Every time she came into contact with someone, she exposed them to her brand of poison.

"Why don't we talk in the morning?" Taggert swayed. She and Durant rushed forward. Durant grabbed Taggert's elbow, but she hesitated.

"Don't pull away." Taggert cupped her jaw, his gaze so direct and so unlike himself that she stiffened. "I like the changes. If you hadn't picked me up at the club, I'd still be there, waiting for my death."

A lopsided smile lit up his face, and her heart thumped hard against her ribs to see him so relaxed and happy despite everything they'd been through.

"I think it's time for you to get some rest before you fall on your face." With everything that'd changed in his life the last few days, not to mention her bringing his wolf to the surface for long periods of time, she was actually surprised he was still conscious.

Durant helped him settle in her bed, double-checking his wounds. She grabbed a change of clothes, stripped what remained of her clothing and cursed the time it took to dress with her injuries.

When she would've sneaked away, Taggert's chocolate eyes follow her movements. Unable to resist, she drew near and brushed her fingers over his sun-streaked hair. With a smile, his eyes closed, his breathing deepened, and he dropped off to sleep.

"I think we should discuss this more." Durant watched her from the bathroom doorway.

"Discuss what? The Pack? The fact you want us to be lovers? Or that if we touch, I could kill you?" Eager to get away from him and the conflicting feelings he invoked, she focused on finishing this case and put it to rest. "I need to review my case file and see if I can fill in some answers. I want to get this settled tonight in time to pick up Jackson." She waited for him to protest or go back on his promise not to interfere in her work. Muscles bunched in his jaw, but he remained quiet when she thought he'd explode.

"As you wish." He unbuckled the first closure of his pants with a lazy smile that made her uncomfortable and nearly stopped her heart, the traitor. "I'll be here if you need me."

Raven swallowed thickly and quickly left before she did something stupid.

Like stayed.

Chapter Thirty-four

DAY 9: PRE-DAWN

Shadowy hallways greeted her, the cold air almost frosting along her skin as she went downstairs. Her mind worried the details of the case. Everything made sense except who killed Jason and what happened to his body.

A light in the study illuminated her desk, and she kept her gaze locked on it. Part of her was afraid to look at the chair where she'd last seen Ross, half-expecting to find his body waiting for her. When she'd gathered enough courage to turn, he was gone. Hell, the whole chair had vanished for that matter.

Finding his body didn't frighten her; it was the fear of accidentally bringing him back to life that scared the dickens out of her. The unease plaguing her since she stepped into the house, strangely, didn't lessen one iota.

Seating herself, she noticed the note on the desk. Dina and London were still with the shifters who'd been rescued from Ross's lab. The house felt silent with everyone gone.

Determined to finish this, she pulled out Lester's file and opened the folder. Jason's photograph arrested her. She pulled out Sarah's picture and recalled the girls abbreviated hospital stay.

Things were becoming heart-wrenchingly clear.

"You got your wolf back." Rylan's voice emerged from the darkness, his face unemotional as he tucked away everything that made him Rylan and her friend.

She mentally reached out for him in the shadows, seeking reassurance. And met a cold wall.

Sorrow crept over her at the distance he was putting between them. "Why didn't you tell me?"

"It's none of your business."

"We're friends!" That hurt, not to mention that his attitude pissed her off. "I had a right to know what kind of life I condemned you to suffer every time you fed."

"Damn it anyway." He rushed across the room in a blur, slamming his fists down on her desk. "That's exactly why I didn't tell you. You think everything's your fault. This has nothing to do with you."

"It has everything to do with me. If not for my blood, none of this would've happened." Just as furious, she stood and planted her palms on the desk, mimicking his posture.

Rylan didn't say a word as he turned and walked toward the door. Her breath hiccupped in her chest.

"Don't leave."

He reached for the knob then paused, keeping his back to her. "You're partially right."

A bubble of pain grew under her ribs. She lifted her chin and pulled back her shoulders, bracing herself against his words.

"If it wasn't for you, I would've died in the labs years ago."

The door shut quietly, deflating her. When he left the house, the hum in the air slowly dissipated. But damn it, between the choice of him being dead or alive, she'd choose alive every time.

Taking a deep breath to deal with another vampire, she dialed the number Lester left for her. He answered on the first ring. "I believe I know what happened to your son."

"You have my attention." His voice was smooth and mellow…like right before a predator would strike.

Her skin tightened uncomfortably despite the distance between them. That was not something you ever wanted to hear from a vampire.

"You're son dated a girl named Sarah Wilson. She was involved in a hit and run, leaving her in a coma that no one expected her to survive." Raven paged through her notes. "They were going to remove her from life support. Her pack was going to claim her body, so he bit her."

"You're sure?" Displeasure echoed through the phone line.

"Yes, but nothing happened," Raven spoke faster. "They took her off life support that afternoon. What happened next is foggy. I believe he thought there was still a way to bring her back. He went to the morgue later that evening." An image of the broken morgue fridge flashed through her mind. "Something went wrong with the transfusion. She had enough human DNA to wake, but the few drops of her shifter blood prevented a full transition." She grew quiet. "I think he recognized what she was in the end."

"A ghoul." The disgust in his voice was obvious.

"He must have found her when she woke, starved and confused. He tried to stop her."

"And died. Thank you for your assistance. I'm sure you understand that this stays between—"

"You misunderstand. He succeeded. While distracted trying to contain her, Jason was murdered. Ghouls are rare. The chance to enslave one is even more so. It was a possibility the killer couldn't pass up."

"They're an abomination." The controlled emotion in his voice boomed in her mind like a bullhorn, the power coming to him automatically. Mind games.

She doubted he was aware of using it this time.

"Be that as it may, your son died trying to save her life." Prolonged silence filled the phone, leaving her uneasy. Smart people knew better than to disagree with a Vampire. You'd think she'd learn sooner rather than later to keep her opinions to herself and just report the facts.

"The killers name?"

"Dr. Patrick Ross. Dr. Ross ran into an unfortunate accident earlier this evening."

Another pause, this one fraught with danger. "I thought we had an understanding."

She had to tread carefully. The last thing she needed was a new enemy. "Our agreement stood until he kidnapped one of mine. I'm sure you understand."

A disgruntled sigh crossed the line. "At least tell me he suffered."

"Yes." She thought back to Ross, his dying mother, his life, and knew it was true. Until his mind snapped. "But not nearly enough." Especially when images of the bloody lab haunted her, the glaringly empty cages, the near skeletal survivors that somehow managed to live.

"And the police?"

"Have no knowledge of your son or his connection to Sarah's resurrection. As far as they know, she's dead."

"You'll keep it that way." It was a command.

"Of course." She debated whether to say anything about Sarah's existence and decided against it. Wolves and vampires didn't mix. He wouldn't care that his son loved her or died for her. To him, she never existed.

"Thank you for your services. We owe you a debt."

An instant later a dial tone rang in her ear.

Raven pulled away the headset and looked at the phone, then slowly lowered it. His gratitude sounded like more trouble than it was worth. Sunrise would be here soon. Her body ached, her head pounded. A couple of hours of sleep would do wonders for her body to heal.

The guys would be asleep upstairs. In an odd sort of way, she was glad Durant had stayed. Without Jackson, her room felt empty. If asked, she'd deny it, but she'd grown accustomed to Jackson's presence. She didn't think she'd be able to relax until she had him home.

Shadows shrouded the room when she turned off the last light. Half asleep, she slipped out to the hall. Her hand was on the railing when the floorboards groaned.

Her brain snapped to full awareness. Someone else was in the house.

"You stupid bitch. You ruined everything."

Chapter Thirty-five

$\mathcal{P}$ure dread raked down Raven's spine. She recognized that smooth, superior voice from the hellish tunnel deep within the bowels of the earth. The analytical observer was gone. There was a wealth of emotion in his voice now.

Grandpa had found her.

She removed her foot from the bottom step, shuffled backwards and turned. Her back brushed lightly against the wall. One second was all it took. Power immediately flared along the wires, dancing behind the sheetrock like it had been waiting for her touch. Her body throbbed at the call, still oversensitive from all the abuse. She refused to absorb any of it for fear that at the first touch, her core would shut down again.

"I thought you and your friend would've been long gone by now." She swallowed with difficulty and took a step closer to him and his silent companion, willing them away from the boys upstairs.

"Not without taking care of a little business first."

"To kill me." The floor trembled beneath her. She resisted a shudder as energy forked its way under the floorboards, slowly snaking its way toward her.

"You were never meant to survive. You succeeded because you cheated. The others showed up to rescue you." Disgust clouded his face, and he spit on the floor.

"You said if I escaped, I was free. You said nothing about rules."

"I lied." He raised the gun in his hand. "I'm going to enjoy this."

Raven raised her hands and twisted sideways to make herself a smaller target. "I don't understand. You didn't care about the hunt. It was more of a means to an end. Why make it personal?"

"The boy was my grandson."

"The pervert?"

He backhanded her, splitting her lip. Blood spilled across her tongue. She used the momentum to twist about, bringing her closer to the door. Then she noticed that the alarm was off.

She froze when she faced him. Those cold eyes latched onto her wound, his breathing erratic. He licked his lips, his tongue flickering like a reptile. His hands curled into fists as if unable to wait for the pleasure of hitting her again. "You created the hunt for him, didn't you?"

"He had an aptitude for it."

A sickening thought took root. "He started killing people, and you needed to find a way to protect him, so you orchestrated this whole thing."

"And why not? There is a whole shifter population that everyone ignores. No one missed them. Hell, they kill their own kind."

"But you found that you liked the hunt."

A smile came to his face. "I find there is a certain justice to cleansing the world so others might live without the stink of your kind." Spittle flew from his lips, his eyes overly bright. He waved to his henchman. "Go upstairs and handle the others."

"No." Raven prayed they heard her shout and got the hell out of there.

The henchman smirked and took the stairs two at a time, pulling a gun out of the waistband of his pants.

Raven halted her retreat, everything in her stilling. The air brushed over her, every inch soaked with power. And she couldn't access any of it. Without a care for the consequences, she ripped open the vault holding the poisonous golden strands. Energy poured into her body, each pore sucking it in like water to desert sand as fury ripped away every ounce of self-preservation.

The gun cocked.

"Once I finish you, I'll go back and skin those pets of yours and use their pelts on my floor."

The deluge of power rippled over her, the pain nipping at her nerves. She lifted her hand to strike first when the door to the kitchen inched opened. A shape entered with a disjointed, awkward gait she recognized.

"Sarah?" Vengeance gleamed in the cloudy eyes when her gaze landed on Grandpa.

She must have followed the men here. Raven instinctively took a step back, trying to pull back the swell of power. She nearly went sprawling on her ass when her foot caught on the rug she used to hide the scars etched in the floor.

Grandpa twisted, firing without hesitation. The first shot struck Sarah high in the shoulder. Her body jerked, then slowly toppled forward.

"No." Raven ran forward to catch her, and the gun swung in her direction.

"Stay back."

Sarah landed on her face with a sickening crunch. Her fingers twitched, her arms slowly moved as she pulled herself forward with her hands.

Grandpa laughed at her feeble attempt, lifted the gun, and shot her again. This time, the body lay still. That little flame of life sputtered then faded.

All the golden cords of power burst out of Raven, including the few remaining blue strands that had kept the lockbox sealed. They swarmed the body on the floor like ants. Drained by the total lack of power, she dropped to her knees with a painful crack. Not even the animals grumbled. Her body felt like someone had taken her out back and kicked the shit out of her.

A roar rang in her ears. A thump vibrated under her hands. She lifted her head to see the mauled body of the henchman two feet away, tossed over the railing like a paper airplane to land in a splatter of blood and bones.

Durant and Taggert loped down the stairs in a blurred speed, half-dressed but none the worse for wear. Blood rushed out of her head to see them healthy and whole. Durant didn't even spare her a glance, his focus centered on the threat. Taggert ignored it all, his attention on her.

"I see your friends have decided to join us." Grandpa waved the gun, the barrel pointed at her head. "Let's keep your distance, now, shall we."

Taggert grabbed Durant's arm, muscles flexing when Durant resisted. Both men halted halfway down the steps. Then Durant's molten gold gaze met hers.

Eager to get the old man's focus away from the guys, she tossed out the theory she suspected the first time she saw him. "I wonder what your friends would say if they knew you weren't completely human. Like how you can pick out shifters from humans."

His reaction was immediate. He lashed out with his boot. The blow caught her in the ribs, nearly picking her off the floor.

A roar reverberated in the room, and Durant leapt over the railing. A bullet cracked in the ceiling, halting all movement.

Grandpa lowered his arm and aimed the barrel at her head. "I'd rather not have any holes in my new pelts. Stand down."

Grandpa walked to the other side of the room to keep them all in view and out of arm's reach. Raven struggled to her feet. Without electricity to hold them back, the shadows at her core woke with a vengeance. Under their influence, the aches faded, and her emotions grew more volatile.

Taggert helped her rise as Durant stood in front of them, his large body protecting her. She grabbed his belt loop, gouging her nails into the hard muscles of his side to prevent him from doing something stupid like attacking. Gunshots at such close quarters could be lethal even for him if the old man got off enough shots.

Durant flinched, but the hum under her hand calmed. Then she saw a movement on the floor.

Sarah.

Though the rims of her eyes remained clouded, they were not that of a ghoul. Raven saw only Sarah. Recognition flashed between them.

The electric charge must have returned her humanity back to her. All the horror she lived through the last few weeks hollowed out her face. Her hand encircled a necklace at her throat, and a bitter smile came to her lips.

"No." But Sarah didn't listen, throwing herself at the old man, her arm raised to strike.

Grandpa turned and fired at point blank range, but she was already on him.

After what felt like an eternity, they stumbled in an awkward dance and collapsed. Blood pooled beneath the bodies, spreading toward Raven in an ever increasing circle.

Durant cautiously knelt to check for life, but she knew it was already too late.

"She tore out his throat." Durant turned Sarah over. Her sightless eyes stared up at them, her body pale and gaunt. "She's gone."

A terrible sadness riddled Raven's heart. She hadn't meant to bring Sarah back. The two powers must have mingled, merging to form an unholy union, one powerful enough to bring Sarah back from the dead and human. No one could ever know the truth.

The horror in Sarah's eyes as she realized what she'd become would haunt Raven for a long time.

Chapter
Thirty-six

Raven stood in the shower, groaning as the heated spray pounded her aches away. Durant had ordered her and Taggert upstairs. Any protests she had died when he warned that time was short if she wanted to be at the police station in an hour to pick up Jackson. A thrill shot through her at the prospect of seeing Jackson again. Of claiming him.

With no threat, her animals were at peace, her power was recharging, taking the time to repair the damage Randolph's power had inflicted. Though the last week had taken its toll, her new pack had been worth all of it. She just had one more task remaining: to prepare for the council meeting.

She reluctantly turned off the water and stepped out of the steam. And found a pile of clothing neatly folded on the sink, including her bra and panties. All the clothes were black, but instead of her normal gloves, she found in their place a colorful red pair that she knew didn't come from her drawers. She fingered the smooth leather, unsure how to handle the little kick of pleasure she got at seeing them.

After dressing, she walked into the bedroom to find Taggert waiting for her.

"Sit."

A little uncertain of his demand, she sat in front of the mirror as instructed. He picked up a brush and stroked it through her hair. On the third pull, her head fell forward, and the tension slowly eased. Everything was finally over. No one would try to kill them today.

"The car is ready when you are." Durant's voice shocked her back to the present. She lifted her head to find him leaning against the doorjamb, his concerned gaze studying her. "I can pick him up if you want to rest. I'm sure he'd understand."

She peered in the mirror at her pale face, bruised eyes, and busted lip. Didn't she look like a treat? "No. I need to finish this."

She twisted her hair up, gritting her teeth as the muscles in her wounded arm and shoulder trembled at the simple move. She had a feeling even a mosquito would win a fight with her today.

Nerves fluttered to life as she rose to leave.

She would take Jackson's blood and make him one of her own. Instead of dread, excitement lashed through her as they made their way downstairs.

The hall was clean like nothing had ever happened. Part of her was grateful. This was her retreat. Her place of peace. That had been shattered hours before, but Durant helped right it.

She brushed against him as she walked, catching the light fragrance of leather. His body tensed, but he didn't pull away. "Thank you."

He didn't reply, only brushed against her in return as they walked toward the car.

The ride to the police station was uneventful. The station was teeming even though it was barely eight in the morning.

As soon as she crossed the threshold, she saw Scotts and knew something had gone terribly wrong. Her feet stopped, and she waited for him to make his way toward them. Before he could say anything, she spoke. "He's gone."

Scotts ran a hand through his hair. The man looked like shit under the unforgiving florescent light, his dark coloring washed out. She doubted he'd gotten a lick of sleep. "He was released into the custody of his pack. With the charges dropped, I had no right to hold him."

Disbelief winged through her. He'd left. Without saying good-bye, he'd left. She nodded at Scotts, too numb to feel anything yet. "Thank you for everything."

"Wait!"

He shoved a packet in her hand.

"What's this?"

"An application. You had four nominations even before the station opened."

"For what?" She didn't bother to open the thick envelope, not even curious of its contents as she battled to keep her composure. The numbness that cushioned her at the announcement of Jackson's disappearance gradually started to fade.

"Thanks to the media coverage on this case, the legislature passed their law to create two paranormal police squads." Scotts looked resigned at the new changes. "A person can apply for the job, then pass the blood tests and formal interviews, or a registered paranormal can be nominated into the position."

Scotts wasn't any more thrilled about her nominations than she did.

She couldn't help but be suspicious of what her mysterious benefactors would want in return. And the last thing she wanted was to register herself in the national database. How the hell was she supposed to fill in the question of species and/or talent?

"Who placed the nominations?"

He just shrugged. "We lowly lawmen don't get to know the details. It's all approved by committee. A human in the government or law enforcement has to vote for you as well as one pack or clan. The catch is the whole pack has to be in consensus for their vote to count. And no member can be nominated by one of their own."

She swallowed hard at that. She either had very powerful friends she didn't know about, or very ruthless enemies. They'd just painted a huge target on her back. "Which means?"

"Congratulations. With your background, you've been grandfathered into the force without all that rigmarole. Sign the papers and you're in. You will be issued a gun, a badge, and the right to review every criminal case involving anything paranormal." Scotts sounded as world-weary and tired as any cop who had over ten years in service. "Oh, and lousy pay."

Raven blindly looked at the innocent crumpled envelope, half determined to toss the thing in the trash.

"Think very carefully before you decide." Scotts disappeared within the bustle of the stationhouse without another word.

She didn't know if the advice was a threat or plea, but she knew that if she didn't take this step, she'd just worked her last case for the police. After the way things had ended last night, she thought maybe that was for the best.

She turned on her heel and left, desperately in need of air.

The bright sun kissed her skin, but did little to penetrate the deep cold leeching away the last fragments of warmth her body had hoarded.

Taggert stepped in front of her, blocking her exit on the sidewalk. "Jackson wouldn't have left voluntarily. If he left at all, it was because he had to follow orders."

"Would he? Now that he has his wolf back, would he really want to stay and do his *baby-sitting* duty?"

Taggert's jaw tightened at her taunt, but he didn't back down. "He wouldn't leave you without a direct order. Even if he'd wanted to stay, they wouldn't have allowed him."

She glanced away, and Taggert shifted to stand in front of her again, his whole body filling her vision. "You can't believe everything you see or hear in other packs. They deal in politics. No pack is willing to work with another without compensation. They deal in lies. They steal. If they see you as weak, they'll attack. He's useful to them again, so they recalled him."

"And the rule about us not being allowed to be alone? The whole reason for the chaperone?" She was grasping at straws, but didn't care.

"Pack can recall their enforcers at any time."

"No matter if it left you in danger or not."

Taggert shrugged. "You can petition the council, but since you already mated me, I'm not sure it would matter."

Determined to retrieve Jackson and fulfill her promise to him, she lifted her chin. "Where did they take him?"

Taggert touched her arm. "If we go now, they'll see it as an act of aggression."

"Jackson's back to being the enforcer. He'll be safe enough for now." Durant spoke for the first time, his voice a rumble at her back.

"The conclave gathers in ten days. You'll have a chance to express your interest in him then."

Though Durant might not like Jackson, he was willing to help her retrieve him. For her. "And they'll just hand him over?" Her hands curled into fists at the thought of being denied, her skin crackling as energy swirled to life around her.

"As long as his alpha or the council approves the mating," Durant replied without inflection.

Durant and Taggert didn't look at each other with so much as a flicker of an eyelash, raising her suspicions. She narrowed her eyes and braced herself. "Tell me the rest."

"You're a new alpha. Though unlikely, someone could challenge your pack status. Another complication is the meeting takes place during a full moon." They both paused and gazed at her as if she was supposed to know what the hell they were talking about.

"And?"

Taggert winced while Durant smiled. "What they say about the full moon having an effect on the shifters is true. The animal side of our nature is more pronounced, and the need to mate increases."

"So?"

"What he's trying to say is now that you're pack, you might be affected as well."

She licked her lips, uncertain where this was heading. "I'm sure I'll be fine."

Durant smiled again, a wickedness gleaming in his gaze. "The meeting will also be a place where other packs scope out potential lovers. If you're there, you'll be sure to receive offers." Then his smile disappeared, and a shiver passed over her when his gaze sharpened possessively on her face. "You will be one of the few female alphas present."

"I can take care of myself." Neither of them said a word. "Anyway, I'll have my hands full focusing on Jackson. No one will approach me."

Durant and Taggert shared a glance that all men share when they thought a female was being unreasonable. She hated that look.

Taggert broke the silence first. "They won't give him up without a price. You didn't mark him when he had leave from the pack, so if you want him, you'll either have to fight for him or bargain with his alpha to get him back."

She winced at the slight incrimination in his voice. He was right. She should've pushed mating Jackson last night, but Jackson had to play the hero and give her time to adjust.

She was a fool. "And if I mark him at the club?"

"Now that he's healed, he's a valued member of the pack again. Without permission from his pack alpha, it's an act of aggression. You'd be risking both his life and your own."

"And both of you in the process." So not an option.

Taggert's phone rang, startling all three of them. He fumbled with it before answering, his eyes locked on hers.

"I'll let her know." He hung up the phone, his face grim. "We have to get back to the house. London found two intruders. They say they know us and are asking for sanctuary."

Raven rubbed her brow, quickly covering the ground back to the car. Disappointment settled on her shoulders, along with a deep anger that another pack was trying to take what was hers.

And Jackson was hers. He knew it. She knew it.

She couldn't help feel that his pack knew it as well and had purposefully recalled him to active duty where she couldn't touch him without a price.

She had ten days to do research, prepare for the conclave, and find out what the hell another pack wanted in exchange for the mate they had stolen right from under her nose.

THE END

ABOUT THE AUTHOR

Stacey Brutger lives in a small town in Minnesota with her husband and an assortment of animals. When she's not reading, she enjoys creating stories about exotic worlds and grand adventures…then shoving in her characters to see how they'd survive. She enjoys writing anything paranormal from contemporary to historical.

Other books by this author:
BloodSworn
Coveted

A Druid Quest Novel
Druid Surrender (Book 1)
Druid Temptation (Book 2)

An Academy of Assassins Novel
Academy of Assassins (Book 1)
Heart of the Assassins (Book 2)
Claimed by the Assassins (Book 3)
Queen of the Assassins (Book 4)

A Raven Investigations Novel
Electric Storm (Book 1)
Electric Moon (Book 2)
Electric Heat (Book 3)
Electric Legend (Book 4)
Electric Night (Book 5)
Electric Curse (Book 6)

A PeaceKeeper Novel
The Demon Within (Book 1)

A Phantom Touched Novel
Tethered to the World (Book 1)
Shackled to the World (Book 2)

A Clash of the Demigods Novel
Daemon Grudge (Book 1)

Coming Soon:
Daemon Scourge (Book 2)
Ransomed to the World (Book 3)

Visit Stacey online to find out more at www.StaceyBrutger.com
And www.facebook.com/StaceyBrutgerAuthor

Made in the USA
Coppell, TX
04 October 2020